His grip on her arms tightened

and he drew her fast against him now. His voice fell an octave, becoming husky and sensual. "I was extremely aware of your physical maturity down by the bathing creek this afternoon."

"You saw nothing!" she snapped, trying to sound indignant but recalling the intimate encounter with an excitement that inflamed her.

"I saw enough. You're a beautiful, desirable, exciting woman . . ."

"You must be insane, Lieu— I mean, Brad. We hardly know each other."

"I've known you all my life. The first day you arrived here at the post, I knew you were the one, the girl I've been waiting for all of my life."

He cupped his hand gently under her chin and tilted it up as he bent to kiss her. Moira was helpless, mesmerized. Desire coursed through her body like a flash fire, obliterating all her senses but one—the sense of touch, touching and being touched.

"Oh, Brad, I'm on fire."

A GLORIOUS PASSION
by Stephanie Blake, author of
FIRES OF THE HEART and CALLIE KNIGHT

Other books by Stephanie Blake

A GLORIOUS PASSION

STEPHANIE BLAKE

A JOVE BOOK

A GLORIOUS PASSION

A Jove Book / published by arrangement with
the author

PRINTING HISTORY
Jove edition / January 1983

ISBN: 0-515-07071-8

Jove books are published by Jove Publications, Inc.,
200 Madison Avenue, New York, N.Y. 10016. The words
"A JOVE BOOK" and the "J" with sunburst are trademarks
belonging to Jove Publications, Inc.

Book One

Chapter One

Dear Diary,

It has been five days since the end of the war, with the surrender of General Robert E. Lee and the Confederate forces at Appomattox. Daddy was there with General Custer to witness the ceremonies—the proudest moment of his life, he says. He is home on a well-deserved leave. Susan, Wendy and I are very concerned about his health. He is so pale and wan, and there are dark hollows under his eyes. He has been a different man since Mama's death last year from influenza. After supper he retires to his study with a box of cigars and a bottle of brandy and stays there long after we go to bed.

Today he is in better spirits than he has been on any day since he came home. We are all looking forward to tonight. It is not every day one has the honor to be in the same theater with the President of the United States. Daddy says that our seats are almost directly below the President's box. What a thrill! Susan says she knows she is going to faint.

The special presentation at Ford's Theater this evening will be an English comedy titled Our American Cousin. *It is said to be very humorous. In a way, though, I feel bad for the actors because most of the audience's attention will be on President Lincoln's box . . .*

Moira Callahan put down the quill pen and closed the cover of her diary at the sound of footsteps ascending the hall staircase. Moments after, her oldest sister, Wendy, entered the bedroom.

"Susan has been in the bathroom for over an hour," she complained. "At this rate you and I will never be ready on time."

"Oh, I've had my bath," said Moira.

"Well, that's something at least." Wendy went to a closet and took out the gown she was going to wear to the theater. "Do you think this is appropriate, Moira?" She pressed the dress against the front of her body, modeling it.

It was a frock sprinkled with petite blossoms in rose and gold, a scoop neckline and a flaring skirt that was trimmed with purple and pink ribbon.

"The sleeves are too puffy for my own taste," Moira replied, "but yes, I think it's very appropriate for such an auspicious occasion. I'm going to wear my new silk." She got up from the writing desk and retrieved the dress from the closet she shared with her sister. She hung it on the closet door and stepped back to appraise it.

"Simple but rather elegant, I think."

The print was a small plaid of gray and wine with white. It featured a tiny stand-up collar, front button placket and narrow shoulder yoke. It was cinched at the waist by a smart bias cummerbund.

"I approve," said her sister.

"Well, I don't. It's too prim, for one thing." Susan Callahan poked her head into the room. Her blonde hair was wrapped in a towel turban, and a larger towel was draped around her body, which was still glistening with beads of moisture from the bath.

The Callahan girls, "army brats" sired by Colonel Patrick Callahan, who had distinguished himself at Gettysburg and Vicksburg, were anything but look-alikes. Moira at fourteen years of age was the tallest of the sisters, a raven-haired beauty with aquamarine eyes, an aquiline nose and flawless olive skin, a legacy of her father's Irish female forebears who had bred with survivors of the Spanish Armada when it had been wrecked off the eastern coast of Ireland in the sixteenth century.

Susan, fifteen, and Wendy, seventeen, were more fragile, small boned and willowy, with delicate features. They lacked the statuesque physique of Moira. Susan was fair and blond and had almond-shaped pastel blue eyes. Wendy was a fiery redhead with green eyes that were speckled with golden, swirling pigments.

Yet there was no denying that the girls were sisters. It could be seen in the tilt of an eyebrow; a dimple in the chin; the long, swanlike neck; the sensuous mouth; the widow's peak above the long, sloping, aristocratic forehead; the high, uptilted bosom; the flex of ample hips when they walked.

Although she was the youngest of Callahan's daughters, Moira possessed native wisdom and wit, coupled with flair and sophistication that made her seem the eldest of the three sisters. "Moira the maverick," as her father labeled her, had been born a generation before her time.

Seething with hostility and indignation against the male chauvinism of the era, especially manifest within the military community, she let it be known in no uncertain terms that she was the equal of any man jack in her father's regiment—"the whole friggin' Union Army" —including Pat Callahan himself! Certainly she could ride with the best horse soldiers in the regiment.

Aunt Tillie Newstrom, who had been keeping house for the Callahans since the death of her sister, was shocked by the attire her young niece wore when she went riding across the rolling hills and green meadows of Maryland on the outskirts of the capital: faded cavalry trousers and scuffed boots and a threadbare officer's shirt. Atop Devil, her great black stallion, she was a common and welcome sight to farmers and field hands, galloping through the tall grass, leaving clouds of dust in her wake, her unfettered breasts straining against the taut, thin fabric of her shirt.

"I've got friends all over the countryside, clear to Baltimore," she liked to brag.

"No doubt most of them think you're a Baltimore wench," her sister Wendy said archly.

Moira's blue-green eyes twinkled mischievously. "Well, I'm not. Listen to Miss Prim, Susan. You'd think butter wouldn't melt in her mouth. Yet when that young Lieutenant Monroe comes to call, I sense a bit of the wench in her as well."

"Every good Irish lass has a bit of the wench in her," Susan offered.

"You're both gauche and uncouth," the older sister chided. "I value Lieutenant Monroe's friendship, and that's all there is to it."

"Friendship, is it?" Moira jeered. "The two of you were awfully cozy for friends on the front-porch glider the other night. You should have heard her moan and groan when he kissed her, Susan."

Wendy blushed furiously, trembling with outrage. It was all she could do to speak. "You—you—you—you're a vile monster, Moira, and I detest you! How dare you spy on me!"

Moira's expression was all wide-eyed innocence. "How do you expect me to learn how to deal with men if I don't learn from my dear older sister?"

The fact was that at fourteen, Moira knew more about dealing with the opposite sex than Wendy did at seventeen or would know even at twenty. In her peregrinations throughout the Maryland countryside, there was one friend who held a special attraction for her, a young farmer named Bob Thomas. He had not been pressed into military service because he was the breadwinner for his widowed mother and two younger sisters. Because of the heavy responsibilities he was burdened with, Bob seemed older than his eighteen years. Tall, blue-eyed, with cornsilk hair that fell low over his forehead, he had perfect white teeth and a shy, winning smile that had thoroughly captivated Moira the first time she spied him laboring in his cornfield. From smiles exchanged and a casual wave of the hand, the relationship progressed rapidly. The summer of '64 would remain a memorable time for Moira for as long as she lived.

She learned the pattern of his workday and made it a habit to ride in his direction whenever the opportunity presented itself. Soon they were exchanging conversation. Then the girl would rein in Devil and dismount to engage in more personal talk. By late July Moira was packing a picnic lunch before she set out, and she and Bob would sit with their backs against the bole of an ancient shade tree and munch sandwiches and drink cold lemonade.

The first time he touched her hand—accidentally, as they were standing up after eating—Moira jumped as if she had been touched by a hot coal.

"Gee, I'm sorry," he said in dismay. "I didn't mean—"

Impulsively Moira placed her hand over his mouth. "No, it's all right. In fact, I rather enjoy having you touch me. I was beginning to think you never would." Their eyes met and held unblinkingly as slowly Bob raised a hand and covered her hand across his lips. He pressed her soft palm and kissed it.

Moira shivered and moved closer to him. She tilted her face up to him and parted her lips invitingly. He started to draw back, but she gripped his shoulder and said, "What's wrong? Do I frighten you?"

He appeared perplexed. "No, of course not . . . although yes, in a way you do frighten me. You're so beautiful . . . so soft . . . almost like a princess out of a fairy tale." He shook his head. "You don't seem real."

She laughed. "Oh, believe me, I am very, very real. Flesh and blood just like you . . . Here, let me demonstrate." She slipped her hand behind his neck and stood up on her toes, offering him her mouth. Almost in a trance he pressed his mouth down on hers. And Moira was thrust into a new enchanted world, like Alice passing through the looking glass. She opened an eye and looked past his cheek upward. Green, leafy treetops and blue sky were whirling around them like the colored blades of a pinwheel.

Moira was aware of her body as she had never been before in all her fourteen years. Hot blood coursed rhythmically through her veins, throat and temples. All her nerve endings were aglow with a tingling, wondrous sensation that she had only been dimly conscious of before on warm spring and summer evenings, lying alone in the dark, staring at her bedroom ceiling.

She was keenly aware of his hard, young, male body, his hand at the small of her waist pulling her urgently against him, his chest against her breasts. Most of all she was aware of the increasing and expanding pressure of his manhood rising along the curve of her belly. Not that it was any great mystery to Moira. Sex was of consuming interest to her and her school chums and dominated much of their conversation. They *knew* what it was that men and women did in bed together to make babies. But knowledge and experience were worlds apart.

When their ardent embrace ended without a word having been exchanged, they walked away from the tree in the direction of the tall corn waving in the gentle breeze. The corn swallowed them up into another world of vivid greens and yellows and golds, with cotton-ball clouds scudding across the blinding blue of the sky. He led her to a small clearing, where they lay down side by side. Moira rolled onto her back and wrapped her arms around his neck, pulling him down on top of her. He kissed her eyes and her nose and her lips and her throat, firing her lust to near-unbearable limits.

She reached a hand between their bodies and grasped the bulge in his work pants. He gasped and recoiled, staring at her with disbelief. His eyes slid away guiltily and his face turned crimson.

"I—I'm sorry," he stammered. "I don't know what came over me. I got carried away. It's like that with men. You ought to slap my face."

"Whatever for?"

"For behaving like some kind of an animal."

"We're all animals, and your behavior is most natural and normal. As for myself, I have such a deep need and craving for you, Bob, that I'm beside myself." With an impish grin she reached out and touched him again. "I'm dying to have a look at that. It's mighty intriguing."

"You *are?*" He was incredulous.

"Of course, I've never seen one before. And don't you have a notion to have a look at me?"

He was tongue-tied.

"Of course you do, so here goes." She unbuttoned her shirt from neck to waist and spread it open. Bob was mesmerized. Without any coyness Moira slipped the shoulder straps of her chemise down over her arms and bared her breasts, high and firm, with upturned perky nipples.

She reached out and clasped his hands, guiding them to her bosom. The touch of his large, callused hands filled her with ecstasy. Her nipples surged against his palms.

With trembling fingers she unclasped his belt and unbuttoned his trousers and drawers. His hard, hot flesh filled both her hands. She stroked him lovingly until he protested.

"I can't hold out any longer. Stop!"

"Then we must hurry," she said breathlessly. "Take off your things!"

Moira kicked off her boots, raised her legs in the air and struggled out of her trousers. Shirt and chemise were flung high in the swaying cornstalks. She lay back on the warm, soft cushion of corn silk and watched him undress. She was entranced by his erect, jutting member.

"That must be quite an encumbrance to carry about," she jested.

He laughed self-consciously. "It isn't always in this state. Only when I'm with you. Or thinking of you at night when I'm in bed."

Moira giggled. "I think of you in bed, too. I've tried to picture what you look like naked. But you exceed my expectations altogether. Come, my darling. I can't bear the agony of wanting you an instant longer."

She opened her thighs to him and grasped his shoulders, drawing him down on top of her.

"I fear hurting you," he whispered.

"No fear, the pain will be exquisite, I know it will."

"Show me the way. Would you believe you're the first girl I've ever been with like this?"

"And you're the first boy for me. How wonderful. We'll lose our virginity together." She guided him to her yearning orifice, gritting her teeth as his hard flesh strained against her unyielding membrane.

"I can't do it," he gasped.

"Yes you can. Push."

She thrust her hips hard and high against him, locking her heels at the back of his waist. He entered her, and the pain was worse than she had expected, but it was quickly dissipated by indescribable pleasure as he and she rocked to and fro in the rhythym of lovemaking. His breath was hot against her throat. She was a helpless leaf flung higher, ever higher, on the crest of successive waves of ecstasy. Her flesh and bone and blood seemed to vaporize in the manner of a comet hurtling into the heart of the sun.

Consciousness and reality were slow to materialize. She felt as if the atoms of her body were reconstructing themselves. A finger, a toe, lips and tongue tingled once more. She turned her head and looked at Bob lying still beside her.

He looked at her and smiled. "Was it good for you, Moira?"

She rolled up her eyes and sighed. "Nothing in my life will ever be better. All this and heaven, too. Oh, Bob, my wonderful, marvelous darling, I'll count the moments until we can be together again. Tomorrow?"

"Tomorrow," he said. "And every tomorrow after that." He bent over her and kissed her gently on the lips.

"I don't know if I can wait until tomorrow." She flung her arms around his neck and clung to him fiercely.

He chuckled. "I don't want to either, but we can't spend all our waking hours making love. I've got a farm to run and a family to feed."

"I suppose you do," she said wistfully. She sat up and

reached for her trousers. "Anyway, thinking about it is almost as good as doing it."

Bob slid a hand along her thigh, raising goose bumps on her satin flesh. "Not quite as good. I've made love to you many times in fantasies, but it's a lonely kind of love."

They dressed in silence, each lost in revery. They left the field hand in hand and walked over to where Moira's horse was grazing in the shade of a tree. Bob kissed her and helped her mount Devil. Then he patted the stallion's rump and watched her ride off.

Atop a distant knoll Moira reined in and looked back. Bob waved to her, and she waved back. Then she rode down the far side and out of sight. It was the last time she would ever see Bob Thomas.

The following morning Bob surprised a Confederate deserter sleeping in the Thomas barn. Johnny Reb scrambled to his feet, pulled a pistol and shot the lad through the heart.

Among her friends and family Moira maintained a brave front. But every afternoon for almost a year she would ride Devil across the fields to the Thomas farm and sit under their shade tree with her back against the bole, just as she and he had tarried on warm lazy afternoons. And she would cry. It was a grief that would remain with her all her life, a jagged scar on spirit and soul, even though time would heal the open wound.

Chapter Two

Supper was served early at the Callahan household that eventful evening. Patrick Callahan sat at the head of the table, resplendent in his dress blues. His craggy face split in a weary smile.

"I don't know which one of you looks the prettiest tonight," he complimented his daughters.

Wendy touched a hand to her auburn locks, gathered up in a chignon snood decorated with colored sequins. "It's truly no contest, Father, and you know it. Tonight Wendy Callahan will be the uncontested belle of the ball."

At the other end of the table, Tillie Newstrom clucked her disapproval. "Vanity does not become you, young lady."

Moira stuck out her tongue at her older sister. "You look like a parlor maid decked out in her mistress's hand-me-downs. And that snood is hideous."

Colonel Callahan frowned, and there was a snap in his voice. "Silence, the two of you. I will not tolerate bickering at the table. Now eat your supper. The carriage will be here for us in a half-hour."

Moira put down her fork and slumped in the chair. "I'm really not hungry. My tummy is full of butterflies."

Aunt Tillie looked affronted. "And after all the trouble I went to cooking roast duck with cherry sauce."

"I'm sorry, Auntie. It's positively delicious, but I can't appreciate it tonight. Save it for me, and I'll eat it cold for lunch tomorrow."

"Did I mention that General and Mrs. Grant will not be attending the theater with the Lincolns?"

"Why not?" asked Susan. "Did he have an accident, as Secretary of State Seward did?"

"No, but I'm certain he offered the White House a suitable explanation. As a matter of fact, I understand from the provost marshal that the President isn't keen about attending himself, but he feels that at such an auspicious time, with the war ending and all, it's imperative that the President put in more public appearances and mingle with his constituents." His expression was grave. "I'm glad this war is over for more than one reason. For the past few months there have been persistent rumors that Confederate sympathizers in Washington have been hatching a plan to commit some dramatic act of treason."

Aunt Tillie was aghast. "Oh, dear me, how dreadful."

"Probably nothing to it, but now, of course, there's no purpose in acting against the President. The South has surrendered, and it's time this whole country united once more and put aside whatever personal differences any of us may have to pull together for the national good." He rolled up his napkin and slipped it back into the napkin ring. "All right, girls, it's time we get ready."

In the hall, as she draped her cape around her shoulders, Moira inquired, "Now that the war is over, what will happen to you? Will we be staying on in Washington, do you think?"

"I seriously doubt it. Right now there are more soldiers in the capital than there are civilians. In my own case, being a regular cavalryman, I imagine I'll be going to the frontier. You know, all these years the cavalry has been occupied with fighting the Rebs, the border Indian tribes have had things pretty much their own way. Time to put a stop to that."

"I feel sorry for the Indians. The whites keep pushing them further and further back into their own territory and

breaking treaties at will. It won't be long before the poor
red men will have their backs to the Pacific Ocean.''

"You've been reading too many of those inflammatory
newspaper editorials by this Horace Greeley fellow. He's
an atheist and an anarchist and he's against country, patriotism and God! Anyway, young lady, politics is not a topic
a woman should poke her nose into.''

Moira drew herself up haughtily and stared her father
directly in the eyes. "That kind of attitude is decadent,
Father, and rapidly becoming obsolete. It won't be too long
before women will demand suffrage and equal rights with
men. Why, one day a woman will be elected president.''

Callahan's gaunt face turned ashen and his eyes blazed
with anger. For an instant Moira thought he would strike
her. Wendy came to her rescue.

"Don't mind the brat, Daddy. She takes a perverse
delight in riling people. Ignore her.''

The colonel regained his composure. "Indeed she does.
But let me warn you, Moira, one more scandalous word
out of you and you'll be spending this night alone in your
room.''

A retort formed on Moira's lips, but she swallowed it.
To be denied this once-in-a-lifetime opportunity was
unthinkable.

"I'm sorry I angered you, Daddy,'' she said meekly.

"That's better.'' He opened the front door and peered
out into the night. "Yes, the carriage is waiting. Hurry
along.'' Moira paused one last time before the hall mirror
to inspect her ribbon headdress of *bouton d'or*.

She smiled in approval. After all, it was the latest
Parisian fashion for theatergoing!

The packed house at Ford's Theater was crackling with
excitement as men and women in uniform, evening clothes
and elegant ball gowns twisted and turned in their seats in
impatient expectation of the President's arrival.

There were two tiers of boxes on each side of the stage,
each tier containing two booths. Top right, from where the
Callahans were seated in the orchestra, the partitions sepa-

rating Booths 7 and 8 had been removed to accommodate the presidential party. The appointments consisted of two sofas and three cushioned straight-back chairs as well as President Lincoln's favorite rocking chair with bright red upholstery.

Decorating the front and sides of the presidential box were two large American flags flanking a picture of George Washington. A smaller flag, the banner of the Treasury guards, hung from a short staff above the picture.

"The suspense is unbearable," Susan whispered.

And then the moment was at hand. Abruptly the orchestra, which had been warming up, burst into the spine-tingling march, "Hail to the Chief." As one, the audience rose and commenced clapping and cheering. The presidential party consisted of the President—his tall, commanding presence towering above the others—the First Lady; Clara Harris, the daughter of a New York Senator; her brother and her fiancé, Major Rathbone. President Lincoln moved to the front of the box, acknowledging the rousing welcome, smiling and waving his hands. When the commotion finally subsided, the party took its seats, with the President seated at the rear of the booth in his rocking chair, hidden from sight now by heavy draperies.

The theater manager came out to center stage and held up his hands for silence: "Ladies and gentlemen, Ford's Theater takes pleasure in presenting a play by Mr. Tom Taylor, *Our American Cousin*, starring that illustrious lady of the theater, Miss Laura Keene."

He walked into the wings, and the curtain went up on what was to be a momentous historical drama that would eclipse the trivial pleasantry taking place on the stage.

It all occurred so rapidly that the people in the audience were thoroughly baffled by the sequence of events. Many believed at first that the action was part of the performance onstage.

Laura Keene had just delivered a line that elicited explosive laughter from the spectators. Moira, as she had been doing constantly throughout the play, turned her head once again for a hopeful glance at the presidential box. To her astonishment a young man with dark, bushy hair and a flowing mustache was standing at the front railing of the box, brandishing a dagger and shouting: *"Sic semper tyrannis!"*

Mrs. Lincoln and Miss Harris screamed, and Major Rathbone leaped up and grappled with the stranger. The intruder slashed his arm with the dagger, shoved him away and with practiced agility, vaulted over the balustrade with the obvious intention of landing lightly on the stage. But as he cleared the rail, his boot spur became entangled with one of the American flags. Flung off balance, he crash-landed on the edge of the stage, smashing his leg. While audience, actors and stagehands watched in immobile silence, never having heard the fatal gunshot and still unaware of what had transpired, he got to his feet, dragging his broken leg behind him, and limped off the stage.

Overnight the city of Washington, D.C., went from euphoric celebration to a state of national mourning. Colonel Callahan escorted his daughters home to their dwelling on the outskirts of town and returned immediately to the capital. He was present when Secretary of War Stanton issued the final bulletin on the President's fight for life:

"President Lincoln died this morning at twenty-two minutes after the hour of seven o'clock." He went on to say: "Gentlemen . . . our intelligence sources have not been idle in the desperate hours since the President was shot last night at Ford's Theater. It has come to light that the assassination of President Lincoln was only part of a massive conspiracy to assassinate Vice-President Johnson, Secretary of State Seward, General Grant and other cabinet officers, with the purpose of throwing the United States into a state of anarchy. . . . The conspiracy was conceived in the twisted brain of a notable Washington actor, one John Wilkes Booth who, himself, fired the fatal shot into the President's brain.

"At two A.M. this morning the War Department's secret service apprehended many of the leading conspirators at a local boarding house run by Mrs. Mary Surrat. . . . John Wilkes Booth and his chief lieutenant in the plot, David

Herold, so far have escaped across the Potomac River, but you have my guarantee that their freedom is only transient."

The secretary's pledge was fulfilled eleven days later, on April 26, when a detachment of twenty-eight soldiers commanded by Colonel E. Conger tracked Booth and Herold to a barn on a Mr. Garret's farm. They surrounded the barn and issued an ultimatum for the two fugitives to surrender. Herold complied, but Booth was defiant to the end. Even after the barn was torched by Conger's order, he stood in the open doorway waving his pistol in the air. Then, in what some consider an act of charity, Sergeant Boston Corbett raised his rifle, took aim and shot Lincoln's assassin through the head.

In July of the same year Colonel Patrick Callahan announced to his family: "It's official. I'm being transferred to Texas along with Phil Sheridan and George Custer. I'll be serving under Custer with the Michigan Cavalry Regiment."

Wendy and Susan were appalled. "Texas!" the oldest sister exclaimed. "It's so primitive in Texas. There's nothing there but desert and savages."

"You're right about that. Lots of desert wilderness, where it's customary in the summer for the temperature to hover at one hundred and ten for days at a time. And Texas abounds with murderous Indians. Now if keeping the Apaches, the Sioux, the Comanches and the Cheyennes under control isn't enough, we may have to contend with the Mexicans. Army intelligence agents down in Mexico City say that the emperor Maximilian is having delusions of grandeur about restoring Mexican rule in Texas."

"It sounds positively horrible," Susan lamented. "I'd rather die than go to Texas."

Moira was silent.

Next Callahan looked at his sister-in-law, Tillie Newstrom. "What do you say about it, Tillie?"

She sighed. "I'm sorry, Patrick, but I can't accompany you. My cousin Maude and her two girls are coming here from New York; Maude was widowed the last month of the war. If she and I pool our resources, we can keep up the house.''

Callahan nodded and looked from Wendy to Susan. "If I sweeten the pot for you and Maude, would you agree to keep Wendy and Susan and Moira here in Maryland with you?''

Tears glistened in Aunt Tillie's eyes, and she wrung her hands with emotion. "Agree? You don't know what a relief it would be. These girls are like my own daughters, and I'd be brokenhearted to let them go off to that wild land.''

Wendy and Susan fairly danced with glee and took turns hugging their aunt and their father. "Oh, thank you, Daddy. Thank you, Aunt Tillie.''

Moira maintained her reserved silence until at last Colonel Callahan looked at her for some response. "Well, young lady, what do you have to say?''

Moira cleared her throat and replied in a casual tone, "Oh, I'll be going along with you, Daddy. After all, somebody has to look after you. As Aunt Tillie says, men are so helpless without a woman's hand to keep their lives and health in order. To be honest, the idea of going to a far-off place like Texas is very exciting to me. So exotic. And all that wide-open space for me and Devil to ride over. And the Indians! My, no, I wouldn't miss it for the world! When do we leave?''

"We'll be shipping out in two weeks.''

"Then I must go shopping for some new outfits. I scarcely believe that female attire in Texas features too many buttons and bows and frill. I'll need work pants and shirts and boots, and one of those wide Mexican sombreros.''

That night the three sisters, wrapped in nightgowns and shawls, sat cross-legged on Moira's bed for a girl-to-girl chat. Somehow Moira's imminent departure for Texas was drawing them closer than they had been in years.

"I never thought I'd ever hear myself say this to you, brat,'' said Wendy, "but I am going to miss you something fierce.''

"Me too." Susan moved closer and put an arm around Moira's shoulders.

Moira could feel tears welling up in her own eyes as well. "The same goes for me. You know, the three of us have never been separated before. I'm going to feel like a part of my own body is missing. You know something else, Wendy—secretly I've always looked up to you, maybe even been a little jealous too, no matter how atrocious I am to you at times."

Susan smiled beneficently at them. "The thing is, sisters, the thing of it is love. We may not always act it, but deep down we love one another very much indeed."

"Love!" Wendy and Moira chorused, and then the three of them laughed, happy in their newly affirmed togetherness.

Alone in his den, Colonel Callahan sipped his bourbon, reflecting on what Moira had said:

"*. . . After all, somebody has to look after you, Daddy. As Aunt Tillie says, men are so helpless without a woman's hand to keep their lives and health in order . . .*"

"Tillie is right," he said, the words directed at his dear departed wife. He glanced upward as if at the heavens. "Since you went away, my darling, I've been like a ship without a rudder."

Moira was the spitting image of her mother, both in appearance and spirit. Yes, she would be a great comfort to him in the lonely wastes of Texas. Patrick Callahan loved all his daughters dearly, but there was a special place in his heart for Moira, although her stubbornness and her unfeminine will and determination constantly exasperated him. Well, he rationalized, in another few years she'd be of marrying age. He smiled ruefully. God help the poor devil who would marry her; he would have to be a special kind of man to cope with a hellion such as Moira!

He covered his misting eyes with a hand. Despite his grief Colonel Callahan considered himself a man well blessed.

Truly my cup runneth over.

Chapter Three

Dear Diary,

We have been at Fort Hempstead for more than two weeks and have been exposed to all the predicted hardships and then some. Life for the cavalry wives on a frontier post is extremely primitive and arduous, and I have unbounded admiration for these dedicated and gallant women, especially for General Custer's wife, Elizabeth. From her appearance it would seem she was born to a life on a royal manor. Petite and very dark, with lustrous brown eyes, she is small-boned and delicate-looking, with skin like fine porcelain. It is a wonder to us all how she tolerates the scorching climate that prevails throughout the summer. The instant the sun emerges from behind the distant mountains it glows brighter and brighter like a fiery coal, ascending slowly to the noon zenith, blistering and splitting the earth and sucking all moisture, color and life out of the countryside. Each morning pick-and-shovel teams turn out to fill in the blisters and splits that reappear day after day in the adobe roadbeds and on the drab parade ground like vast, erratic spiderwebs. Nonetheless, Mrs. Custer— she's asked me to call her Elizabeth—bears up under

*the unceasing ordeal with stamina and good cheer
that put many of the other wives to shame.*

*There is a total dearth of creature comforts at this
godforsaken post. Ice is almost as rare as a snowball in
hell, although, upon our arrival, the then-commanding
general gave a party for General Custer and his
officers and had three small pieces of ice sent by
express from San Antonio for the occasion. Daddy
says they cost ten dollars apiece and were packed in
huge crates insulated with sawdust.*

*What passes for butter here tastes like axle grease,
and the milk is thin and watery and flavored with the
wild garlic that the cows graze on. Meat, beef and
lamb taste as musty as if they had been resurrected
from the grave. There are no fresh vegetables. Yesterday a shipment of potatoes arrived, and every
single one was decayed. It is impossible to grow
flowers. The sole vegetation that thrives here in summer is Madeira vine. It grows thickly on trellises that
flank the sides of the small porches that front the
officers' bungalows.*

*Quarters are allotted by rank, and if a new officer
is assigned to the post or a bachelor marries, it
means a general shifting of quarters all down the
line. A hapless second lieutenant and his family often
find themselves out of the frame homes and pushed
into the tent city with the noncommissioned officers
and enlisted men. Some of the new wives are already
talking about going back East. It is difficult to blame
them. Aside from the heat, the post is besieged by
ants, ticks, buggers, chiggers, snakes, scorpions, ta-
rantulas and creatures I cannot identify.*

*Tonight Daddy and I are invited to the Custer's
home for supper. It is an occasion that all the officers
here and their families look forward to, an invitation
to one of their dinner parties. Elizabeth and her black
cook Mary always manage to come up with some
special treat, some delicacy brought in from San
Antonio.*

I must stop now. There is still time to ride down to a creek about four miles from the post and take a bath.

A small pool had been scooped out of the creek by the enlisted men, and once a week the women on the post were transported there by wagons and allowed to bathe. It was an isolated spot hidden by trees and knolls and surrounded by a detail of armed guards in case there were marauding Indians in the vicinity.

"It wouldn't surprise me if the guards spy on us from the weeds atop those hills," a lieutenant's wife observed the first time she visited the pond.

"Don't dwell on it, dearie," a veteran wife advised her. "Not a thing we can do about it, anyway. It's either this or no bathing."

Another woman laughed. "Listen, it's harder on them than it is on us. Remember, the enlisted men don't have any women to go home to."

One bath a week was not enough to suit Moira. She didn't sit around on the Madeira-shaded porch all day like most of the women. There wasn't a day that she didn't go riding on Devil, either alone or with the scouts who made daily patrols of the border, seeking out bands of hostiles. It was her custom at the end of the afternoon to ride out to the creek and have a quick bath in privacy, never wandering too far from the pile of clothing on the bank with the Spencer army carbine atop it. The Spencer rifle could fire seven rounds in quick order. Even in the short time she had been at the post, Moira was becoming an excellent marksman. Or "markswoman," as she liked to call herself to tease her father.

She donned her riding clothes and boots and walked down to the corral, whistling the battle march of the cavalry, "Garryowen." Corporal Keller, one of the regimental grooms, tipped his square cap to her.

"Afternoon, Miss Callahan. I guess you want me to ready up old Devil for you?"

"Thank you, Tom." While she was waiting she checked

her saddlebags: clean underwear and outerwear, towel, soap, ammunition. She loaded the Spencer rifle just as Keller walked Devil over to her.

"Better not wander too far today, miss," he warned her. "Scouting party reports a Cheyenne war party is casing the fort."

"I'll take care, Tom." She jammed the rifle into the saddle boot and swung herself aboard, light as a feather. She felt Devil's sides quiver against her thighs, and the big stallion shook his mane, swinging his head around to her. She bent over and stroked his long sleek muzzle, the texture of moire.

"Good boy, you want your treat, don't you?" She took a piece of rock candy from the pocket of her shirt and held it out to him in the palm of her hand. Devil's tail lashed in pleasure. She patted his neck lovingly. "Giddap."

Moira rode over a dry stream bed that traversed a rolling hillside. On the ridge of the hill she reined Devil and patted his sweaty mane. The sun beat down mercilessly, so dry and stifling that her breath seared her lungs. Devil's breathing was labored, too.

"We're both new here, feller. This climate is going to take some getting used to." She took off her stetson hat and wiped her forehead with a sleeve.

To the south a flash of motion caught her attention. She squinted at a distant ridge through a shimmering haze of heat waves rising from the parched earth. It took intense concentration to make out what was there: a band of mounted Indians, motionless against the azure sky, looking like the lead toy soldiers and Indians that she and her cousin Jeb had played war games with when they were small children. Far off as they were, she sensed that they were watching her as attentively as she was watching them. Her cotton shirt, wet with perspiration, felt icy cold against her backbone. Fleetingly she considered forgoing her bath this day. Then, to her surprise and relief, the Indian at the head of the column waved an arm in salutation. Grinning now, Moira waved back. And with a parting wave the band disappeared down the far side of the ridge.

"It's all right, Devil. They're a friendly tribe for sure. Let's get on with it."

Some time later Moira reined in her mount on the high ground overlooking the creek. She looked down at the grove of stunted trees where the post women bathed. At intervals along the winding banks of the shallow stream there were little oases where, over the centuries, certain hardy specimens of foliage had survived the murderous heat, drawing life through long, multibranched root systems at the river's bottom. She urged Devil down the slope and into the grove and its welcome shade. She dismounted and tethered the horse to a thin tree where he could munch on the dry duff that layered the ground beneath the branches. She scanned the terrain on all sides. Sand, leaves and grass emitted a strange eerie whisper, stirred by the gentlest of breezes. Satisfied that she was alone, Moira undressed and placed her clothes on the edge of the bank, with her rifle on top of the pile. Being naked in the wide-open spaces under the uncritical scrutiny of nature, with the gentle wind caressing her body like a lover's touch, was a stimulating and sensuous sensation; not the prosaic act of undressing in the cloistered privacy of one's room. Soap in hand, she waded into the tepid stream. At its deepest level the water just covered her hips.

She soaped her arms and breasts, buttocks and belly, shivering not from cold but from the memory of her one grand passion with Bob in the tall golden corn. Her craving for love was becoming more urgent with every passing day.

Her reverie was shattered by the sound of hoofbeats from behind the hill, heading in the direction of the stream. She waded back to shore, but before she could emerge and reach for the rifle, a horseman appeared on the top of the ridge. He wore the uniform of the US Cavalry, not a Cheyenne headdress. Relief flooded over her, only to be succeeded by growing mortification. It had never occurred to Moira when she came to bathe that such an embarrassing predicament would ever befall her.

The cavalryman cupped his hands to his mouth and called down to her: "Who the hell are you and what are you doing down there?"

"Who the hell wants to know?" she shouted back.

"Lieutenant Bradford Taylor of Fort Hempstead. I asked you what you were doing."

"What does it look like I'm doing? I'm taking a bath. And I'll thank you to leave me alone so I can get on with it. I'm the daughter of Colonel Patrick Callahan."

His long, shrill whistle of surprise pierced the still air. "Moira Callahan, is it? You must be daft, miss, to come all the way out here by yourself." He dismounted and started down the hill in her direction.

In dismay Moira grabbed her clothing off the bank and covered her breasts with the articles. Below the waist she was concealed by the high bank. A rosy blush suffused her face, neck, shoulders and torso all the way down to water level. Bradford Taylor was the most dashing young officer on the post. He was the object of attention of every single woman on the post and several who were not single, as well as the secret passion of Moira Callahan. Her emotions fluctuated from love to hatred, for Bradford treated her as if she were a child.

"If he sees me in this naked state," she reflected, "he'll well lose the notion that I'm a child!"

Bradford Taylor was, as Elizabeth Custer put it, "handsome to a fault"—tall, slender, with classic features, wavy brown hair and a square jaw that had a deep cleft in the point. He had perfect white teeth, a roguish smile and green eyes with a glint of lechery in them.

He entered the grove and stopped alongside Devil, who whinnied and welcomed him with a cold nose on his neck. Taylor patted his flank and contemplated Moira with a mixture of amusement and disapproval.

"Wait until your father hears about this," he said. "Suppose it had been an Indian buck instead of me coming upon you like this?"

"He'd have got a bullet right between the eyes. Now turn around and let me get dressed."

"Glad to oblige." He did an about-face.

Hesitantly Moira climbed onto the bank, still shielding her body as best she could with her discarded clothing. She cleared her throat.

"Lieutenant, in one of my saddlebags there are some clean clothes. Would you please hand them to me?"

"At your service." He unfastened the saddlebag and extracted the newly laundered garments. "Well, what have we here?" He held up a pink shirtwaist and lace panta-lettes. "Who would have thought that underneath that tomboy exterior there lurks a streak of frivolous femininity?"

Moira's cheeks flamed. "Don't get funny with me, Lieutenant. You could get that slug between the eyes just as well as any Indian buck!"

"Tsk, tsk . . . Temper, temper, temper."

"Give me those clothes!"

He started to turn around, and Moira screamed: "Don't you *dare!*"

"My dear child, I find myself in a dilemma. First you tell me to bring you your clothing, then you countermand the order. You remind me of an old platoon leader."

Moira took a deep breath to calm herself. In a steady voice she directed him, "Put the clothes behind you and then back toward me."

He laughed mockingly. "I say now, I'm likely to break my neck if I can't see where I'm headed."

"I'll tell you where to step."

"My life is in your hands."

"All right, now start walking. Straight on. That's it. Now a step sideways to the left, so you don't trip on an exposed root . . ." He kept backing toward her. "There now, stop."

She took a step forward and grabbed the clothing from him. "Now walk back to Devil." As he proceeded, Moira ducked behind a thick thistle bush. Quickly she put on the shirtwaist and underpants, followed by a white silk blouse and riding britches of soft chamois, and lastly her boots.

"All right, you can turn around now." She walked toward him, her eyes downcast on the ground, self-conscious over this unexpected encounter with Lieutenant Taylor. There was an enforced intimacy about it that annoyed and embarrassed her. She could hear him recounting the episode at the officers' mess, as well as the laughter it would evoke. Every time one of the cavalrymen glanced in her direction, she would read silent mirth in his eyes.

At her approach, he flashed his dazzling smile. "Feeling more comfortable, Miss Callahan?"

"Considerably."

She stooped to gather up her dirty clothes, walked stiff-legged to Devil and stuffed the bundle into the saddlebag. Not once looking at Lieutenant Taylor, she placed a foot in a stirrup and vaulted into the saddle.

"You're quite a horsewoman," he said. "I've watched you."

"Thank you."

"It's hard to believe you're only fourteen."

"Fifteen. I had a birthday last week."

"Did you now? Well, many happy returns of the day. I guess we'd better be getting back to the post." He started up the slope to where his mount was waiting patiently. Moira followed at a slow gait.

On the ride back to the post there was a barrier of tension between them; more accurately a barrier that Moira had erected. It was sustained until Lieutenant Taylor casually said: "If you're worried that I'm going to relate this anecdote at your expense, forget it. Because that's exactly what I am going to do—forget it ever happened. Incidentally, I wouldn't mention it to your father. I don't believe the old boy would appreciate the humor of it."

Suddenly Moira burst into laughter. "I don't imagine he would. He'd no doubt believe that you took advantage of me and throw you into the post stockade."

Lieutenant Taylor threw back his leonine head and joined in the laughter.

"Another thing, Lieutenant . . ." He looked at her,

and she raised an eyebrow and said solemnly, "I promise I won't mention to my father either that you referred to him as the old boy."

Now the two of them laughed so hard that their horses looked back at them uneasily and snorted. And by the time they rode into the post, Moira Callahan and the lieutenant were good friends.

Chapter Four

While she was dressing for the dinner party at the Custers', Moira surveyed herself in the mirror and reflected: "Do you know, this is the first time I've worn a dress since we left Maryland?"

She had brought three dresses from home for such occasions as this. The one she had chosen for this evening was a summer ball gown printed with colonial wild flowers on porcelain blue; a wide floral border went around the softly shirred bouffant just above the hemline flounce. She smoothed out the horseshoe collar and bowed the waist sash. Her long black hair was gathered at the nape of her neck with a blue ribbon and cascaded down her back almost to her waist.

She turned at the knocking on her door. "Are you almost ready, my dear?" her father called to her.

"I'm ready when you are." She went to the door and opened it. His face was radiant.

"I've never seen you look lovelier—the image of your mother when we were first married."

She rewarded him with a dimpled smile and a curtsy. "Thank you, Colonel Callahan. You look very handsome yourself."

The colonel was wearing his dress uniform, a snug dark blue jacket with brass buttons to the throat, over light blue trousers with yellow stripes running down the outside seams. Atop his head was a spiked dress helmet with a yellow horsehair plume.

Colonel Callahan snapped his heels together and offered her a crooked arm. "Shall we be off, then?"

She slipped a hand inside his elbow. "We shall be the handsomest pair at the party."

"It's not a large party, you know. Besides you and me, there will be Major Simpson and his wife, Mrs. Simpson's sister Bea and one of the younger officers, I forget who. George believes in encouraging a spirit of camaraderie among his officers of all ranks."

Elizabeth Custer greeted them on the front porch, where she was seated with Sara Simpson and her sister, who had arrived from St. Louis to spend the month of August with the Simpsons. Another of the thousands of American woman widowed by the heartbreaking War Between the States, she was a striking woman with auburn hair curled up in twin barrettes at the back of her head. Her gown was a deep-cowled flow of velour with a subtle flaring that suggested a flawless figure beneath.

Moira's feminine instinct told her that Elizabeth Custer was endeavoring to make a match between Bea and her father. Furthermore, it would not surprise her if Elizabeth harbored a similar intention in inviting a junior officer to be her escort for the evening.

"You look divine, Moira," Elizabeth said, clasping both her hands.

"I love your gown, Elizabeth," Moira countered. The general's wife was wearing a heavy satin skirt and a satin blouse with a V neckline and a ribbon over the waistband.

"I think it's about time we roused the men out of George's study. You'd think after being together all day, they'd be sick of masculine society. But no, they are talking military shop. Well, come along, girls, we shall rectify that promptly."

She seated her guests in the small but elegantly furnished parlor and went down the short hall to the general's study. She rapped smartly on the door.

"Rise and shine, you horse soldiers. We ladies crave your companionship."

A short time later the men trekked into the parlor. General Custer was not a handsome man in the usual meaning of the word. His appearance—long blond hair, piercing blue eyes, strong aquiline nose and a mustache shaped like a scimitar—was intimidating, yet Moira felt a strong fascination for the man.

On Custer's heels was rolypoly Major Simpson. And behind him was Second Lieutenant Bradford Taylor. Moira's eyes were round with surprise, and her mouth formed an oval.

Custer greeted her jovially. "By God! I can't believe my eyes. What a remarkable transformation. Major . . . Lieutenant . . . would you recognize this fairy princess as the same hellion who rides like a Comanche and wipes down sweaty horses in the paddock with as much verve as the grooms?"

"Mercy, no." Major Simpson honored her with a low bow.

"What about you, Lieutenant?" Custer demanded of Lieutenant Taylor. "Isn't she a dream?"

"Enchanting . . ." The lieutenant's smile was conspiratorial, and his left eye twitched in a wink that only Moira could detect.

Elizabeth addressed Lieutenant Taylor: "Lieutenant, would you do the honor of escorting Miss Callahan into the dining room?"

"I would be delighted." He extended his arm, and Moira grasped it with a gracious smile.

Colonal Callahan escorted Beatrice Carter, and they made a very handsome couple indeed, Moira observed, not without a trace of anxiety. She and her sisters had often discussed the possibility that their father would remarry. After all, he was only in his early fifties and a strong, virile man who led an active life. Bea Carter would tempt any unattached red-blooded male.

General Custer sat at the head of the table, with Moira to his immediate right and Lieutenant Taylor beside her. Her father and Mrs. Carter sat directly opposite them. Major Simpson and Mrs. Simpson sat across from each other to the left and right of Elizabeth Custer.

At first the conversation was light and animated, filled with anecdotes about daily life at the post, familiar laments about the quality of the food, the lack of fresh vegetables and the abominable weather.

"They should have named it Hades instead of Hempstead," Custer declared.

In comparison with the everyday fare, the meal was sumptuous: Gulf shrimp with creole sauce; baked ham with raisin gravy; candied yams; and rice pudding laced with hard sauce, not to mention Mary's famous homemade rolls.

"I forgot there was food like this," Lieutenant Taylor complimented Elizabeth. "A feast fit for gods."

"I hope nobody minds if I open my jacket," said the portly Simpson.

"Take it off if you'll be more comfortable," the hostess offered.

Simpson was going to assent until his wife gave him a reprimanding look. "No, this will be fine," he said regretfully.

"Shall we retire to the parlor for coffee and brandy?" Elizabeth asked.

"Good idea," her husband agreed.

They followed the general and Mrs. Custer into the sitting room and sat around a large round coffee table that Custer had commissioned some friendly Cheyennes to construct upon their arrival at Hempstead. They had barely been seated when the charge of quarters appeared on the Custer front porch.

"Sorry to interrupt your party, General, but I knew you'd want to see this special bulletin from General Sheridan's headquarters. It arrived by courier about fifteen minutes ago. It's marked 'Urgent—Top Priority.'"

"By all means, Sergeant." Custer opened the screen

door and took the manila envelope. The sergeant saluted and departed. Frowning, General Custer opened the dispatch and removed the contents. He read in silence as an expectant hush settled over the others. Finally he cleared his throat and addressed them.

"I think you should hear this, my fellow officers. Looks like the Sioux and Cheyennes are stepping up their war games. Let me quote: 'August 20, near Lake Station, J. H. Jones, stage agent, reported a woman and child killed and scalped and thirty head of stock run off by Indians; at Reed's Springs three persons were killed and three wounded; at Spanish Fort four people were murdered, eight scalped, fifteen horses and mules run off and three women were raped; one of these women was raped by thirteen Indians, who afterward killed and scalped her and then killed her four little children.' "

The cavalrymen listened in stoic silence while the women emitted exclamations of shock, outrage and horror. Moira bit her underlip and said nothing.

"Those brutal savages—they're not human," Mrs. Simpson shrilled, her voice trembling.

Quite casually Moira interjected, "Wasn't it a Cheyenne village—Sand Creek, I believe—that was totally massacred by a cavalry regiment under the command of a Colonel Chivington? If memory serves me, the good colonel said: 'Kill and scalp all Indians big and little. Nits make lice.' His men murdered three hundred Indians, only seventy-five of whom were warriors."

There was a sharp intake of breath from Elizabeth Custer and the two other women. Colonel Callahan leaped to his feet and thundered at his daughter: "Moira, your insolence is inexcusable. To equate a legitimate battle with irresponsible acts of unprovoked barbarism, why, it's—it's—words fail me. I think you owe everyone in this room an apology for making such a mindless statement."

Custer held up a hand. "It's all right, Pat. There's a good deal of truth in what the child says. Those Cheyennes were a peaceful group; in fact, they were under the protection of Major Wynkoop's command at the time. Chivington was a fanatic, a crazy man; he was deposed from the clergy. Do you know what Nelson Miles said of the massacre at Sand Creek? He called it the foulest and most reprehensible and unjustifiable crime in the annals of the United States."

"I think we must all agree, sir," Moira said quietly.

An uncomfortable and strained hush settled over the assembly until General Custer continued. "No, the Cheyennes have never forgiven the United States for that bloodthirsty crime. They've sat on their grudge for a long time, but now it seems they intend to repay the debt in kind. I won't distress the ladies by exposing them to any more of this sordid and grisly report, but, gentlemen, tomorrow I would like all company commanders to report to regimental headquarters for a thorough briefing on the matter." He thumbed through the documents in his hand. "August twenty-first, more of the same. And on the twenty-second, twenty-third, twenty-fifth . . . it goes on and on." He dropped the report on the coffee table and sighed. "It's been a quiet summer, comparatively speaking, but it appears all that is about to change."

Understandably the remainder of the evening was conducted on a subdued and somber note. At a point during a lull in the conversation, Lieutenant Taylor suggested: "Perhaps you'd care to accompany me for a stroll, Miss Callahan? I really need to work off that superb but rather filling meal."

"I could use some exercise myself," she assented. "If General Custer and Mrs. Custer will excuse us."

"By all means, my dear," Elizabeth said. "You young people take your stroll."

Outside the house Moira looked up at the sky. "Billions and billions of sparkling diamonds on a black velvet background."

"It's amazing—even though there's no moon one can see as clearly as if the moon were full."

"It's softer and more soothing than moonlight."

"Well, where shall we walk?"

Moira laughed. "There are no surprises on the post. I

could find my way around blindfolded. So why don't we go down to the corral and visit the horses? I find their company very agreeable."

"Aye," he agreed. "Far more agreeable than some humans." He added slyly, "Such as your Colonel Chivington."

"Inhuman beast! No, I take that back. Beasts don't kill and torture for the love of it, the way humans do. They only take life for food."

He offered her his arm and they commenced walking. "You're a spunky one, you are, talking up to all that top brass." He chuckled. "I thought your father was going to have apoplexy."

"I love my father dearly, but I find it totally unthinkable that I would ever marry a military man."

His smile was rueful. "And why would that be?"

"My sisters and I have been military brats since birth. We grew up living, breathing cavalry. I saw the hardships that being a military wife and mother wrought on poor Mama. And mind you, my father was an officer for most of his career, and a high-ranking one. Look around you here at Hempstead. The younger wives of junior officers, hoardes of new little army brats tugging at their skirts and bawling about the food, the heat, the insects, complaining about everything, and rightly so. Life down here is pure hell."

"The condition is temporary. They will eventually get on to better assignments. The juniors will rise through the ranks."

"Do you really think so? Daddy says now that the big war is over and once the Indian issue is resolved, there won't be any need for so large an army. Some will be discharged; the regulars will be reduced in rank. You know, of course, that the general is no longer officially a major general?"

"I know, he's a brevet major general, but on the books he's rated a colonel."

"Yes, and out of respect for his brave exploits during the war, his men would never call him anything but General Custer . . . But what about you, Lieutenant Taylor, what are your future plans? You appear to me to be too bright and ambitious to want to make the cavalry your career.''

''Oh, but I do. War may go out of fashion, but there will always be an army, a navy, a cavalry. And the services will always provide opportunities for ambitious and superior officers.''

Moira teased him. ''And naturally you consider yourself a superior young officer?''

He stopped walking and turned her to face him. ''Indeed I do, and before too much longer I intend to prove it to you. I've set my sights on foreign service, say as military attaché to the Court of St. James's or at Versailles. Now that's where the power is. Oh, I'll keep an open mind, watching the way the wind is blowing militarily for the United States. If we ever get into a major war—and I believe there is every likelihood that we will—I can always switch directions and become a war hero like Custer and Sheridan and Grant, but in the interim I'll be scoring political victories. Look at Grant—he has his eye on the presidency, and damned if I don't believe he'll succeed.''

''Your modesty does become you so, Lieutenant,'' she mocked him. ''Why, I can see the headlines now, say in 1880: BRADFORD TAYLOR ELECTED PRESIDENT BY AN OVERWHELMING MAJORITY.''

Taylor laughed, and even in the starlight his smile was brilliant. Moira shivered as he drew her closer to him. ''Well, I wouldn't go that far, Miss Callahan, but it's not beyond the realm of possibility.''

She tilted her head and looked up into his face curiously. ''What did you mean before about proving your superiority to me?''

''Oh, can't you hazard a guess as to what I had in mind?''

She shook her head. ''Not remotely. Sooner or later you and my father will be reassigned, and our paths will diverge.''

Now Lieutenant Taylor shook his head, and the smile

faded from his face. Quite solemnly he said. "I don't see it that way, Moira. No more false formality; call me Brad. I have no intention of letting our paths diverge."

"Nonsense, whatever do you mean?"

"Quite simply, I intend to make you my wife one day. And the sooner the better. I realize you're only fifteen, but years are meaningless. You are a grown woman in every condition of the term. Intellectually and physically." His grip on her arms tightened and he drew her fast against him now. His voice fell an octave, becoming husky and sensual. She could smell the afterdinner brandy and tobacco on his breath, and it did not offend her the way it did when she walked into her father's airless study. In fact, it acted as a mild aphrodisiac.

"Physically . . ." he repeated, and his gaze was drawn to her bosom, heaving against his chest. "I was extremely aware of your physical maturity down by the bathing creek this afternoon."

"You saw nothing!" she snapped, trying to sound indignant but recalling the intimate encounter with an excitement that inflamed her.

"I saw enough. You're a beautiful, desirable, exciting woman, and I want you to be my wife for ever and a day."

"You must be insane, Lieu—I mean, Brad. We hardly know each other."

"I've known you all my life. The first day you arrived here at the post, I knew you were the one, the girl I've been waiting for all of my life. It's true. Don't deny that you haven't been aware of me as well, that you haven't sensed the mutual attraction between us."

She lowered her eyes demurely. "One can't help but notice you, Brad. You're a very attractive man."

He cupped his hand gently under her chin and tilted it up as he bent to kiss her. Moira was helpless, mesmerized. When their lips touched, she closed her eyes and was transported back in time to that glorious interlude with Bob, lying in the tall corn with the sun glowing on their bare backs. Desire coursed through her body like a flash fire, obliterating all her senses but one—the sense of touch, touching and being touched. She was deaf to the background sounds of the summer night: the chirping of crickets, the drone of locusts, the distant barking of dogs and howling coyotes, the sound of accordion music from the enlisted men's quarters accompanying a chorus harmonizing to the lyrics of "Garryowen."

Moira wrapped her arms around his neck and abandoned herself to passion. Brad lifted her off the earth and ground his pelvis against hers. She thrilled to the urgent thrust of his manhood and the tender strength of his hands kneading the soft globes of her buttocks. Their mouths parted briefly in order that they might regain their breath. She slipped a hand between their bodies and caressed him.

"Oh, Brad, I'm on fire."

"So am I, but where can we go?"

The issue was decided for them as a voice called out from the corral, "Who's that back there by the barn? Come forward and identify yourself."

Moira and Brad broke apart, and after a moment he found his voice; just barely. "It's all right," he answered in a hoarse voice. "Lieutenant Taylor here with Miss Callahan. We're getting a breath of air." He took Moira by the hand and they continued on to the corral.

At their approach the armed sentry lowered his rifle to port arms. "Evenin', Lieutenant . . . Miss Callahan . . . Sorry to challenge you like that, but the general gave strict orders. We're on full alert, with the sentries pulling double duty. Mason's on the far side. Cheyenne war party in the neighborhood."

"I think I may have seen them earlier today," Moira said, pointing in the direction of the hill from which she had spied the distant Indian column. She described the event.

Lieutenant Taylor was shaken. "Good Lord, girl! It's a wonder you weren't captured!"

"No danger of that; they were too far off. I could have easily ridden back to camp if they had shown any hostility.

In fact, one of them waved to me and I waved back. Then they rode off out of sight.''

"Don't be misled by the wave of a hand. They're deceitful buggers, miss,'' the sentry told her.

"Same as the white men who make treaties with them knowing full well they have no intention of keeping their promises.''

"Miss?'' The sentry was bewildered by her candor.

Brad laughed. "Never mind, Saunders. Resume your duty.''

"Yes, sir.'' The private saluted, and Taylor returned it. Then he and Moira made their way back to the Custer home.

"I don't know what came over me, Brad. Another few minutes and we might have been caught in the act.''

"*Flagrante delicto,* as they say.'' It struck him as amusing. "Can you imagine how that would have looked included in Saunders's morning report to Georgie-Porgie?''

"Georgie-Porgie?''

"Yes, of course, you are not privy to barracks banter. General Custer is quite a ladies' man.''

Moira was genuinely shocked. "Oh, I don't believe it. He and Elizabeth are devoted to each other.''

"I'm sure they are, but possibly their life in the bedroom leaves something to be desired. I'm fairly certain he's having a go with a half-breed barmaid in town as of now.''

Moira shook her head in disbelief. "Men!'' she said with ill-concealed contempt. "Their relationships with women are so shallow—no more than skin-deep. All they've got on their minds is sex and war!''

"I've seen some females like that myself. But you and I are not of that ilk, my darling. I shall love and honor and treasure you until the end of time.''

"And I you.'' They walked with an arm around each other's waist in silence, almost a reverent silence, as if they were awed by the new element that had been introduced into their lives with such breathtaking suddenness.

She spoke for the first time when they reached the Custers' front steps. "I'll be bathing at the same time tomorrow afternoon. Would you care to join me?"

"An army of Cheyenne braves couldn't keep me away."

Chapter Five

Moira felt as jittery as a bride on her wedding night on the ride out to the creek the next afternoon. Her stomach was growling, and she was keenly conscious of her heart thumping against her breastbone.

"It's not as though it were the first time for me, Devil," she confided to her stallion. "But it's been such a long time." She debated whether to tell Brad that she was not a virgin and came to the conclusion she would remain silent unless he asked her outright.

"After all, Devil, it's not as though it will be the first time for him. It's a well-known fact that cavalrymen are a lecherous bunch." It made her wonder about her father. Was it possible that he and Bea Carter were indulging in some hanky-panky? She doubted it; there was scarcely any opportunity for them to be alone. It saddened her somewhat because she wished her father would find a more satisfying interest in life than drinking and smoking and talking war with his fellow officers.

She reached the creek, dismounted and debated whether to undress now or wait for Brad. She concluded that it would be less embarrassing for her to be in the pond when he arrived. Removing one's clothing while a man was watching could be so awkward; especially when it was a man she had spoken to for the first time less than twenty-four hours ago. It had been different with Bob Thomas. Their friendship had progressed slowly to a stage of comfortable, casual intimacy before they engaged in sex.

She removed her shirt, boots and trousers and lastly her shocking pink chemise; later, when it was over, she wanted Brad to see her in it. It was a frothy lace frippery with see-through panels, which she had purchased on her last visit to the nearby town of Barstow from a traveling salesman who had been passing through with his horse and wagon. She'd carried it home in a brown paper bag and hidden it in a dresser drawer at the bottom of a pile of her everyday underthings. She wondered what she had been thinking of when she bought the intimate item, so incongruous compared to the attire women wore on a primitive cavalry post. At the back of her mind had there been a spark of precognition that had anticipated her whirlwind romance with Bradford Taylor? Moira was a strong believer in premonition; not in a superstitious sense; merely that it was a honing and extension of one's five physical senses.

She tied her hair with a red ribbon and waded into the pond. The air was still, and Moira, floating on her back, could not detect any motion at all in the canopy of leaves overhead. The sun filtered through the sparse branches, a coruscating, molten ball that hypnotized her. She closed her eyes, savoring the weightless buoyancy of her body in the temperate water. A sensual lassitude pervaded her limbs.

She smiled at the first sound of hoofbeats coming down the trail behind the hill to the west. One hand slid down the swell of her belly and trailed between her open thighs. Her heart accelerated as he crossed the ridge and rode down to the creek. He tied his horse alongside Devil and came toward her. Reveling in her wantonness, Moira lay spreadeagled on the surface, breasts floating free, thighs spread provocatively. She saw the excitement in his eyes, the physical hunger in his expression and posture as he stopped at the edge of the creek and devoured her with his gaze.

"Well, what are you waiting for?" she demanded in a sultry voice. "Don't you know it's impolite to keep a lady waiting?"

"You vixen," he said huskily, and he began to undress.

Moira watched him with undisguised delight and admiration as he bared his chest and broad shoulders, hard and lean muscled. The mat of thick blond hair on his chest was like golden down in the slanting rays of the sun through the foliage. He stepped out of his buckskin trousers; his legs were long and straight, the thighs firm and strong. Moira held her breath as he kicked off his drawers and stood before her as unabashed by his nudity as she was. He stepped into the pond and came toward her.

"Come to me, my darling," she whispered and held out a hand to him, at the same time spreading her thighs wider apart. He took her hand and came between her parted legs. An electric current coursed through her body as his hard, throbbing manhood probed the portals of her womanhood.

"Oh, God! I feel as if I am about to enter heaven," she moaned, wrapping her legs around his waist, with her heels locked at the small of his back. Brad put his hands underneath her armpits and lifted her out of the waist-deep water. She wrapped one arm around his neck and, with her trembling free hand, grasped his rigid shaft.

It had been so long since her initiation to sex with Bob that she might as well have been a virgin. He strained and pushed, teeth gritted, making little headway.

"Harder, harder," she urged him, thrashing about in the water in her uncontrollable desire. A concerted effort by the two of them broke the impasse, and she shuddered as the full length of him penetrated her. Joy burst through her flesh from an exploding rocket at the very core of her. The increasing tempo of his thrusts induced a higher plateau of pleasure, measure by measure, until the excruciating intensity of her ecstasy almost made her lose consciousness. They thrashed about in the water like two wild sea creatures locked in mortal combat, moaning and groaning, muttering things to each other that were unintelligible. At last their passion subsided, and they stood close together with their arms around each other, her cheek resting on his heaving chest. Ripples emanating from them spread across the surface of the pond in ever-widening, concentric circles.

After a while he gathered her up in his arms and carried her onto the bank. The forest floor was thick and soft and warm. He lowered her gently, his eyes adoring.

"I love you, Moira Callahan," he said.

"I love you, Bradford Taylor." She sighed and put her arms around his neck. He bent and kissed her lips and chin, and his lips trailed down the swanlike curve of her throat and into the cleavage between her breasts. His mouth closed over her left breast, his tongue teasing the nipple until it swelled in his mouth like a hard, ripe strawberry. And then he gave the same attention to her other breast.

Lust flamed within her again, no less insistent than the first time. Strange new sensations engulfed her as his loving ministrations continued down the length of her torso, pausing to titillate her navel with his tongue and then lavishing kisses between her thighs. Moira cried out in joy as he straddled her and slipped his hands under her legs and up so that his hands were clasping her inner thighs. Ablaze with passion, she urged him down further. It was an utterly unique experience, subtly different and more erotic than conventional lovemaking.

His loins were poised directly above her face. Her greedy hands captured his tumescent phallus and guided it to her ravenous lips. It was all she could do to accommodate him. Her tongue was a thing gone wild. Their paroxysms began simultaneously. Moira's blood was a thunderous crescendo in her ears; her heart raced out of control and the pulses pounded in her temples, her throat, her wrists and her groin.

For a long time afterward neither of them spoke. They lay side by side, hip to hip, thigh to thigh, holding hands with the innocence of two sleeping children.

At last Moira roused herself and bent over him, her face radiant with adoration. "I have never felt more alive, more vibrant or more conscious of my identity as a woman. It's as if up until now some part of me was missing, some mysterious part of the whole woman.''

"I know what you mean," he agreed, stroking the fine down on her back. "I have always sensed that lack myself. The first time I set eyes on you, darling, an inner voice whispered to me: 'She is what has been missing from your existence.' I've told you that. My instincts told me that from this point on our destinies would merge and pursue life's course as one mind, one body, a single human entity.''

On the ride back to the post, Moira laid a hand on his thigh. "Brad, my dear, wonderful husband.''

He looked at her and smiled. "Aye, and you are my precious wife. The vows we swore today weigh stronger in the eyes of God than any rote sacrament pronounced in a cathedral or any affidavit issued by some legal bureau. Yet we must abide by the mores of the society we inhabit. If I didn't make an honest woman of you, I'd be drummed out of the service.''

Moira laughed. "Not to mention the horsewhipping you'd be getting from my father.''

Brad laughed. "Yes, I suppose I'll have to do it proper and ask him for your hand.''

Near the end of November and through December life at Hempstead took a turn for the better. As the zenith of the winter sun declined, the parched earth could breathe once more, dissipating the volcanic heat entrapped in the earth's surface. Like the legendary phoenix, southern Texas was resurrected out of its own ashes. The rains came and barren sand was converted to fertile soil. Crops flourished and game became plentiful; deer, wild turkey and fish abounded in the rivers that had been dry beds for most of the summer. Behind their cottage Moira cultivated a garden that produced potatoes and yams, enough to feed the entire company. The weather was brisk and exhilarating, and general morale improved tenfold. Social life flourished. Elizabeth Custer organized teas, card parties and, just before Christmas, a full-dress military ball. A canvas dance floor was staked out on the parade grounds and Japanese lanterns were hung from ropes strung on poles set up around the perimeter. A band was hired from San Antonio, and for weeks before the occasion the women spent most of their free time designing and sewing the gowns they would wear at the gala event.

Moira wore a silk crepe georgette blouse with a flower print and a broomstick skirt, brightly banded in yellow, blue, red and green, of crisp seersucker.

"You're sure to be the belle of the ball tonight," Brad told her when he arrived to escort her.

"Thank you, but Elizabeth must walk away with that honor. Wait until you see the gorgeous gown she's wearing. Do you like my hair?" It was piled high on her head and fastened in place with barrettes shaped like miniature boomerangs.

"Regal, very regal." He embraced her on the dark front porch. "Although I prefer it free flowing down your naked back."

"We'd better be off," Moira said. "As it is we're late."

"It's fashionable to be tardy. Has your father left yet?"

"He's at the Custers'. Bea is his date, you know."

"I think there's something going on there, don't you? He's been in excellent spirits of late."

"Has he ever! And he's gained weight and cut back on his drinking and smoking."

"The influence of a good woman will do it every time."

They went down the steps and headed for the parade grounds. When they arrived, the band was playing Strauss's "Blue Danube" waltz, and the canvas dance floor was a swirling kaleidoscope of color under the Japanese lanterns. Military blue and gray and brass were overshadowed by the women's dazzling gowns, skirts and tartans of lightning blue, lapis lazuli, cardinal's purple, peacock green, mandarin red and old tapestry; high boots with tassels, cloth slippers with patent-leather toe caps, stockings striped in peacock blue and golden yellow.

"It's breathtaking," Moira exclaimed.

"I'd swear I was in the grand ballroom at the May-flower Hotel in Washington," Brad said.

General Custer and his wife swept past them, an accomplished pair in the dance. Elizabeth was looking majestic in a ball gown of Lyons silk overlaid with a shadow decoration of flowers trimmed in white lace and green ribbon, the regimental colors. Her hair was contained by an ivory tiara encrusted with semiprecious stones.

Beatrice Carter was stunning as well in an empire gown of blazing scarlet with a high neck and high waist, dancing close to Colonel Callahan.

"Shall we dance?" Brad said. Moira came into his arms and he led her onto the dance floor. "Never was one much for dancing," he apologized as he stepped on her foot.

"Never mind," she whispered in his ear. "Dancing is only an excuse for men and women to have body contact."

During an intermission the celebrants gathered around a long refreshment table laden with cakes, cookies, petit fours and a huge punch bowl adorned with the luxury of a large block of ice. Moira conversed with Elizabeth, Bea and several other officers' wives while Brad drifted to the end of the table, where a group of officers were clustered around General Custer. The conversation here was anything but festive.

"We were just discussing what happened at Fort Phil Kearny early this week," Custer addressed Brad. "Have you heard?"

"No, but they should be able to handle any trouble that comes their way. Hell, they're garrisoned by five companies of infantry and the Second Cavalry."

"Well, they got more trouble than they could handle. Captain Bill Fetterman took out a work party to cut wood— eighty-three men. On the way back to Kearny they were ambushed by a large war party of Sioux and killed to the last man."

"My God!" Brad turned ashen.

"What's even worse, the word is going to spread like wildfire among the Indian nations and they're going to get the idea that they can all whip the US army and cavalry.

Gentlemen, I foresee that this incident will open the flood-gates of Indian resistance. It's going to mean full-scale war. The word is that the Sioux alone have mobilized eight thousand crack warriors and all are well equipped with contraband army weapons.'' Custer downed a half tumbler of whisky. ''Unless I miss my guess, it won't be long before our regiment will be heading northwest. There's going to be a mess in the Black Hills the like of which this country has never experienced. There's been a big gold strike up there, and the damned irresponsible fortune hunt-ers are pouring into the hills in droves in direct violation of the treaty the government just concluded with the Indian Council of Tribes.''

Brad shook his head, still stunned by the news of the massacre of Fetterman and his men. ''Totally wiped out at Kearny. It's unbelievable.''

''Believe it,'' Custer said grimly. Then he added what was to become an irony that Lieutenant Taylor would remember all his life. ''Well, gentlemen, it's a lesson we can all profit by. No way that's ever going to happen to a regiment of mine!''

Chapter Six

July 4, 1866

Dear Wendy and Susan,

Daddy and I were both delighted to learn of Wendy's engagement to Carl Collins. Daddy says you made quite a catch, that your Carl is one of the most promising young politicians in Washington. Of course we will come East for your wedding next June.

You will both be surprised to hear that Wendy is not the only Callahan sister planning on matrimony. Inasmuch as I mention him in almost every letter I write to you, you no doubt have deduced that Lieutenant Bradford Taylor is a special person to me. In fact, dear Wendy, if things go according to plan, your younger sister will be tying the marital knot before you do! And to a career military man at that; you know how I always vowed I would never marry a soldier. Well, none of us is ever in full control of our own lives and destiny. I am madly in love with Brad and would marry him even if he were a ragpicker.

We don't expect you two to travel to this hellhole for the wedding. It will be a very simple military ceremony at the home of General Custer, and later in

*the day we will take the train to San Antonio for a
brief honeymoon.*

*Daddy has not been the same since his lady love
Bea Carter returned to St. Louis. He plans to take a
furlough in September and visit her. Maybe he will
return to Texas with a bride of his own.*

*Today is Independence Day and there will be a big
celebration commencing at noon. All the regiment
contributed to a general fund, and three days ago.
Brad took a ten-man detail to San Antonio to fetch the
food and drink and fireworks which General Custer
commissioned General Sheridan to purchase several
weeks ago. This is one occasion that rates six blocks
of ice.*

*I will cut short this missive because at ten o'clock I
am to accompany Brad and his platoon on a scouting
mission to the south, where a band of marauding
Cheyennes have been terrorizing the settlers. It is a
frustrating business for the cavalry, for by the time
we get there, the Indians will be long gone.*

*Once again, dear sisters, Daddy and I love you
and miss you, but we send our heartfelt congratulations, Wendy, to you and to Mr. Collins on your
engagement, and we look forward to attending your
wedding and to being together again, even if it only
will be for a short time.*

> *Your devoted sister,*
> *Moira*

Moira folded the letter and put it in an envelope. On her
way to the corral she posted it at the orderly room.

"Won't be no post until next Monday, Miss Callahan,"
the charge of quarters informed her.

"The mail can't be rushed," she said cheerfully and
left, whistling a happy tune. The day was gorgeous, one of
the coolest July days that Texas old-timers could recall.
Moira's exuberance showed in her bouncing gait.

The cavalrymen were saddling up when she arrived at
the formation area paddock. Brad greeted her with a smile

and a kiss on the cheek. "You look fat and sassy this morning."

Moira sniffed. "Fat indeed! You certainly know how to deflate a girl's spirits, Lieutenant Taylor."

He bent to whisper in her ear. "It's all in the right places, at any rate."

Moira feigned a pout. "Well, it will be a long, long time before you get your hands on any of those places, Lieutenant Smart Aleck!"

A groom brought Devil over to her. "He's feeling skittish this morning, miss.".

"Just like me." Moira stroked the stallion's snout and he nuzzled her on the cheek, whipping his tail and whinnying. She put a foot in a stirrup and vaulted aboard.

Moira wore the same frontier field uniform as the cavalrymen—buckskin trousers and jacket decorated with heavy fringe and wide-brimmed campaign hat. The platoon filed out of the post at a leisurely gait, a long column with men riding two abreast. Moira was alongside Brad at the head of the column.

"Are you sure you want to come along on this scout?" Brad inquired. "You're going to miss a lot of the early holiday activities. I don't expect we'll be back before four this afternoon."

"If I can't share them with you, I may as well miss them. Whither thou goest, I goeth. My biblical terminology may be a bit off, but the meaning is clear."

He laughed. "You're going to make a perfect army wife, like Elizabeth."

The compliment somehow rubbed Moira the wrong way. "Not quite like Elizabeth. I love her dearly, but she is much too passive for my taste. I mean, she is more of an appendage of the general than a whole woman in her own right." When she was angry or indignant the green predominated in Moira's eyes. "So if Elizabeth fills the criteria of the perfect army wife in your view, then you're marrying the wrong gal."

Brad reached over and put a hand on her shoulder. Very seriously he said: "My dear Moira, there is no man on this post who could doubt that you are a whole, individualistic woman in your own right and in every way.''

She smiled a trifle self-consciously. "Sorry, love. I know I can be overly sensitive and defensive about the place of women in modern society, but for every reasonable, fair-minded male such as yourself there are a score of men who still live in the dark ages where women are concerned."

Brad gazed at her, his expression registering affectionate amusement. "Moira me darlin'. It wouldn't surprise me at all if someday you run for public office."

"I couldn't do any worse than the male politicians we have in Washington now. Namely President Johnson."

"He never was much of a vice-president, much less a president. Did you know he was drunk on the day he was inaugurated?"

"So Daddy told me. And they say his present feud with Secretary of War Stanton is bound to spell trouble for him in the Congress."

Their conversation was terminated when one of the advance scouts came galloping back down the trail. "War party of Cheyenne has got Jesse Smith's place under siege. Jesse and his family and the hired hands are holed up in the barn. Don't know how much longer they can hold out."

"That's about two miles up Shoshone Creek," Lieutenant Taylor said. He rubbed his hard jaw and looked at Moira. "Darling, this is no place for you to be. Better hightail it back to the post."

Moira's jaw jutted out belligerently. "Not on your life, Lieutenant. I wouldn't miss this for the world. Besides, you're going to need all the firepower you can get."

"Damnit, Moira!" he snapped. "I won't let you take the risk. Back to the post. That's an order!"

Her eyes glittered like twin emeralds now. "I'm not under your command, Lieutenant. If I were a cavalrywoman, then I'd be bound to obey. So let's get on with it."

Brad winced as muffled laughter could be heard clear to

the end of the column. Taking a deep breath, he addressed the bugler. "Sound 'To Arms,' Mason!"

Mason put the mouthpiece to his lips, puffed his cheeks and sounded the call to arms; the shrill, urgent, staccato notes caused the fine hairs at the base of Moira's neck to bristle. With the scout leading the way, the platoon set out at full gallop.

Half a mile away from the Smith homestead they could hear the insistent crackle of rifle fire and the banshee war cries of the Indians. Another sound made Moira shudder— human voices screaming in terror. The din enabled the cavalrymen to approach the battle scene by means of a dried-up creek bed whose banks concealed them. From a position no more than two hundred yards off, Brad surveyed the action. His voice trembled with outrage.

"The red bastards. They've boarded up the barn door and windows and set it afire." He turned to his second in command. "Sergeant Yates, dismount and take five men around that curve in the creek bed and disperse in the sagebrush to the east. As soon as you hear the bugler sound the charge, commence firing, all the while circling back behind the barn. That way the Cheyennes will think we have a lot more firepower than we do and figure they're surrounded."

He ordered the standard bearer, "Unfurl the guidon." He drew his saber from its scabbard and lifted it high in the air. "Raise the guidon." The regimental colors snapped in the brisk wind coming through the gulch. The sight of it made Moira's blood tingle.

Brad turned to her. "For God's sake, Moira, at least do me the favor of staying back in the rear."

"Don't worry about me, darling. I'll be just fine." She drew her Spencer rifle out of the saddle boot and cocked it.

"Sound the charge!" Brad bellowed. The shrill bugle notes sounded above the Indians' war cries, and for an instant they were immobilized like figures in a tableau. An eerie hush settled over the battlefield. Then, flourishing his saber, the lieutenant urged his mount over the bank and led his platoon, deployed on either side of him. Simultaneously Sergeant Yates's detail commenced firing from the flanks, catching the confused Indians in a brisk enfilade of fire and moving constantly to reinforce the impression that the Cheyennes were surrounded. The thick dust kicked up by the charging cavalrymen was a screen that prevented the Indians from determining just what the size of the enemy force was.

Recovering from the initial shock, the Cheyennes rallied to meet the cavalry charge. They broke into two groups; one advanced toward the horse soldiers while a larger group retreated to a ridge north of the burning barn, where their horses were tethered. They were demoralized by the cross fire laid down by Yates and his men.

The charging platoon was assailed by heavy rifle fire and a barrage of arrows. Alongside Lieutenant Taylor a trooper took an arrow in the chest and toppled from his horse. The lieutenant felt the breeze of an arrow grazing his hat. Then they were in the midst of the Indians, the onslaught of their horses decimating their ranks and sending warriors tumbling to the ground like bowling pins.

A savage Cheyenne fired from the hip at Lieutenant Taylor. It missed, and before he could get off a second round, the lieutenant decapitated him with a slashing sweep of his saber. He dispatched another brave who had grabbed hold of his bridle with the pistol in his other hand. The wild melee did not last very long, but before the Cheyennes retreated in panic, Moira downed two of the enemy with coolly placed shots in the head and heart. Lieutenant Taylor had no intention of pursuing them yet; his first concern was the men and women trapped in the burning barn.

"Sound the recall," he ordered the bugler, dismounting and running to the barn. "Tear down those beams across the door and windows!"

Employing their rifles like crowbars, the cavalrymen labored desperately to free the prisoners. By the time the farmer and his family and hands ran staggering out of the barn, the roof was a crown of fire, and smoke was pouring out the windows and door. Assisted by the troopers, they reached a safe distance from the blazing structure and watched in dazed silence as it collapsed in a shower of burning embers that cascaded high into the air in the manner of sky rockets.

"Let's go back to the farmhouse and I'll make coffee and sandwiches for you nice young men," Mrs. Smith said. "I don't know how we'll ever repay you."

"That's mighty kind of you, ma'am," Lieutenant Taylor said to her, "but we have to flush that war party clear out of this part of the country or they might come back and finish what they started."

Jesse Smith put an arm around his wife. "We all would have been goners if them Indians hadn't forgot about the loft doors at the back of the barn. At least we had some ventilation." He chuckled. "We'd planned to celebrate the Fourth with a big blowout tonight, but this wasn't exactly what we had in mind."

Moira marveled at how nonchalantly these settlers accepted the Indian raid and the fact that two of their group had been killed along with two of the cavalrymen. The dead troopers were tied across the backs of their horses while Jesse Smith and his men prepared to bury their dead and sixteen Indians.

The settlers said their grateful farewells to the cavalry as the platoon rode off to follow the trail of the Cheyenne ponies. They followed the tracks about ten miles to a high hill overlooking a broad river. The Indians had made a crossing here, and far to the south, the dust churned up by their horses was a low cloud over the desert plain.

"I don't think they'll be coming back this way for a while," Lieutenant Taylor surmised. "They must have thought the whole regiment was after them." To one of the scouts he said, "There's a running creek somewhere about. Let's head for it and water the horses; then we'll return to the post."

The scout shook his head. "Yup, Kinkypoo Creek. 'Bout six miles to the northeast."

Brad turned the platoon and they started for the watering place.

"Why so silent?" he asked Moira, as they rode off.

"I was thinking about the Smiths and their people. How can they act so festive when they narrowly escaped being slaughtered?"

He sighed. "Yeah, it takes some getting used to. You see, on the frontier death is as much a part of life as eating, drinking, breathing and making love. The trick is to count your blessings, not your losses."

Kinkypoo Creek had been a broad river before a drought struck the region; what remained of it was a channel in the middle of the otherwise-dry riverbed some forty feet wide. The water was clear, and as was the cavalry custom, the troopers attended to the needs of their horses before they filled their canteens and washed some of the sweat-encrusted dust off their faces and hands.

"We can follow the riverbed almost back to Hempstead," the scout advised Taylor. "It curves due west about two miles down and will take us within ten miles of the post."

"Then let's get moving," Taylor said. "We want to get back in time to join in some of the celebrating."

They rode off in column formation, two horses abreast, with Taylor and Moira at the head once more. They made excellent time, for the smooth bed felt good to the hoof-sore horses. They had covered roughly five miles when they came upon an island that was covered with green foliage such as none of them had seen in almost a year.

"I'll be damned!" Taylor exclaimed. "That's a regular oasis!"

"Underground spring," the scout explained. "Even when the creek is dry, the spring feeds the vegetation. Look at them wild plums." He rode his horse through the shallow water to the island, picked one of the small but ripe fruits and bit into it. Juice spurted all over his face. "Nectar of the gods," he said with satisfaction.

Starved for fresh fruit for so many months, the troopers headed for the island in a mad stampede. While they were overindulging themselves on the delicious fruit, disaster struck with the shock of lightning. From the low hills on both sides of the creek, mounted warriors came charging down the slopes, firing rifles and arrows and screaming the familiar, bloodcurdling Cheyenne war chant. After an instant of shocked indecision, Lieutenant Taylor's trained reflexes went into action.

"Dismount and deploy the horses around the perimeter of the island!"

The troopers responded in quick and orderly fashion, and not a second too soon. The heavy barrage of rifle and arrow fire the Cheyennes directed at the besieged island killed all the horses in less than ten minutes; their dead bodies formed a natural breastwork around the island, behind which the cavalrymen took cover. Though they were heavily outnumbered, they put their sole advantage to good use.

Three times the Indians charged the little island, and three times they were driven back with heavy losses. On the final charge one warrior's pony cleared the breastwork, and Brad placed a bullet right between his eyes. The dead Indian was thrown back into the water, and his mount continued galloping downstream. They counted scores of Indian corpses floating in the same direction. Although small in number, the troopers with their repeating Spencer rifles had devastated the enemy. Marksmanship was irrelevant, so closely packed had been the ranks of attacking Indians. The cavalry had suffered its losses as well. Six men dead and another dozen wounded.

Their respite was short-lived. A half-hour later a trooper sounded the alarm:

"Here they come again!"

"I don't believe my eyes!" Moira exclaimed.

Leading the charge was the biggest Indian that any of them had ever seen; he was awesome, almost supernatural. His chest was naked and painted with garish colored designs; a genuine living work of primitive art. He wore a feathered war bonnet that trailed down his back and rested on the horse's rump. And as a final bizarre touch, he held a cavalry bugle to his lips, the highly polished bronze flashing in the sunlight. They could only stare in mute wonderment as this magnificent savage blew a "charge" that the best bugler at West Point would have taken pride in.

The Cheyennes swept toward the island like a human tidal wave, ranging from one bank of the dried-up riverbed to the other. When he estimated their front rank to be within five hundred yards, Lieutenant Taylor gave the order:

"Fire at will!"

The withering fire from the troopers mowed the attackers down like a scythe cutting through grass, but they came on relentlessly. They were almost at the barricade now, and Taylor yelled to his men:

"This is our last chance, so make it a good one!"

The Indians were at point-blank range now, and the cavalrymen threw aside their rifles and commenced firing their Colt pistols.

The conclusion of the battle was as unexpected as had been the initial attack. The giant Indian chief with the bugle faced Lieutenant Taylor across the barricade of dead horses, their eyes locked in mutual hatred and fury. They fired their weapons simultaneously. Brad was hit in the left shoulder and hurled backward against Moira. The slug from his Colt struck the chief in the chest. He clutched his heart with the bugle still clenched in his huge hand; his eyes glazed over and he toppled from his horse into the shallow water. Then, as in many Indian tribes who regarded their chieftains as immortal, the attack was broken off as swiftly as it had begun, and the demoralized warriors fled in a blind rout.

The astonished cavalrymen watched them drive their horses up the bank and across the rocky ridges flanking the river.

"It's a miracle," Moira said.

Taylor struggled to his feet, holding his wounded shoulder, and watched the chief's corpse, regal even in death, float facedown away from the island. "Not from their viewpoint it isn't. They saw his downfall as the will of the gods. A man like that—a magnificent fighting machine who has no doubt lived through scores of battles—his people must have regarded him as invincible, invulnerable to mere mortal weapons. Today his charmed life was snuffed out; not by us but decree from the heavens."

He looked around at the shambles of the island, surrounded by dead horses and littered with the bodies of dead troopers, eight in all after the final onslaught. He spoke to his chief scout. "We can't carry out the wounded or the dead. Our best bet is for you to round up one of those stray Indian ponies grazing in that field at the foot of the hills. Ride back to the post and have them send out a rescue party with fresh horses for those of us who can ride and a wagon to transport the dead and wounded. And damnit, Charlie, on the double."

It was dusk when the first horsemen came in sight from a bend downriver. "There they are!" an elated trooper shouted. A mighty cheer echoed off the foothills on either side.

As the column drew closer, Moira exclaimed. "That's Daddy leading them!" It was true, and never had she seen Colonel Patrick Callahan sit taller in the saddle. Relief spread across his face as Moira ran through the shallow water to greet him, but he was damned if he was going to condone his daughter's maverick behavior by displaying just how happy he was to see her alive and safe.

"Another pretty mess you've gotten yourself into, miss. You're lucky your scalp isn't adorning some brave's loincloth at this very moment."

Moira attempted to look contrite, but she was too happy and excited. "I wasn't in any more danger than Brad or the other troopers. And I killed my share of Cheyennes. Isn't that so, darling?"

Lieutenant Taylor cowered under the colonel's stern gaze. "That she did, sir. That's quite a daughter you have, sir. I—I—that is . . ." He faltered. "I apologize, sir. I know I shouldn't have permitted Moira to accompany us, to expose her to this awful danger, but. . . ." He shook his head and looked down at the water swirling around his knees.

Colonel Callahan cleared his throat. "Lieutenant Taylor, at ease, son. If a chicken colonel can't make this brat—this willful brat—tow the mark, how can I expect a mere second lieutenant to tame her?"

Lieutenant Taylor looked up, startled, as the other troopers enjoyed a hearty guffaw at his expense.

The dead and wounded were loaded into a wagon, and the remainder of the survivors mounted the fresh horses that had been brought from the post by their rescuers. Despite his shoulder wound Lieutenant Taylor insisted upon riding back, ignoring Moira's protests.

"Listen to me, dear girl. You don't like the idea of being ordered around by men," he told her. "Now hear this: I don't like the idea of being ordered around by a spoiled army brat such as you. Agreed?"

She appraised him uncertainly for a moment, then her eyes lit up and she laughed. *"Touché!* I agree. Let's shake on it." She extended her right hand to him.

Brad pushed the arm aside and stepped closer to her. "I'd rather seal it with a kiss." She tilted her face up to him, and as other troopers looked on approvingly, he kissed her full on the mouth.

"All right, you two lovebirds, *attenshun!"* Colonel Callahan said dryly. "Time to move out. They'll be waiting for our return before they set off the fireworks."

Moira snorted. "For all I care they can start without me. I think the boys will agree that we have had enough fireworks this one day to last us for the rest of our lives."

The ayes were unanimous!

Chapter Seven

March 21, 1867

Dear Wendy and Susan,

It may seem strange to you that on the morning of the most momentous day of my life, I am calm enough to take time to write this letter to you. Yes, it's hard to believe that the moment is at hand. In a few more hours I will become a bride: Mrs. Moira Callahan Taylor. I wish with all my heart that you could be here, my dear sisters, to share my happiness. In a way, writing this letter helps me impart to you a small measure of my joy and to join hands with you both, so to speak, across the vast distance that separates us. Just think, though—in another three months we will share a wonderful reunion when Daddy and I return East for Wendy's wedding. How I do look forward to being together with all my wonderful family.

Here in Texas throughout the winter we have enjoyed the best weather since our arrival. Winter rains have settled the dust and filled the dry riverbeds, which abound with fish. Game is plentiful, especially wild turkey and deer. Our backyard gardens are flourishing, and we have delicious meals almost every night.

*Everything about the post has undergone an aston-
ishing metamorphosis. Drunkenness and brawling are
all but eliminated; the personality of the troopers has
improved along with the weather. Our stockade holds
only a handful of prisoners. At least two or three
times a week we have balls, masquerades, community
dances and theatrical plays. Last week we performed
the play we were watching when our beloved President Lincoln was assassinated,* Our American Cousin. *Elizabeth Custer played the leading lady. You
won't believe this, but she wore a blond wig made, of
all things, from General Custer's golden locks. "Shorn
like Samson by Delilah,"* he joked ruefully.

*The Indian situation here on the frontier degener-
ates systematically month by month, year by year. I
can't help but entertain deep sympathy for the red
man's plight. Despite treaties and repeated assurances
from the United States that their hunting grounds will
be respected, the white settlers here are conscience-
less. Motivated by greed and in total defiance of the
government officials stationed here—and with the tacit
support of the military establishment—they keep pushing further and further into Indian territory. One of
the biggest factors inflaming Indian hostility is the
construction of the Union Pacific Railroad, which
goes straight through the heart of the buffalo country.
Hordes of commercial buffalo hunters following in
the wake of the rail workers are slaughtering the
animals by the thousands for their valuable hides. In
truth, the buffalo for centuries has been the staff of
life for all the Indian tribes: their primary source of
food, clothing and shelter provided by the hides, and
their ribs and bones are shaped into tools. The entire
frontier from Canada to Mexico is aflame. As General
Phil Sheridan, who commands the military division of
the Missouri, expressed it to General Custer: "Were I
to send cavalry to every sector of the frontier where
they are clamored for, we would require on the plains
alone a hundred thousand cavalrymen."*

*But on to more pleasant topics. Daddy and Beatrice
Carter are in love, I am sure of it. He's always
finding one excuse or another to visit St. Louis. I
hope they one day marry, for he has been a new man
since their romance; he looks ten years younger.*

*And speaking of marriage, it is time I start prepar-
ing myself for my own. Once again I wish you could
be here to witness the ceremony, but I know you both
will be at my side in spirit. Give my love to Aunt
Tillie and her cousin Maude, and God bless you all.*

> *Your loving sister,*
> *Mrs. Moira Callahan Taylor*

She chuckled and put down the pen. "Aren't you jump-
ing the gun a bit, Moira my girl?" she mused aloud. "Not
really. I have to get some practice in writing it; besides,
Brad and I have been husband and wife in body and spirit
and soul for a long time. The rite of passage from maiden
to Mrs. is a mere formality, a piece of paper and a minister
saying a few words over the pair. Oh well, it will make
Daddy happy."

The marriage of Lieutenant Bradford Taylor and Moira
Callahan took place in the living room of the Custer home.
The bride wore her mother's wedding gown, antique white
satin over a crinoline to emphasize the full skirt; the tight
bodice was embroidered with tiny seed pearls and trimmed
with Valenciennes lace. The bridal veil fell to her waist
from a simple white ivory tiara.

Elizabeth Custer, the matron of honor, wore a gown of
mauve flowered brocade with a full three-tiered skirt. Her
hair was folded close to her head in a chignon snood of
crocheted gold thread.

Colonel Callahan, standing at his daughter's side, wore
the full dress uniform of the Union Cavalry, as did the
groom and his best man, Lieutenant Seth Monroe. Major
Alonzo Wilson, a chaplain attached to General Sheridan's
headquarters, officiated at the ceremony.

No more than a dozen officers and the wives of those

who were married attended the affair and the small reception afterward, a buffet laid out on the Custers' dining room table, served with champagne punch. Soon after, Moira and Brad said their farewells and departed for San Antonio.

The trip by stagecoach and train lasted two days, and Moira and Brad were both exhausted by the time they registered at their hotel; their stay in the bridal suite was a gift from General Sheridan, and the bathroom proved a source of pure delight to Moira.

"Imagine, a bathtub!" she exulted.

"With hot water." He patted the little iron boiler beside the tub, and, bending over, he lit the gas flame that heated the water.

"Shall we draw straws to see who goes first?" Brad jested.

Moira's aquamarine eyes faded to a sultry deep blue and narrowed, felinelike. "I have a much better idea. Suppose we share it?"

Brad took her in his arms and kissed her lips. "You are a wicked, wicked Jezebel. Well, what are we waiting for?"

They undressed in the bedroom and walked naked into the bathroom, now misty with steam from the running water. Moira stepped daintily into the big metal tub, followed by Brad. They sat facing each other with their legs stretched out.

"Cozy, isn't it?" he said.

"It reminds me of our baths together in the lagoon," she said.

Brad smiled. "This is somewhat more crowded."

"Are you complaining?"

"Not on your life." He reached out and caressed her breasts with his large hands, his desire quickening at the sight of her nipples becoming erect.

She slid her hands up the inner sides of his thighs and touched him with an expertise that had him quickly erect. "I love you, Brad," she whispered. "Come to me, my lover." Closing her eyes, she moved against him in rhythmic, undulating motion.

"Sheer paradise," she murmured.

He kissed her neck. "My garden of paradise."

After their lovemaking they bathed themselves and went back into the bedroom. They lay side by side on the big canopied bed, holding hands and luxuriating in the warm afternoon sun that splashed across their bodies through a wide bay window.

"Do you want to have supper out?" Brad asked her.

"Not really. I just want to relax. Daddy says there's a fine restaurant in the hotel. We can have our supper sent up and eat right here in our room. Just the two of us, over a bottle of good wine."

"Sounds good to me." His green eyes glinted lecherously. "And then to bed for some additional diversion."

Moira giggled. "Additional diversion, that's a euphemism if I ever heard one. But as the bard said: 'A rose by any other name . . .' In any case, I'm all for it." Abruptly she became serious. "Brad, what about the future? Have you given much thought to what is going to happen to us now? I mean, we're certainly not going to spend the rest of our lives out here on the Texas plains."

"Damn right we're not. You know I have plans. My ultimate ambition is not exactly the goal of most shavetail lieutenants: that is, to win my colonel's eagles, command a battalion and plant my rump behind a desk until retirement. No reflection on your father, darling. It's just not my idea of career fulfillment. By the way, your father told me my promotion to captain has been approved by the War Department."

"That's quite a feather in your cap, darling, leapfrogging from second lieutenant to captain. But you deserve it after the heroism you displayed against the Cheyennes last Fourth of July."

He discounted the compliment. "Heroism, like any other form of success, is being in the right place at the right time, where one can have the opportunity to make his or her own luck." He sat up, and she had never seen him look more intense or determined. "This chap your sister is marrying—your father thinks he's one of the young turks destined for big things in politics. Apparently he's got a lot of friends in the War Department and State."

"Yes, Carl has many of the same characteristics that you have, Brad, from what Wendy tells me about him in her letters. He knows exactly where he's headed. She said that one of the most important tenets he lives by is Browning's: 'One's reach should always exceed one's grasp.' "

Brad smiled. "I like that. Yes, when we go to Washington for the wedding, I intend to cultivate the friendship of my future brother-in-law with a will and a way."

Moira rolled over on her side and ran a hand through the matted hair on his chest. "That axiom applies to women as well as to men, you know. All my life I've aspired to things that are beyond my reach, but I keep stretching and straining, and one day all the things I want will come within my grasp." She clenched her fingers against his chest.

Brad bellowed in pain. "What are you trying to do, rip my chest hair out by the roots?"

Laughing lightly, she ran her hand down across his belly and between his thighs, fondling him. "Now that I've got you in that happy state again, let's have another go at it, shall we?"

"It will be my pleasure."

"And mine." To his surprise she pushed him back on the bed and straddled his hips.

"What on earth are you up to?" he demanded.

"Variety is the spice of life. I thought it would be an innovation if I were to assume the aggressive position once in a while."

"What the devil are you talking about? Why is being on top an aggressive position? I never think of it in those terms. You're daft."

"You may not think about it consciously, but it's there at the back of your mind. Right now I can tell that the idea of my being on top bothers you in some nagging, indefinable way."

"That's untrue," he denied it, but halfheartedly, she noted. Moira grasped his erection and guided it between her thighs. Then, pressing herself down upon him with her breasts flattened against his chest and her elbows braced on either side of him, she commenced the rhythmic piston strokes of love.

"Now is that so hard to take?" she asked, kissing him gently.

He gasped, matching his strokes to her own. "Now I know what they mean when they say, he had his way with her."

She smothered his mouth with hers and thrust her tongue deep inside him, teasing the inside of his mouth with the fluttering tip. She rode him as she would ride Devil, driving him faster and harder until he collapsed beneath her in exhaustion.

Moira was wildly exhilarated as she contemplated the long future that lay ahead of them. It was going to be a good life, of that she was convinced.

Chapter Eight

Carl Collins and Bradford Taylor formed a mutual admiration society from the day they met. Although there was slight physical resemblance between the two, they were very much alike in temperament, personality and thinking. Collins, a nephew of Secretary of War Edwin Stanton and a second cousin of Chief Justice Salmon Portland Chase of the United States Supreme Court, was a Radical Republican legislator from the state of Tennessee. A confirmed imperialist, he was a staunch admirer of the British Empire, and it was his fervent ambition that one day the United States would become a colonial power of the same magnitude as England.

Moira Taylor did not share her husband's enthusiasm for her soon-to-be brother-in-law. He was an attractive and magnetic man, she had to concede; slender, of medium height, with pale blue eyes and a winning smile rather like Brad's. His mass of thick black ringlets and his haughty, upturned nose were his most distinctive physical characteristics. What she found unattractive about Carl Collins was his politics and his social philosophy. Although he was an aristocratic Southerner by birth, the only vestiges he retained of his heritage were his courtly manners and his sense of chivalry. During the war he had been a major in the Confederate army, but midyear of 1864 he had perceived the futility of the South's cause and had defected to the North. In the postwar period of Reconstruction he was totally insensitive to the plight of the impoverished homeland he had once championed and was one of the loudest proponents of imposing severe sanctions and retribution against the vanquished Confederacy. There were many Republicans as well as Democrats who disliked and disapproved of Carl Collins, but they concealed it out of fear of and respect for the impressive political clout he had amassed in the few years since the cessation of hostilities in the nation's capital. His presence was felt keenly in all three departments of government—the executive, the congressional and the judiciary.

At supper in Collins's stately Georgetown town house on the eve of the wedding, Moira and Collins got into a heated discussion of the United States' Indian policy and his vision of what role the United States should assume in the near and distant future in world affairs.

"There is only one inevitable final solution to the Indian problem," he discoursed while chomping on a cigar in the drawing room over demitasse and Napoleon brandy. "We've got to put our minds to it once and for all, concentrate all our military might on crushing the red insurrectionists. Destroy the incorrigibles and herd the docile Indians together on reservations as wards of the nation."

"Insurrectionists?" Moira exclaimed. "This is—this was—their land for centuries before the white man invaded it and plundered it. A handful of our forefathers rose up against the once-proud Indian nation and have been irrevocably trampling those noble people into the dust ever since. In truth, it is the white man who fomented insurrection."

"Rubbish!" he snapped, cocking a haughty eyebrow in her direction. "Noble people, indeed! That nauseating pap the liberals have been trying to force down the throats of the public for years. Ah, yes, the noble savage compelled into servitude by the villainous white man. Miss, if that pretty little head of yours had a gram of sense in it, you'd realize that what I am proposing for the Indians is the most charitable solution to their worsening plight. They are children intellectually and they will remain children because they are a mentally inferior race. And as we do with our children, we must harbor and protect them against the mounting threats to the safety and well-being of individuals who are incompetent to deal with the mature problems of a complex society such as ours: advancing technology, expansion, international politics, our constantly expanding sophistication. Yes, it is our duty to look out for their best interests.''

Wendy Callahan, his bride-to-be, only too aware of her sister's militant liberalism and hair-trigger temper, tried to avoid the impending clash. "Dear, can't we discuss lighter and happier topics tonight? After all, tomorrow is our wedding day and tonight we ought to be gay and cheerful.'' But there was no way to avoid combat between Collins and Moira.

Her eyes casting lightningbolts at Collins, Moira exploded, "Carl, I find you to be a condescending, patronizing, insufferable boor!''

Wendy gasped and clasped a handkerchief to her mouth. Brad's expression and his tone of voice expressed severe disapproval.

"Moira, have you taken leave of your senses? We are guests in Carl's home. You have not only overstepped the bounds of good taste, but it is inexcusably audacious for a young, uninformed woman to challenge the views of a learned and experienced statesman like Carl!''

Moira slapped a hand to her forehead. "My God! You are beginning to sound as stuffy and pompous as he is. And let me tell *you*, *Mr*. Collins, don't you concern yourself about my 'pretty little head.' I think very well for myself, thank you; well enough to realize that you and your kind are the real enemies of this country, far more dangerous than the poor Indians.

"Peace and prosperity, the pursuit of happiness—have you forgotten the Declaration of Independence, *Mr*. Collins? '. . . We hold these truths to be self-evident, that all men are created equal, that they are endowed by their

Creator with certain inalienable Rights, that among these are Life, Liberty and the pursuit of Happiness . . .' God is the Indians' Creator as well as ours, and they are entitled to the same inalienable rights as we are.

"No, Mr. Collins, you don't give a damn for the principles that this nation was founded upon. You don't want peace and prosperity or happiness for the American people. All that matters to you is the acquisition of power and wealth—ever more power, ever more wealth. But what is worse, you want to extend that power beyond our borders, beyond this continent. First it was the threat posed by the French when they installed Maximilian as emperor of Mexico. The hue and cry from the radical politicians was 'Invade Mexico and rescue it from French Imperialism.' Luckily the Mexicans took care of Maximilian themselves, thereby saving themselves from enjoying the dubious benefits of having American imperialism installed as an alternative to the French brand. And now the new threat to American democracy is to be Spain. All those diabolical Spaniards poised just off our shores in Cuba, waiting for the right moment to invade the United States."

Collins regarded her with his smug, supercilious smile. "I could not have expressed it more incisively myself, my dear Moira. The Spanish presence in Cuba is clearly a violation of the Monroe Doctrine."

To the relief of both Wendy and Brad Taylor, the heated debate between Collins and Moira was terminated by the arrival of guests who had been invited to a champagne buffet to be served later in the evening. Among the distinguished assembly was Secretary of War Edwin McMasters Stanton and Chief Justice Salmon Portland Chase; foreign notables included the French ambassador to Washington and the British vice-consul.

Brad was awestruck at being part of such eminent company. "Never figured we'd be rubbing shoulders with so many power barons," he said in an aside to Moira.

"You are impressed, aren't you, Brad?" she said irritably.

"Well, of course I'm impressed," he said hotly. "Don't you realize that Carl's influence in the capital can serve to further my career, broaden our lives? Why on earth do you go out of your way to insult the man?''

"I didn't insult him. I merely argued with him on his own terms. And if, indeed, you regard that as an insult, I certainly didn't have to go out of my way. Carl Collins stands squarely in the way of everything I believe in and aspire to for this great nation.''

"There's no reasoning with you," he said in exasperation. "At least try and keep your mouth shut for the remainder of our visit here.''

"That's a tall order, my boy," commented Colonel Callahan as he joined them. "Brad is right, you know, Moira. Why alienate a man who's in a position to advance your husband's career? Not to mention the fact that you are upsetting your sister by your behavior. Is that what you want to do, spoil her wedding?''

"Of course not," Moira replied contritely. "All right, from now on I'll play the role of an obedient little wife and sit primly on the edge of my chair with my hands folded in my lap and keep my mouth shut in silent worship of you big, strong men while you decide the fate of the world.''

It was a herculean task, keeping that promise, and she became increasingly frustrated and infuriated listening to her husband pander to the power barons, as he referred to them. It was an apt description, she had to admit—power barons, robber barons. They were the same the world over; a relatively small clique of men controlled the lives and destinies of millions. There was a fascination about the casual and almost indifferent manner in which the men in this group discussed events that were of grave import to the nation.

"It's pretty much a fait accompli." Secretary Stanton was addressing a group that included Brad Taylor. "The Old Man has me marked for the guillotine.''

"The Old Man?" Brad said in bewilderment.

His naiveté evoked hearty laughter. "President Johnson, dear boy," Collins said jovially. "He's about to dismiss Edwin and install General Grant to replace him as interim secretary of war.''

"Over the dead body of the Congress," declared a senator from Kentucky. "We will impeach the incompetent boob if he makes such an attempt."

"I hope he does dismiss Edwin," said the chief justice, biting the end off a fresh cigar and spitting it out on the expensive Persian carpet. "And I hope to have the honor of presiding at the impeachment proceedings."

The assembly was joined by the French ambassador and the British vice-consul. It was Carl Collins who pointedly steered the conversation to China. In 1839 China's government banned the import of opium, which was the most lucrative trade for Great Britain as well as other Western importers, whose warehouses were confined to an international settlement on the outskirts of Canton. For a long time the Western traders had been chafing under the limitations that prevented them from extending their influence throughout China. When the Chinese army raided the island of Lintin, headquarters of the opium trade, drove out the British and dumped six million dollars worth of the drug into the Pearl River, it provided the British with a golden opportunity to realize its ambitions to expand trading operations in the East.

In the ensuing Opium War, the British soundly defeated the ill-equipped Chinese army and extracted humiliating concessions as the price for peace. The island of Hong Kong was ceded to the British, and the coastal ports of Canton, Shanghai, Amoy, Foochow and Ningpo were declared open-treaty ports, thus opening the floodgates for greedy and avaricious merchants from France, Germany, Holland and other European nations to set up shop all along the coast and exploit the new free market to unconscionable excess.

"Last year our Chinese trade achieved its highest peak since the treaty of 1842," boasted the French ambassador.

"But you didn't top our gross," the British vice-consul countered good-naturedly.

The Frenchman shrugged. "The pie is big enough and rich enough for all of us to share." He inquired of Collins, "I'm surprised you Yanks haven't had a go at sticking your own fingers in the pie. Don't tell me you're all that altruistic.''

It was true that the United States had steadfastly maintained a hands-off policy with regard to China, except for conducting a brisk trade in tea and Eastern spices.

Collins chuckled. ''Altruism has nothing to do with it. Actually we've been too overwhelmed with our domestic affairs to pay attention to China; the slavery issue and then the war, and now we're faced with a showdown with the Indian Nations.'' He winked. ''But don't write us off in the future, gentlemen. When the time is right, the American flag will be flying in all the open-treaty ports. By the way, I understand there may be trouble brewing for you chaps in China. Verging on open resistance in some provinces.''

The French ambassador tugged at his mustache. ''Yes, there has been a bit of a problem. Troublemakers have always been part of Chinese tradition—one warlord vying with another, or subjects rising up against their warlord. This movement appears to be better organized and more cohesive, an underground group that has attracted followers from all the provinces. They call themselves the I-Ho Ch' üan; roughly translated, it means 'the Fists of Righteous Harmony.' We don't expect anything serious to come of it. They march and chant and sound off with dire threats against us foreign devils.'' He laughed. ''The truth is, if they do gain enough support to put the foreign delegations in real danger, it could work to our advantage.''

''Bloody well right!'' the British vice-consul agreed. ''It would be a replay of the Opium War. Provide an excuse for the European nations to move troops into China in force.''

His audience thought his assessment of the Chinese situation was highly amusing, and no one laughed louder than Brad Taylor.

After the party Moira and Brad and Colonel Callahan returned by coach to the old Callahan homestead in the Maryland countryside. Collins was escorting his bride-to-be home in his private coach.

When they were finally alone in their bedroom, Brad asked Moira, "What the devil has gotten into you? You haven't spoken a word to me since we left Carl's place."

"When I don't have anything positive to offer, I choose to remain silent. I don't give a fig for Carl or his atrocious opinions, but you, Brad, are my husband. I care for you. I respect you. But of late you seem to be doing your best to undermine that respect."

She was sitting at her dressing table, brushing her hair, and she watched him in the mirror as he came up in back of her and bent to kiss her neck and caress her breasts through the thin nightgown.

"Listen to me, my little spitfire. I don't give a fig for Carl Collins either, but it serves no purpose to reject an influential man who is in a position to advance my career. The least you can do is be civil to the man for my sake, for Wendy's sake. Tomorrow she'll be his wife."

"Poor girl; I pity her."

His blue eyes, reflected in the glass, were flint hard. "You can be an exasperating bitch, do you know that? Willful as well. There's an old saying: Don't cut off your nose to spite your face. You take masochistic delight in self-destruction. Remember what you said on our wedding night? You asked me about our future. You said you didn't want to spend the rest of our lives on some frontier outpost. Damnit, woman, neither do I! And if it takes a bit of ass-kissing to achieve my ends, so be it!"

What he said was true; she wanted Brad to get ahead in the service, and it softened her resentment about his lack of principle, his deceit in cultivating the favor of the power brokers. His persuasive hands kneading her breasts and stroking her nipples were thawing the coldness she had felt toward him earlier in the evening.

"All right," she said grudgingly, "perhaps I have been headstrong and unreasonable tonight. From now on I will treat Carl with civility. And I will avoid discussing politics with him. But I will never embrace or tolerate his distorted, self-serving philosophy or his contempt for the masses, especially those of color other than white. And did you hear what he said about the future intentions of the United States toward Cuba—that the Spanish should be forced to withdraw from the island?''

"Now, he didn't say that at all."

"Not in so many words, but his meaning was very clear. And that French ambassador and the British consul— what insufferable imperialists, the way they've been riding roughshod over China all these years."

His hands slipped inside the bodice of her gown and moved down across her belly to settle on her hips. "Moira, you can afford to be an idealist, but I cannot. Like your father, I am a soldier, and my first duty is to my country. It isn't my prerogative to decide what is right or wrong. I obey orders and do not pass judgment on my superiors. You've been an army brat all your life; you should appreciate that."

"Yes, I know." She slumped on the bench. "My father must have repeated the same words to my mother a thousand times."

"You accepted me as your husband on those terms." Now one hand wandered over the floss of her pubic hair and between her thighs.

Moira shivered with pleasure, and her surrender was complete. She swung around on the bench and held up her arms to him. "Oh, Brad, I do love you. I know I'm a silly dreamer. It's an imperfect world, and none of us is a perfect human being."

"A wise man once said: We love people not because of their virtues, but in spite of their imperfections." He pulled her to her feet and held her close to him. Then, arms around each other's waists, they walked to the bed and Moira removed her nightgown.

He gazed at her with desire and admiration. "Your body comes as close to perfection as anything could be."

Caresses between Moira and Brad were never prolonged; their flesh demanded quick fulfillment.

In the middle of the night Moira awoke abruptly and with a start, deeply troubled by a force she could not determine; a pinpoint of light in the darkness of her mind as elusive as a firefly. Did it have something to do with the disagreement she had had with Brad earlier? A peripheral factor, to be sure. Was what she had said about Brad undermining the respect she had always harbored toward him true? And his statement:

"We love people not because of their virtues, but in spite of their imperfections."

More than anything else, it was the realization that had come to her after her spat with Brad that there was a side to him she did not know. You could love and live with someone all your life, and still there were facets of a person's character and mind that were only revealed in brief flashes of insight. It left Moira feeling insecure and shut out of that private world of Brad Taylor. Then, by natural progression, she applied the same logic to herself. It dawned on Moira, with misgiving, that there was an inner self of her own that Brad would never fathom, a secret self. Her passionate romance with Bob Thomas so long ago; Brad would never know about that cherished interlude. The resurrection of the memory of that glorious day in the corn with Bob caused a lump to form in her throat. She stared at the ceiling, sad and empty, until merciful sleep overtook her.

Chapter Nine

The day before Moira and Brad were scheduled to take the train back to Texas, a special military courier delivered an invitation from Secretary of War Stanton to Captain Brad Taylor:

> *Dear Captain Taylor:*
> *I am giving a small luncheon in the private dining room assigned to the War Department. It would please me if you would see fit to join us there at noon today.*
>
> > *Respectfully,*
> > *Edwin McMasters Stanton*
> > *Secretary of War for the United States*

"My God!" Brad exclaimed. "It's almost eleven now. I've got to hurry."

"Then you plan to attend?" Moira said.

"Of course I do. This isn't an ordinary invitation to lunch. It's more like a command performance."

"I know, and that's what I don't like about it. What does he want to see you for?"

Brad swept her off her feet into his arms and spun her around. "Whatever it is, you can bet it's going to work out favorably for us."

"I wonder. . . ." For no valid reason an uneasy depression settled over Moira.

At ten minutes before the hour of noon, Brad presented himself at the offices of the secretary of war. An aide to Secretary Stanton escorted Brad down a long hallway and into the private dining room, where Secretary Stanton was seated at the head of an oval banquet table with sixteen place settings. He was alone, reading a newspaper and sipping wine from a crystal goblet, along with his ever-present cigar. He rose when Brad entered the room and offered his hand.

"I'm pleased you could oblige me, Captain. Please sit down." He addressed the aide. "Send the waiter in, Hawkins. What will you have to drink, Captain?"

"Bourbon and branch water, if I may. We don't see much of it in Texas."

"I suppose not. Well, possibly that situation can be rectified."

Brad took a place to the left of the secretary and looked around at the otherwise empty table. "It appears I'm early."

"No, you were right on time."

"What about the other guests?"

Stanton placed his hands on the table and leaned back in his chair, laughing. "I specified in my invitation that it was to be a small luncheon, didn't I? I would say that the two of us constitute a small luncheon."

"Sir? I don't understand."

"My quixotic method of avoiding the inference that it was a command performance."

Brad suppressed a smile. *A command performance, indeed*—his own words. "I must confess my curiosity is mightily piqued, Mr. Secretary."

"Well, I will relieve your suspense. Just a minute, here's the waiter." A handsome Negro wearing a white jacket and black trousers took Brad's order and withdrew.

Stanton relit his cigar and cleared his throat. "Carl Collins speaks glowingly of you, my boy, and I liked the cut of your jib the moment I met you." He chuckled.

"Cut of your jib, odd phraseology for an army man, no? Anyway, I have made a careful study of your military records, and you come off A-number one. Yessir. Every commander you've served under, including Custer and Sheridan, gives you high marks. And what's more, I get the distinct impression that you are a man of integrity, a man who can be trusted with vital confidences." He pushed his chair back from the table and crossed his legs so that he was looking directly at Brad. His shrewd black eyes noted every nuance of the captain's expression. "Tell, me, Brad—you don't object if I call you Brad?—what would you say if I told you that you do not have to go back to Texas?"

"Sir?"

"My chief military aide was forced to resign because of his wife's illness. Consumption, I believe. They took her out West. Now, I cannot think of a more qualified man to fill the post. Will you accept the position?"

Brad could only stare at the secretary of war in mute astonishment.

"Say something, man."

"I—I—I am overwhelmed, sir," he stammered. "I never expected to be so honored when I came here." He shook his head, still scarcely believing his good fortune. It proved beyond all doubt that the life strategy he had espoused to Moira was gospel. No man, particularly an army man, could realize his highest ambitions without influence.

"Then you accept the appointment?"

"I do, sir. And thank you, sir. I can't wait to tell my wife. She'll be overjoyed to be spared the ordeal of returning to Texas."

"Yes, your wife. Moira, I believe? Lovely girl, and a lovely name. Colonel Callahan's daughter, isn't she?"

"Yes, she is."

"Good man, Callahan. Custer's right arm."

The waiter returned with Brad's bourbon and took their luncheon order.

"I don't mind telling you, Brad, that your assignment is going to be a rigorous job. For a while, at least. Now, what I am about to tell you is in the strictest confidence. And when I say confidence, I mean you must not tell even your wife.''

"Understood, sir," Brad retorted.

"Good . . . the other night at Carl's soirée, you were aware of the joking about my relations with the President. I don't mind admitting that I hate his guts, and he returns the compliment. Johnson is an ignorant clod. Would you believe he couldn't read or write until after he was married? His wife taught him, of all things. It defies all logic that a man such as he should be president."

"That's remarkable, sir."

Stanton continued. "I have secret sources in the White House who keep me informed of every move that scoundrel Johnson is about to make before he takes action. Well, what was said the other night about him dismissing me—it's all too true."

Brad was shocked. "Do you know when he intends to do it?"

"Almost to the day. He will make my dismissal official some time early in August, either the tenth or the twelfth."

"This is all very bewildering, Mr. Secretary. That's barely two months off. If you won't be secretary of war after that, then why are you offering me this appointment?"

Stanton reacted with a smug and confident smile. "Because, my boy, my absence will only be temporary, until the Congress convenes in January. They will unanimously declare the President's action in dismissing me illegal, and I will be reinstated to the post of secretary of war. That's where you come in. During the interim appointment of my successor, you will serve as my eyes and my ears in this office. You will observe and pass on to me each and every detail of business conducted by my successor."

"What if your successor chooses to dismiss me from the post and replace me with a man of his own?"

"Ahhh, there's the beauty of it, my boy." He leaned forward and slapped Brad on one knee. "I know definitely that President Johnson intends to install General Ulysses S. Grant as the new secretary. So, with Custer and Sheridan behind you, General Grant will retain you as his chief aide, there's no doubt about it.'' He lifted his glass. ''To our mutually profitable and enduring relationship, my boy.''

Brad touched his glass to Stanton's goblet and they each took a healthy swallow of spirits.

The waiter reappeared with a tray bearing two platters of roast beef, Yorkshire pudding and red-eye gravy in a separate cauldron.

''Thank you, Wallace,'' the secretary said after he had served them. ''And please bring us another round of drinks.''

Throughout the meal Stanton informed Brad as to the duties of his new office. ''The War Department really has to keep on its toes to ensure that that weak sister Johnson doesn't undo what it has taken the army all these years to accomplish. If he had his way he'd administer a slap on the wrist to those damned traitorous Confederate states and say 'Forgive and forget.' Well, by God, I'm determined that the Rebs are going to get everything that's coming to them! If I had my way I'd turn over all the local governments to the Negroes and let them teach the bastards how it feels to be the underdog!

''Oh, by the way, Mrs. Stanton and I are having a few guests over for dinner this evening. Would you and Mrs. Taylor care to join us?''

''We would be honored, sir. What time should we arrive?''

''Let's make it seven thirty. Time to have a few bourbons before we sit down.'' He winked and clapped Brad on the shoulder. ''Yes, siree, I really am grateful to Carl for bringing you to my attention.''

''And I am grateful to him as well for giving me this splendid opportunity to serve you, Mr. Secretary, and to serve my country.''

To Brad's disappointment, Moira received the news of his appointment with something less than enthusiasm. ''As much as I dislike Texas, I think I prefer it to Washington. Politics is such a seamy business, and politicians are all poseurs and hypocrites, including Mr. Stanton and Carl Collins."

Brad was infuriated. He grabbed her roughly by the shoulders and shook her. "For Christ's sake, Moira! Ever since we've been married, you've provided me with no support! You bitch constantly about being an army wife. You keep nagging me about the future. Now this fantastic opportunity is presented to me—the chance for us to get out of the drab routine of army life—and you belittle it and me! Is there nothing that will ever satisfy you, damnit?"

"Get your hands off me, damnit! And don't talk to me like that ever again!"

"You bitch!" He backhanded her across the face so hard that she was flung onto the couch. Her eyes blazing green with rage, she struggled to her feet, seized a vase from the end table and rushed at him. She swung it at his head, but he caught her by the wrist in midair and wrenched it loose from her grasp.

"Want to play rough, do you?" he muttered through gritted teeth. "So we'll play rough." He picked her up and flung her back across his shoulder. She flailed at his back with her fists, but he was too powerful for her.

"Put me down, you bastard, or I swear to God I'll kill you!" She tried to dig her knees into his torso, but he pinned her legs fast against him. He carried her into the suite's bedroom and across to the bed.

"You're long overdue for this, my girl. In fact, your father was remiss for not administering a sound paddling to your bottom years ago."

Moira redoubled her struggles and shrieked in outrage. "Don't you dare touch me, you brute!" He sat down on the edge of the bed and flung her across his lap.

Moira kicked and pounded her fists, to no avail. He lifted up her skirt and her petticoat, exposing her satin-encased bottom. "Lovely, very lovely indeed. A trifle pale perhaps, but we will shortly rectify that." He lifted his right hand high in the air and swung it down smartly on her quivering buttocks. The *thwack* resounded throughout the room.

"Owwwwwwwwwwww!" Moira wailed, and it was all he could do to restrain her. Again and again and again he spanked her until abruptly her resistance slackened. He became alarmed when she commenced writhing against him; at first he thought she was crying, then realized that it was laughter.

"What the hell!" he exclaimed in bewilderment. He could not imagine what had evoked this unexpected display of merriment.

"You're a pervert, a degenerate," she accused, still giggling. "Beating a poor helpless female arouses you sexually, doesn't it?"

"What are you talking about?" She kept rubbing her hips back and forth across his lap, and with a jolt he became aware of his burgeoning erection.

Moira rolled off his lap and onto the bed. "Well, at least something good developed out of this spat." She wrapped an arm around his waist and grasped the bulge in his trousers.

Her humor was contagious, and suddenly Brad burst into laughter. "You hussy! Just when I was winning for a change, you resort to dirty tricks to twist me around your little finger."

She pinched him. "Well, *this* isn't little, and isn't it about time we put it to good use?"

With shameless abandon they peeled off their clothing. Her desire was at fever pitch even before he mounted her, and as he entered her, her orgasm began. It was a sexual experience that neither of them would ever forget, of white-hot intensity, of a rare quality that could never be recaptured.

And maybe that was a good thing, Moira reflected as she lay in the aftermath swoon of glorious passion.

After a time she sat up and nudged Brad with her knee. "Think I'll take my bath now and get ready for Mr. Stanton's party."

When she came out of the bath with a towel wrapped around her, he sat on the edge of the bed smoking a

cigarette. He watched her get dressed with hungry eyes.
"God! I can never get enough of you."

She dropped the towel and stepped into a silk chemise
of tawny hue with diaphanous panels. She sat at the dressing table and slipped on long black silk stockings that
fastened to garters on her undergarment. Next came a
corselet, which lifted her breasts and bunched them together, and a shirtwaist and petticoat. Careful not to muss
her hair, which was swept back in a pompadour and
fastened with barrettes at the nape of her neck, she put on
her gown. The bodice of the gown was a festoon of
colorful flowers on a black background, skirted in shimmering blue silk taffeta.

"How do I look?" She did a pirouette.

"Good enough to eat." He reached for her and put his
arms around her hips, squeezing the firm globes of her
buttocks. His voice fell an octave. "And I think I will."

Moira laughed and pulled away from him. "Not now
you won't, my lad. Don't you want to make a good
impression on your new boss by being on time?"

"A good point." He rose and went into the bathroom.

They arrived at the Stanton town house at precisely six
twenty-five. "Minutes to spare," Brad said as he paid the
coachman.

They were greeted by a liveried butler, who took Moira's
black mantilla shawl and Brad's cavalry hat. Secretary
Stanton came out of the parlor into the hallway to greet
them. He shook Brad's hand vigorously and honored Moira
with a slight bow. "I can't tell you how delighted we are
that you could join us this evening, Mrs. Taylor."

"And we are delighted to be here, Mr. Secretary," she
answered with a gracious smile. She had made up her
mind that no matter what the topic of discussion was that
evening, she would bite her tongue and abstain from
interjecting her own views.

Stanton introduced them to the other guests, many of
whom they had met at Carl Collins's nuptial-eve affair. As
was the custom at these get-togethers, Brad drifted off to

join the men conversing animatedly around the sideboard, where drinks were served by a white-jacketed black man, while Moira joined the ladies. Carl's sister, Charlotte, whom they had met at the dinner party, looked stunning in a mauve silk gown with contrasting balloon sleeves of a lilac rosebud print, which was wasp-waisted, with a long, slim, sinuous skirt. Her pale blond hair was a golden beehive piled high on top of her head. Her high, prominent cheekbones and almond-shaped eyes gave her an exotic, somewhat Slavic mien.

"So good to see you again, Moira." She extended her hand, a rare informality among women of her class. She had a firm handclasp and an open smile, and Moira liked her a good deal better than her brother. She could not help but wonder why such an attractive woman was unattached.

They chatted for a time; then Charlotte excused herself. "I must go over and say hello to that handsome husband of yours." As if she had read Moira's mind concerning her single status, she added mischievously, "The great advantage of not being romantically involved is that you get to share the men of all the other women."

Although she was rarely at a loss for words, Moira could offer no rejoinder other than, "A girl could get her eyes scratched out for that." She watched Charlotte walk across the room to join the group of men; the exaggerated sway of her hips was calculatingly provocative. Yes, she decided, that one would require careful watching!

At dinner Charlotte was seated next to Brad, while Moira was relegated to the opposite side of the table between a fat banker and a pompous senator, an arrangement she was positive had been arrived at by Charlotte's instigation.

It annoyed her that Brad appeared to be enjoying her company with so much enthusiasm; they kept up an incessant stream of chatter punctuated with much laughter, occasionally lowering their voices to exchange a conspiratorial aside.

When they left the table, Charlotte took hold of Brad's arm possessively and led him back into the living room.

Well aware that petty jealousy was not worthy of her style, Moira nevertheless found herself smarting at the oversolicitous attention Brad was bestowing on the blond coquette.

Later, in the hansom cab on their way back to the hotel, she remarked more offhandedly than she felt, "Well, you and Miss Collins certainly hit it off very well tonight. I felt like a wallflower."

He laughed. "You a wallflower—that will be the day. Every time I looked your way, you were surrounded by a gaggle of panting males."

She sniffed. "Fat old men with false teeth and bald heads."

"Don't knock those eminent gentlemen, darling," he said seriously. "The power lies in their hands."

"You're becoming obsessed with power, Brad, and I don't like it."

"I keep everything in perspective," he assured her and took her hand. "Incidentally, I'm very grateful to you for being so scintillating, even if it was an act. Nothing is more beneficial to a man's advancement in life than a pretty and intelligent wife. You were the belle of the ball, no doubt about it."

"Not of your ball I wasn't. That blond hussy had her claws in you all night."

Brad was very pleased with himself. "I really turned on the magnetism and charm, didn't I?"

"And you have the gall to admit it? You were playing up to her, weren't you?"

"Of course," he admitted. "She's Carl's sister. And, by the way, did you know that she and Carl are distantly related to General Grant's wife?"

"You're such a snob and social climber, I can't believe you." The dark side of his nature, the canny, calculating manipulator, was emerging with greater frequency since their arrival in Washington. It disturbed Moira.

More disconcerting, he remarked with a patent note of pride, "Do you know, I think Charlotte feels some attraction to me?"

Moira had never backed off from a challenge in her life;

no conniving woman was going to steal her husband away
from her, of that she was supremely confident. The irony
of it was that she was not competing with a rival in the
conventional sense. It was not Charlotte's beauty or sensuality that she had to contend with. Brad wasn't attracted to
her because of her physical attributes. Charlotte Collins
was a symbol in his eyes of status and power!

"Oh, yes, Miss Collins has her eye on you, no doubt
about it. Just make sure that when your eye is on Charlotte, you keep everything in perspective, as you neatly put
it."

Chapter Ten

Three weeks later Moira and Brad bid farewell to Colonel Callahan and Bea Carter at the railroad station. The colonel embraced his daughter, his eyes misty.

"I'll miss you, my dear. This will be the first time you and I have ever been separated for any span of time."

She kissed his damp cheek. "And I'll miss you, Daddy." She smiled at Bea. "I don't know how he'll ever get along without a woman to take care of him."

Bea winked. "I'm trying to convince him that he can't. Maybe now that you've left him on his own, he'll be more receptive to the messages I've been sending him."

The colonel blushed like a schoolboy. "Really, we must be getting aboard, Bea." He kissed Moira again and shook hands with Brad. "Once again, congratulations on your new assignment, my boy. This is the opportunity of a lifetime. No telling where it could lead."

"Thank you, sir; and I assure you I will capitalize on it to the full extent."

Bea and Moira embraced, and the older couple climbed the steps of the Pullman car. They stood on the rear observation deck, waving as the train rumbled out of the station.

Brad consulted his gold pocket watch. "Where can I drop you, dear? I have a noon luncheon appointment with the undersecretary of state."

Moira raised her eyebrows. "The undersecretary of state. Well now, isn't the State Department out of your baliwick?"

"Not in the least. I intend to keep on top of anything and everything that even remotely reflects on the War Department. Those are my orders from Stanton."

Moira was bemused. "Maybe I'll take a cab out to Georgetown and look at that house Wendy was telling us about. If we have to stay cooped up in that hotel room for much longer, I'll go dotty."

"Good idea. If you like it, go ahead and make the arrangements to rent it. I'm amenable to any decision you make." He hailed a passing carriage and helped her up the steps. "I may be back late tonight—special staff meeting at six. So why don't you go ahead and eat without me?"

"I hate to eat alone, but we'll see."

As the carriage drew away, he exhaled with relief. A rueful grin spread across his face. "The undersecretary of state . . . well, in a sense she is."

At noon he arrived at an old English inn named the John Peel Tavern on the outskirts of Washington. The interior was dimly illuminated by gas lamps, and due to their effect along with the dark wood paneling and the cavernous beamed ceiling, Brad was momentarily blinded, after coming in out of the bright sunshine. The maître d'hôtel, clad in a red velvet frock coat, tight black knee-length trousers and white hose, bowed low.

"Can I be of assistance, sir?" he inquired in a voice with a faint accent.

"Yes, I'm to meet a Miss Charlotte Collins here at noon."

"Of course, you must be Captain Taylor. Please come this way, sir." He led Brad to a booth in a dark corner of the dining room, where Charlotte was already seated, sipping sherry and smoking a long Turkish cigarette. She held out her hand to him, and he bowed and kissed it.

She smiled and nodded to the maître d'hôtel. "Thank you, Jimmy. Please send over a bourbon and branch water for the captain."

When he had departed, she reached across the table and took Brad's hand. "You look very dashing today, Brad."

"And you look ravishingly beautiful."

Her gaze swept past him and fixed on two women who had just entered the restaurant, one fair and blond, the other dark and olive complexioned. They were elegantly attired in gowns glittering with semiprecious gems, low cut in the front to reveal their ample bosoms. Both wore ostrich-feather boas curled around their long, swanlike throats and wide-brimmed hats decorated with peacock feathers.

"Excuse me, Brad; I must have a word with Carole and Eileen." She rose, bent to kiss him on the cheek and sauntered off, wagging her magnificent backside. She returned to the table a few minutes later, beaming.

"Carole and Eileen are my bankers," she explained. "They own the Georgetown Federal Bank."

Brad's eyebrows lifted deferentially. "Highly unusual. You don't often hear of women bankers."

She leaned toward him confidentially. "They are highly unusual women. Few people know what I'm about to tell you. Although they now travel in the most elite social circles in the capital, rumor has it that they once were the co-owners of the fanciest bordello in Baltimore. One night some years back, one of the richest and most powerful figures in Washington accidentally killed one of their girls in a drunken orgy, and in return for hushing up the tragedy and disposing of the corpse, they have extorted huge sums of money from the gentleman ever since." She laughed. "And in the process of setting themselves up as wealthy widows here in Washington, they just happened to marry the Willoughby brothers, who were the former owners of the Federal Bank."

"Former?"

"Decidedly former. Not a year after the double marriage, the Willoughby brothers went fishing in the Potomac River one Sunday and never returned. Their boat was found overturned twenty miles downriver, but there never has been a trace of their bodies." Her eyes shone wickedly.

"It's my opinion that the party or parties who disposed of the murdered prostitute also took care of the Willoughbys."

Brad was aghast. "You mean they—" He paused and turned to survey the merry widows, who were chattering gaily with a large, dour-looking man with thick black hair and heavy eyebrows who had recently joined them at the table.

Charlotte nodded. "And it wouldn't surprise me if Ben Calluchi was one of the aforementioned parties who did the dirty job for them—he's the one sitting with them at the table. And the irony is that Ben is the federal marshal of this district. He's quite a character, Marshal Calluchi. He hails from the island of Sicily. It's common knowledge that he was forced to flee the country after seducing the wife and the daughter of one of the most notorious Black Hand chieftains. For some reason his intimate friends call him the Big C." There was a naughty glint in her eyes. "I can't imagine why."

Brad took a healthy swallow of his bourbon. "You certainly have a quaint assortment of friends."

"They're so much more alive than those mealy-mouthed political fops like my brother. As a matter of fact, the John Peel Tavern boasts a wide array of odd characters.

"Take Jimmy, the maître d', for example. Like Ben, he was deported from Greece for throwing tomatoes at the king in the midst of a parade. And the bartenders—they're a motley crew for sure. George was banished from Portugal for making obscene advances to a group of novitiates at a convent. And Valentine was sentenced to hang for fomenting revolution in Cuba; fortunately he escaped. Then there's Bill; he did time in the New South Wales penal colony in Australia for trying to rob the Tower of London. Just turned loose a year back. Now Mickey, a nice young chap who's been with the John Peel for years, he squanders every penny of his pay at the bordello the girls used to own in Georgetown. Ah, yes, that's why it's my favorite barroom, the Peel; it's such a wicked, wicked place." Her eyes were hot with excitement. "And I feel very wicked myself, being here alone with you today, darling."

"No reason to," he said lightly. "After all, this is a business luncheon, isn't it?"

"Well . . ." Her mouth shaped into a pout. "Business before pleasure, isn't that what they say? That doesn't rule out the latter, though." She stroked his hand, which was lying on the table. "Do you find me attractive, Brad?"

"You know damn well I do. I wouldn't be a man if I said otherwise. But back to business. What did you want to discuss with me?"

"All of Washington is abuzz over your love affair with Secretary Stanton." She laughed. "No, darling, don't take it the wrong way. What I mean is that in the short time you've been his aide at the War Department, you are already making a reputation for yourself."

"I do my best." He took a cigar from his inside pocket and bit off the tip. Charlotte removed a cigarette from a slim gold case. He struck a wooden match with his thumbnail and held the flame to her cigarette, then lit his cigar.

"I know that, and I'd like to ask a favor from you. Actually it's not for me personally, but for a good friend of mine who is with the State Department."

Brad was amused. "How good a friend?"

She smiled. "Once we were very close, but that's long over. The point is, he's the one who influenced Secretary of State Seward to purchase Alaska from the Russians last March. That deal is causing a great furor in the Congress. Most senators and representatives feel that it was sheer folly to buy a tract of land whose only resources are seals, polar bears and snow and ice. Seward's Icebox, they call it."

Brad frowned. "They're a bunch of fools! Resources be damned! Purchasing Alaska from the Russians was one of the best strategic moves this administration has made. Don't those idiots realize that it dispossessed Russia from the North American continent once and for all? As long as they had that foothold here, they would always pose a threat to Canada as well as the United States."

"You are positively clairvoyant, darling. You've anticipated the problem and solved it all in one breath. As you know, Secretary Seward and Secretary Stanton are barely on speaking terms. Jealousy within the cabinet has been rampant throughout Lincoln's administration and right into Johnson's. Do you think you can persuade Stanton and the War Department to support the Alaska purchase and back up Seward and my friend, on the grounds that it was in the best interests of national defense against foreign aggression?''

Brad grimaced and massaged the back of his neck. ''That's a tall order, Charlotte. Seward and Stanton mix like oil and water.''

''If Stanton goes along with it, the State Department is prepared to acknowledge that it was the War Department and Secretary Stanton, a patriot of great wisdom and vision, that inspired the State Department to enter into the initial negotiations with Russia.''

''That's a feasible approach, I must admit. Look, let me feel my way along with Stanton over the course of the next few days, and I'll get back to you.''

''I am deeply grateful to you, darling, for your help. And let me assure you that if you can bring Stanton over to our side, State and Seward will not forget the favor.''

''Can I count on that?'' Brad said, his heart racing in contemplation of this further access into the inner circle of political power.

''You have my word for it. And now for lunch.'' She signaled to a waiter. ''Elliot, we'll order now.''

When he had taken the order, Brad asked Charlotte, ''What manner of felon is Elliot?''

''Nothing too colorful. He was formerly employed in the congressional dining room and was accused of poisoning the soup of two Democratic senators for a fat fee from rival Republicans. However, he was acquitted for lack of evidence.''

Brad grinned. ''I'm glad I skipped the soup course.''

Over lunch she invited him to attend a small gathering she was having that evening at her home.

''Thanks, but it's awfully short notice. I have to keep an appointment with Secretary Stanton at three. Then by the time I get back to the hotel and advise Moira—well, as you can see, there just won't be time. Maybe some other time."

He could feel her shrewd eyes contemplating him, evaluating him, sensing the measure of his unbridled ambition. Casually she said, "Tell you what, then—why don't you stop by after you leave Stanton for a quick drink? General Grant and his wife will be there. It will give you two a chance to get better acquainted." She smiled, confident that the bait was irresistible.

"That might not be a bad idea. To be sure, I'd like to stop by for a quick drink and get acquainted with Grant."

"Good, we'll expect you whenever you get there. And I am sorry that Moira can't join us."

As soon as he got back to the War Department, Brad informed the secretary that he had lunched with Charlotte Collins and that she had invited him to her place to meet the Grants.

"Excellent, my boy!" Stanton clapped him on the back. "Yes, sir, you're learning fast, Brad. Sucker up to your future boss before he's appointed. Good thinking."

Brad decided to put out a tentative feeler about the Alaskan matter. "Incidentally, do you know what Miss Collins told me at lunch—in the strictest confidence, of course? She said there's an undercover move afoot in the State Department to diminish Secretary Seward's credit in launching the Alaska negotiations."

"Oh?" He was about to add that acquiring Alaska was indeed a dubious credit, but Brad said quickly, "They're saying that Seward was influenced by an offhand remark you made at a cabinet meeting over a year ago, something about Alaska standing as a buffer between Canada and the United States against Russian imperialism. There is a striking parallel between Alaska and our acquisition of Oregon; shrewd of you to recognize it before anyone else, sir."

Seward stroked his beard thoughtfully. "Hmmmm . . . seems to me I did remark on the strategic value of Alaska at a cabinet meeting. Naturally that idiot Johnson was oblivious to the significance of what I said." He was beginning to look extremely pleased and smug. "So Seward's own people recognize that the idea of purchasing Alaska did not originate entirely within State?''

"Too bad there isn't some way for us to get our fair share of the credit," Brad mused. "I mean, Seward issued a gag order once he heard of the small mutiny within State, so there's small chance it will receive any publicity outside the family, as it were."

"Well, now, don't be too certain, my boy. As you are aware, there is a good deal of controversy within the Congress about the Alaska purchase. Obviously we can't be too incursive, but what's to prevent the War Department from sneaking the word to Congress that we have been behind the Alaskan negotiations all along? Because long before Seward thought of it, we here at War had foreseen the vital strategic value that Alaska holds to the future self-defense of the United States."

"Brilliant, Mr. Secretary. I couldn't have phrased it better myself."

"All right, then." The secretary rubbed his hands together, gloating over this unexpected development. "Let's get to work on it at once. Brad, draft a letter to Senator Burton; he's the department's big man in the Congress; drop the hint that we've been monitoring the Alaska business from the beginning."

"Yes, *sir!*" Brad labored to subdue his elation. He'd estimated that it would take days to manipulate Stanton to embrace this line of thinking when, in fact, it had required no more than one subtle hint.

"I'll get right on it, sir." As he was leaving Stanton's office, the secretary called after him, "Will Mrs. Taylor be accompanying you to Charlotte's place?"

Brad turned back, hesitating. "No . . . Moira's been out shopping for a house to rent. She'll be too tired."

"Oh?" Stanton's raised eyebrow and lecherous smile were far more eloquent than words. Brad hurried out of the office.

After Brad put her in the carriage, Moira gave the address that Wendy had written on her calling card. To her surprise, the man said, "That would be the Clinton place, ma'am?"

"Yes, you're familiar with it?"

"Yes, ma'am, everybody in Washington knows Sam Clinton. It's said that Sam made a fortune smuggling contraband during the war; played both sides, he did. It's said but never been proved. Giddap!" He slapped the reins down on the mare's broad back.

The ride into the suburbs took longer than Moira had anticipated. At last the carriage veered off the main road and rumbled down a country lane lined on both sides with maple trees. Their branches arched over the roadway, creating a feeling that they were passing through nature's cathedral. When they emerged at the other end of the lane, the sight that greeted Moira made her exclaim: "Oh, dear. Is this the Clinton place?"

"Yes, ma'am." ·

"Goodness gracious, my sister told me it was a town house. This is more of a baronial mansion." It was an impressive sight, a sprawling Georgian structure sitting in the center of a huge lawn like a gem displayed on green velvet. There were innumerable windows and small balconies on the upper story. A broad portico ran almost the full length of the house, supported by stately Doric columns. The porch and the balconies were overgrown with pink crepe myrtle, magnolia and wisteria with purple, white and yellow flower clusters.

"There must be some mistake," Moira told herself. "Wendy gave me the wrong address. Possibly Sam Clinton owns a smaller dwelling somewhere else in the neighborhood." She and Brad could never afford such extravagance on a captain's salary.

The driver pulled around a long gravel drive and stopped the carriage at the front steps. "Care to have me wait, ma'am?"

"By all means. This shouldn't take very long." The driver hopped to the ground and opened the carriage door; he assisted her to disembark.

Taking a deep breath, Moira mounted the steps, feeling insignificant and out of place in such grandeur. She was wearing a simple town dress of gray flannel with a cashmere shawl draped about her shoulders. She patted the twin buns at the nape of her neck, then rapped on the brass knocker. The door was opened by a black butler in full livery.

Moira swallowed hard. "I would like to see Mrs. Clinton. My name is Moira Callahan Taylor."

A redheaded woman came up behind him. "It's all right, Amos." She held out both hands to Moira. "Do come in, Mrs. Taylor. Your dear sister, Wendy, has told me so much about you. We were so disappointed not to be able to be present at her wedding. Carl and Sam are very old and close friends. Unhappily Sam had to be in New York on that date on some very urgent business. We've just returned. Come and meet Sam. We're having a mint julep on the patio. By the by, my name is Thelma."

She led Moira through the living room and dining area, whose appointments more than justified the promise of the house's exterior. Sam Clinton rose from his lounge chair at their arrival. His wife introduced them.

"Well, this certainly brightens up what up until now was a decidedly mundane day. It's a great pleasure to meet you, Mrs. Taylor." He inspected her from head to toe with the same unabashed boldness he would have lavished on a piece of fine horseflesh.

He was a striking-looking man, although not handsome in the way that Brad was. His features might have been carved out of hard wood or stone. He had an eaglelike nose and a square granite jaw. His hair was light, curly and close-cropped. His most striking feature, his eyes, were pale blue, not unlike Brad's, but his gaze was more penetrating. He was wearing a suede shirt open at the throat and riding breeches and boots.

He held a chair for her. "Sit down, Mrs. Taylor."

"Thank you. And please call me Moira."

"Moira it is, and I'm plain old Sam." He snapped his fingers, and as if by magic a young black page boy appeared, clad in dark trousers and a white serving jacket. "Thomas, fetch Mrs. Taylor a julep, please."

"It's rather early in the day for me," she said self-consciously.

"Nonsense, it's never too early to partake of a classic Kentucky julep. My home state, Kentucky." She never would have guessed it; there was a genteel quality to his voice, but nothing like the distinctive Southern drawl she was accustomed to.

"To what do we owe the honor of this visit, Moira?"

"I think I can guess, dear." Thelma looked at Moira. "It's about renting the house, I imagine."

"Yes it is, but—" Moira was flustered. "I had no idea it was anything like this—so large, so grand. I fear my husband and I are thinking in more modest terms."

Sam grinned, showing gleaming white teeth that lent a sardonic cast to his face. "Why drink beer when you can sip champagne? I'm sure your husband would be very comfortable here. And there are the horses. I understand you're quite a horsewoman?"

"You don't understand. Our finances are strictly budgeted."

Sam and Thelma exchanged amused glances and commenced laughing.

"I beg your pardon?" Moira said a little icily.

"It's you who doesn't understand. It won't cost you a red cent to stay here at Briarcliffe while Thelma and I are in Europe."

"The fact is, Moira, you'll be doing Sam and me a favor," his wife added. "We want someone responsible here while we're away to oversee the household, keep the servants in tow and see that things run smoothly."

Moira was stunned. She clasped a hand to her throat and finally regained her voice. "I think I can definitely use that mint julep now."

Sam put an arm about his wife's waist, and they both laughed gleefully.

Suddenly Moira remembered the cab that was waiting for her outside the house. She leaped to her feet. "Oh dear, my driver. I told him to wait for me. I didn't expect to be here so long."

"I'll take care of him." 'Sam motioned for her to sit down. "You drink your julep; I'll be right back." He went into the house.

Moira shook her head. "I still can't believe it. This gorgeous house, and no rent to pay. Brad will be flabbergasted."

Thelma smiled. "You can move in anytime after the first of next month. In fact, you and your husband are welcome to come and stay with us until we leave for Europe. There's ample room, as you can see."

"That's awfully generous of you. I'll discuss it with Brad tonight."

The page boy served a round of drinks, and Sam returned to the patio. "It's all taken care of. I sent him back to town."

"But how will I get back to Washington?" Moira asked.

"No problem. I have a supper date with a business client at the Mayflower Hotel. You can ride back with me in my hansom." He lifted his glass. "I'd like to propose a toast. May you and your husband be very happy here at Briarcliffe, and may all of us become good friends. Now if you ladies will excuse me, I'll bathe and change for my appointment."

"Would you like a tour of the house, dear?" Thelma inquired.

"Oh, I'd love it."

By the time her hostess had shown her the house and the exquisite gardens that occupied four acres behind the house, Sam Clinton was ready to leave.

"Are you ready, Moira? One of the boys is bringing the carriage around to the front."

"I'm ready." She averted her eyes from the couple as Sam embraced his wife and kissed her tenderly on the lips.

"You look very dashing, darling. I wish I were coming with you tonight," Thelma said.

He did look debonair, Moira had to agree. Sam wore a brocade burgundy frock coat with fawn-color trousers and soft suede boots. A high silk hat that matched the jacket was set at a rakish angle on his leonine head.

Thelma stood on the front veranda, waving good-bye as the hansom cab rolled down the circular drive and plunged into the heavily wooded lane.

"She's a charming woman, your wife, and so gracious," Moira observed.

"That she is," he said in a stern voice. His rugged profile looked particularly sharp and grim. "I don't know what I'd do without Thelma."

For some reason his manner made Moira feel subdued. She made no reply.

After a lengthy silence he said, "But I'm going to have to learn how to do without her."

"I don't understand."

He turned to her, and to her dismay she saw a tear roll down one cheek. "What is it, Sam?"

"Thelma is going to die unless a miracle saves her. That's why we're going to Europe. There's a tuberculosis sanitarium in Switzerland that's supposed to be the best in the world. It's our last hope."

Moira was shocked and distressed. "I can't believe it. Thelma looks the picture of health. Oh, I just know that she'll recover."

He smiled wanly. "Pray for her, Moira. It's a very deceptive disease, consumption. At this point the disease is in remission. Each time that happens the period of reactivation that inevitably follows becomes more critical."

Moira slumped in her seat, totally depressed. "I don't understand life. The two of you, so devoted and so happy, with so much to live for . . . it isn't fair."

"Whoever said life was fair?" He patted her knee. "But enough of this gloomy talk. Tell me about you and your husband. You don't strike me as being a typical army wife."

She laughed. "Army brat, army wife. But no, not typical. And Brad is not a typical career military officer. He has extravagant plans." She recited a capsule life history: the early years in Maryland, the sojourn to Texas and how she and Brad had met and married.

"So now he's an aide to Secretary of War Stanton. Very

impressive. I know Edwin well, and he's a stern taskmaster. I know your brother-in-law, too, Carl Collins.''

"Yes, I know,'' she replied noncommittally.

He regarded her thoughtfully and said with keen insight, "You don't like him, do you?''

She shrugged. "I barely know the man.''

His laugh was deep and masculine. "Don't pretend. You hate his guts, and so do I.''

Moira was startled. "Thelma said you were good friends.''

"Politics and big business make strange bedfellows. A marriage of convenience, you might say. You know, I'd be deeply appreciative if you and Brad would move in with us until we leave for Europe. Thelma is so lonely and apprehensive. You'd do worlds to cheer her. Keeping one's morale up is so important in the treatment of tuberculosis. What do you say?''

His hand was lying on the seat between them, and she placed her hand over it and smiled. "I'll have to speak with Brad, but I'm sure he'll be amenable. I'll let you know tomorrow.''

"Good; I'll count on it. Tell you what—let's have lunch. I'll be in town all day, half a dozen conferences. And I deserve one interlude of pleasurable self-indulgence.''

"I don't see why not.''

"Good. I'll call for you at your hotel about noon.''

By the time they arrived in Washington, Moira knew a great deal about Sam Clinton; in fact, she felt as if they were old and intimate friends. He had had a long and varied career, commencing at the age of ten, when he ran away and became a cabin boy aboard a clipper ship. A ship's officer before he was twenty, he declined an opportunity to become a ship's master and became an importer of tea and spices from the Far East and then a plantation foreman in Borneo, where he cornered the European market on rubber and tin. At the onset of the Civil War he was already a millionaire. At this point his account of his business activities began to sound vague and even a little devious.

"I served as an intermediary between the North and South and the European markets, notably England."

She did not press him for details. "Well, here we are at the hotel. Time passes so rapidly when you're enjoying yourself."

He smiled. "I thank you for that, Moira, my dear. But the pleasure was all mine." He took her hand, raised it to his lips and kissed the palm.

Moira shivered and felt the color rise in the slim column of her neck and suffuse her cheeks. She pulled her hand away and said briskly, "Well, I thank you and Thelma for everything. You are most generous."

"Can I see you inside?"

"That won't be necessary, thank you." The hotel doorman helped her down the steps of the cab.

"Don't forget our luncheon date," Sam called after her.

Moira was irritated with herself for reacting as she had when he kissed her hand. She was sure Sam had observed her perturbation. She finally had to acknowledge to herself that the reason she found Sam Clinton so disturbing was that a strong physical attraction existed between them. He was a highly exciting man. Yes, she reflected, he was undoubtedly a very accomplished lover, a man who could help a woman achieve the acme of her sensuality.

Later, in her bath, she rationalized to herself that visualizing sex with a man other than one's husband in a fantasy did not mean that a woman would actually be unfaithful to her mate. No, she and Brad had a good, solid marriage, and Moira intended to keep it that way.

Chapter Eleven

Brad was more than willing to move into Briarcliffe, and one week after Moira's visit to the Clintons, they packed up and left the Mayflower Hotel.

"This is my lucky year," he exulted during the carriage ride into the suburbs. "First the appointment with the War Department; then becoming chummy with Ulysses S. Grant; and now we're going to live with Sam Clinton. I can't believe it." Impulsively he grabbed Moira and kissed her. "And I owe it all to you. If your sister Wendy hadn't married Carl Collins, we'd still be roasting our butts in Texas."

"You hardly owe your friendship with General Grant to me," she said snidely. "That was Charlotte's doing. By the way, how is the dear girl?"

It was plain to her that the question flustered him. His face became flushed, and he refused to meet her steady gaze. "Charlotte? How the devil should I know how she is? I haven't seen her since the night she introduced me to Grant."

"What a shame. Incidentally, I'm going to have to buy some new things now that we are part of the Washington social whirl."

"By all means. And I must pick up some evening clothes for myself. Wearing my uniform everywhere we go is beginning to make me feel gauche."

Brad was overwhelmed when the Clinton mansion came into view as they emerged from the wooded lane. "It's a palace! Can you imagine what an estate like this must have cost him? He must be as rich as an Indian potentate."

"He doesn't play that role. Really, he's very down to earth."

"That's right, you had lunch with him last week. God, you must have been the envy of every woman in the dining room."

She looked at him. "Yes, you and Sam should get along famously. After all, he's an idol and you're an idol worshipper."

He gave her a surly glance. "That's not a bit funny, Moira."

The carriage drew up to the front steps, and the cabby jumped down from the driver's seat and opened the door. Then he retrieved their luggage from the boot at the back. Brad paid him and gave him an extravagant tip.

Moira frowned as the carriage pulled away. "Aren't you forgetting something, my dear? Just because we are going to be staying here for a while, it doesn't mean that you are Sam Clinton. We can't afford that sort of gratuity."

He laughed and slapped her on the behind. "Nonsense; we've got an image to live up to." He picked up his portmanteau and her valise and they climbed the steps. "I feel like Alice walking through the looking glass," he said with awe. "Yes, sir, from here on it's going to be all uphill."

As Moira had predicted, Sam and Brad hit it off from the start. By the time supper was served by a staff of four servants, the two men had polished off several bourbons and numerous cigars.

It was a lavish feast; pâté from Belgium; trout as a second course; roast pheasant with chestnut-and-raisin stuffing served with baby carrots and potatoes. There were three varieties of French wine and an English trifle for dessert. After dinner they retired to the music room, where Thelma entertained them at the harpsichord.

"I adore the Turkish Rondo," Moira complimented her first selection.

The men withdrew to a corner of the room and sipped brandy with their cigars. "It's my judgment that you have a bright future ahead of you, Brad," Sam said.

"I couldn't agree more with you, Sam."

Sam laughed. "No false modesty about you, is there?"

"If you don't blow your own horn, you can bet that no one else will."

"Bravo! My sentiments exactly. All right, what's next on your timetable, Brad? A man like you won't hold still in a petty bureaucratic job in the War Department for too long."

"Hell, no!"

"Plan to stay in the service?"

Brad frowned. "Now that will depend on what kind of opportunities I'm confronted with."

"I like that word—'confronted.' It's not the usual term one connects with opportunity."

"No, but it's more appropriate than any other word I can think of. Opportunities are always confrontations, challenges."

Sam narrowed his eyes and thrust his cigar in Brad's direction. "If you do stay in the service, there's only one way for you to go—into foreign service."

"What type of foreign service?"

"Military aide to an ambassador or military adviser attached to a foreign military delegation. I think I have just the right post for you, Brad. Do you have any idea what is about to take place here in the United States now that the war is resolved? Expansion—no, let's call a spade a spade. We are about to embark on a long-overdue campaign of imperialism. Build ourselves a foreign empire like the British have done in India, Egypt, Canada, Australia. Imagine, of all the world's major powers, the United States is the only country that does not possess any territory beyond its own continent."

"I've heard that view expressed recently at a party we attended at Carl's. Cuba was mentioned."

"Precisely. That is a situation that cannot be tolerated any longer—the Spaniards ensconced in an island only miles off our coastline. And the Philippine Islands—what right do the Spanish have to rule the Philippines? Consider the threat they pose to Hawaii. That will come to pass in time. We'll kick their butts out of our hemisphere. It calls for patience. However, what I have in mind for you is China."

"China?"

"China. The British, French, Germans, Russians, Japs have had things all their way in China since the Opium War. Now it's our turn to get a piece of the action. China is a virtually unlimited market for foreign trade. The groundwork for American intervention in China is being laid at this very moment. What would you say to heading a delegation of industrial and military advisers who are being sent to Peking to discuss American participation in the lucrative China trade market?"

Brad poked a finger into his chest, slightly incredulous at the suggestion. "Me head a delegation? You can't be serious. What do I know of China or trade or politics?"

"What was it you said earlier this evening? Your credo in life? 'Ah, but a man's reach should exceed his grasp, Or what's a heaven for?' You will learn about China on the job. Trade, politics—they're only tools of power. Power—that's the bottom line, my boy." He thrust out a hand full-length, clutching at empty air. "Reach, damnit! Now what do you say?"

Brad laughed. "Where do I apply?"

"That's the spirit. Let me mull it over for a few days, and then I'll set you on course."

Brad was sincerely grateful. "You're quite a man, Sam. You barely know me and yet you are willing to go out of your way to help me further my career, my very life. I will be eternally in your debt."

Sam contemplated the younger man thoughtfully. "Eternally grateful, my ass. You figure I'm doing this out of altruism? Shit! I'm the hardest horse trader this side of Laredo, Texas. There's a price on everything worthwhile in life, and I intend to levy my price on you when the right time comes. If things go as planned in the next ten, twenty years, you will be my man in the Far East. You'll be representing Sam Clinton's international cartel in that neck of the woods—in an unofficial capacity, of course.''

Later that night when Brad and Moira were getting ready for bed in the guest bedroom that had been assigned to them, he related to her his conversation with Sam Clinton with mounting excitement and ebullience.

''Can you picture it in your wildest imagination? You and I in China, as important foreign dignitaries? It's positively fabulous.''

The prospect excited Moira, too, only she approached the issue with more caution than Brad. ''It certainly sounds like a marvelous opportunity, if it does work out.''

''Of course it will work out! How can I fail, with Sam behind me?''

''It's solid backing, all right, but remember what Sam told you. There's a price on everything worthwhile in life. Just make certain that the price isn't too exorbitant.''

After one week at Briarcliffe, Moira found herself becoming more accustomed to living the good life of luxury than she should have. She slept as long as she cared to in the mornings on the huge canopied bed that was soft as a cloud; breakfasted in bed at Thelma's insistence; took a leisurely bath before lunch. Then, in the afternoons, she and Thelma would stroll through the estate gardens and feed dry bread to the ducks and swans in the pond. When Sam arrived home in the late afternoon, the three of them would sit on the patio and enjoy a predinner drink. Moira saw less of her husband than when they had resided in Washington. He went to the War Office early in the morning and rarely got back to Briarcliffe until nine or ten at night.

''Brad is certainly industrious,'' Thelma commented when he had missed supper for the fifth straight time. ''He'll wear himself to a frazzle if he doesn't let up.''

''He's a strong young buck,'' Sam drawled.

Moira thought she detected a veiled innuendo in his tone and in his sly smile. "He's doing very well, thank you. I keep hearing complimentary things about Brad all over the capital."

One of Moira's favorite pastimes at Briarcliffe was riding. Sam Clinton's stables were among the most prestigious in the state and included three racing champions. She and a young palamino gelding named Rex took to each other from the first day she led him out for a canter. There was a bridle path that ran around the perimeter of the estate. Frequently when Sam came home early in the day, he and Moira would ride together.

"Quite the tomboy," he remarked the first time he watched her ride. "Man's shirt and trousers, boots. You ride like a cowpuncher. You even look like a boy from a distance." His rugged face cracked in a smile. "But not close up you don't."

She felt his gaze move from her breasts, straining against the thin fabric of the shirt, down to her thighs, molding the tight denim pants. She sensed that at that instant he was lusting for her and eased the tension by galloping far out in front of him, shouting back: "C'mon, I'll race you back to the stable!"

On the following Friday Sam decided to take the day off. He came down to breakfast dressed in his riding togs, and after a meal of beef-and-kidney pie, sweet rolls, and coffee laced with cognac, he invited Moira to go riding.

The sun was warm on her head and back, and the crisp breeze caressed her cheek. Her body was tingling with life. She urged Rex on ever faster until the trees on either side of the path were a blur of brown and green. When she reached the pond, she reined in and waited for Sam to catch up.

"You ride like a demon," he told her. "Poor old Samson here can't keep up with the likes of your young gelding."

She bent over Rex's neck and hugged him. "I love him; he reminds me of my horse Devil back in Texas." A wistful note crept into her voice. "How I miss him, old Devil."

"Send for him. You can keep him here at Briarcliffe."

His penetrating gaze made her uneasy. "I couldn't do that, Sam. You and Thelma have done far too much for us as it is."

He laid a hand gently on her arm. "I like doing things for you, Moira. You know, if you'd like, you and Brad can stay on here as long as you wish. Until we can get him appointed to that China delegation."

"No, we've imposed on you enough already. Do you really think Brad will get that post?"

"If I say so, he'll get it, you can be sure." His grip tightened on her arm. "I meant what I said. I wish you'd consider it carefully. It's not easy to say this, but the chances that Thelma will be making the return trip to Briarcliffe are mighty slim. This big place is going to be terribly lonely for me, living here all by myself."

She didn't want to shake off his hand, but his touch made her uncomfortable. "I want to stretch my legs, Sam." She dismounted and walked out on the little rustic footbridge that spanned the pond. Sam followed her. She tensed as he came up in back of her and put his hands on her shoulders.

"It's been a long time since I've been with a woman," he said in a quiet voice. "The doc said some time back that she and I had to stop—well, you know what I mean."

"It's hard to believe that a man like you would have any difficulty finding someone. There must be hundreds of women who would jump at your beck and call."

"Maybe so, but you see, I'm not interested in women who would jump at my beck and call. I like a special kind of woman. Strong, honest, with a mind of her own. A woman of strong passions and sensuality. A woman like—"

"Don't say it!" She turned and pulled away from him. The green in her eyes intensified. "Sam . . . you are a very fine man. You're attractive, charming and I'm flattered at your attention, I really am. But I have a husband whom I love and cherish very dearly, and I would never be unfaithful to him so long as we stay married. I'm sorry, Sam.''

He shook his head sadly. ''Not as sorry as I am. Let me tell you, Moira, I respect fidelity in a marriage. The thing is it should work both ways.''

''Of course it should. What are you leading up to, Sam?''

His gaze was cool and dispassionate. ''Moira . . . are you aware that Brad is having an affair with Charlotte Collins?''

A physical blow would have been less punishing. She recoiled and placed her hands against her cheeks. ''That isn't true, Sam. Why did you have to say that and lower my high esteem for you? It's contemptible to slander my husband just because I rejected your advances.''

He massaged his jaw with thumb and index finger, studying her with his head cocked to one side. ''I'm not lying, and I have no wish to harm or slander Brad. I think a good deal of him or I wouldn't be sticking my neck out to wrangle this post for him on the China committee. What I don't like is that he would cheat on a splendid woman like you. Charlotte Collins isn't fit to shine your shoes. She's a calculating wench and a man-eating barracuda.''

''I refuse to listen to any more of this.'' She strode past him and off the bridge and vaulted onto the horse's back.

Sam leaned against the bridge rail and called after her. ''Why don't you ask Brad, Moira? I have a feeling he won't deny it. In his own way he's got integrity; I'm a keen student of human nature. Ask him, Moira! Ask him!''

That night when they were alone in their room, Moira did just that, in an indirect way. ''Brad, I feel like making love tonight. You haven't touched me in days.''

''My darling, it's just that I'm under so much pressure at the department, working nights, getting up at dawn. Tell you what—I'll make it a point to come home early tomorrow, and we'll spend the entire night partying, as the good ol' Southern boys say.''

"Are you sure it's the job that's exhausting you?" she asked archly. "I thought it might be that that little ol' Southern gal Charlotte Collins is too much for you to handle."

The vacuous expression on his face and his evasive eyes answered the question even as he was denying it. "Charlotte Collins? Where on earth did you get such a preposterous notion? Oh, I know Washington is the metropolis of the world when it comes to rumor and gossip. The only reason I see Charlotte is because she has an inside track to the State Department, you know that."

"Do you know what, Brad?" she said tonelessly. "The terrible part is that I do believe you. There's nothing personal between you and her, not on your part, that is. I've no doubt that Charlotte finds you very attractive, and, cold logician that you are, you aim to please the power brokers, male and female. Is there no Machiavellian depth you won't sink to in order to satisfy your ambitions?"

He sat down on the edge of the bed and stared at the carpet. "All right," he said in resignation, "so I've had a fling with Charlotte. It has nothing to do with us. I love you and I always will. Charlotte is a flash in the pan. She can't hold a candle to you, darling."

"I know, she isn't fit to shine my shoes," was her sarcastic retort.

He looked up, frowning in uncertainty. "That's an odd way to put it. Look, Charlotte has had her fun with me. Now she'll drift on to more challenging encounters. Why can't we forget about it once and for all? Look, if you still feel like making love. . . ."

"No thank you," she said acidly.

When Moira went down to breakfast the following morning, Thelma was sitting alone in her dressing gown. "Brad and Sam off to work so soon?" she inquired.

"No, as a matter of fact, Sam is giving Brad instructions about some construction work he's having done while we're in Europe. He wants to make sure it's done exactly the way he wants it. A new boat house down by the river. Did you sleep well, dear?''

''Like the proverbial log. How are you feeling, Thelma?''

''Exhausted. I was up half the night with a coughing fit. Sam has to refill my laudanum prescription when he goes to town. Have some breakfast; I'll call Melissa.''

''No, thank you. I believe I'll skip breakfast today.'' She patted her tummy. ''I must have put on five pounds in the short while we've been staying here. You treat us too well.''

''Nonsense, you have a figure like Aphrodite . . . goddess of love.'' The expression of wistful envy in her eyes saddened Moira.

Moira put a gentle hand on the other woman's shoulder. ''I'm going to change into my riding togs and look for Sam and Brad down by the river.''

Fifteen minutes later she was aboard Rex, heading at a leisurely canter toward the river. After a mile she left the bridle path and rode up a grassy slope and over a knoll. From the ridge she could see the river a half-mile off and the rough skeleton of what was to be a new boat house. Two horses were grazing nearby, but there was no sign of their riders. She nudged her knees into Rex's sides, and the big gelding took off down the far side of the hill and through high grass that brushed Moira's legs with a feathery touch. She had covered half the distance when Brad appeared from behind a pile of lumber and mounted his horse. They met and reined in.

''Morning, darling,'' he greeted her. ''Sam's been filling me in on the blueprints for the new boat house. Now I've got to hurry and dress and start for Washington. There's a staff meeting at the department at eleven o'clock.''

''You do that, dear . . . Where's Sam?''

''Making a count of the lumber that was hauled in yesterday. He thinks maybe they gave him a short count.''

''I'll go join him. Maybe there's some way I can help.''

''Good . . . and remember, I'll be home early this evening.''

She watched him ride off, her eyes aflame with anger, then rode up just as Sam came into view from behind the lumber. He was so involved with a pencil and clipboard that he didn't notice her until she called to him: "What are you so preoccupied with, Sam?"

He looked up. "Oh, hello, Moira. Just finishing my inventory. I was right; it's a short count. Well, they won't get away with it." His eyes were flint hard. "I don't cheat on my business deals, and I don't like getting cheated. I'll horsewhip that SOB Tim Maloney!"

He lapsed into silence, making careful notations on the paper in the clipboard. Without warning he looked up at her. "Did you ask him?"

"I did."

"I told you he wouldn't lie to you, didn't I?"

"How do you know he didn't lie?"

"Because he told me all about it."

She dismounted and faced him, her aquamarine eyes searching his face. "Exactly what did he tell you?"

"That he was having a fling with Charlotte Collins and that you had confronted him with it. He wanted to know if it was common gossip in D.C. I told him that Charlotte's affairs have ceased to be news in Washington, they're so repetitious. And what did you say to him about it?"

"Not much."

"What do you intend to do about it?"

"Take your recommendation. You know what they say: What's sauce for the goose is sauce for the gander." His eyes widened as she began to unbutton her checkered shirt. She flung it open to bare her breasts.

"Damn! You're beautiful," he said.

Sam moved closer to her and bent his head to her breasts, kissing one and then the other. Her nipples rose and hardened against his tongue. Moira moaned and closed her eyes. She unfastened her belt and unbuttoned the fly of her trousers, letting them fall about her ankles. She wasn't wearing any underclothing. Trembling like tall grass in the wind, Sam sank slowly to his knees. His arms went around her hips and his hands cupped her buttocks. He buried his face in her pubic hair and adored her mound of love. Moira's hands locked at the back of his head and pulled him fast against her, her hips writhing to the tempo of his tongue.

"I'm ready, Sam," she sighed. "Hurry and undress." She lay down in the sweet, soft, warm grass on the riverbank and watched him fling off his clothes. A short distance away, her gelding whinnied and pawed the earth. No gelding, Sam Clinton! He had the lithe, muscular build of a man half his age, a physique that reminded her of Michelangelo's statue of David. His erection, standing up almost straight against his ridged belly, suggested a hunger and urgency that came from lengthy deprivation.

Moira opened her thighs to him and he kneeled between them. He cried out in sheer delight at her gentle fondling.

She suddenly thought back to the first time with Bob Thomas. It had happened in a place very much like this; warm sun; cornsilk and wind-whipped grass.

With Bob making love had been like slaking a desperate thirst with a dipper of cold water from a sparkling spring. Sex with Brad was exciting, titillating, intoxicating, like drinking champagne. With Sam it was altogether different. Sam was a patient, tender lover with vast experience and a confident knowledge of how to please women. Sam made love to her with the artistry of a musician playing a violin, strumming all the notes in the scales of carnal pleasure up and down her body. Love with Sam was like sipping fine, aged brandy from a crystal snifter, so that every nuance of the bouquet could be totally appreciated.

When it was over, he smiled and leaned across her to kiss her lips. "It was wonderful for me. I'm very grateful to you, my darling, for taking pity on an old man's infatuation."

Moira laughed. "Old man! Now that's a laugh. You are a highly accomplished lover."

"As accomplished as Brad?" he asked slyly.

She shook her head. "There's no comparing lovers,

whether they are male or female. We are all individual and
unique in everything we do in life, including sex.''

"I expect you're right about that." His eyes narrowed.
"Do you feel guilty about cheating on Brad?"

She sat up and put her hands on his shoulders. "Oh, but
I'm not cheating on Brad. I am merely paying him back in
kind for his infidelity." She drew her knees up to her chest
and wrapped her arms around them, struck by the irony of
the situation.

"You're smiling like the Cheshire Cat," he remarked.
"What are you thinking?"

"It's funny when you consider it. Brad was never serious with Charlotte. Sleeping with her is merely a favor in
return for help in furthering his career. When I tell him
about you and me—never while Thelma is alive—I'll say
that sleeping with you was for the same noble purpose. Or
to employ one of his favorite phrases, you're stroking him
in offering him this China assignment; now it's only fair
that you should be stroked in return." She showed him the
feline grin once more and caressed his phallus, which was
prompt to react.

That same afternoon Brad had an appointment to meet
Charlotte at the John Peel Tavern. When he arrived, he
was shocked to find her seated at the bar; it was scandalous to see a woman alone in a tavern, much less sitting at
a bar. There were two men standing on either side of her;
good friends, he assumed from the animation of their
conversation and their hearty laughter.

"Darling." She rose at Brad's approach and kissed him
on the cheek. "I'd like you to meet some friends of
mine." She indicated a good-looking young man of Latin
complexion wearing a rakish smile. "This is the tavern
manager, Louis." Louis was stylishly clad in a blue swallowtail coat, yellow knickers and knee-length stockings of
a vermilion hue; his patent leather shoes boasted glittering
brass buckles. "Louis, this is my good friend Captain
Taylor."

Louis smiled perceptively and bowed. "A great pleasure

to serve you, Captain.'' He signaled for the bartender. ''Terry, the drinks are on the house . . . Now, if you will excuse me, *señores* and Señorita Collins, I must get back to my duties.''

Charlotte introduced Brad to the other friend, a tall, dark man with a saturnine face, introspective eyes and the general look of a man who had seen everything and traveled everywhere. ''Captain Taylor, I'd like you to meet Al Valli.''

''Pleasure to meet you, Captain.'' They shook hands. ''By the way, if you ever get down to the Riverboat Club, look me up. I'll buy you a drink.'' He bowed and excused himself. ''I have to go to work at three o'clock.''

After he had departed, Brad commented. ''Seems like a decent chap. What line of work is he in?''

''Al's a professional gambler. And I would advise you to steer clear of the Riverboat Club. Al is one of the most notorious dealers this side of the Mississippi. In fact, he's been barred from playing cards on every steamer sailing the Mississippi.''

Brad shook his head. ''They certainly are an unprincipled lot who gather here, clientele and staff alike.''

Charlotte smiled. ''Let he that is without sin . . . *Comprends?*''

His smile was sheepish. ''Touché! I suppose my character is not without reproach. Incidentally, Moira knows about us.''

He might as well have been announcing the time of day, for all the interest she evinced. Shrugging, she said, ''I shouldn't concern myself about it if I were you. Be assured I couldn't care less who knows it.''

He nodded wearily. ''To be sure, I'm just one in a long succession of your conquests.''

There was a tinge of contempt in her voice. ''You don't have to play games with me, my boy. You know damned well it is not you who has been conquered! You used me to gain a private end, and that's fine with me. You're a good companion, a handsome escort at parties, and a good stud. By the way, I have a confidential message for you from Secretary of State Seward. He is well aware that the recent overwhelming support the Alaska Purchase gained in the Congress is largely due to the positive results of your campaign initiated in the War Department.'' She took a cigarette out of her case and put it to her lips. ''The secretary asked me to assure you that his department will support you in your bid for nomination to the elite China Committee.''

''I appreciate that, darling, and I owe it to you and to Sam Clinton.'' He took a box of wooden matches out of his pocket, but Terry the bartender was ahead of him, thrusting a lit match under the tip of her cigarette. ''Miss Collins, please permit me.''

She inhaled. ''Thank you, Terry, and please bring the captain a tumbler of bourbon and branch water.''

Brad looked after him. ''And what's his unique vice?''

''Near the end of the evening, Terry is famous for spiking the drinks of transient customers and then slipping out the back way when they stagger out of the tavern, sandbagging them and robbing them of all their possessions.''

''Nice chap, isn't he? And he looks so innocent with that blond hair, genteel voice and pince-nez.''

Later, drinking and eating at their favorite corner table, Charlotte said, ''I trust the fact that Moira knows about our little affair won't disrupt the relationship. I haven't grown tired of you yet.''

He shriveled inwardly and could not meet her cold, blue-eyed stare with any self-respect. And deliberately demeaning his esteem even lower, he replied complacently, ''No, I don't see why it should.'' His gaze rose to meet her eyes now. ''As long as we can be useful to each other.'' He could have slapped her for her mocking laughter, but instead he gripped the edge of his bench until his knuckles ached with strain.

As they departed the tavern, Louis bade them farewell. ''I trust I will see you again, Captain Taylor.''

''I am certain that you will, Louis. The food and the service were excellent.''

"Despite his respectable appearance, Louis is a thoroughly disreputable fellow," Charlotte observed.

"Why should he be any different from the rest?"

"He's Puerto Rican by birth, and for half a century his father and uncles sailed under the Jolly Roger."

"Pirates?" Brad said incredulously.

"The most feared throughout the Caribbean. Eventually they were caught and all were hanged, with the exception of Louis. They say there is still a warrant out charging him with piracy, murder and other reprehensible crimes."

As he helped her into the carriage, she inquired, "Will I see you tonight?"

"Not tonight," he said firmly. "Especially not tonight."

She smiled, comprehending his meaning. "Tonight is for mending fences, is that it?"

"It is imperative."

"I understand. Well . . . have fun and give my love to dear Moira."

That night, as he had vowed, Brad returned to Briarcliffe in time for supper. All four of them were in high spirits, and Brad had never seen Moira look more aglow. Sam was in fine fettle, jocular and humorous. And even Thelma had more color in her cheeks and drank two glasses of sherry.

"We've had to delay our traveling plans by two weeks," Sam announced. "There are things in Washington that must be resolved before I leave—including your appointment."

Brad protested, "Please, Sam, not on my account. I realize that time is of the essence and—" He broke off without completing the sentence, and all three of them glanced furtively at Thelma, wondering if she had anticipated what he had been about to say.

In a firm voice Thelma answered: "Nonsense! A week or two more or less isn't going to make a bit of difference. Sam, pour me another glass of wine. I feel festive tonight."

When they were in bed, Brad fulfilled the promise he had made the night before and made passionate love to Moira. He was relieved to find her so responsive; it appeared that her discovery of his infidelity with Charlotte Collins had not diminished her sexuality. On that night and on all the nights to come she never brought up the subject again.

After their lovemaking, she announced to Brad rather casually, "You know, it wouldn't surprise me if I was pregnant."

He was thunderstruck. "Are you serious? I can't believe it!"

She giggled. "It is not an uncommon result of the strenuous activities we've been indulging in in the bedroom all these months."

"I realize that. It's just that I never expected it would occur so soon."

"Are you sorry?"

He hugged and kissed her. "Sorry? What a ridiculous thing to suggest. Why, it's always been my dream to have a son who would follow in my footsteps."

"I'll do my best to have it turn out a boy."

Brad swung his legs over the side of the bed to the floor and took a cigar from his nighttable. He was intoxicated by all his recent good fortune: the appointment at the War Department; meeting Charlotte Collins and Sam Clinton; their combined efforts that had produced his imminent appointment to the prestigious China Committee. And now this above all—he was about to become a father!

His eyes were glowing with excited speculation about the future that lay ahead of them, him and Moira. Turning to her he said, "All this and heaven too! You know what they say in romantic novels?"

". . . *And so they lived happily ever after . . .*"

"By God! I'm going downstairs and tell Sam the good news. He's working late in his study." He put on his robe and slippers, knotting the sash.

Moira watched him with a combination of pleasure and satisfaction at the joy she had bestowed upon him. He kissed her again before leaving the bedroom.

She lay there staring at the ceiling, recalling what he had said:

"*. . . And so they lived happily ever after . . .*"

"And why not?" she said, turned on her side and fell asleep.

Book Two

Chapter Twelve

Dear Susan,

 I can't tell you how delighted we all are to learn of your engagement to Major Thomas Shaffer. Wendy and I were beginning to fear that the last of the Callahan girls would end up an old maid. Major Shaffer was always one of Daddy's favorite officers. It was indeed fortunate that Major Shaffer was transferred from the Seventh Cavalry Regiment before it went west to the Dakotas. Almost certainly he would have been with Daddy and General Custer at the tragic massacre of all those brave troopers at the Little Bighorn. My heart goes out to dear Bea. They were together as man and wife for only four years. I am glad that she and Elizabeth Custer are together to lend comfort to one another.

 Time goes by so rapidly; with each passing year the process seems to accelerate. Would you believe that our Patrick is six years old and little Desiree is three? Pat is the image of his father, and they worship each other. There is no doubt in my mind that he will choose the army as his career. Speaking of careers, Brad is doing very well in his post here at

129

Peking as chief of staff of the military mission at the American Legation and was recently promoted to full colonel. Wendy, in her last letter, informed me that Carl told her President Grant is very impressed by Brad's ability as a leader and administrator and feels that he could become a top-notch politician if he so chooses and could win the firm support of the Republican Party. I suspect he is accurate in that assessment. Brad possesses that indispensable quality of a political leader—Machiavellian amorality.

Life here at the foreign colony within Peking's walls is tranquil and comfortable—almost too comfortable and serene, even monotonous. Sometimes I feel that all of us here—Americans, French, Germans, Russians, Italians, English and Japanese—are an exotic community of sybarites. Outside of the few hours of each day that are occupied in official business, we spend most of our time in every form of self-indulgence imaginable. It is ironic that this society of self-styled elitists occupies a small, privileged island in the midst of an impoverished giant of a nation. The decadent monarchy is indifferent to the sad plight of its starving, desperate people, who continue to breed like rabbits despite the country's bankruptcy.

The royal family quite literally lives in an "ivory tower," The Forbidden City, a walled city within the city of Peking. The emperor is only four years of age, and the real power is wielded by his tyrannical aunt, the so-called dowager empress. As long as she reigns, China will stand still in a world that is changing and modernizing at a pellmell pace. The empress is fanatical in rejecting all foreign influence on the ancient customs, religion and mores; she is determined to keep the sleeping giant chained to its primitive agrarian past.

However, despite the atmosphere of tranquillity that has prevailed in China since the Taiping rebellion in 1864, I feel intuitively that we are living in a time that is the calm before the storm. Antagonism toward the foreigners who have been exploiting the Chinese since the Opium War in 1842 with ever-increasing flagrancy grows and spreads throughout the provinces. Isolated acts of violence against Occidentals are mounting all over China. Then there is the as-yet-intangible menace of a secret organization designated as ''the Fists of Righteous Harmony,'' reputedly thousands of peasants, soldiers and common workers who take a blood oath to purge their homeland of the foreign devils. It is astonishing to Brad and to me what ostriches our fellow expatriates in the colony are. They casually dismiss the reports of this expanding organization of dissidents as ''pure poppycock,'' as the British minister decries it.

It is time I close this missive and start preparing for the big party at the English Legation tonight. I don't remember what the occasion is. The fact is, no occasion is required for ribald revelry here at Peking. Love and good wishes to you and Carl from Brad and myself as well as from little Patrick and Desiree. How I regret that we cannot attend your wedding. It would be much appreciated if you could send us a wedding photograph. Good-bye and good luck.

Your loving sister,
Moira

Moira took her bath and put on her finest silk chemise and a satin corselet, both handmade by her lady's maid, Lotus, who was a classic beauty with skin the shade of Burmese light tea. Her hair was straight and black, meticulously rolled at the back of her neck and fastened with ornate Oriental combs made of pure ivory. Her figure was slender and fragile like the bloom that was her namesake, but she was every inch a woman. Lotus was bright, alert, sensitive and highly intelligent. Although she had no formal education—her parents were both field workers in the rice paddies outside of Peking—she had taught herself to read and write, and her English was excellent. If she had been born in any other culture, Lotus would have had unlimited opportunities to achieve success in any vocation she chose, but in China she had gained the loftiest ambition available to an Oriental woman—handmaiden to the wife of a Western civil servant.

There was a knock on Moira's bedroom door; it was Lotus with her freshly ironed ball gown, a Hong Kong copy of the latest Parisian fashion at the Tuileries, a princess gown that was an explosion of multicolored blossoms, molded to the torso to give a woman's figure a triangular silhouette, flat in front and flaring behind. Moira slipped it on over her crinoline petticoat and surveyed herself in the mirror.

"You look beautiful, madam," Lotus complimented her.

"I'll pass," Moira said dryly. "Frankly, I'd rather stay home and lounge about in a kimono." She sat down at her vanity and began to brush her long black hair.

"Let me do that for you, madam." The Chinese girl took the brush from her and commenced brushing with long, vigorous strokes that produced a radiant sheen.

"How should I do my hair, Lotus? A pompadour should go well with this gown."

"If you don't mind my saying so, madam, I'd like to try something different that will set you apart from the other women at the party."

"Fire away, my girl."

She marveled at the adroitness of the girl's slim hands, her fingers flying, curling dark strands around thumb and forefinger and arranging them in concentric circles, piled one on top of the other and held in place by jeweled combs until the finished coiffure resembled a perfect beehive atop her head.

"It's absolutely stunning, Lotus. I never cease to wonder at your varied talents," Moira said.

The girl was pleased, but compliments made her shy and self-conscious. "It is nothing, madam. I try to please."

"Above and beyond the call of duty."

A half-hour later she descended the staircase to where

Brad was waiting for her in the hall. His gaze was admiring. "You're positively ravishing. The other wives will detest you for monopolizing all the males' attention."

"You look rather handsome yourself," she told him. He was wearing the dress uniform of a cavalry officer, embellished by a a red cummerbund and a sash slashing across his chest. He offered her his arm. "Shall we be off?"

The ball was held in the British Government House, a palatial residence that was equal to any elegant Edwardian mansion situated on the outskirts of London. Its rooms were richly appointed, and fine paintings and silk tapestries adorned the walls. A marble staircase descended to the ballroom. At the far end of the large rectangular room, on a dais beneath a bower of shimmering silk, was a ten-piece orchestra. The dance floor, crowded with couples, was an ever-changing montage of colors; gowns of tulle and voile, velvet and brocade, silk and satin and paisley; of every shade—vivid reds and greens, peach and orange, apple green, melon, lightning blue and gold. As they whirled around the room to a fast-tempo waltz, the women's skirts ballooned so that from the balcony they resembled a sea of colored flowers. There were naughty glimpses of shapely limbs through draped skirts, revealing silk stockings of every design and hue.

The civilian men were all in evening wear, with long swallowtail coats that flapped behind them like blackbirds' wings; the military men were in dress uniforms—British, American, Italian, Russian, Japanese, French—their contrasting shades and design rivaling the plumage of the women.

In the years they had been stationed in China, Moira had seen the same familiar faces so many times that they had almost become faceless out of monotony. So, when on the rare occasions that a stranger did join the assembly, he or she presented a highly vivid profile.

Even as she descended the staircase on Brad's arm, her attention was captured by a man in uniform who literally stood head and shoulders above his military peers. He was tall, at least six-feet four, with an imposing physique that flattered the uniform of a British light cavalry officer: French gray with buff plastrons and the golden belt buckle flaunting crossed sabers. He had sharp, bold features and fair, curly hair, and when he smiled, his blue eyes and his mouth conveyed impudence and sardonic wit. Moira knew, too, that she had captured his attention. His gaze fixed on her across the powdered shoulders of his dancing partner.

"Who is that attractive man?" she asked Brad.

"Who? Which man? Oh, you must mean Major Sean Flynn. He's to be stationed temporarily here at Peking on his way to permanent assignment as military attaché to the British viceroy at Calcutta, India."

"Is his wife here as well?"

"No, he's not married. Quite a catch for one of the single ladies here. Possibly the German minister's daughter, Brunhilda, whatever her name is."

Moira laughed. "I don't think she is quite the major's type."

Major Flynn joined them at the beverage table. He clapped Brad on the shoulder. "I say, old chap, aren't you going to introduce me to your daughter?"

Brad and Moira laughed, and she wagged a finger at Flynn. "Knowing the name is Flynn should have prepared me for that bit of blarney," she jested.

"Flattery will get you everywhere, Sean," Brad said. "Daughter, indeed!"

"Will you do me the honor of having the next dance, Mrs. Taylor?" he inquired.

She looked at Brad, who assented. "You dance with Sean, Moira. I have to see Baron von Kessler on a matter of business. I'll see you later."

Major Flynn swept her into his arms and onto the dance floor. "I always thought of myself as tall for a woman, but next to you, I feel positively puny."

His white teeth flashed in a crooked smile. "You, puny? Lass, you are as fine a figure of a woman as ever I've seen. Perfect in every way."

Moira rolled her eyes at the ceiling. "Here it comes

again—the blarney. What's a Flynn doing in the British service anyway?''

''My family are members of the Ascendancy, I confess with some guilt.''

''The Ascendancy?''

''Yes, English landlords who were assigned huge land grants by the crown. They settled in Ireland and made serfs of the true owners of the land. Generation after generation of them, until they became Irish natives, although lacking the real Irish spirit and soul. My maternal grandfather, he was a Limey, and my father was a schoolteacher who was lucky to fall in love with his master's daughter, as it were.

''When the potato famine struck, there was little need for teachers in Ireland. Those children who didn't die spent their youth working in the fields twelve hours a day. My parents had the means to emigrate to England, where my father secured a job teaching physics at the Royal Military Academy at Sandhurst. My alma mater, incidentally.''

There came a faraway look in his blue eyes, uniquely Irish blue, she thought.

He sighed. ''I serve the queen, it's true, but deep down I'm a son of Erin.'' He laughed without mirth. ''Enough of my biography. I must be boring you to tears.''

''On the contrary. I find it fascinating. What will you be doing in India?''

''Forming a special regiment to deal with the *thugs*. Not that it will do much good. Like trying to exterminate cockroaches. For every one you kill, there are two more to take his place.''

''I recall reading somewhere about the *thugs*. They're professional murderers, aren't they?''

''Yes, they strangle their victims.''

''Do they kill for profit?''

''Of course. Money and revenge, the two notable reasons that motivate all killing, whether on the personal level or the grand scale of nation against nation. Naturally the *thugs,* like everyone else, rationalize their deadly activities; they elevate their crimes to a noble cause in the name of religion. Reminiscent of the Christian Crusades, come to think of it.

"*Thuggee* is an ancient cult that precedes Christianity, actually. Its followers worship the mythical black goddess Kali, who, according to tradition, requires human blood to assure her immortality. However, in pursuit of their obligation to Kali, the *thugs* acquire a horde of filthy lucre. That is understandable too."

"How will you go about dealing with these *thugs?*" she asked.

"Oh, the regiment will concentrate on the high-risk areas along the Ganges River and the foothills of the Himalayas. We'll kill a good many *thugs* and capture a few who will promptly turn informers—approvers, as they're called. They will reveal the identities of high-station members, many of the government officials, police and military men; the whole damned system over there is corrupt and chaotic; we should have pulled out of India years ago and thrown the ruling power up for grabs, let them kill themselves off. In any case, the miscreants exposed by the informers will be hanged or thrown into military prison. Then we sit back and wait for the next uprising. Cockroaches . . ." He shook his head despairingly. "I say, would you like a breath of fresh air? It's getting a bit foggy in here."

"I'd like that."

Adroitly he steered her across the dance floor, wending their way through the jam of humanity in the direction of wide French doors that led out to a balcony. For a big man he was remarkably light on his feet. Outside they stood by the marble balustrade overlooking the delegation garden, drenched in moonlight. Moira inhaled deeply of the crisp night air and hugged her arms tight against her sides.

"What a gorgeous night," she said. "Look at that shooting star!" No sooner had she spoken when, to her amazement, the sky to the west put on a display of pyrotechnics the like of which she had never seen.

"A meteor shower," he informed her. "It's a common phenomenon in this part of the world in certain seasons."

She chanted the childhood rhyme: "Star light, star bright, I wish I may, I wish I might, Get the wish I wish tonight."

Flynn laughed as he lit a cigar. "At least you have the odds on your side with all those buggers flying about. What did you wish for?"

Moira smiled. "You can't reveal your wish or it breaks the spell."

She was standing with her back leaning against the balustrade so that, when he unexpectedly moved closer to her, she could not retreat. His eyes shone eerily in the reflected light of the full moon, like an animal's eyes. In a low voice he said to her, "I'm not afraid to reveal my wish, Mrs. Taylor." His gaze was fixed on the cleavage of her breasts, bunched together and lifted high by her corselet. "In a word, my dear, I wished for you. I want you in the very worst which way, as they say in County Cork."

Moira was stunned by the cheek of the man, whom she had met less than an hour before. She stiffened as he pressed himself against her, his hard, muscular body conveying an urgent message to hers. The quickened tempo of his breathing swelled his chest rhythmically against her breasts. Hard thighs strained against her loins. The heat of his flesh was a palpable force against which she was powerless. The turgid insistence of his manhood against her belly helped her muster the willpower to brace her hands against his chest and shove.

"Let go of me, you brazen bastard!" she snarled.

He cast down his cigar and embraced her in a hug. From behind, one big hand grasped her head and pulled it back so that her face was uplifted to him. His wide, sensual mouth closed on her lips. She ceased struggling and hung limp in his arms. To her shock and dismay, she was engulfed by a rising tide of emotion that could not be subdued. Without volition her arms snaked up and around his neck, one hand caressing the curly hair at the nape of his neck. She writhed against him as his tongue probed the inner recesses of her mouth; her own tongue squirmed like a snake gone wild. In another minute she would have reached the point of no return; would have lain with him here on the hard balcony as indifferent to the celebrants just inside the French doors as a bitch in heat is to idle onlookers in the streets.

She found the strength barely in time. Wrenching her mouth from his, she turned her head aside and hissed. "Noooooooo! Stop it, you nasty brute!" She jerked her knee up into his groin with all her power.

"What the hell!" he cried out in pain and staggered backward, crouching and holding himself to recover from her onslaught. "Jesus, Mary and Joseph!" He was gasping for air, and tears of pain sprang to his eyes.

Moira combed her hair back in some semblance of array with her fingers and smoothed down her gown. She leaned back against the railing, holding on to it for dear life. She was afraid that if she let go, her legs would give way. This encounter with an oversexed Englishman had been the most traumatic experience of her life. An unparalleled ordeal! The worst part of it was the nature of the ordeal— overcoming her irresistible lust to commit public adultery!

At last he recuperated enough to speak, still bent over and holding his private parts. "What the devil did you do that for, you damned wildcat? Is sadism part of your mating ritual?"

"That was to show an egotistical, cocky Limey stud that he can't treat a lady the way he treats a barracks whore. It requires a good deal more than a large prick and a full moon to woo me into a roll in the hay so soon after a casual introduction!"

He straightened up and took his first full deep breath since Moira had delivered her foul blow. Slowly a smile spread over his face.

"What are you grinning at, you big baboon?"

"Self-mockery, mostly. You're quite right. I should have known better than to push my luck so fast. I had it coming, and I won't hold it against you—no, no!" He backed away, holding his hands up to fend her off. "I swear there was no pun intended."

Fully recovered, Moira walked around him, chin tilted up haughtily. "I'm going back inside."

As she was marching toward the doorway, he called after her: "Mrs. Taylor . . . what you were saying about the full moon, the you-know-what and a roll in the hay . . . *so soon* after a casual introduction . . . *So soon,* now there's the key phrase. Over the long haul it tends to leave me with a glimmer of hope."

Moira blushed to the roots of her hair.

Chapter Thirteen

Brad Taylor and Sean Flynn stood on the veranda of the American Legation house, drinking Scotch and sodas, staring out into the heavy rain.

"I've never seen such a deluge," Flynn observed. "It's like standing behind a waterfall and looking out. Can't see more than ten feet."

"Makes one think about building an ark, like Noah," Brad said wryly. "For all intents and purposes, China's weather can be described simplistically as dry in the winter and wet in the summer . . . You'll find more of the same in India. Yearly monsoons, typhoons."

"Well, I'm not looking forward to that." He paced back and forth restlessly. "I feel like a prisoner—a prisoner of the elements."

"I expect it will break in a few days. Then we'll really break loose, let off steam."

"How do you go about that?"

"We've a club here made up of officers from the various legations, all good horsemen. We ride into the back country and bivouac in the field. Makes you feel like a soldier again. You're welcome to tag along, Sean."

"I'd love it; get the ants out of my pants."

Moira came out of the house and joined them at the porch railing. She was wearing a checked tunic with a skirt draped to show the crimson petticoat underneath. Her hair was tied at the nape of her neck with a matching ribbon and hung almost down to her waist.

Flynn cocked an admiring eyebrow. "Don't we look chic today, Moira?"

"Thank you."

Flynn put a hand on his host's shoulder. "You must be the envy of every man in the colony, old man, possessing such a lovely wife." He sighed. "If I could find another like her I would gladly foresake the blissful state of bachelorhood."

"If she were indeed like me, Major Flynn, she wouldn't have you," was her tart reply. "And mind you, Major, *nobody* possesses me!"

"I say, Moira, Sean was merely jesting," Brad said self-consciously.

Flynn laughed. "Don't trouble yourself over my feelings, old man. I've got a thick skin." His blue eyes twinkled. "Anyway, your wife and I share the Irish gift and liking of banter."

"Let me get you another drink, Sean."

"I'm never one to decline a drink." Brad took his glass and went into the house.

"To what do we owe the honor of your presence here so early in the day?" she inquired.

"Came over to show Brad the new uniform issue we'll be wearing in India, the latest design in field garb."

Moira was not impressed. "It certainly lacks the glamour of your lancer's uniform."

The trousers and jacket were loose and baggy, with large patch pockets across the chest and a brown leather strap that ran diagonally from one hip to the opposite shoulder and fastened to the broad Sam Brown belt in front and at the back.

"It's called khaki," he explained. "Dyed with *majari* from the dwarf palm tree. The helmet and puttees are stained with tobacco juice. Helps the troops blend in with the drab, muddy Indian terrain. Camouflage."

She folded her arms beneath her breasts and shook her

head. "And you couldn't wait to show off that monstrous uniform?"

"No, the uniform was only an excuse to see you. The very sight of you makes my whole day."

"You must have shallow satisfactions, Major."

He smiled. "Now, don't deny that you're just a wee bit flattered by my fawning attention, Moira. After all, I am a handsome, dashing fellow with a dynamic personality. I mean, a woman wouldn't be normal if she didn't have some positive response to my devotion."

"What conceit," she said, displaying more annoyance than she truly felt.

"You could invite me to lunch," he said.

"I could, but I won't. Now if you'll excuse me, Major, I have more important matters to attend to than standing here playing word games with you."

"Word games . . ." He studied her thoughtfully. "We are playing games with one another, that's true. . . There are more pleasurable games we could play together, though."

She spun on her heels and stalked off the porch.

Later that night as they were preparing for bed, Brad mentioned casually that he had invited Flynn to join the colony bivouac into the Chinese countryside after the cessation of the rains. Moira was the only woman in the foreign compound who joined the men on their periodic treks; she had not lost her love of the great outdoors. To her husband's surprise, she threw her brush down on the vanity and swung around on the stool to face him, the fathomless green of her eyes mirroring her displeasure.

"You didn't! How could you possibly invite that insufferable English bastard to take part in our group outing?"

"Yes, don't forget that, my dear," he retorted smartly. "*Our* group, not *your* group. In the short while he's been at Peking, he's become popular with the members of every legation here. And you are undoubtedly the sole female inhabitant whom he has not charmed the pants off." He cackled salaciously. "That may be a slight exaggeration, but I'll wager he's seduced a fair number."

"You're disgusting," she said coldly and resumed brushing her hair. He lay in bed, hands folded behind his head, watching her slip into a pair of red silk mandarin's pajamas.

He rolled over on his back and lay there staring at the ceiling, frowning. Moira sat on the edge of the bed and blew out the oil lamp on the night table.

The rains ceased the following week, and two days after that the cloud cover lifted, unmasking the red, coruscating sun. The following Sunday, the International Riding Club, as the members referred to themselves, gathered in the community square to begin their trek into the hinterland. Despite the fact that Major Flynn was accompanying them, Moira awoke that morning full of anticipation and elation. Life in the wilderness would offer a welcome contrast to the cloistered atmosphere of the colony at Peking. She dressed in a white linen blouse, hip-hugging breeches of black broadcloth and riding boots, and went downstairs singing the anthem of the Seventh Cavalry:

> *"Instead of spa we'll drink down ale,*
> *And pay the reckoning on the nail;*
> *No man for debt shall go to jail,*
> *From Garry Owen in glory . . ."*

Kim the houseboy met her in the lower hall. He placed his hands together, palms touching, and bowed. "Good morning, Madam Taylor."

"Good morning, Kim. It's a wonderful morning. Is the colonel at breakfast?"

"He has long since eaten and is working in the den. He asked to see you as soon as you arose."

Moira marched down the hall to the rear of the house with a mounting premonition. Brad was hunched over his desk, riffling through a stack of documents. She was startled to see he was wearing a white linen suit, shirt, collar and tie. He glanced up at her entrance and smiled.

"Morning, dear."

"Brad, what on earth are you doing in that ridiculous garb? We're due to ride out in another half-hour."

He rose and came around the desk and took her in his arms. "I won't be riding out with you, I'm afraid. The minister wants me to complete the secret paper for the State Department that will be leaving on a ship this afternoon."

Moira was outraged. "Damn it, Brad! It's not fair. He knows how much we've been looking forward to this adventure."

"I'm sorry, sweetheart; but you are not to be deprived of your excursion. You go ahead without me."

"It's out of the question." She picked up a riding crop from a chair and beat it savagely on the desk in frustration. "Damn! Damn! Damn!"

"No more tantrums, Moira. Get your gear together and convene with the others in the square. Tell you what—after I wrap up this paperwork, I'll ride out tomorrow and join you."

That possibility pacified her somewhat. "You promise?"

"My solemn oath . . . Oh, by the way, Major Flynn will replace me as leader of the expedition. He is the senior officer of the group."

She stared at him, mouth agape. "Major Flynn! Oh no!"

"Protocol, darling. I know how you dislike him, but please don't let your emotions interfere with your enjoyment of the outing."

"I wouldn't give him the satisfaction." She slapped the crop against her thigh. "Well, I'd better be on my way. Don't forget your promise."

He placed a hand on his heart. "Believe me, I'll see you tomorrow without fail." He kissed her and went back to his work.

Wearing a pith helmet tilted rakishly over one eyebrow, Moira left the house. Kim was waiting at the foot of the steps, holding the tether of her mount, a large, rawboned roan named Big Red. She checked her saddlebags and the Spencer rifle in the rifle boot and mounted.

"Good-bye, Kim. Take good care of things until I get back."

He bowed low. "Farewell, madam, and may the gods of good fortune watch over you."

Moira was the last member of the group to arrive at the square. There was Lieutenant Santini of the Italian delegation; Major Schultz of the German contingent; Fouche of France; Spassky of Russia and the redoubtable Major Flynn of Great Britain. Japan was not represented.

"You're late," Flynn said cheerfully. "Just like a woman."

She glared at him. "I understand you are in charge of our party, Major Flynn, but let's get one thing straight at the onset. Don't pull rank on me!"

"Cheerio." He touched the bill of his cap in a mock salute. "Sound the 'Advance.' "

They were accompanied by a detail of Chinese servants riding on mules and bearing gear and provisions. There was a good deal of banter and joking throughout the morning. For the most part the journey was as monotonous as the landscape; dusty plains and fields of rice and poppies as far as the eye could see.

Flynn was puzzled. "Do my eyes deceive me or are those poppies?"

"They are indeed. Since you English won the Opium War, it's been open season on the peasants of China and Asia."

They passed through a small village of dung hovels teeming with scrawny, naked children with swollen bellies. "Good God!" Flynn muttered. "I've never seen such filth and poverty. It's an abomination!"

"Wait until you get to India," she told him. "I hear it makes China look like a land of plenty."

The quality of the scenery improved as they reached the foothills of a great mountain range. They followed a trail along the bank of a sinuous river. The traffic on the river was heavy with squat ugly Chinese junks propelled by primitive membranous sails battened with bamboo and by oarsmen sculling at the stern. The countryside was colorful; craggy mountains in the distance splotched with green forests. The ascending riverbanks on both sides were a series of terraces on which barefoot men, women and children labored in the rice paddies with their trousers rolled to their knees.

"Not a foot of arable land goes to waste in China with so many millions to feed," she informed him.

In the late afternoon they rounded a bend in the river and saw a Buddhist temple sitting on a patch of high ground overlooking the terraced rice paddies, a pagoda in the shape of an octagon constructed in three stages: the base, a shaft and a crown topped by a sharp spire.

"Up there on the mountain above the pagoda, I say we make camp for the night," said Flynn. "See, there's a water hole in that grove of trees."

They rode up the hill and made camp in the middle of a grove of mulberry trees alongside a small pond surrounded by lush ferns. While the servants were staking out the tents and lighting the cook fires, Moira gathered the petite red berries that grew on the mulberry trees; she held out the canteen cup to Flynn.

"Try them; they're delicious."

He accepted a handful and tasted them. "Ummmm. They remind me of raspberries."

"These are white mulberry trees. The leaves sustain the silk worms," she explained.

Moira's tent was larger and better appointed than the men's quarters. Pyramidal in form, it boasted an army cot with a blanket and a sheet, a small table, a chair and a washstand. After inspecting it, Major Flynn observed:

"I say, this is very cozy. No comparison to a bedroll. Large quarters for one little girl such as yourself. If you'd care to have company, I'd be happy to oblige."

"No thank you, Major. I prefer my solitude."

His smile was saucy. "The nights get rather cold up here in the mountains. One of the boys was telling me that it is not uncommon for the snakes and rats to crawl into

the sack with a warm body." He winked. "Which, incidentally, is a pastime I am not averse to myself."

"You're quite a card, Major. In fact, I think you would
have done very well in the entertainment business instead
of the cavalry. A circus performer; namely a clown . . .
Now, if you will excuse me, I think I'll take a bath."

"Are you serious? A bath in a wash basin?"

"No, there's a natural bathtub down at the far end of the
pond where it overflows into a rock basin."

"You mean to say you are about to cavort naked with
all these military types looking on?"

"As officers and gentlemen, they should not be 'looking
on.' "

Major Flynn, Major Schultz, Lieutenant Santini and
Captain Fouche posted themselves around the site with
their backs turned to the waterhole while Moira splashed
about in the rocky basin.

After the long hours in the saddle Moira was exhilarated
by the crystal-clear, cool water. Because of the high min-
eral content, the water had a soft, oily texture; it caressed
her skin like liquid silk. If Brad were here, she would have
gone directly back to the tent and made passionate love to
him.

She emerged from the pool and dried herself with a
fleecy towel. The feel of the nap on her bare flesh height-
ened her sensuality. Through the trees she had a glimpse
of Major Flynn's broad khaki back; he was standing at
parade rest, with his hands folded at the small of his back.
She speculated that almost surely he had sneaked at least
one peek while she was bathing. A man like Flynn would
have to succumb to such a temptation. Curiously, the idea
stimulated her.

Steady, Moira, me girl, she warned herself. *You're
sleeping alone tonight, and that is that!*

When she was through drying herself, she put on a
butterfly peignoir with wing sleeves and a long floating
skirt and started back to her tent.

"All clear," she shouted to Flynn. As she walked past

him, she noted the expression of undisguised desire on his face. It felt good to be a woman.

Back at the tent, she wrapped a dry towel around her head like a turban. She peered out from behind the tent flap and called to Flynn. "What time do we eat? I'm famished."

"Dinner should be ready by the time you're dressed."

"I don't believe I will get dressed. I'm cold and tired, and I think I'll turn in as soon as I eat."

"Fine, I'll have one of the boys bring you up a mess kit and a pot of tea."

Moira withdrew into the tent and lit the oil lantern that was hanging on a spike in the tent's center post. She finished drying her hair, and by that time one of the servants had arrived with her supper. The tin mess kit was mounded with steaming meat, vegetables and brown rice, all of it highly seasoned and covered with a spicy pepper and curry sauce.

She was idling over her second cup of tea when Flynn called to her from outside. "Everything all right?"

"The meal was delicious."

"Yes, and it tasted even better than it would have back at the colony. All that fresh air and exercise really stimulates the appetite."

"I'll leave the utensils outside the flap for the boy; then I'll turn in."

"Sleep tight. I'll see you in the morning."

He walked away from the tent, stopped and turned around impulsively. Moira was standing at the side of the cot between the lantern and the tent wall, a dark, vivid silhouette on the translucent canvas. He experienced a sharp intake of breath as she removed her robe. The profile of her nude body was captivating. As she leaned over to remove her slippers, her pear-shaped breasts dangled from her body like ripe fruits on a vine.

"Good god!" he uttered in awe and sheer physical torment. She walked back to the lantern and blew it out. The tent was dark now, but the voluptuous image of what he had witnessed was vividly branded on his mind's eye more vividly than a shadow on a canvas wall. Now he could envision the real woman. Bare, bold breasts upturned to his lascivious gaze, the nipples red and stiff. The dimple of her navel, her belly softly curved and enticing. The plump curly mound of her *mons* and between her thighs . . .

He turned and joined the other officers, who were drinking brandy and beer around the roaring fire on the shore of the pond.

Eventually the men drifted into their tents until only Flynn was left, chewing on his dead cigar butt and pacing restlessly until the campfire dissipated into a heap of glowing embers. Silence enveloped the mountain like a shroud; the only sounds were the chirping of the night birds and the complaints of monkeys vying for the best perches in the mulberry trees. Flynn strolled among the horses, answering their whinny of welcome with a pat on a rump or a gentle tug on a mane.

Time and time again he would glance across the clearing at Moira's tent, set apart from the rest. In a trance he walked slowly toward it; stood before it, staring at the tent flap. He was powerless to overcome the fire in his blood. With deliberation he threw down the cigar butt, reached inside the flap to unfasten the drawstring, and stepped inside. He stood quietly in the Stygian darkness until his vision adjusted. A full moon playing on the translucent canvas lent a luminous sheen to the tent's walls. On tiptoe he walked to the cot and looked down at the sleeping woman. He could make out the gentle rise and fall of her bosom beneath the thin blanket.

Consumed by lust, he unbuttoned his trousers and unbuckled his belt. Flynn had crossed his Rubicon; there would be no retreat now. He must possess the succulent body of Moira Taylor. He removed his trousers and drawers and prepared to do battle. He carried his erection like a lance. Moira was lying on her back, her arms and legs askew. He took a deep breath, bent over and pulled back the sheet and blanket. She was naked. The moonlight filtering through the canvas caused her flesh to glow like an alabastar statue of a goddess in a Grecian garden. Ravenous with desire, he fixed his gaze between her spread thighs.

Moving swiftly, he kneeled on the cot and wedged a knee between her knees, spreading them further apart. Simultaneously he clamped a hand over her mouth.

Moira had finally descended into restive slumber after tossing and turning, troubled by the hot tingling in her loins. If only Brad were here to relieve the tension she was enduring. She visualized how it would be. He was hovering over her, positioning his rigid member, sturdy as steel, yet soft as velvet to the touch. She welcomed him ardently. She thrilled to his lips nibbling on her aching breasts.

No dream this! she realized with a start. It was real! It was happening to her. Her immediate thought was that Brad had decided to ride out to join them after dark. What a romantic way to surprise her.

"Oh, darling, my prayers have been answered." Her arms snaked around his neck and her hips thrust up with an ardor equal to his.

I must be dreaming, he thought. *Or going mad!*

She was smooth and dewy, fully prepared to receive him, almost as if she had been waiting in excited anticipation. She was all that Flynn had conjured up in his wildest imagination. And much more. She ground her pelvis and belly against him, murmuring lusty obscenities to him in the near-unintelligible language of love, the tempo of their pumping parts carrying them from white-hot frenzy to insupportable ecstasy.

"Oh, my sweet adorable husband!" she cried out as her orgasm peaked.

In the aftermath of his miraculous bliss, Flynn collapsed alongside her, limp and weak. Then as she kept speaking, he stiffened and bolted upright on the cot.

"Husband!" It was the most traumatic moment of his life.

"Brad?"

Flynn was speechless with terror. Now that his lust had been satiated, the full gravity of what he had done came down on his shoulders; he was Atlas bearing the weight of the earth on his back!

"Brad?" She reached out and touched his chest.

Flynn swallowed hard, determined to meet his fate like a man and a soldier. "I'm afraid not, luv. It's me—Sean."

Moira was shocked and incredulous. "Sean? Sean Flynn! You *bastard*."

"Jesus! Do you want to advertise this to the whole camp?"

"You rotten son of a bitch!" she hissed angrily. She sat up and beat on his chest with fists. "Wait until Brad hears what you did to me, you goddamned rapist. The British minister at Peking will have you flogged; hanged if I have my way." A strong, athletic woman, she cocked back her right fist and slugged him on the jaw.

Flynn fell off the cot onto the floor, and before he could recover, she leaped off the cot and kicked him in the groin.

"Ahhhhhwwwwwgggggghhhhh!" He muffled his howls of pain, pushing his mouth into the dirt. The pain was every bit as intense as the delight he had experienced only moments before. Yes, it was truly an orgasm of agony. Gradually it subsided and his eyes stopped watering.

He held up his hands, begging for mercy as she prepared to kick him again. "Stop, please! And let me tell you, for a woman who is crying rape, you certainly acted as if you were enjoying it as much as I was. You were ready and eager for it in every way."

Moira withheld her assault, staring down at him confused, flustered, stunned by an astonishing burst of self-revelation. Flynn had a point. There was no denying that she had enjoyed it, had wanted sex desperately since her afternoon bath in the pool!

To Flynn's astonishment, Moira began to laugh. She lay down on the cot and buried her face in the pillow, her naked body shaking with mirth. Believing that she was hysterical, he kneeled beside her.

"Calm yourself. Hysterics won't solve this mess."

She turned her head and gasped, "I am not hysterical, Sean, at least not in the way you think. I'm sorry I struck you and kicked you. I had no right."

He was thoroughly confounded. "I don't understand. What's got into you?"

She reached out and stroked his blond hair. "All right, don't just sit there looking at me like a fool. Come into bed, the night is young!"

Chapter Fourteen

The next day they delayed their departure until Brad caught up with them. Major Flynn walked away from Moira as Brad took her in his arms and kissed her.

"Miss me, sweet?"

"Terribly." She looked across his shoulder at Flynn, who was standing by the bank of the pond. He stooped, picked up a flat stone and skimmed it across the placid surface of the water. It took four bounces before sinking. Flynn's shoulders slumped. His heart felt as heavy as that submerged stone.

Inwardly Moira's heart was heavy, too. She chided herself for not feeling more guilty about her affair with Major Flynn. Yet she was always the realist. What cannot be cured must be endured. Besides, it was not the same as if she had invited the encounter with the handsome Englishman in her tent. She may well have provided provocation by undressing with the lamp on, but her seduction had not been brazen and overt.

"How did your work go?" she asked Brad lightly.

"Splendid. The State Department will be very pleased."

Ever since he had been invited to attend the coronation of the three-year-old Emperor Kuang-Hsü in 1875, Colonel Bradford Taylor had been one of the few foreigners who was welcome at the royal palace within the Forbidden

City, at the center of Peking. There was the outer wall; then within still another wall lay the Imperial City; and finally there was the walled Forbidden City.

The real power in China was the Dowager Empress Tz'u Hsi, who would rule until Kuang-Hsü came of age at fifteen. The dowager empress was a domineering, implacable woman who was largely responsible for China's backwardness in the modern world. However, a new breed of "Young Turks" was emerging from within the ranks of mandarins who served as advisers at the court and provided liaison between the palace and the foreign element at the delegations within the colony. Brad, more than any other foreigner stationed in Peking, was on intimate terms with some of the most powerful young mandarins. Among the advancements they advocated were the building of roads and railroads and stringing of telegraph lines across the country to improve communication among the cities. They were also determined to modernize the Chinese army and navy against the threat of Japan, a nation once considered barbaric by the Chinese and now outstripping its former "big brother" by leaps and bounds in every phase of development.

Brad considered one member of the royal court his strongest ally and direct line to the imperious empress— Tz'u Hsi's favorite niece, Sun Ying. Sun Ying was a princess in every respect. A petite woman of twenty-four years of age, her well-rounded body appeared boneless, so exquisitely did skin and flesh flow over her frame. Her complexion was flawless, with skin like porcelain and the hue of light sandalwood. Her eyes, slanting up to the corners of her graceful, finely plucked eyebrows, were the shade of dark jade. The confidences that Sun Ying imparted to Colonel Taylor made him the most highly qualified China expert in all the foreign delegations.

As they broke camp, they observed that a large crowd was congregating around the holy pagoda down the hillside.

"Wonder what's going on?" Flynn said.

"I aim to find out," said Colonel Taylor, who had assumed command of the expedition.

They rode downhill and stopped on a ridge overlooking the temple. The peasants were kneeling and praying silently when unexpectedly a strange, disembodied voice issued forth from within the temple, a voice that smote the sun-drenched hillside like thunder:

"I am Yu Ti, god of the unseen world. If you submit to the sacrilege the foreign devils plan to inflict on your sacred land, I will stop the rains from falling and your crops will shrivel up and die. You must resist their efforts to desecrate our land with their railroads and their telegraph lines. You must resist their efforts to convert you to their pagan religion. You must exterminate the foreign devils, decapitate them. Then you will win the favor of Yu Ti and the land shall prosper as before."

"Now that's what I call a pretty piece of legerdemain," Brad said with genuine admiration. "Whoever's behind the trick has surely put the fear of the gods in those poor ignorant devils."

The crowd rose up now and commenced clapping their hands and chanting: "Yu Ti is almighty . . . Yu Ti is eternal . . . Yu Ti is invincible . . . Drive out the foreign devils . . . Kill! Kill! *Kill!*"

"Not a reassuring demonstration," Moira commented.

"Schweinhundes!" Major Schultz spat on the ground. They will learn a painful lesson if they try to drive us Germans out of China!"

"Oui, they are filthy *merde!"* Fouche concurred. "Ahhhgh, those sheep would never have the will or the courage to stand up to Occidentals!"

"Don't be too sure of that, gentlemen," Brad said grimly. "Come on, let's be on our way."

They spent two more days riding through the mountain wilderness, then headed back to Peking. Along the way they shot two wild pigs and a dozen wild ducks.

"We'll have a royal feast when we get back to the delegation," Moira said.

"Am I invited?" Flynn inquired with his little crooked smile.

"By all means, old man," Brad said as Moira was

about to make an excuse. Since she and Flynn had made love, she felt even more uncomfortable in his presence than when their relationship had been one of cool formality. With the insight gained that passionate night, she realized now why she had kept him at a distance since his arrival in Peking. Her instincts had warned her that if he got too close to her, the strong physical attraction he exerted on her could get out of hand, as indeed it had, though quite by accident. But now that Moira had acknowledged her vulnerability to the masculine charms of Sean Flynn, in the future, she would have to redouble her defenses so that there would be no repetition of her indiscretion.

She was uncertain whether there was a connection between her troubled state of mind, her lingering guilt and the decline in the quality of her love life with Brad, both in frequency and pitch of ardor.

Early in September, Brad informed her, "I'm going down to Tientsin for a few days. Special mission for the minister. I've given orders to Major Flynn to take care of you while I'm away."

She glanced at him in disbelief and not without real trepidation. Did he suspect what had happened that night in her tent? Was he making a sly allusion to it in order to observe her reaction? No, it was impossible—unless Flynn had betrayed her. Moira studied his expression for some clue. There was no trace of guile reflected in his eyes or in the open smile he showed her. She relaxed and said flippantly:

"Now that's a strange thing for a man to tell a friend. 'Take care of my wife while I'm away.' Really, I can make out very well without the ministrations of Major Flynn."

Brad laughed. "You're still down on the poor blighter. What's he ever done to you?"

Moira merely shrugged and turned away in silence.

The same morning Brad set out for Tientsin, Major Flynn put in an appearance at their quarters shortly after noon. Moira was sitting on the small porch that fronted the dwelling, a porch that reminded her of the one on the bungalow at Fort Hempstead. It was shaded by trellises overgrown with thick vines clustered with small yellow blossoms that smelled like honeysuckle.

"Thought I'd look in on you, see if I could be of service." He removed his helmet and stood uncertainly with one foot on the bottom step.

Moira put down her sewing and regarded him with anger darkening her eyes. "Is your choice of phrase deliberate? 'Service,' as in the way a stud services a mare?"

"Oh, Moira." His face became beet red. "I had no such intention, please believe me." He wiped a sleeve across his sweaty forehead. "It's still nagging at me, too. It makes me feel like such a cad—I mean on top of all the courtesy Brad has shown me." His jaw jutted adamantly. "One thing I must tell you—I can live with the guilt and self-contempt because I'm not sorry for what happened. It's an experience I will cherish for the rest of my days."

She was touched by the ring of truth in his voice. "Come sit down. I'll have the houseboy make us some tea. I'll be right back." She got up and went into the kitchen, where Kim was polishing the wood cookstove with blackener. When she returned, Flynn was slumped in a rattan chair, looking the epitome of dejection.

"Cheer up, Sean. It's pointless to brood over it after the fact. Spilled milk and all that, you know."

He looked up and frowned. "No, you don't understand. I told you I wouldn't take back what you and I shared for all the tea in China." He reached out and took her hand. "Don't deny it, luv, you were every bit as blissful as I was."

"I don't deny it," she said firmly. "Although it can never happen again."

His grip tightened. "Why not, Moira? You are a vibrant, earthy woman, and I know damn well Brad doesn't satisfy you in bed."

"Brad is an accomplished lover or I wouldn't have married him."

"Maybe that was true in the past, but he hasn't the time anymore to pay attention to his husbandly duties. How the hell could he? He's always working, or gadding about the Forbidden City; right now he's on his way to Tientsin, and you probably won't see him for a week or more."

Moira couldn't deny it. Flynn was right. Brad was totally consumed by his work and ambition. The fact was, the dissatisfaction she sensed in their marriage could not be blamed on her affair with Flynn; the seeds had been germinating for more than a year. Flynn stood up and, before she could stop him, he folded her into his arms. She struggled to free herself.

"Are you mad? Kim will bring out the tea any minute!"

"This won't take but a minute." He crushed his mouth down on hers, his tongue probing between her parted lips. It was only a brief kiss and then he released her.

Stunned, Moira touched her fingers to her lips, still hot, wet and tingling from his kiss. Desire was stirring in her loins; she was powerless to quench it.

"Well?" he asked quietly. "You feel it too, I can see that. Moira, my darling, I've never felt about a woman the way I feel about you. It's the first time in my life that I've been in love."

"That's absurd, Sean. It's a physical thing you feel, an infatuation." She met his gaze squarely. "No, I won't deny that I feel physical desire for you, but that's not love."

"Do you love Brad?"

"Of course I love him; he's my husband."

"The two are not synonymous. Have you always loved him?"

She thought about it; it was difficult to find words. "No . . . not in the beginning . . . I took him to be a swaggering, cocky young man, too well pleased with himself and his ability to charm women."

Flynn smiled. "Very much the first impression you had of me, isn't it?"

Moira was taken unaware. "I never thought about it,

but you're right in a way. The two of you are very much alike.''

"No, we're night and day, Brad and myself—deep down, that is, beneath the facade. I have nothing but contempt for his obsessive ambition. I don't want to be a leader of men, a bastion of power. The only ambition I have is to put in my time and retire from the service and then settle down on some remote Irish loch with a girl like you, and spend the rest of my life making her happy.''

It was a pretty speech and it evoked a lump in her throat. "That's a beautiful sentiment," she said wistfully, "but there's one thing you are overlooking. One of the attractions I felt toward Brad from the start was his ambition. You see, I am an ambitious woman, and life on an isolated Irish loch would not be my cup of tea.''

"Then I'll become ambitious," he said airily and flung up his hands. "But not so ambitious that I'll ever neglect you.''

She gaped at him. "Me? What the devil are you talking about?''

"What I said about a girl like yourself, it's not true. It's you I want to settle down with, Moira. You and only you.''

"Sean, you've got to stop this silly talk. It's childish. I'm a married woman.''

"You may belong to Brad under the law, but in the eyes of Almighty God you belong to me. Heart and soul, we belong to each other. There's an ancient Greek myth that at the beginning there was only one sex in the world, creatures reproduced by parthenogenesis. Then God split them in twain as male and female and scattered them at random all over the globe. He decreed that they should wander the earth until they had sought out the missing half, the man and woman who are true mates to each other.'' He smiled and took both her hands in his. "You and I, we've finally found each other.''

They separated at the sound of footsteps coming down the inside hall. Kim served the tea and bowed to Moira:

"Madam . . . there is a request that Lotus and I would

beg you to consider. There is a high religious service at the Tonglong temple up the hill to honor the birth date of holy Buddha. If you would permit us to leave at sundown and attend, we would be most grateful.''

"To be sure, Kim. In fact, you can leave before sundown. I won't need you until tomorrow morning.''

"Thank you so much, madam.'' He bowed and went back into the house.

Moira poured the tea, keenly aware of Flynn's hungry eyes on her bosom as she bent over the table. She was wearing an Oriental kaftan of dazzling browns and golds and crimson, with a billowy skirt and a deeply cut V bodice. She sat down and pulled at the neckline self-consciously.

"What are you blushing for?'' he asked.

Her face flushed hotter. "I am *not* blushing,'' she snapped. "And stop looking at me in that lecherous way.''

"That is not lechery, it's love, though the loved one must expect to be desired as well as loved.''

"Can't we change the subject?''

"With the servants gone for the night, you'll be alone.''

"You can't be serious. It's out of the question.''

"If it will assuage your conscience, I'll break into your bedroom in the dead of night as I did before.''

"I think you had better leave now, Sean. I have a splitting headache.''

"As you wish.'' He rose and put on his helmet. On his way down the steps, he turned and said, "If you change your mind, leave the door unbolted when you retire.''

Moira's nerves were so frazzled, her body felt as though it had been abused by nettles. A cool bath didn't help either. The feel of the rough terry-cloth towel started erotic impulses coursing through her breasts and buttocks and between her thighs.

She had read about certain women who were obsessed with sex. Could it be that she was turning into such a woman? No, she denied it; she was a healthy, normal, highly sexed female who of late had been neglected by her husband. Her physical and mental frustration were quite normal.

Moira ate a light supper of leftover beef and kidney pie. Afterward she sat on the veranda and watched night creep over the settlement. It was a dry, clear darkness, which encouraged various members of the legations to take leisurely evening strolls. Some of them stopped at the front steps to chat with Moira for a time and to exchange gossip. Two of the passersby were the American minister and his wife.

"Feeling lonely with the colonel away to Tientsin, eh?" the minister inquired.

"A bit, but I shall survive for a few days. How long will Brad be gone, do you think?" she asked.

The minister looked puzzled. "Well . . . I would think you'd know more about that than I do."

"I beg your pardon?"

"It's not as if he's off on official business. He requested a few days' vacation to attend to personal business." Abruptly he cleared his throat and said, "Nice to have spoken with you, Mrs. Taylor. We really must be off. Cheerio, as our British friends say." He and his wife set off briskly.

"My dear, how could you?" the minister's wife hissed at him when they were out of earshot. "Personal business, indeed! Monkey business with that little Oriental slut, I'll wager!"

"Hold your tongue! If a Chinese spy working here at the compound reported that you referred to a royal princess as a slut, the two of us would be on the next ship out." A note of serious concern sounded in his voice. "I have warned Colonel Taylor that his relationship with the dowager empress's niece is not looked upon with favor by some of the mandarins at the royal court. Oh, he's got powerful friends, including the good graces of Tz'u Hsi herself. But the empress is notorious for her unpredictability and fickleness. If she can be persuaded that the friendship between her niece and Colonel Taylor is anything more than platonic, the good colonel might find himself in very, very serious trouble. I mean, the idea of a royal princess involved with a commoner—an Occidental at that— would be intolerable, even criminal.''

Moira was completely bewildered by the incident. The minister must have been mistaken. What personal business could Brad have in Tientsin? Could it be that he was engaged in some scheme to further his high prestige with influential Chinese officials to even loftier goals? No, why would he seek favors from lesser mandarins in Tientsin when he was firmly entrenched with the high mandarins in the Forbidden City, including—including—And suddenly the parts fell into place like the letters in an anagram! Brad's friendship with the niece of the dowager empress! It came back to her vividly that he had once mentioned casually that Sun Ying had a summer palace near Tientsin. She was strikingly reminded of the dalliance he carried on with Charlotte Collins in Washington in order to curry favor with the State Department. There was no doubt that his relationship with Sun Ying was a replay of his affair with Charlotte.

"You amoral, conniving, ruthless bastard!'' she said aloud.

Her anger dissipated quickly. Brad was Brad. He would never change, anymore than the proverbial leopard could change its spots. She would have to be realistic. Resigned- ly, she rose and went back into the house. Halfway up the staircase she paused, pondered an instant and then came back downstairs slowly. Smiling purposefully, she unbolted the front door.

Chapter Fifteen

She lit a candle on the bedside table and climbed into bed naked. She lay there in the stillness, staring at the flickering image the candle cast on the ceiling. Part of her hoped Flynn would not come to her; another part was desperate with desire for him. The question of infidelity was purely academic now. Her heart accelerated as she heard the creak of footsteps on the stairs, coming down the hall, pausing at the door, which was slightly ajar. He pushed it full open and entered, a dark, faceless figure in the shadows beyond the penumbra of the candlelight.

"Sean . . ." Her voice quavered.

"I almost turned about and left when I reached the door," he said.

"Why?"

"I was afraid it would be locked, and that would have indicated that you had made up your mind to reject me permanently."

She held out her arms to him. "I made up my mind, all right. No more deluding myself that my marriage is sacrosanct. Tell me the truth, Sean. Do you know about Brad and that Chinese woman, the niece of the empress?"

He sat down heavily on the edge of the bed, averting his eyes from her questioning gaze. He rubbed his jaw thoughtfully; his lips were compressed.

"What's wrong?" she asked. "Cat got your tongue?"

His hand moved from his jaw to the back of his neck. "I'm hard put to give you an answer, Moira. There is a code among military officers. One simply does not tell tales about a brother soldier."

"What childish rot! You've already slept with his wife, and now you get finicky about answering a simple question. Look, my lad, you owe me a lot more than you owe Brad. Besides, I already know the truth. All I'm seeking is confirmation."

He looked at her steadily and sighed. "Yes . . . it's so. I've known about it since my arrival, that first night. Brad is not very discreet when he's drinking. He wanted to impress me with his influential connections within the inner sanctum of the monarchy. Sun Ying is a very impressive woman, even aside from her status in the power hierarchy. Yes, Brad is having a torrid affair with the lady. That's where he is now, at her summer estate at Tientsin."

"I thought as much . . . Now that's out of the way, let's attend to the business at hand. I feel particularly wanton tonight. Take off your clothes."

Moira's breathing quickened as he removed his shirt and jacket. The candlelight cast a sheen on the rippling muscles of his chest and biceps. She wet her lips as he stepped out of his trousers and undershorts. His erection thrust toward her, an erotic obelisk that took her breath away. She reached out and drew him gently toward her.

"I want very much to please you tonight, darling. Lie down on your back and relax."

She knelt beside him, and he watched her, hypnotized, as she bent her head. Her parted lips enveloped his manhood.

"Dear God!" he moaned in rapture as her hair fanned out across his loins and belly. She was a high priestess paying homage at the altar of Eros. He was racked by spasms of an intensity he had never before experienced, drained as he had never before been spent.

Moira raised her head. "Did I please you, my darling?"

Still floating in a state of holy bliss, he rolled his eyes up so that the pupils almost disappeared; it was not an incongruous term—holy bliss. Their love was sacred. She did love him as he loved her; he knew that without a doubt.

"And now I will please you." He sat up and grasped her by the shoulders, drawing her down beside him on the bed. He lavished kisses on her face, her throat, her breasts, her belly and her thighs. But when his mouth sought out the sweet bower of her womanhood, she stopped him.

"No, my darling, not now."

Flynn was bewildered and hurt. "But why?"

She smiled and stroked his cheek. "Once in a while a man and a woman must give freely of themselves merely for the simple joy of giving love and pleasure without claiming retribution. A pure, unselfish act. I can't describe the satisfaction I derived from your enjoyment. Do you understand?"

He lay down and took her in his arms. "Yes I do, my sweet." They cuddled together, silent, each wrapped in his and her own reveries. At last he asked her, "What time are the servants due back?"

"Not until morning. They're staying with friends who live close by the temple so that they can attend another sunrise service."

"What about the children?"

"Pat and Desiree are spending a holiday at the Christian mission."

"Moira . . ." She felt him tense against her. "In another two weeks I'll be leaving for India. My special orders came through today."

She clung to him fiercely. "Oh, my darling, life will be unbearable here without you."

"I can't live without you, Moira, not after tonight. You've got to leave Brad and come with me to India."

Tears blurred her vision. "Sean, Sean, Sean, if only life were that simple. If only we were two wild larks sailing along free on the wind currents. But we are bound to earth. We grow roots. I realize now that my love for you is deeper than the love I had for Brad. But he is still my husband. He is the father of my children. As dearly as I love you, Sean, I would give up anything, even you, darling, before I would give up my flesh and blood. They grew in my womb; I suckled them at my breasts. No, Sean, ours is a star-crossed love, a meteor that blazes brilliantly across the dark universe and vanishes as dramatically as it appeared.''

"Aye . . . I guess that sums it up pretty well." He sighed, then raised himself up on an elbow and peered intently into her eyes. "Just one thing, darling. I've got a gut instinct that one day you and I will be together for all eternity. I don't know how or where or when, but we are destined to be reunited.''

She smiled and put her arms around his neck. "Until that day, we should make the most of the short time allotted to us before you ship out for India. Make love to me now, my sweetheart. Adore every inch of my body with your hands, your lips, your eyes and with this.'' She took his limp penis in her hand and stroked it to life.

Before dawn they had made love four times, renewed each time by intermissions of blissful sleep, locked into each other's arms. After the last time she cautioned him:

"You had better leave while it's still dark, my love, so no one will see you.''

Flynn dressed and took her in his arms one last time. "That Greek myth—it's true you know. When I leave you, I have truly left a part of myself behind.''

Her smile was wan. "That must be where the old expression derives from—the better half.''

"You are the better half of the entity.''

She shook her head. "No, it works both ways. To me you are the better half . . . I still can't believe it. In a few short weeks my original dislike of you has undergone an incredible metamorphosis. Now I love you with all of my heart . . . Good night, my beloved.''

She went downstairs with him and let him out the front door. She stood in the doorway, watching until he melted into the night. To the east there was a thin silver line limning the mountain ridges, presaging the imminent dawn.

Moira was in deep sleep when Lotus entered her bedroom. The girl approached the bed and shook her gently. "Madam, there is someone here to see you. The American minister."

Moira sat up in bed and smoothed back her hair with her hands. Still half-unconscious, her eyes refused to focus on Lotus. She shook her head to shake the cobwebs out of her brain. "The American minister . . ." she said groggily. "What on earth . . . does he want?" Reason returned with the shock of ice water dashed into her face; her throat constricted.

"Hand me my negligee, Lotus."

She ran a hair brush quickly through her hair and prepared to meet the American minister. He was pacing up and down like a lion in the small parlor, and when she saw his face, she was certain that her worst fears were justified. Never had she seen this commonly jolly man so grave.

"Mrs. Taylor . . ." He came toward her. "Is there someplace we can speak privately?"

"To be sure; in Brad's study." Heart hammering against her breastbone, she led him down the hall to the small cubbyhole of a room where Brad kept his books and legal papers. She sat down behind the desk and beckoned to the minister to sit in the single leather chair beside the desk.

The minister sat on the edge of the chair, with his hands braced on his plump knees. He opened his mouth, closed it, licked dry lips, opened his mouth again, coughed and finally got it out:

"I find it very difficult to speak of this to you, Mrs. Taylor. It is very bad news. You must brace yourself, madam, for a terrible shock."

Moira was bewildered. It certainly would come as no shock to her to be told that she and Flynn had spent the night together. But she had badly misinterpreted the minister's purpose in visiting her.

"Mrs. Taylor, your husband . . . Colonel Taylor . . . He has been arrested by the Chinese police in Tientsin."

She reeled as if he had dealt her a physical blow. "Brad

arrested? There must be some mistake. Why would the Chinese police arrest my husband?''

He was unable to look her in the eyes. He shook his head dolefully as he explained. "Colonel Taylor was arrested by direct order of her majesty the Dowager Queen Tz'u Hsi.''

It was inconceivable to her; the dowager favored Brad over any other foreigner in Peking. "On what grounds?''

He seemed to shrivel in his dire distress. "There is no easy way to break this to you, madam, but for some time Colonel Taylor has been carrying on a clandestine affair with the dowager's niece, Sun Ying. Last night the Chinese secret military police caught the two of them together in Sun Ying's bedroom at the summer palace in Tientsin.''

Moira could think of nothing to say. The minister leaned toward her and extended one hand in a gesture of solace.

"I realize what a shock this must be, Mrs. Taylor. I have every sympathy—''

"What's going to happen to Brad?'' she interrupted.

The minister threw up his hands. "Quite frankly, I have no idea. The crime—consorting with a princess of the royal family—well, it is a very serious offense.'' His color waned, and his voice was weak. "He could be executed.''

"Oh, no! They wouldn't dare! He's an American citizen and a member of the United States army!''

The minister was pessimistic. "Mrs. Taylor, need I remind you that the Chinese government is not fond of us Americans to begin with? It is not likely to show any charity toward a foreigner, American or otherwise, who has violated their highest holy mores by molesting a royal princess. Another thing—we do not have a military posture in China as yet.''

"What about the other legations? Surely they will commit forces to ensure the safety of another Occidental?''

The minister wiped his brow with a white handkerchief. "I think not. I've already spoken to the British minister, and he informed me bluntly that England would not jeopardize its own interests in the East, secured at such high cost, to save the hide of a man who is such an 'unscrupulous bounder,' as he put it.''

"There must be something that we can do."

"I'm off for Tientsin as soon as I leave here, but I caution you not to be too optimistic. I have also telegraphed the State Department and asked for their counsel."

"I'll come to Tientsin with you."

"I don't think that is advisable. Quite frankly, as Brad's wife, you would be in great danger. Certain militants with a fanatic hatred for the Westerners here in China might take reprisals against you."

Moira recalled the ceremony they had witnessed that day at the pagoda and the hatred mirrored in the faces upturned to their party.

The minister consulted his watch. "I must be going. The train to Tientsin leaves within the hour."

She accompanied him to the door. "Thank you, Mr. Minister, for all that you have done and will attempt to do in the future to secure Brad's release."

"Sadly, I have done precious little, Mrs. Taylor. My hands are tied, but, as they say, where there is life there is hope. Good day."

Moira went back upstairs. Lotus was waiting for her in the bedroom. "Madam's bath is drawn. Now I will make the bed and tidy up."

"Thank you, Lotus," she said listlessly. She did not mention Brad's trouble to the girl. With any luck, Brad's indiscretion might be kept in confidence.

That slim hope was shattered later that afternoon when Sean Flynn called to offer his sympathy in the crisis.

"I was hoping it wouldn't become common knowledge."

"No chance. The mandarins from the Forbidden City are making full use of the propaganda value of the incident to heat up the hostility the Chinese already feel toward us."

"Oh, Sean, what am I to do?" She came into his arms and pressed her cheek against his chest. "Oh, I know he's an unprincipled bastard, but Brad just can't help himself when it comes to playing power politics."

"He's really put his head in the noose this time."

"Don't say that even in jest," she said.

"Darling, I don't think they would go so far as to execute him. That would be too much of a risk—the kind of thing that could lead to another big conflict like the Opium War. He could go to prison. My guess, though, is that he will be deported back to the States."

"Good God! I hope it's that simple."

She lived on that hope through that day and into the next. That afternoon when the minister returned from Tientsin, she read the bad news on his face even before he told her.

"What's happened to Brad?" She was trembling with trepidation.

"The very worst, Mrs. Taylor. Last night there was a glimmer of hope in my negotiations with the Chinese military police and other officials at Tientsin. When we broke up the conference, I was of the opinion that they would show leniency toward him. But what happened in the middle of the night was beyond official control. Overwhelming numbers of revolutionaries stormed the jail, overpowered the guards and spirited Colonel Taylor into the hills." He exhaled loudly and shook his head. "A lynch mob is what they were."

Moira collapsed on a sofa and buried her face in her hands. Sobs racked her body. The minister put a hand on her quaking shoulder. "I'm so sorry, Mrs. Taylor. It's a true human tragedy. Colonel Taylor was a fine man, of noble character and great courage and abilities. To think that this one indiscretion—this one human weakness—could have brought on such terrible consequences, yes, it is a tragedy."

She looked up at him through her tears. "Is there no hope at all? Maybe they're going to hold him for ransom?"

"I entertained that thought briefly, but the Chinese officials assured me that it is a forlorn hope. These radicals aren't interested in money. They're out for blood. Look, I must get back to the delegation and telegraph Washington. If there is anything that my wife and I can do for you, please let us know. When are your children returning from their holiday?''

"The day after tomorrow."

"I imagine you'll want the delegation to make plans to ship you back to the United States as soon as possible?''

"I'm not sure. I'm not sure of anything. Suddenly my whole world has been turned topsy-turvy. I think I'd like to remain in Peking until there is definite proof of Brad's fate—that is, if it is permissible, sir.''

"My dear, you're welcome to stay here as long as you like, but in my opinion it will be a lot easier on your children to put Peking and its sorry memories behind them. And for you, too, Mrs. Taylor.''

"Of course, you're right. Just a little time, then. If we haven't heard anything within another week, we'll depart as quickly as we can.''

He patted her hands and walked stoop-shouldered down the hall and out of the house.

Chapter Sixteen

Life was a nightmare for Moira for the remainder of the week. She attempted to break the news to the children of their father's abduction by the revolutionaries as gently and tactfully as she could.

"Your father is a brave man who served his country loyally and unselfishly, just as my father did. It is not an easy thing to be a soldier."

Desiree was inconsolable, and Moira could say and do nothing to stem her tears. "My daddy's dead!" she lamented. "We'll never see him again, Pat."

Patrick was a staunch little soldier throughout the ordeal. His eyes misted over and there was a lump in his throat, but he refused to cry. "They can't be sure he's dead, Desi," he consoled his sister. "Maybe they're holding him in captivity."

Moira encouraged that hope, even though she had just about resigned herself to the hard fact that Brad was lost forever. The final glimmer was dispelled a few days later when Sean Flynn visited the house. He nodded gravely to Moira, tousled the boy's unruly hair and swung little Desiree high into the air.

"Just like Daddy used to do," she chortled.

Patrick fixed her with a disapproving frown. "Nobody does anything quite like Daddy did."

"To be sure," Sean agreed lightly. "Your father was a wonderful man and you're going to grow up just like him. You're the picture of him now." He set down Desiree. "And you, young lady, what a charmer you are going to be when you're grown up. That copper hair and green eyes—wherever did you inherit them?"

"From my mother," Moira said.

Flynn turned to her. "Can I speak with you alone?"

"Children, go out back and play. Major Flynn and I have business to discuss." Reluctantly they departed, and Moira took a deep breath. "What is it—bad news?"

"I'm afraid so." He shut his eyes and pinched the bridge of his nose in a gesture of distaste. "The authorities at Tientsin found Brad's body in the hills. I don't care to go into the grisly details. His uniform, his identification— there's no mistake, it was Brad . . . This is extremely difficult. The final positive identification was made by Sun Ying herself."

Moira was consumed with outrage and hatred. "Damn! Damn that bitch! The greatest indignity of all, that he should be identified by the woman responsible for his death!"

"I know how you must feel. It's a rotten business all around." He tried to embrace her, to comfort her, but she backed off. "What about his remains?"

"They're shipping his body back to Peking by train, where he will receive the funeral of a military hero. The casket will remain closed; the body was badly decomposed."

Moira bit her lips and pounded her fists against her thighs. "The sooner it's done, the better, so the children and I can return to the United States."

"That's something I want to talk to you about. I don't want you to return to the States."

She was dumbfounded. "What on earth would I do here in China?"

"Not in China." He took her by the arms. "Moira . . . I want you and the children to come to India with me. I want to marry you and adopt Pat and Desiree. I promise you they will receive the same love and care as if they were my flesh and blood.''

She closed her eyes and put a hand to her forehead, swaying. ''So much has happened in such a short time, one thing on top of the other. I don't know what to say.''

''Let me help you, my darling. You need a strong shoulder to lean on.''

''I can't deny that.'' She pressed herself fiercely against him, holding on for dear life. It was exactly how she felt, that she was hanging onto life by her fingertips, gripping the edge of a bottomless abyss.

''Will you marry me, Moira?''

''I don't know what to say.''

''Say yes; it's that simple. Don't deny that you love me. You've admitted it.''

''I do, but—''

''No buts. We love each other and we want to be together for the rest of our lives.''

Tears blinded her. ''Brad and I said the same thing when we first married.''

''That was a long time ago. Life does not stand still. What's done is done, and your marriage to Brad is a thing of the past. No looking back, luv; just look to the future. Our future.''

''It seems so wrong. I mean, he's not even buried, and here we are talking about marriage. I need time, Sean.''

He was understanding and full of sympathy for her sentiments. ''Take all the time you need. We won't be married here. We'll go to India, and when you feel the time is right, we'll tie the knot all legal and proper.'' He smiled mischievously. ''We'll even sleep in separate rooms if you fancy.''

''We'll talk about it after Brad's funeral. Meanwhile I want to sound out the children on how they'd feel about such an arrangement. I must warn you, Sean, you can never replace Brad in Patrick's affections. He worshipped his father.''

"Aye, as he should. I have no intention of taking Brad's place, but I think I can win over the boy to love me like a favored uncle."

"That sounds reasonable. I'll discuss it with them tonight before bedtime."

"Fine. And now I've got to get back to my legation, do some sounding out of my own. I'll need official sanction in order to take you to India with me."

Later, after supper, Moira introduced the subject to Patrick and Desiree. "How would you feel if we took a new father into the family?" She saw the stricken look on Pat's face and amended hastily. "No, not a father but a kind uncle."

Pat eyed her suspiciously. "Are you talking about Major Flynn?"

"Yes, the major is a fine man, and your father thought the world of the major. Now that your father is no longer with us, Major Flynn wants to take care of the three of us."

"We can take care of ourselves," the boy said sullenly.

"I like Major Flynn," Desiree said.

"Who cares what you think?" he shot back.

"We'd be traveling to India with him and live in Calcutta. You know about India—an exotic land of mystery. Tigers and elephants and king cobras. It would be exciting, wouldn't it?"

She rejoiced at the ray of interest that shined in his eyes. "India . . . tigers . . . elephants . . . cobras . . . Could I ride on an elephant?"

"I'm sure that can be arranged."

"Do you really want to marry Major Flynn, or are you just doing it so that there'll be someone to take care of us?" the boy wanted to know.

Moira knew she had to be very careful how she responded to the question. "There is that to be considered. There won't be enough in your father's army pension to live on. But aside from that, I admire and respect Major Flynn very much." She did not want to introduce the matter of love into this conversation; they were both too young to understand.

Patrick smiled, and briefly he was the reincarnation of his father; it wrenched her heart. "I guess it will be kind of fun living in India, at that. And I really do like Major Flynn."

"Of course you do. And I know he's going to be a good—a good uncle to you both."

Brad was buried with full military honors on a Sunday morning in the little colony cemetery outside the north wall. As the casket was lowered, a bugler blew taps over the grave site. Major Flynn removed the American flag from the coffin at the last moment, and he and the German Major Schultz folded it in the traditional military triangle. Then Flynn presented it to Moira.

For the first time since learning of his father's death, little Patrick broke down and began to sob along with his sister. Moira kneeled down beside them and comforted them as best she could. On an impulse she handed the flag to the boy.

"Daddy would have wanted you to have this. After all, you are his little soldier."

Flynn turned away and wiped a tear from his cheek with his sleeve.

As they walked back to the American delegation, Moira said, "The last page turned in yet another chapter in our lives."

"It's a good way to look at it," Flynn said. "Now we begin with page one in a new chapter." He took her hand and raised it to his lips. "I love you, my darling."

"And I love you."

When they were back at the house and the children were in the kitchen teasing Lotus, who was preparing tea and crumpets, Flynn took her in his arms on the shaded porch. "I can't wait until we are one—man and wife."

They arrived in India in the midst of the monsoon season. For the first month they were the guests of Lord Harry Chesterton and his wife at the Government House, a

spacious mansion such as might be seen in an affluent
English surburb. Moira and her children were billeted in a
two room suite with beamed ceilings and oak-paneled
walls arrayed with silk tapestries and paintings of the
English countryside. An enormous four-poster bed was the
focus of the tastefully appointed master bedroom.

"How I'd like to get you into it, luv," Flynn whispered
when he first saw it. "But so long as we remain here at the
Government House, my hands are tied and my fly stays
buttoned."

Moira slapped his face playfully. "Deprivation is the
anvil on which character is formed."

"The hell it is! Nevertheless, it will only be a short time
until we are man and wife."

Moira had decreed that a two-month grace period should
be observed before they were married.

One week after their arrival, the viceroy, Lord Chesterton, gave a ball to celebrate Major Sean Flynn's appointment as vice-commander of nearby Fort William, under
General Archibald Sideny, a stout martinet with bulging
eyes and a walrus mustache.

The ballroom of the Government House was large and
pretentious. An enormous crystal chandelier was suspended
from a vaulted cathedral ceiling over the center of the
dance floor. It had taken five native servants to replenish
and light the candles in its glittering sconces. The walls
were adorned with large tapestries depicting the history of
the British colonization of India: a turbaned raja laden with
jewels, receiving an English military delegation in his
throne room; colonial and Hindu troops clashing at the
Khyber Pass; two generals in a gondola atop a bull elephant, firing rifles at an attacking tiger; an intimidating
coiled king cobra doing combat with a wily mongoose;
other breathtaking works of historic art, all of them woven
by native craftsmen and artists.

On a raised dais at one end of the room, beneath
an oversize Union Jack, a string quartet was playing
Haydn's Russian Quartets, Opus 33. The four musicians

were dressed in courtly velvet breeches and jackets and powdered wigs.

Moira was impressed with the high fashion of the women's gowns, not to be expected in this far end of the world: satin, velvet, tulle, voile, patterned chiffon in a galaxy of colors. Many of them were daringly low cut in front, and some were even strapless. Moira wore a long, white, flowing Grecian gown and an emerald pelisse trimmed in gold lame to match the gown's hemline. Taking her cue from the headwear of the other women of the British settlement at Calcutta, she wore a turban, green like the pelisse and slippers, and decorated with four feathers; her attire was an exotic combination of Western and Eastern culture.

Major Flynn wore the dress uniform of the Eighteenth Bengal Lancers: a double-breasted scarlet tunic with turned-down lapels that matched the gold facing on the breast that resembled a butterfly; two rows of gold buttons ran down the jacket. A crimson sash wound around his waist. His trousers were blue with gold stripes down the sides of the legs.

Moira took his arm as they descended a marble staircase to the ballroom. The arrival of Flynn and Moira was a signal for the music and dancing to cease. The viceroy greeted them at the foot of the stairs and made a formal introduction to the assembly:

"Ladies and gentlemen, it is a distinct pleasure for me to present the new vice-commanding officer of the Fort William military post, Major Sean Flynn, and the lovely lady who will soon become his bride, Mrs. Bradford Taylor, widow of the late Colonel Bradford Taylor, chief of the American military delegation at Peking, China."

"May I have the honor of the first dance, Mrs. Taylor?" the viceroy inquired.

"I'd be delighted." She offered him her hand, and as they advanced onto the dance floor, the music resumed. Now the ensemble played a lively English reel. There followed a succession of dances with General Sideny, other officers and British civil servants. Moira was at the point of exhaustion when she was finally rescued by Sean.

"I'm parched," she said. "Can we get something to drink?"

He led her to a long table against a wall, which was laden with beverages, hors d'oeuvres and sweets. Moira's eyes lit up at the sight of a huge crystal punch bowl containing an amber-color beverage with a large block of ice floating in it.

"Ice—I don't believe it!" she said.

"In honor of this special reception to welcome us to Calcutta," he informed her. He filled a cup for her, and she downed it in one gulp.

"Nectar of the gods," she exulted. "I'll have another, please."

"All right, but don't down it so fast. These exotic punches taste like fruit juice, but they pack a wallop like a mule's back foot." He refilled the cup and took her arm. "There's someone over there who is very desirous of meeting you."

"And who might that be? Just so he doesn't ask me to dance."

"The sultan of Delhi. He's here on official business. I imagine it has to do with the resurgence of the Thuggee cult in his province."

She picked him out immediately, outstanding among the group of army officers he was conversing with. He was a tall, bronzed man of indeterminate age with a regal bearing. He was wearing a red military tunic over a black waistcoat. His black turban had a gold medallion on the front and a steel ring on the side that resembled an oversize earring.

Sean and Moira stood unobtrusively on the fringe of the grouping until he was finished speaking:

"Yes, the downfall of India has been that there are too many politicians and too many religions—the Muslims; the Buddhists; the Jainists; many, many minor sects. And last but not least, we have the black goddess Kali, who is feared and revered by the masses far more than they regard their own respective gods. It's the major reason the damnable *thugs* are so hard to exterminate. Their patron Kali is the one unifying symbol behind which the people rally . . ." His eyes focused on Moira and he stopped his discourse. He made straight for her, his smile a wicked scimitar beneath his bushy mustache.

"Ahhhhh . . . at last I have the great pleasure. Madam Taylor, your wish is my command. I am your eternal slave. For surely one who possesses such heavenly beauty is a goddess come down to earth." He took her hand, bowed low over it and pressed his lips to the slim fingers.

Sean and the other officers laughed while Moira blushed. "I am deeply flattered, Your Highness, but I fear you are the dispenser of what in Ireland is called blarney. Are you familiar with the word?"

The sultan looked puzzled. "Please translate."

One of the officers cupped a hand to the sultan's ear and whispered, "An Irish euphemism for 'bullshit,' Your Highness."

The sultan roared with laughter and slapped his leg. "My dear Madam Taylor, there are many occasions when I deserve that appellation, but what I have just spoken to you is untainted by hyperbole."

"That's very gallant, Your Highness, and please continue with what you were saying about Kali and the Thuggee cult. I find it fascinating."

"I was about to say that military force is powerless against any underground guerrilla movement in the long run. What is required is to improve the lot of the impoverished, uneducated populace, endeavor to cure their fatalistic sense that there is no hope for India or its people. Restore in them a love and loyalty for the motherland. Instigate a campaign of land reforms, redistribution of wealth. Stamp out the outrageous corruption that is a cancer on the Indian society; stamp it out on every level and caste from the wealthiest rajas and princes down through the ranks of the revenue collectors.'' He smiled sarcastically. "And yes, gentlemen, not excluding the British army and magistrates and merchants. What India requires is fewer cooks to spoil the broth and more agrarian and economic experts.''

"Touché, Your Highness!'' Moira said.

"Don't misunderstand me. I am not laying the blame for the Thuggee movement on the English doorstep. Thuggee was an institution in India for generations past, a secret society of murderers who take an oath in blood to rob and murder unwary travelers to honor and sustain Kali.''

"What is the derivation of the term *Thuggee*?'' she wanted to know.

"*Thag-lana* . . . In Hindustani it means 'to deceive.' The *thugs* roam the countryside in packs of two, three or more in the guise of travelers and merchants. When they confront potential victims, they strike up a close camaraderie with the unsuspecting ones. Usually they feign fear of their own kind and suggest they all travel together for protection against the *thugs*. They play out the charade for one or two days, and then when they have lulled their prey into complete vulnerability, the *thugs* will whip out their *rumals* and destroy the hapless victims before they have any chance to defend themselves.''

"What is a *rumal*?'' Moira asked.

He touched his turban. "A turban folded to a length of exactly two feet and knotted at both ends. A sacred silver rupee is tied in one end, as prescribed by Kali when the world was new and she came down to earth to initiate the Thuggee gospels.''

"I'll never look at a turban again without that thought in mind. A murder weapon—who would have ever guessed it?''

"A purely improvisational device conceived by the *thugs*. Actually the true purpose of a turban is quite practical. In the Sikh faith it is sacrilegious for a man to cut his hair—any body hair—during his lifetime. So a turban satisfies this inconvenience by providing a receptacle into which the hair can be rolled up and contained. In my own case, not embracing my faith strictly, it is merely ornamental.'' He clapped his hands together. ''But enough of my boring chatter. Madam Taylor, may I request the honor of the next dance? They are playing my favorite Strauss waltz.''

''I'd be delighted, Your Highness.'' She offered him her arm, and they floated out onto the dance floor.

Chapter Seventeen

During the four days that the sultan of Delhi spent conferring with the viceroy at the Government House, he became good friends with Moira and Major Flynn. The night before he departed for Delhi, the three of them sat on the veranda drinking brandy and soda and watching the rain cascade off the broad eaves.

"This is worse than the rains in China," Sean said. "I can't see three feet beyond the railing. How will you travel in this downpour, Your Highness?"

"It will have ceased by dawn," he assured them.

"How can you be so certain?" Moira asked.

His smile was cryptic. "One of the mysteries of the Far East. We Hindus possess special powers of perception. It will stop raining by morning . . . I have intended to bring up another subject for some time. I would consider it a privilege to be your close friend. Friends do not stand on formality, so, please, will you refrain from addressing me as Your Highness. My given name is Rai."

Moira smiled. "And I would consider it a privilege if you called me Moira and Major Flynn, Sean."

The sultan smiled. "Now that we are close friends, I would like to issue an invitation to you both. When you are married, I would be honored if you visited me in Delhi. How do you say it, on your honeymoon? The trip will afford you an opportunity to become acquainted with our country, and when you arrive in Delhi, you will be treated like a raja and his princess."

Moira was enthusiastic. "It sounds wonderful to me. What about you, Sean?"

"Indeed it does," he said speculatively. "Kill two birds with one stone, as it were. The viceroy met with General Sideny and me this afternoon. Tentative plans were made for me to take a regiment of Lancers into the interior and look for a band of *thugs* who are raising hell in Rajputana."

"Splendid," said the sultan. "Delhi is in close proximity to Rajputana. From time to time I dispatch my own Ludhiana Sikhs Sepoy cavalry to support the Rajputana army in putting down native uprisings. . . . Then I can expect the pleasure of your company at my palace."

"We'll be there with bells on," Moira promised.

Two months and one day after Brad was buried, Sean and Moira were married in a quiet ceremony performed by the regimental chaplain in the parlor of the Government House. Present were General and Mrs. Sideny, the viceroy and his wife, four troop captains and, of course, Patrick and Desiree. After a champagne luncheon, Sean and Moira and the children returned to their new quarters at Fort William.

The neat row of officers' houses at Fort William gave the impression that an English street in some small Surrey village had been transported intact and set down in this alien land: modest Georgian houses with gabled and gambreled roofs, surrounded by white picket fences overgrown with lilacs and roses, and shaded by oak, elm and lime trees. The house assigned to the newlyweds had a hawthorn hedge in lieu of a fence.

Sean said, "Wherever Englishmen travel around the world, they always manage to take a small part of England along with them. They drink Scotch whisky and soda; they dress for dinner the same as they would in London. It holds the empire together in some curious fashion."

They ate an early supper, put the children to bed and

retired early to their own bedroom. Sean took her in his arms.

"My blushing bride?" he joked.

"I almost feel like a virgin bride," she said. "It's been over two months since we've made love."

"We'll make up for it tonight."

Moira removed her wedding dress, an informal, white gown with off-white stripes and pearl buttons running down the front. She posed for him in her clinging pink-silk chemise, so sheer that, as Sean put it:

"It shows more than it conceals."

He came to her and slipped the straps of the chemise down over her shoulders and arms, baring her breasts. He bent his lips to one soft globe and then to the other, teasing the nipples with his tongue until Moira moaned and writhed against his face with fast-mounting desire. Kneeling, Sean pulled the diaphanous garment down over her hips and let it billow around her ankles. He slid his hands around her quivering hips and caressed her buttocks, all the while lavishing kisses on her satin-soft belly.

"Oh, my darling, I can't stand it any longer! Please hurry."

He undressed quickly. Moira's eyes fairly glowed as his sturdy, turgid phallus burst out of the confinement of his drawers. He carried her to the bed and gently placed her down. Her parted thighs and outstretched arms pleaded with him.

"Sean, my darling, this is the first time you come to me as my husband."

"My virgin bride." He positioned his erection at what he thought of as the gate to paradise and entered her.

He was a gentle lover, and pleasure radiated from the cores of their manhood and womanhood, wave after wave of soaring pleasure, like the waves spreading from a stone dropped into a placid pond.

She peaked a first time, subsided for but a few moments, and then surged to a second peak, relishing the rhythmic pumping of Sean's climax, expanding and contracting within her own singing flesh. It seemed an eternity before their desire was completely satiated and they collapsed side by side in exhausted bliss.

Moira slept fitfully that night, troubled by vivid nightmares in which she died and went to hell. Naked and stumbling through a gutted, moonlike landscape, with plumes of fire spewing from crimson fissures and craters bubbling with sulfur and brimstone, she saw a figure in the distance standing atop a giant skull, fire blazing from his eye sockets and grinning, fleshless mouth. It was Satan himself, with horns, swishing forked tail and trident pitchfork. She tried to flee, but there was no escape. He exuded a force field that drew her to him like flecks of steel to a magnet, her terror rising with every forward step. She could not make out his features, distorted by smoke and flickering shadows, until she was almost upon him. Then recognition overwhelmed her: the face of Rai, sultan of Delhi! Blazing, demoniac eyes, scimitar eyebrows, scimitar leer—the face of evil incarnate.

Moira sat up in bed screaming.

Sean bolted up beside her. "What the devil is it, Moira?"

She stopped screaming and flung herself into his arms, trembling as if she had palsy. "It was so terrible, darling. My dream. I was dead and went to hell."

He began to chuckle. "As well you deserve, performing all those acts of perversion last night. It's a wonder we both are not turned into pillars of salt."

"It's not funny, Sean. The worst part came when I met the devil. You'll never believe who it was—the sultan of Delhi."

"Rai?" Now he erupted into hearty laughter. "Now that is one for the books. You must tell him when we reach Delhi."

"I will not, and don't you dare either. He'll think I'm an idiot."

"Well, it's over now, so let's salvage what we can of this night. We've got a long day ahead of us."

She didn't sleep a wink until dawn, when she lapsed into restless slumber. An hour later Sean woke her.

"Time to get up, sleepyhead. Pat and Desiree are dressed

and ready to go to the Government House.'' The viceroy and his wife had generously offered to take care of the children while Moira and Sean were honeymooning. Moira bathed and dressed, then she and Sean saw Pat and Desiree off in Lord Chesterton's private carriage.

She kissed them both; Sean kissed Desiree and shook hands with Pat. "Now be a good soldier and take care of your sister."

"And do exactly as you're told," Moira cautioned as the carriage pulled away.

They walked back into the house, arms about each other's waists. "Well, Mrs. Flynn, are we ready to leave? Our escort is already assembling at the drill field."

"Just as soon as I gather up my saddlebags and rifle."

"I've already sent down our gear with two of the orderlies. So we're all set."

Major Flynn was in command of two troops of the Eighteenth Bengal Lancer Regiment. The troopers were wearing their field-khaki uniforms. Before they mounted, Flynn inspected the ranks, then the horses. All had Lee-Metford rifles in the saddle boots. The men also carried British service revolvers holstered to their cartridge belts.

The onset of their long journey reminded Moira of the dull, barren plains of the Chinese lowlands. Dusty plains stretched off to the distant foothills of the mountain country. Barley and poppy fields abounded; the mud and dung hovels and the scrawny children with swollen bellies and skeleton arms reached out for food.

Moira shuddered. "It's outrageous! How can the British colonials here permit human beings to live in such squalor and starvation?"

"That's the point," he said grimly. "The British do not consider these poor wretches human."

Moira removed a tin of biscuits from her saddlebag and threw it to a group of the children who were running alongside the mounted column.

"You shouldn't have done that," Sean told her.

"And why not?" But she saw why not all too quickly,

as the children began to fight over the biscuits like a pack of snarling dogs.

"One or two of the poor little beggars may well be killed because of your misdirected generosity."

"Dear God!" She wiped her eyes with her sleeve.

As they approached the foothills of the Himalayan mountains, the landscape became more scenic. There were fertile oases at intervals along the dusty trail, *beles,* as the natives called them. In the late afternoon they came upon a particularly lush *bele,* aromatic with the spicy scent of lime trees and the sweet nectar of lotus blossoms.

"Kali blossoms, these beggars call 'em," a veteran trooper informed them.

Moira stroked one of the blood-red flowers. "How apt; a reminder of Kali's blood lust."

Flynn examined a white bloom. "In Greek mythology the white lotus is the source of the drug of sweet forgetfulness that almost did in Ulysses and his crew."

As it turned out, there were two water holes about one hundred yards apart, screened from each other by a sunbaked plain bounded by tall trees and a jungle of lush vegetation.

The tents were erected and the horses were watered. Moira decided she would have to make do with a sponge bath, inasmuch as the *bele* was teeming with Muslims from the other party, so there was no chance of privacy. While she was washing in the tent, Sean visited the other campsite to learn if the members had encountered any trouble with *thugs* during their journey. When he returned, his face was beaming.

"Would you believe it? The Muslim party is being led by Sheikh Rai Sing, a distant cousin of Rai, the sultan of Delhi. We're invited to have refreshments with the sheikh and his wife."

"Delightful. Is he as handsome as his cousin?"

"There's a family resemblance, but this Rai is older."

Moira chose the kaftan she had worn that memorable night in the Chinese wilderness when she had mistaken Sean for Brad. He grinned at her.

"That garment looks remotely familiar. Yes, it's the same one you wore to seduce me."

Moira pretended to be indignant. "I seduced you? That's funny. You bullied your way into my tent and took me by force, like the oversexed maniac you are. I didn't enjoy a moment of the ordeal."

"Like hell you didn't, you wench." He took her in his arms and kissed her, running his hands over the round, soft globes of her buttocks.

"Hold on, my lad. We don't want to keep the sheikh waiting." She wrapped her hair in a black velvet turban bedecked with seed pearls and wore a plain golden bracelet around her left wrist.

"You look stunning," he said.

"Thank you. I hope you're going to change out of those sweaty khakis. Later on I'll wash them for you in the pool."

"That's what I have a batman for. Yes, I'll dig out my dress uniform."

When he had changed, they left the tent and walked through the trees and the silvery, plumed grass to the other pool. They observed, with no particular interest, that there were two separate parties camped on opposite sides of the *bele*.

The sheikh's tent was large and rectangular, made of varicolor silk. Emblematic pennants flew from its four corner posts.

Sheikh Rai Sing was a tall, storklike man with a handsome, saturnine face and a sharp widow's peak; his long mustache was waxed and curled up at the ends. Moira was reminded of her satanic dream and shivered. His wife, Jasmine, was a petite, dark woman with eyes like shiny black buttons. Her sari was coal black and trimmed with gold leaf. The sheikh, too, was dressed in voluminous black robes set off by a gold burnoose.

The interior of the tent was carpeted with heavy Oriental wool, and silken pillows were arranged in a circle about a low table with a mosaic top. They sat around the table cross-legged, and Rai clapped his hands. Three servants immediately appeared.

"Refreshments for our honored guests."

The sheikh was delighted to hear they were visiting his cousin in Delhi. "Rai and I, we do not get to see one another as much as we should. Responsibilities, always responsibilities. We're on our way to Jodhpur to arrange for the wedding of our daughter to a rich merchant. Of course, we will invite Rai, but I do not think he will accept."

The refreshments were brought into the tent and placed on the round table: cakes, coffee, tea, various sweet liqueurs and a cool fruit punch.

The smoke from the campfires across the water was pungent, and Moira was charmed by the haunting strains of sitar music and voices chanting what sounded like religious liturgies.

"A merry bunch they are, merchants from Baghdad," the sheikh told them. "We joined up with them yesterday, at their request. They are strangers in this country and have been badly frightened by the many tales they have been told about the murderous *thugs*. Quite frankly, I welcome their company. Safety in numbers. It is a comfort, too, Major Flynn, to have your troops present. You can believe the *thugs* have been alerted through the grapevine that you are in the area and will give this place a wide berth."

They engaged in idle conversation for another hour, and then Moira said, "I think we have taken up too much of your time already."

"Quite to the contrary. In the presence of such charming company, time flies by too fast."

"We do want to get to bed early," Moira said and rose from her pillows.

Moira and Jasmine were the first to emerge from the tent. Across the pond, fires blazed, and the concert was louder than ever.

"It's so black," Moira observed. "I hope we don't get lost on our way back."

"Or get ambushed by *thugs*," Flynn joked.

The words were barely out of his mouth when it happened. Materializing from out of the darkness like wraiths came a band of men naked except for loincloths. Moira, in the lead, was paralyzed by terror as two men dropped to their knees behind the sheikh and his wife, wrapping their arms around their legs to immobilize them. At the same time two more assailants leaped on their backs, catlike. Accustomed to the darkness now, Moira saw the dreaded yellow silk garrotes, weighted by the rupees bound in one end, curl around their victims' throats before they could cry out. Rai and Jasmine were flung facedown on the ground and throttled to death in moments. Flynn made an effort to go to their rescue but was grabbed by two men, while a third struck him savagely on the back of his neck with the edge of one hand. He fell to the ground, unconscious. It all happened with such stunning swiftness that before Moira found her voice, a white *rumal* was tied over her mouth and her hands were bound behind her with still another *rumal*.

She was forced to look on in horror at the bodies, lined up side by side, of the sheikh and his wife, as well as six servants who had been executed while they chatted within the tent. Then in the grisly *phansigar* tradition, a high-ranking member of the cult, who was authorized to wield the consecrated pickax of the goddess Kali, dug eight shallow graves in the soft sand outside the tent. At the same time the other *thugs* disemboweled and dismembered the bodies as nonchalantly as a butcher dissecting a side of beef. The purpose of it all was to make compact bundles for fast and simple burial. Before the corpses were covered with sand, the torsos were stabbed innumerable times so that the noxious gasses caused by decomposition would not bloat the remains. As a final touch, a mound of wet sand was piled on each grave. Within hours after sunrise the mixture would be baked as hard as clay.

Throughout the massacre the *thugs* kept up their loud singing and laughter. Even had she managed to scream, it was doubtful that the Bengal Lancers at the other *bele* would have heard her. Their own singing of army ballads carried through the trees.

Bound and gagged, Moira was thrown across a horse's back, and the assassins skirted the pond and rejoined their conspirators. The fires were piled high with wood, and several of the tents were left behind to maintain the illusion that there was still a camp there in case any of the troopers should wander across from the other campsite. Sooner or later the lancers would become curious about Major Flynn and Moira, but by that time the *thugs* would long have melted into the night.

In spite of her uncomfortable position, all Moira's strength and mental resources had been exhausted by this living nightmare she was enduring. Lulled by the rhythmic sway of the horse's back, she fell into a trancelike sleep.

She had no way of knowing how long she had been asleep, but it was still dark when the sound of raucous, angry voices woke her. Through slowly returning consciousness she was aware that the horses had stopped and their riders had dismounted. They were arguing with another band of men, whom she assumed were also *thugs*. Always a quick study when it came to language, Moira had picked up an astonishing amount of Hindustani, and she was able to understand small snatches of the heated conversation.

"You really botched up the job, Alee . . . stupid pig of a dog. You are not fit to wield a *rumal* . . . even unworthy to hold the victim's feet!"

The *thug* to whom this tirade was directed tried to defend himself in a scared, trembling voice. "But it was so dark and she was wearing a *sari*. You said yourself that we need more women for pleasure."

"Son of a jackal!" There was the loud crack of a whip, and the erring *thug* let out a howl of pain.

"Silence! Take your punishment like a man!"

Moira counted nine more lashes, and then it ceased. She heard muffled weeping from the beaten man, and then rough hands removed her from the horse's back and carried her through a dense forest and into a narrow defile in the rocky base of a mountain, barely wide enough to accommodate one person walking single-file. As they proceeded, the fissure grew wider, and then her captors put her down on a couch of soft cushions.

In perfect Oxonian English, the angry *thug* who had inflicted the beating on his colleague ordered: "Remove the blindfold and untie the *memsahib* immediately!"

It was done, and Moira sat up, experiencing no small wonder. They were in a high, domed cavern with stalactites of varied sizes and grotesque shapes reflecting a rainbow of color in the light of flaming torches that were wedged into recesses in the stone walls. She sat up slowly, rubbing her wrists and contemplating the ring of *thugs* around the couch. But for three men who were apparently the leaders of the gang, most of them wore peasant garb and turbans of a color signifying the lowest caste of Hindu.

The Thuggee chieftain addressed Moira, after giving her a small bow. He was a tall, slender man who bore a strong resemblance to Sheikh Rai Sing, with sharp black eyes and a full beard and mustache. He was wearing a black vest over a white silk shirt, white baggy trousers and black shiny boots. His yellow silk turban was wound in an elaborate fashion so that it came to a point at the top, forming a cone. It was fastened with a gold ring, the sign that he was a Hindu of high caste, possibly even of royal blood. His two lieutenants were similarly attired, except that their vests were yellow—of the same shade they had employed in such bloodthirsty fashion against Sheikh Rai Sing and his party.

"My dear madam, a thousand apologies for what these *dhokurs* have subjected you to."

"I don't want your apologies," she said coldly, "and for all your drawing room manners and speech, you are nothing more than a savage murderer like all the rest!"

He sighed and lofted his hands in a gesture of resignation. "I have every sympathy for your chagrin, but we are all murderers in this violent world. The British murdered thousands of Indians in the conquest of this sad nation. All over the world, there is killing taking place with each tick of the clock. England, France, China, America—there are no exceptions. Given a cause to rally around—power, wealth, freedom, revenge—there will be millions all eager to kill, be it with the gun or the saber.'' He smiled, but it was more of a sneer. ''Or by pounding nails into a cross!''

Moira was baffled by his self-righteous discourse. It had a familiar ring, but she could not bring the notion into focus.

''This bloody fool is responsible for the unforgivable abomination of treating you as if you were some village slut. You, an Englishwoman of high caste and refinement.''

''I am *not* an Englishwoman. I am American, but my husband is Major Sean Flynn of the Eighteenth Bengal Lancers stationed at Fort William, and when word of this reaches Calcutta, every British Lancer and every other soldier will be on your heels like a pack of hounds.''

His face became contorted in fury, and he whirled and backhanded his miscreant lieutenant, who wore only a steel ring in his turban, across the face so hard that the *thug* was flung to earth. ''*Munjwar!* You bloody fool. On top of everything else, she turns out to be the wife of Major Sean Flynn, the vice-commander of Fort William!'' He launched into a rapid tirade in Hindustani that she could not follow. Then he looked back at Moira. ''There is no excuse for his behavior, but I must say one word of defense in his favor. My men did not kill your husband; he was merely knocked unconscious. Believe me, even a foolish dog such as he does not want to antagonize the British to the extent that they would inflict major reprisals on our organization.''

''Organization? Now there's a euphemism if I ever heard one. An organization of professional killers is what you really are.''

He shrugged. ''I do not deny it. Killing is our profession. Now, if you will indulge us with the *tuponee*. It is a form of Thuggee religious ceremony. It should be of interest to you.''

The *Thugs*, who had taken part in the massacre, seated themselves cross-legged on a circular carpet with a woven

design, the artist's conception of the terrifying countenance of the goddess, with her tusked jaws dripping blood.
At a signal from an older man, the leader and a younger
man stood up and faced each other. They advanced to the
center of the ceremonial carpet, and the younger man got
down on his hands and knees.

"On this day the young fellow becomes a *bhurtote,* a
member of the elite few among us *thugs* selected to use the
sacred *rumal.* He is paying homage to his *guru,* his teacher."

After kissing the guru's feet, the new *bhurtote* stood up
and removed a silken garrote from his robes, the one he
had initiated in the murders back at the *bele.* He unfastened the knot containing the sacred rupee and presented it
to the old guru. Now the guru handed him a small pack-
age, which the pupil opened and placed on the carpet. To
Moira it looked like the coarse yellow sugar peddlers sold
in the marketplaces. Then the guru placed the silver rupee
and a consecrated pickax on top of the sugar.

"The rupee and the *kusee,* the ax, will be delivered to
the high priests of Kali at the next general services," the
sheikh explained.

Now the remaining *thugs* rearranged themselves so that
seven men were sitting with their backs to the carpet,
facing west. The guru led the group in a religious chant
that was largely unintelligible to Moira, though she understood enough words to glean the symbolism of the ceremony:

" . . . nought else is in our hearts, O Mother Kali . . .
The ashes of the dead are strewn . . . Kill! Kill! Kill!
Fulfill our hearts' desires, Mother Kali!"

Now the *phansigars* turned around, and each partook of
a small portion of the consecrated sugar and washed it
down with consecrated water. Then the remaining sugar
was passed out among the *thugs* who were standing around
the rug.

"After the ceremony, sugar that has not been blessed
will be given to those members of our group who have
been denied the honor of strangling with their bare hands
because of fear, weakness, youth and other defects. My
dear Mrs. Flynn, will you do me the honor of quaffing a

bottle of wine with me before you retire to your sleeping quarters?''

She would have preferred to sit down with the devil himself rather than with this beast, but curiosity overcame her repugnance. ''I am a bit parched, and a drop of wine would contribute to soothing my frayed nerves.''

He escorted her to a table set in a small chamber off the main cavern. An underling served them a sweet nectar in heavy golden goblets.

''These goblets are magnificent,'' she said, sipping the wine; it was quite delicious.

''The spoils of war,'' he said with a supercilious smile. He studied her with the eye of a connoisseur. ''You are even more beautiful than our *burka, our baroo*, claimed you to be. He—'' He broke off frowning, as if vexed with himself. ''Never mind, let us drink.'' He lifted his glass. ''To beauty.''

There it was again, the elusive firefly that evaded her mind's grasp. She made word associations.

''. . . *more beautiful than our* burka, *our* baroo, *claimed you to be* . . .''

Burka . . . it came to her—a high-ranking *thug* celebrated for his own feats and for the feats of his illustrious ancestors.

Baroo . . . a chieftain.

Together: Our celebrated and famous chieftain.

''Tell me, Sheikh—I don't know your name.''

''Futty Sing.''

''Sheikh Futty Sing . . .'' Her hackles bristled. ''Sing . . . You bear the same name as the murdered sheikh, Rai Sing.''

He seemed uneasy. ''A common name in India. Like Smith or Jones in your country.''

''You even bear a strong resemblance to Rai Sing.''

He smiled, but she sensed his restlessness. ''As they say about the Chinese, we all look alike to you Occidentals.''

She pressed ahead. ''How is it that you selected Sheikh Rai Sing's party as your victims?''

He shrugged. ''Random selection.''

"I don't believe that, somehow. I think it was a deliberate act and that robbery was only a secondary motive to cover your tracks. Did you know that Rai Sing was a cousin of the sultan of Delhi?"

"I know nothing of Rai Sing or about the sultan of Delhi, aside from his reputation." He finished his wine and rose.

"I think it is best if you go to your bedchamber and get some rest now, Madam Flynn."

"The sultan of Delhi and Sheikh Rai Sing and you, Sheikh Futty Sing; all three of you look so much alike. What a remarkable coincidence."

"Yes, a remarkable coincidence. Come now, we retire."

Moira got to her feet and held onto the table. Suddenly her body felt as heavy as lead, and there were blue and green halos around the torch lights on the walls. Her tongue was thick, and her head commenced spinning. Fear rose in her throat like bile. She tried to focus on Sing's face; it was a shimmering, satanic mask, the one she had seen in her nightmare.

"You . . . you . . ." She staggered toward him. "You . . . you poisoned me!"

Unconsciousness descended across her vision and brain like a black curtain into a bottomless void.

Chapter Eighteen

The hot morning sun slanting through the tree branches onto her face woke Moira. The scent of lotus blossoms and tangy limes wafted into her nostrils on the gentle, warm wind. As her thoughts slowly came into focus, the harrowing experience of the previous night was brought home to her with such devastating impact that she sat up, startled, and cried out.

She looked around wildly. She was no longer in the *thugs'* lair! Where were Sheikh Futty Sing and his cutthroats? Where was she, and how had she gotten here? All manner of questions presented themselves. Bewildered, she got to her feet and walked through the trees and high grass until she broke out into the open. She blinked in shocked disbelief at the sight of the smooth pond and the army tents. It couldn't be! It was a mirage conjured by her tortured mind and nerves. But no, it was daylight and it was real. The area appeared to be deserted. Where were the Bengal Lancers of the Eighteenth Regiment? Where was Sean? Panic rising, she ran toward the tents. As she drew close, she looked across the water in the direction of the road and saw a group of troopers speaking with a group of Indian troops. She recognized Jock Mahoney and called out to him:

"Sergeant Mahoney! Sergeant! My God! What's going on here?"

Mahoney and the other lancers whirled around and looked in her direction. From the stupefaction reflected on their faces, they might have been staring at a ghost. She ran to them and put a hand on the sergeant's arm, felt him recoil. Not a word was uttered.

"Sergeant Mahoney, say something! Yes, it's really me. I know I must look like the wrath of God, but truly it is me, Moira Flynn."

"Ma'am, I don't believe it," he croaked. "I never figured to see you again—alive, at any rate. Where have you been?"

"I'm not quite sure myself. It's a long story. Where is Major Flynn?"

"Out searching for you with the troop. We stayed behind to strike the tents and stow the gear on the pack mules. This here is Captain Buram of the Twelfth Ludhiana Sikh Sepoy Regiment. His troops are going to join up with our boys and raise some hell with those damnable *thugs*. How the devil did you escape from them killers?"

"That's the strange part. I didn't escape. The last thing I remembered last night was drinking wine with their leader, Sheikh Futty Sing. He must have drugged the wine. Then, for some inexplicable reason they must have brought me back and left me in the trees sometime after that."

"The *memsahib* is a very fortunate woman," said Captain Buram, a dashing fellow in his crimson jacket with its stiff white collar and cuffs and white crossbelts slashing across his chest from either shoulder; he wore a purple turban with a jade ring on one side. "Futty Sing is one of the most notorious *thugs,* a fanatical killer. You must have charmed him the way a fakir charms the king cobra with his lute."

Moira laughed. "It's an interesting metaphor, Captain, and I know it was intended as a compliment. Sergeant Mahoney, while you get ready to move out, I'll wash and change in my tent." She looked down the length of herself and could have wept. The once-gorgeous gown was torn in countless places and filthy with grime. "Well, old friend," she soliloquized, "I guess you've been to your last party."

"Ma'am?" Mahoney blinked.

"Nothing, Sergeant, I was merely talking to myself. I'm a bit mad after what I've been through."

"I don't wonder, ma'am. Well. Men, let's get on with it."

Moira went back to the tent and washed as best she could in a basin and cold water. She took off her gown and packed it in a saddlebag for old times' sake. Then she donned her riding habit and brushed out her long hair, fastening it back with a red ribbon. She had a mild headache from whatever drug had been administered to her in the wine.

Moira's tent was the last to be loaded aboard the mules. The horses were saddled, and they mounted to ride after the rest of the troop.

"Captain Buram and his men have ridden ahead to look for Major Flynn and the rest of our lads."

About an hour after they had departed the *bele*, they spied a huge cloud of dust far down the country road.

"Horsemen," said the sergeant, "and if I don't miss my guess, it's the Eighteenth Regiment."

He proved to be correct. The lancers came riding toward them at full gallop, with Major Flynn far out in the lead. Even before his horse came to a stop, he vaulted out of the saddle and ran toward them. Moira dismounted and ran to meet him.

Oblivious to their grinning audience, they flung themselves into each other's arms and hugged and kissed in the way lovers do when they have been separated for a long time. In this case they had been parted less than twenty-four hours, but it seemed an eternity.

"I've never been more happy and relieved in all my life than when Captain Buram gave us the good news. Good news, no, spectacular news! My darling, I have never believed in miracles, but now I am a true believer." He placed a hand over his heart reverently.

Moira was thoughtful. "It wasn't quite a miracle. The Thuggee attack was a bad blunder. Apparently they had no intention of harming us."

He rubbed the back of his neck and winced. "No? Well they came damn close to breaking my neck."

"They mistook me for a native wench because of my kaftan and had plans to put me in some sheikh's harem. When their chieftain found out who I was, he was furious; he gave the fellow responsible a ferocious beating."

Flynn addressed Mahoney. "Let's take a ten-minute break. I want to hear all about what happened to Mrs. Flynn."

When she had finished her rendition of all that had befallen her since the *thugs* had slain Rai Sing, his wife and their servants, Sean tried to refute her suspicions that there was some relationship between the dead man and Sheikh Futty Sing, who had ordered his assassination, and that the sultan of Delhi had some vague place in the complicated scheme of events.

"Darling, don't you think you're being melodramatic?" he reasoned. "After all, what this *thug* chieftain told you is accurate. Sing is a highly common surname in India. And as for the resemblance between the two sheikhs and the sultan, try and be objective. Here we have three dark-skinned men, all three with heavy beards and mustaches and wearing turbans. All right, of course they resemble one another. I'll wager that if I grew a beard and mustache and wore a turban and darkened my skin with tobacco juice, you'd swear I, too, was related to the sultan of Delhi."

"I suppose you have a point," she admitted uncertainly. "And the sultan's name is Rai Om Pragash. Still, what Futty Sing said about his *burka,* his *baroo* claiming I was so beautiful bothers me."

Sean laughed and slapped her thigh. "Don't you know your ethereal beauty has become legend the length and the breadth of the land?"

She slapped his hand. "You're positively exasperating! How would this Thuggee chieftain know anything about me or the way I look? It's not as though you and I are celebrities.''

"Oh, I don't know about that," he replied airily. "After all, we are going to be honored guests of the sultan of Delhi at his royal palace. And by the by, I think it's time we were on our way. Sergeant Mahoney, have the troops fall in and we'll ride on.''

They proceeded at a leisurely pace for Delhi, following a circuitous route to search out the elusive *thugs,* who, intelligence sources claimed, were infesting the region. Working in conjunction with the Twelfth Sikh Sepoy Regiment, they captured two *thugs* posing as tax collectors in a native village.

Captain Buram meted out justice instantly. "As judge and jury trying this case, my decision is that these swine are guilty as charged. Serving as executioner, I will now carry out the sentence." He drew his pistol from its holster and cocked it.

The two prisoners threw themselves down on their hands and knees, weeping and begging for mercy.

"Considering they're such ruthless killers, they do not evidence much courage when the tables are turned," Sean observed.

"He is not a *bhurtote,*" she explained. "Only the elite *thugs* have the license to use the *rumal,* to strangle victims. These two are lackeys, no doubt.''

And this turned out to be the case. Under threat of death they readily turned informer against their brethren, providing vital information to Captain Buram.

He turned to Sean and Moira. "The *thandar* of this district—the chief of police, actually—is a cousin to Sheikh Futty Sing, the *jamadar* of the *thugs* who murdered Rai Sing and a cousin to Rai Sing as well. There has been bad blood between the cousins for years, that is, Futty Sing and Rai Sing. Up until this gory event, the *thandar,* Sanjay Inaent, has been successful in moderating the feud. I wonder what happened, why he failed on this occasion.'' He stroked his beard thoughtfully. "It is strange that Futty Sing would indulge in such drastic measures over a family feud. The *thugs* practice a strict code; no harm or violence is to be directed to a blood relative except in the most extreme circumstances. Well . . . I'll bring this Inaent back to headquarters for questioning.''

''Do you want my company for further support, Captain?''

''I think not, Major. We've delayed your visit to Delhi long enough as it is. I want to thank you for your cooperation.''

''And I want to thank you for being the bearer of the happiest item of news I have ever received.''

''My pleasure, Major.'' The two men shook hands, and Buram bowed to Moira. ''Madam Flynn, may the rest of your journey and your stay at Delhi prove to be more harmonious than what you have suffered so far.''

''Thank you, Captain Buram. I'm sure our troubles are over.''

The remainder of the journey to Delhi was accomplished in another day and a half. Their first glimpse of the royal palace was from the summit of a grassy knoll. It burst upon the eyes like the blinding flare of the sun emerging from behind a cloud. An opulent mausoleum of white marble inlaid with infinite resplendent gems, was flanked by twin minarets, dazzling gold in the midday sun. Between the minarets was a massive, tapering dome topped by a golden crescent, and on either side of it were smaller twin domes. At the foot of the palace's wide marble staircase was a rectangular pool at least two hundred yards long, flanked by grassy swaths on all four sides. A hedge of close-set evergreen trees ran around the pool's perimeter. The palace was reflected in the placid water of the pool with mirror fidelity.

''What a magnificent edifice!'' Sean exclaimed, stating an opinion that was echoed by his troopers.

When Moira expressed their awe to Rai, he belittled the grandeur of his palace. ''A potpourri of Indian and Moslem and Hindu architecture. It blinds one with its rococo clutter. Only slightly less pretentious than the Taj Mahal. Yes, a splendid place in which to be entombed, but I do not relish living in it.''

Moira laughed. "Years of exposure to Western culture seem to have jaded you, Rai."

"We shall see if your admiration for the palace remains constant after you have inhabited its hallowed halls for a few weeks."

Along with Rai, they were welcomed by a score of servants lined up with military precision in the huge navel of the entry hall. Like soldiers executing a drill command, they salaamed as one at a wave of the hand from the sultan. He introduced them to his prime minister, Karoom.

"Not only my right hand, but my good friend as well."

Karoom was a short stout man, bald as a billiard ball, with enormous jowls and eyes like blue marbles. From his appearance and his garb, Moira deduced that he was not Indian. He wore baggy white silk trousers, a blue tunic and a fez instead of a turban, red with a gold tassel.

The sultan confirmed it. "This Lebanese *Burgeela* was run out of his own country by a coup. Lebanon's loss has been India's gain."

Rai had discarded his royal raiments in favor of a London-cut white linen suit, shirt and tie, except for the required turban. "Karoom, will you see to it that Major Flynn's troopers are escorted to the royal barracks we have readied for them?"

The minister bowed. "At once, sire. It has been a great pleasure to make your acquaintance, Major and Madam Flynn. I hope to be of service to you during the course of your stay." He bowed to them again and left.

"Before I take you on the grand tour of the palace, perhaps you'd prefer to bathe and change." He dismissed all but two of the female servants, who were clad in blue saris wrapped around their bodies from the ankles to the neck, with the ends draped adroitly over their heads. "Vijaya, Dalia, you will attend to the *memsahib's* needs during her stay here. Now, show the major and the *memsahib* to their quarters. Sean and Moira, when you are ready, join me in my study for refreshments."

In every doorway and arch within the palace, servants

stood at rigid attention like sentries. Their eyes stared sightlessly off into space.

"They make me shiver," Moira whispered to Sean as they ascended one of two curved marble staircases to the palace's upper story. All the servants wore white saris, unlike the two assigned to be Moira's handmaidens; the men wore white uniforms and white turbans. When Moira questioned Vijaya and Dalia about it, Dalia explained:

"There are three classes of servants at the palace; white is the lowest caste, lemon signifies second class." And with a distinct note of pride: "Blue represents the highest order of royal livery."

The suite assigned to the Flynns was breathtakingly lavish, like everything else outside and inside the royal palace. A large bedroom had a high, domed ceiling, at the top of which was a translucent glass mosaic skylight; the sun's rays shone through, casting a rainbow across the enormous circular sleeping couch that occupied the center of the room. There was a second bedroom of equal size and grandeur.

"The master's bedroom," Vijaya informed Sean with a curtsy.

"You mean we are expected to sleep alone?" Sean asked with a stricken look that made Moira choke on her laughter.

"Is that not customary?" the girl inquired. "There is only one occasion when a man wants his wife in bed with him." She lowered her eyes shyly and blushed.

"There are men like that in our society, but my husband is very democratic. He tolerates me beside him most of the time."

"Very funny," he said with a pout.

Moira pushed him in the direction of the door between their adjoining rooms. "Now, suppose you leave us three girls alone while I make my toilette. You could use a tub yourself, mountain goat."

Reluctantly he entered his own quarters, grumbling to himself. "I hope those damned slave girls aren't going to dog Moira's heels the whole while we're here. Wouldn't surprise me if they intend to sleep in the same room with her. Hell! If they do they'll have to watch; teach 'em some new postures they won't find in their *Kama Sutra!*''

"I will draw your bath while you remove your clothing, *memsahib*,'' Dalia told Moira. "Vijaya, you will draw the *memsahib's* bath and I will be in presently to help you.''

Moira was amused. "I never realized that bathing could be a group enterprise.'' She undressed, and Dalia put the dirty articles into a wicker hamper.

The girl appraised Moira's naked body with frank admiration. "You are very beautiful, *Memsahib* Flynn. You must bring your husband a good deal of pleasure.''

"Your candor is quite refreshing, Dalia, although women's bodies were not created for the exclusive purpose of giving pleasure to men. Men and women should complement each other, give pleasure each to the other in total equality.''

Dalia was nonplussed. "You speak such to *Sahib* Flynn?''

"I do indeed.''

"And he has never beaten you for your defiance?''

"No, and he'd better not try.''

The two women's philosophies and life-styles were literally worlds apart. Moira knew it and patted the girl on the shoulder. "Never mind, Dalia, lead me to that bath.''

The bathroom was a work of erotic art. The floor and the walls were decorated with tile mosaics depicting men and women engaged in every imaginable sexual act. As in the bedroom, there was a lead-glass skylight in the domed ceiling; sunlight filtering through the colored panes cast a rosy glow over the room that created a mood of sensuality, which was enhanced by the scented steam issuing from an immense sunken tub. Moira felt giddy, euphoric. She stepped into the tub and lowered her body into the perfumed water, just a perfect temperature to bask in. She lay back and closed her eyes, savoring the buoyancy of her breasts floating lazily on the surface.

She started and opened her eyes as a hand touched one breast. To her astonishment, the two handmaidens had removed their saris and were kneeling alongside her in the tub.

"We will bathe you now, *memsahib*," Dalia said. They began to massage her with fleecy sponges anointed with thick, aromatic oil. Moira lapsed into a trancelike state, and with every gentle stroke of the sponges her will and strength ebbed. Rainbow whorls of the oil created bizarre designs on the surface of the water. Her imagination ran wild, translating the images into grotesque imitations of the erotica that plastered the walls and ceiling. As they washed her, their fingers teased her breasts, her belly, her buttocks, between her thighs. Moira was helpless against the intense lust that was kindled within her. She was mesmerized by their firm, youthful nude bodies glistening from the unguents.

Dalia began to anoint Moira's breasts with a green oil taken from one of the many bottles lined up on the jade coping around the tub. "This is pleasurable to the *memsahib*?"

The abrupt realization of just how pleasurable the experience was becoming jolted Moira back to reality. She was enlightened enough to accept that there were men and women who preferred sex with partners of their own gender. But never in a million years would she have dreamed that her own body would respond to the erotic manipulations of feminine hands and fingers.

She sat up and gently pushed the girls away. "I think *memsahib* has had sufficient bathing for one day. Thank you very much, ladies. This has been a thoroughly novel experience." She stood up and got out of the tub, followed by Dalia and Vijaya.

They began to rub her dripping body with enormous soft terry-cloth towels. Moira rejected their ministrations as kindly as she was able. "I really don't think I need any further assistance. I've been doing this for myself for years. Thank you nonetheless."

They withdrew and commenced to dry their own bodies. When Moira returned to the bedroom, she gaped in surprise at a black sari laid out on the bed; it was truly stunning, of handwoven silk bedecked with seed pearls and genuine gold leaf.

"A wedding gift from His Highness," Dalia informed her.

"It's magnificent," Moira said. "I will wear it this very night."

The girls helped her dress, showing her how to wrap the sari in evenly placed swaths around her ankles, her thighs, her hips, to nip it in tightly at the waist and under her breasts to lift them; the final wrap pinned at one shoulder with a ruby brooch and then draped casually over the head, leaving one shoulder bare. Dalia did Moira's hair in their own fashion, pulled back sleekly across her head and wrapped tightly in a bun secured by gold and ivory combs.

They stepped back and admired her. "You look like a goddess, *memsahib*," Dalia said.

Moira surveyed herself in a mirror above the dressing table. The girl's statement triggered a subliminal flash across her mind:

The Black Goddess Kali!

It occurred again while she was applying lip rouge to her mouth. A blood-red gash across her lower face.

Kali's slavering jaws dripping blood!

Desperately she scrubbed her mouth clean with a hand-kerchief coated with cream.

The two handmaidens looked at each other, mystified.

Chapter Nineteen

When she was finished dressing, Moira dismissed Dalia and Vijaya and went into Sean's room. He was lying on his bed, clad only in white cotton undershorts, smoking a long thin cigarette with a gold tip.

"Where on earth did you get that?" she asked.

"They come with the room. Damned fine smoke, too, Turkish tobacco. They're in that white ivory box on the dresser if you'd care for one."

"Not at the moment."

He sat up and looked her up and down. "You are positively gorgeous."

"A wedding gift from Rai. It is lovely, isn't it?" She sat down on the bed beside him and placed a hand on his thigh. Her eyes flared as she noticed the bulge in his drawers. "I do declare, what's got into you?"

"It's all those lewd murals in the bath. Do you have them in yours?"

"Yes, and I must confess they stimulated me, too." She discreetly did not describe her own unsettling experience in the bath. "Well, you had better get dressed. Rai is waiting for us downstairs."

He unpacked his regimental dress uniform from his portmanteau and laid it out on the bed. "Somewhat wrinkled, but it can't be helped."

Moira tried one of the Turkish cigarettes while she waited for him. "Whew. They're too strong for my taste."

"Takes some getting used to. All right, I'm ready for action. Let's go."

When they joined him in the study, the sultan was standing at a wide window overlooking the palace gardens and drinking a Scotch and soda. He turned at their entrance and beamed at Moira. "You look positively ravishing, my dear."

"It's such a beautiful sari. Thank you so much, Rai."

He walked to her and took her by the hand. "Sean, you lucky dog. If only I had met her before you, I should have made her my queen. What would you like to drink? I have chilled champagne for this auspicious occasion."

"I'd love a glass of champagne," she acknowledged.

The words were scarcely spoken when a servant came into the study pushing a silver tea cart. On it was a magnum of champagne nestling in a silver bucket of ice, and three goblets. Moira was struck by the resemblance they bore to the goblet in which Sheikh Futty Sing had served her the drugged wine. The servant popped the cork expertly and poured the sparkling wine. He served Moira and Sean and the sultan from a gold tray.

"You haven't been entertaining any *thugs* in the palace of late, have you, Rai?"

"I beg your pardon?" She noted the sharp edge in his voice with interest.

"I'm joking, of course. I recently saw goblets very similar to these, solid gold. I'm certain they were stolen goods."

"Stolen goods? Moira, I must confess you have me befuddled."

Sean laughed. "To be sure. You have no idea of the harrowing experience Moira was put through on our way to Delhi."

"Do not keep me in suspense. What happened?"

Moira narrated the sequence of events, beginning with their visit to the tent of Sheikh Rai Sing at the *bele,* her abduction at the hands of the *thugs*, her brief incarceration in the Thuggee lair and her eventual release.

Rai Om Pragash was flabbergasted. "Rai Sing dead! I can't believe it! We haven't had much association in recent years, but he was a cherished cousin. And you, poor Moira! You must have been frightened out of your mind, being a prisoner of those abominable savages. Oh, this is too much. Major Flynn, all my armed forces are at your disposal. Once and for all, a concentrated effort must be made to stamp out this pestilence."

It was the first time in their brief acquaintance that Moira had seen the sultan fly into a rage. The first time they had discussed the Thuggee movement at the viceroy's ball, Rai had been pragmatic and philosophical about the *phansigars*. He had all but implied that they were a necessary evil in strife-ridden, impoverished, divided India.

"I'll order Karoom to mobilize all our military reserves in the province first thing tomorrow," Rai ranted, pacing up and down, shaking his fist. "Damn! Damn! Damn! I'll have that scoundrel's head mounted on a spike in the city square, I vow it. What did you say his name was?"

"Sheikh Futty Sing. I thought he might be related to your cousin, Sheikh Rai Sing."

"I think not. Sing . . . it's a common name in India."

"So everyone informs me. Well, enough of this gloomy talk. This is a holiday for us."

"Of course." Rai seemed more relaxed now. "Now suppose we begin with the tour I promised you." There were 102 rooms and chambers in the royal palace, each one more enthralling than the one preceding it.

"I know I would get lost wandering around here without a guide. It's a veritable maze."

"As I said before, it is not a home, it is a mausoleum," Rai said wryly.

When they had seen the final room in the palace, he led them onto a terrace and through the royal gardens. Gravel pathways traced a sinuous and circuitous route among the most vast array of trees, shrubbery, and flowers that Moira had ever seen or even imagined in a garden: cedar, jute, fig, date palm, the camphor tree, mulberry, dog rose, banyan, oak and olive; lush tropical blooms that dazzled the eye with their spectrum of colors.

"This is a veritable Garden of Eden," Moira exulted.

They crossed an Oriental arch bridge over a still pond that reflected all the verdant grandeur around it. On the other side of the bridge, a small pagoda stood in a grassy clearing. There was a tapering obelisk of masonry and marble with a frieze running around it, exotic sculptures, and glittering mosaics inlaid with tile and gold.

"How quaint," Moira said for lack of a more enthusiastic expression. There was a foreboding air about the holy temple that made her uneasy.

"It was built over two thousand years ago," the sultan informed them.

"Is it a Hindu or Muslim temple?" Moira inquired.

"Neither, as a matter of fact," he said offhandedly. He looked her straight in the eye. "This temple is dedicated to the worship of Kali. At least it was before my troops dispersed the congregation and moved it here from Allahabad. I think it makes a decorative garden piece, don't you?"

"Can we have a look inside?" Flynn asked.

"Of course," and he added slyly, "Note the Arabic watchword above the doorway. It says: 'Those who pass through these hallowed portals must forever more serve Kali, the greatest goddess of them all.' Do you dare?"

Flynn laughed and put an arm about his wife's waist. "Shall we give it a go, luv?"

Her smile was forced. "I believe we can hold our own with the lady."

"Then we shall proceed." Rai put a shoulder to the massive bronze doors. "Lend a hand, Sean. It's been years since they were opened."

With both men shoving as hard as they could, the doors gave way slowly, with a metallic rasping that sent goose bumps racing up and down Moira's arms. She followed Rai and Sean across the threshold into the musty interior. Dust swirled in the shafts of sunlight refracting through the stained-glass windows set high in the walls. It was silent as a tomb. They walked into a court with slender minarets at the four corners flanking two arcaded porticoes. In the center of the court was a small fountain, dry and corroded after years of neglect.

"In its heyday this charming contrivance used to spew forth sacrificial blood to sooth Kali's savage breast."

"How horrible," Moira said in a small voice, subdued by an atmosphere of intangible menace that was as thick in the air as the dust.

"Over here we have the prayer hall, Kali's *maksoura*." Rai led them through an archway into a smaller room with stone niches lining the walls for the worshippers to sit on. "Rather like church pews, aren't they? They're called *mihrabs*."

At the front of the chamber there was a stone podium on a raised marble dais. "The *dikka* and *nimbar*," Rai explained. "An altar of sorts."

At the back of the dais, shrouded in the shadows of a circular recess in the wall, was a statue. "And now you shall meet Kali." He hopped onto the stone platform and walked to the rear wall, which was covered by a wide drapery. The sultan took hold of a velvet pull cord, and slowly the curtains parted, unveiling a spectacular stained-glass window in the shape of a half-moon. Moira shielded her eyes against the glare of reds and blues and greens and violets streaming through the colored panes. Then her eyes were drawn downward to the statue in the recess, huge, and so ugly it was a visual assault. She had gazed upon grotesque conceptions by artists and sculptors of Medea, Hydra, the gorgon, the minotaur and other monsters of history. But none of them was as repulsive and hideous as Kali.

It was a grotesque distortion of the female form hewn out of glittering obsidian. The blasphemous effigy had ruby eyes—blood-red rubies that impaled Moira as if they were alive. A twisted gash of a mouth, with sharklike fangs and a swollen tongue, dripped blood. The torso was deformed, a three-armed monster, each arm wielding the symbolic weapons of the Thuggee, a club and a sword and a noose.

"They represent the Thuggee instruments of murder," Rai said. He glanced sharply at Moira. "What is it, my dear? You look distressed."

"This temple, everything about it contrived to create illusion, to instill one with an acceptance of supernatural powers at work. Do you know, just now I could have sworn that that monstrosity was winking at me, beckoning to me."

Rai smiled. "Who is to say, Moira? Perhaps you are one of those chosen to win the favor of Kali."

She shook her head in disbelief. "What a barbarous faith."

Rai raised a disapproving eyebrow. "All faiths are rooted in barbarism. Quite frankly, the legend of Kali and Thuggee does not strain my imagination any more than the Christian myths of Adam and Eve and the forbidden apple, the Immaculate Conception and the Resurrection. Tommyrot, all of it.

"The difference between Western and Eastern religion is measured on a yardstick of economics, the difference between enduring centuries of tyranny, starvation and incessant pain and heartbreak, and the comparative life of luxury that is the Western heritage. The Eastern mind has become desensitized, creating a mental state that serves as a buffer against madness.

"It requires more drastic religious fictions to command the respect and reverence of a Hindu or a Muslim than to capture Western imagination. You tell an Untouchable that God is charitable, good, compassionate, forgiving, full of love and kindness for his faithful subjects, and he would think you were insane.

"He damned well knows from a lifetime of bitter experience what the deities who direct human fortune are like. The gods are cruel, unmerciful, vengeful, full of hate and sadism toward those who fear and worship them and with an unquenchable thirst for human blood. God is fear, not love, in the East."

There it was again, the nagging uncertainty at the back of Moira's mind. Rai Om Pragash, a leader of men, with reason, wisdom, education, refinement; one who publicly decried the bloody crimes of the *thugs,* one who, just a short time earlier, had vowed to exterminate the Thuggee cult once and for all. Now, as in the past, when discussing the subject in private with friends, Rai appeared to be offering in a subtle, oblique fashion a tacit approval of their methods, a rationalization for the *thugs'* vicious acts.

The sultan drew the curtain, and Kali receded into the shadows. "Enough of this bloody mythology," he said lightly. "I fear I have little patience with religious zealots of any denomination."

"But you do understand and appreciate what their motivation is?" Moira said pointedly.

His laughter was harsh. "I think I do. Don't you agree, my dear? We all strive to become omniscient observers of life and humankind. . . . Shall we return to the palace? I could use some more of that champagne. What about you two?"

"Sounds fine to me," Flynn agreed.

Moira was silent as they departed the temple and Sean and Rai closed the creaking doors. Outside in the warm sunshine with puffy cottonball clouds sailing through the firmament, sapphire blue and reassuring, Moira's doubts and apprehensions receded. Walking between Rai and Sean, she took each by an arm and they strode off briskly along the gravel path, three friends on a lark.

It was three days since Flynn and Moira had arrived in Delhi. That morning Major Flynn had taken his troops into the field, along with two troops of the sultan's Ludhiana Sikhs Sepoy Regiment, commanded by Captain Buram, to track down a gang of *thugs* who had murdered two tax commissioners on their way from Calcutta to Delhi. Moira lunched with Rai, then went riding on a black stallion from the royal stables. When she returned to the palace, she took a bath and spent a pleasant late afternoon sunning herself naked on the secluded private balcony off her bedroom. In the few days she had been serving Moira,

Dalia, one of her handmaidens, had formed a strong attachment for her mistress. At four o'clock she came out onto the balcony with a bottle of thick purple oil.

"Does the *memsahib* want me to anoint her delicate skin with this mulberry elixir to ward off the sun's harmful rays?" the girl asked.

Moira smiled. "Thank you, no, Dalia. My skin may look delicate, but I assure you it is not. If one can survive the broiling sun of Texas, one can certainly bear with the Indian sun. Besides, there is much moisture in the air at this time of year."

She deemed it would not be wise to encourage another episode like the *ménage à trois* in the bathtub the day they had arrived. Dalia sat down beside Moira cross-legged, looking very introspective.

"You're very quiet and thoughtful, Dalia," Moira observed.

The girl hung her head and pouted. "I do not like that fat toad Karoom."

Moira's eyes widened. "Now what on earth made you think of Karoom? He seems personable enough."

"He is two-faced, *memsahib*. How to say in English? He runs with the foxes and hunts with the hounds."

Moira sat up, suddenly interested in the girl's preoccupation with Rai's minister. Intuitively she asked. "Karoom said something bad about me, perhaps?"

Dalia's eyes would not meet her own. Moira grasped her arms. "Look at me, Dalia. I was right, wasn't I? Karoom spoke meanly of me."

"Karoom despises all Westerners."

"But me especially?"

"You especially. Also he fears you and your husband."

"That's absurd! Why should he fear Major Flynn and me?"

"He is angry with the sultan for inviting you to the palace. He says you pose a danger."

"What sort of danger?"

"I cannot say."

"Or is it that you *won't* say?"

"When I entered the royal service I took a blood oath before the Great God Vishnu to be loyal to the sultan."

"I won't ask you to break that oath, Dalia, never fear. And thank you for telling me about Karoom, in any case."

"Be careful. I think he poses danger to you."

"I hardly think so, Dalia. Rai Om Pragash, the sultan, is my friend." She got up. "I think I'll get ready for dinner. I expect Major Flynn to return shortly. You may go now. I won't be needing your services until after we eat."

Dalia curtsied and left.

With the sun almost touching the horizon, the air cooled rapidly. Moira closed the French doors leading out onto the balcony and began to dress. Moira's brow was furrowed as she thought about what Dalia had told her about Karoom. She could understand his mistrust of Westerners, but what reason would he have to fear Sean and her? She was still pondering it when Sean returned. His face was extremely grim, and his kiss was a mere salutation.

"From your expression, darling, I take it you did not have a very satisfactory day."

"Highly unsatisfactory. When we got to the city of Meerut, Captain Buram and I deployed our forces. His men circled to the west while our lancers circled to the east. When we linked up afterward to the north, the Sepoys were interrogating a band of suspicious-looking bastards at a *bele* where they were camped. And I damned well know that Buram addressed one of them, the leader, as *Futty Sing!*"

Moira swung around on the vanity bench, her eyes wide. "Futty Sing! That was the name of the Thuggee *jemader* who murdered Rai Sing and kidnapped me!"

"Yes, and it had to be he. As you said, he looked like Rai Sing and the sultan. What's more, as they rode off, I saw a yellow *rumal* sticking out of Futty Sing's back pocket."

"They rode off!" Moira was incredulous. "You mean to say you let them go free?"

"It was Buram's decision. He claimed to have searched

them and their gear before our troop arrived on the scene and to have questioned them without discovering any incriminating evidence. It all transpired so fast, I had no chance to collect my thoughts. I accepted Buram's word, but now I'm convinced he was lying through his teeth. I'm going downstairs right now and have a talk with Rai. I think he's got a traitor in his ranks.''

"Or else. . . ." She didn't complete the thought.

"Or else?"

"Never mind; let's go and confront Rai."

The sultan was conferring with Captain Buram and Karoom in the palace library. The door was shut, and two Sepoy troopers were standing guard outside. They tried to bar Flynn's way, but he shoved them aside roughly and knocked sharply on the oaken panel. The door was opened by Karoom, who made no pretense of covering his displeasure over the interruption.

"I wish to speak to the sultan. It's extremely important."

"We are engaged in private negotiations, and His Highness does not want to be disturbed."

Sean looked across the little man's head and saw Rai sitting behind his desk and Buram standing at attention in front of the desk.

Sean called out: "Rai, I regret disturbing you but this is a matter of enormous importance and it concerns Captain Buram."

The sultan was not pleased. "Cannot it wait until I hear a briefing from Captain Buram about today's scouting detail?"

"That is why I'm here, Rai, and I'd like to be present when he gives that briefing. I may be able to add some comments and observations, which, I believe, Captain Buram may omit from his briefing."

Rai took a Turkish cigarette from a gold box on one side of the desk and lit it with a sulfur match. He leaned back in his chair. "All right, Major Flynn, what have you got to say? At ease, Captain Buram."

"After you hear the treachery that Captain Buram perpetrated today, I believe you will relieve him of his command and place him under arrest.''

Rai and Captain Buram exchanged insolent smiles. The sultan sneered at Flynn. ''I doubt that very seriously, Major Flynn. Well, get on with it.''

Flynn took a deep breath. ''On the outskirts of Meerut, Captain Buram and his troops interrogated a group of men whom I have reason to believe were the same Thuggee death squad who murdered Sheikh Rai Sing and his party and abducted my wife.''

The sultan was unimpressed. ''Now what good reason do you have to believe that, Major?''

''The name of the *jemader* was Futty Sing, and he fit the description that Moira gave. Interestingly, he bore a striking resemblance to you and to your murdered cousin, Rai Sing.''

Captain Buram was agitated. ''Your Highness, I must protest this—''

''That's enough, Captain,'' Rai interrupted. ''I see no reason to perpetuate this ruse any longer. Yes, Major Flynn, it was the same Sheikh Futty Sing who killed Rai Sing and abducted your wife. Captain Buram issued a stern warning to Futty Sing and his *phansigars* to get out of Bengal within twenty-four hours or face extermination. He put them on probation, as it were.''

''Probation? Captain Buram released that crew of wanton killers on probation? Why, it's sheer madness!''

''You don't understand, Major Flynn,'' Buram interjected. ''The *thugs* we encountered at the *bele* were a splinter group of one of the most powerful Thuggee contingents in all India. Two or three hundred of them are hiding in the forests, monitoring our every move. If we had taken Futty Sing into custody, they would have ambushed us on our way back to Delhi.''

''You acted very sensibly, Captain,'' Rai told him. ''Look at it this way, Flynn—we put the fear of God in Futty Sing and his men. They will spread the word throughout the province, and the *thugs* will curtail their operations temporarily. That will give us precious time to achieve full mobilization.''

"You're lying, Rai!" Moira said with contempt. "It does not become a sultan to speak with the forked tongue of an Untouchable! You knew about the attack on Rai Sing's camp. In fact, I believe it was carried out with your approval.''

"You're raving mad, Madam Flynn," he said stiffly.

"Am I, Rai? Oh, yes, you knew, all right. But you did not expect Futty Sing to kidnap me; that wasn't part of the plan. So you ordered Sing to release me.''

"My dear Moira, you have the wildest imagination of any female I have ever met. You should become a novelist." He appealed to Flynn. "Really, Major, certainly you don't believe your wife's outlandish hypothesis?''

"I believe every word of it.''

Moira stalked over to the desk and shook a fist at the sultan. "Futty Sing was stricken when I identified myself. He administered a savage thrashing to the man responsible for abducting me. But the point is, he *knew* who I was and that we were bound for Delhi. He said that his *celebrated and famous chieftain* had told him that I was a ravishing beauty, or some such drivel.''

Rai stubbed out his cigarette and rose from the chair. "I find that positively fascinating, Moira. Did he perchance give you any hint of who this mysterious leader is? One of the deposed princes of Maratha, no doubt.''

"I don't think so, Rai. There is no longer any doubt in my mind. The famous chieftain is none other than the sultan of Delhi—*you!*''

The sultan pressed his eyelids with the fingers of both hands. He said nothing for a long while. Finally he lowered his hands and looked at her. The sadness reflected in his eyes and in his voice was sincere.

"Why, Moira? Why? Why did you pursue this feline curiosity? This knowledge you have obtained—you both must realize I cannot permit you to return to Calcutta and reveal my secret to the government. It is not myself I am thinking about. My fate—the fate of any one individual—it is insignificant. What matters above all else is the cause.''

"The cause?''

"The future of India. Independence from the colonial despots. I told you when first we met in Calcutta that the Thuggee movement is the closest thing to a united revolutionary army in the long, lamented, fragmented history of this crippled giant, India. It has taken half a century to nourish this feeble seed into a young and fragile vine that is just beginning to entwine its tendrils around the pikestaff that flies the Union Jack. The cause of freedom must be preserved at any cost. So . . . I have no alternative than to do away with you and Captain Flynn, my dear.''

"How do you propose to get away with it, Rai?'' Flynn demanded. "I've got a troop of Bengal Lancers billeted on the palace grounds. Do you expect them to accept whatever fabrication you cook up to explain our demise?''

The sultan stroked his beard. "I wouldn't be surprised if Sheikh Futty Sing can be persuaded to engineer another abduction. I am not sure about the details as yet, but I will work it out with Karoom.''

"Inasmuch as the cat is out of the bag, why don't you tell us why you murdered Rai Sing?''

"For the same reason I have to dispose of you, my dear. Rai was power hungry. A mere sheikhdom no longer satisfied his ambitions. He had his sights set on becoming a sultan, preferably right here in Delhi. He had uncovered incriminating evidence of my place in the Thuggee movement from a high-placed informer. This informer, for a handsome reward, was prepared to return to Calcutta with Rai Sing and betray me to the viceroy.'' He threw up his hands. "No matter, we are all playthings of the gods, but with the grace of the goddess Kali we shall overcome. Captain Buram, see that Major and Mrs. Flynn are escorted to their quarters and placed under guard for the time being.''

Captain Buram drew his pistol, but to the astonishment of Moira and Sean, he pointed it at the sultan. "Your narration has been highly enlightening to me as well as to the major and his wife. It ties up all the loose ends. The case is now conclusive.''

Rai Om Pragash gaped at him in utter disbelief. ''Loose ends? What case? Have you gone mad, Buram?''

''No, Your Highness, I am sane. It is you who are mad. The sultan of Delhi allying himself with the infamous *phansigars!* To speak of the noble cause of independence in the same breath as you speak of the *thugs,* that is high treason. India may be a crippled giant as you say, but the Thuggee subculture is a terminal cancer on the invalid.''

Rai Om Pragash was livid with rage. ''Buram, you traitorous swine, I will have your head for this treason!''

''No, Your Highness, you have reversed the roles, I think. It is *you* who will lose your head for treason. You and Futty Sing and his legion of mad *dhokurs*. You know me as Captain Buram, but the truth is I am Major Pindares of British Military Intelligence. You have been under our surveillance for two years now, Your Highness, but until today you have always managed to stay beyond our grasp. Om Pragash, sultan of Delhi, I hereby place you under arrest.''

Rai regarded him scornfully. ''You'll never get away with it, Buram—Pindares—whatever the hell your name is. My Sepoys will remain loyal to their sultan, their *baroo,* their *burka!*''

''It's no use, Om Pragash. By nightfall a full regiment of lancers and another of mounted infantry will reach Delhi and surround the palace. Until then you will remain in this room under arrest. Major Flynn, *memsahib,* you are free to go to your quarters. Upon your return to Calcutta, you will be subpoenaed to testify before a military tribunal to what you have heard and witnessed here today.''

''With great pleasure!'' Moira said. And to the sultan, she said, ''I truly feel sorry for you, Rai. What a waste that your intelligence, statesmanship and patriotism could not have served your beloved land instead of exploiting it by championing a tyranny of violence and murder.''

The sultan was suddenly docile and softspoken. ''Moira,

Sean, I would appreciate it if I could have a few words in private with Major Pindares.''

"To be sure.'' Sean took Moira by the elbow and escorted her out of the room. The military sentries stood like statues on either side of the portal.

"Let's wait here until Pindares has something to tell us,'' Sean said.

They did not have to wait long. The door opened and Pindares emerged from the library.

"What now, Major Pindares?'' Sean inquired. "Did he have anything pertinent to relate?''

Pindares stood facing them, hands folded behind his back, his legs spread. "A man of Om Pragash's eminence is entitled to exit this vale of tears with dignity.''

Moira's gaze was drawn to his holster. It was empty!

A heartbeat later a single shot rang out inside the study. Pindares sighed. "And so it is done. Better this way than the humiliation of a public trial and ignoble execution. The ends of India have been better served this way. Major, *memsahib,* there are matters to arrange before our reinforcements arrive. I'm sure you want to make preparations to return to Calcutta with your lancers.'' He honored Moira with a stiff bow and went back into the study.

"All's well that ends well,'' Sean quoted as they climbed the marble staircase.

"Nothing ever ends in this world, except life itself,'' Moira said. "There are only new beginnings.''

Book Three

Chapter Twenty

January 1, 1890

Dear Wendy,

And so we enter a new decade. It is astonishing—and a little frightening—how the passage of time accelerates as the years pass. Sean tells me I don't look a day older than when he first saw me. I know it's his Irish blarney at work, but it's nice to hear anyway. After all, I don't let on to him that his waist is somewhat less lean than it was when I married him. I truthfully don't feel that I am aging. At thirty-nine my weight is the same as it was at nineteen, and I have no trace of gray in my hair as yet. The real yardsticks of how we are maturing are the children. I received a letter from Patrick at the United States Military Academy at West Point. As you know, he is pursuing his childhood dream to become a cavalry officer like his father. He is the mirror image of Brad, as you must have noticed last summer when he visited with you in Maryland.

Desiree, on the other hand, bears little resemblance to me that I can see, although other people say our features are as unmistakable as our physiques. She did inherit Grandmother Callahan's red hair and green cat's eyes. And she has the temperament that supposedly goes with red hair and green eyes. Desiree is a bit of a spitfire, quick tempered, strong willed, a true army brat. Then again, I recall that that appellation was applied to me long ago.

Last year Sean was promoted to brigadier general. Strange how things happen; he had no intention of making a career of the military, but as in other facets of life, there are a variety of complex forces that shape our lives. I'm afraid Sean and I are in a rut. Life has been comfortable, satisfying and uneventful these past ten years, not at all like the initial nightmarish first year we spent in India. We've become typical colonials; we dress for dinner, play whist at the club and ride with the hounds on Sunday mornings.

At the end of this year Sean will have completed twenty-five years of service in the lancers, and he has already applied for retirement. We plan to reside in England or possibly Ireland, buy a small farm and grow old gracefully.

Tonight we are attending a masked ball at the Government House honoring the new viceroy, Sir Sydney Farnsworth. I am appearing as Marie Antoinette, and Desiree is masquerading, of all people, as Salome, who you will recall had John the Baptist's head served to her on a silver tray. Sean says there is something symbolic in our respective choice of costumes, since both John and Marie lost their heads. Sometimes Desiree behaves as if she would not be averse to having my head. I love Desiree, and I know she loves me, but too much of the time we get along like oil and water. Sean has spoiled her worse than if she were his natural daughter, and she adores him. She calls him Daddy, which, I regret, Pat has never been able to bring himself to do. He worshipped Brad far too much to allow another man to replace him. He has always called Sean Uncle, and the two of them get along famously.

I am so looking forward to a marvelous family

reunion next year after Sean retires and we stop over in the States on our way to England.

Please give our love to Carl and to your children, who, no doubt are growing up too fast, as mine are; and of course to Susan and her younger brood. Please write soon.

Your devoted sister,
Moira

Moira sealed the letter and went down the hall to Desiree's bedroom. She knocked.

"Come in, Mother."

Moira stood spellbound in the doorway as her daughter did a pirouette, modeling her ball costume.

"What do you think, Mother?"

Moira blinked. "Well, it's a very lovely costume, quite appropriate for a sheikh's harem, but the Government House—really, my dear. The poor viceroy will have apoplexy when he sees you in that outfit."

"Sir Sydney will adore me, the old lecher."

"You're outrageous."

"Well, it's true. When I took those papers over to the Government House last week, he pinched my cheek." Her eyes flashed wickedly. "And I don't mean these cheeks." She touched her face.

Moira could not suppress her laughter. "You are a naughty, naughty girl, Desiree, and you should be spanked."

Desiree giggled. "I bet Sir Sydney would jump at the chance."

Moira shook her head and came into the room for a closer inspection. Her daughter wore a knee-length toga of scarlet silk over a pair of loose, diaphanous harem pants of white silk that revealed more leg, Moira reflected, than the viceroy had gazed on in many a year. The pants complemented brass breastplates and a short black velvet jacket. A daring expanse of bare flesh showed between the hem of the jacket and the top of the harem pants.

"I don't approve, and neither would your father. I only

wish he were here to discipline you, young lady. I know it's hopeless for me to try."

"Don't act so self-righteous, Mother. I've heard all about your youthful escapades." She looked in a mirror and ran her fingers through her bronze locks, which curled loosely about her round shoulders. "I think I shall let my hair hang loose tonight. It makes me look more abandoned, as Salome must have looked."

Moira had explained the nature of sex to her daughter when Desiree reached puberty, but in an impersonal manner. The two of them had never been close enough to exchange intimacies. She had never discussed her experiences with her lovers with Desiree, just as she had never inquired about the younger woman's experiences—if indeed she had had any. Instinctively she believed that Desiree had lost her virginity in her mid-teens. She had been nubile at fourteen, just as Moira had been, and Moira smiled, recalling her wondrous introduction to lust in the corn with young Bob Thomas. Certainly there was ample opportunity for the young unmarried women at Fort William and its environs to engage in surreptitious affairs if they so desired. There were scores of eligible bachelors among the ranks of the dashing lancers and some of the younger civil servants.

There were always hordes of young men congregating around Desiree at the post's social functions, and she flirted with them all. And after the fashion of certain proud, pretty, popular females, she favored most the one who paid the least attention to her, one Lieutenant Farley Johnson.

Moira had to admit that he had the good looks and charm to set feminine hearts aflutter, old as well as young. The wife of Sean's adjutant, a sultry brunette of forty-five, had once confided to Moira:

"Gad! I'll bet that one is something! He can put his boots under my bed anytime he pleases."

Although he was ten years her junior, Moira confessed to herself that he exuded an aura of masculinity that fired any normal woman's blood. She did her best to keep her distance from Lieutenant Johnson. He, however, had made it very obvious from the day he arrived at Fort William that he found the wife of his commanding officer far better company than most of the younger women. This unfortunate condition served to aggravate the normal tension that existed between Desiree and her.

"I must dress myself now, dear. Would you help me with that Marie Antoinette costume? It's monstrous."

"Glad to." She followed Moira down the hall to her bedroom and sat on the bed while Moira removed her negligee and put on her undergarments.

First she put on the white pantalettes, knee-length and embroidered with lace and colored ribbons. Over that came a thick crinoline petticoat made of horsehair and wool; on top of that a second petticoat, padded from the knees down. From knees to waist it was reinforced with whalebone; then still a third petticoat, white with starched flowers; and last of all a muslin underskirt. By the time Desiree and Moira had accomplished the feat of getting her into the voluminous gown—yards of white ruffled satin and satin supported in back by a bustle and ballooning over an enormous hoop—both mother and daughter were panting from exertion.

"It's a monster all right," Desiree muttered. "Did the women of Louis XVI's court always dress like this?"

"I don't imagine so. Probably for grand balls."

"That's good, because if they did they would have been sexually deprived. I can't imagine any man having the patience or fortitude to battle all those layers of material to get his hands on some maiden's lily-white body."

Moira laughed. "Desiree, you are impudent, precocious and have a mouth like a fishwife."

"Well, at least Farley Johnson will have to keep his distance tonight. No man can get within three feet of you wearing that hoop." The casual tone of her voice belied her malicious smile.

Moira scowled and said sharply, "What is that supposed to mean, young lady?"

The girl shrugged and cupped her hands over her brass

breastplates. "Nothing, except that he's always simpering over you." The smile grew meaner. "And do you know what? I think you're flattered by his attentions, Mother."

"Don't be ridiculous. Farley is almost young enough to be my son."

Desiree's eyebrows arched. "Well, *hardly!*"

"I find your sense of humor highly distasteful!"

"Even Daddy says he's infatuated with you."

"I don't want to listen to any more of your precocious claptrap. Act your age."

"Why don't you act your age, Mother?"

Lips compressed into tight lines, Moira walked to her daughter and slapped her across the face. "Any further insolence out of you and I'll forbid you to attend the ball!"

Green eyes ablaze with fury showing through her tears, the girl spun on her heels and stalked out of the room. Moira rolled her eyes at the ceiling. "Sean . . . where are you when I need you?" General Flynn was attending an honorary supper for the prince of Wales aboard a British battleship anchored in Calcutta Harbor.

Sir Sydney Farnsworth and his wife, Helen, greeted Moira and Desiree at the foot of the great staircase that led down to the Government House ballroom. The viceroy was wearing the garb of a Chinese mandarin, complete with skullcap and a fake pigtail dangling down his back. His wife wore a colorful kimono, and her hair was done in an elaborate Oriental hairdo piled high on her head.

As a final concession to modesty, Desiree had draped a long scarf around her bare shoulders; nonetheless the viceroy and his wife were obviously taken aback by her brazen costume.

"You look lovely, Mrs. Flynn," he said in a thin voice, and, after clearing his throat, he said to Desiree, averting his eyes, "And you, my dear . . . you look . . . charming, yes, charming."

Helen Farnsworth's expression would have frozen hell itself.

Moira and Desiree circulated among the visitors who

were standing around the dance floor, the girl creating a mild sensation wherever she went. Moira winced at some of the disapproving comments directed their way.

"Even for the bedroom that would be vulgar."

"Bedroom? Why, my husband has never seen me in less than what she has on. It's disgusting."

Desiree enjoyed the commotion she had caused with a relish that recalled to Moira some of her own youthful pranks calculated to shock her elders. Desiree's face lit up as she spied Lieutenant Farley Johnson standing tall among a group of fat clerks and office soldiers. He was ruggedly handsome, with blond hair that hung lank over his forehead, fair-skinned and freckled. He had a wide, sensual smile, merry blue eyes and a pair of shoulders that Desiree frequently fantasized naked and rippling with muscle, and encompassing her own nude form. Moira was accurate in her assessment that Desiree was no longer a virgin. A young corporal who was in charge of the stable hands had "taken her" as he later put it in a ribald cockney accent, when she was just fifteen years old. There had been two other men since then. But none of them had stirred her passions like Johnson. And she was insanely jealous of the attentions he showed to her mother.

Lieutenant Johnson and the others lapsed into uncomfortable silence as Desiree sauntered up to them, swinging her hips seductively.

"My word!" an elderly clerk whispered. "It's Flynn's girl."

A colonel stuck a monocle in his eye to have a clearer view and promptly dropped it as Desiree came into sharp focus.

Johnson was masquerading as a pirate, wearing a striped seaman's shirt, duck trousers cut off at the knee and a red bandana wrapped around his head; he had a black eye patch over his left eye. He stood with his arms folded across his chest, appraising her with amusement.

"Well, well, well, if it isn't Miss Flynn."

She lifted her black mask briefly. "How did you ever

recognize me?" she asked flippantly. "You've never seen me without my clothes before."

The colonel choked on his whisky and soda, and in no time, with the exception of Johnson, the assembly had scattered in all directions, leaving the lieutenant alone on the field. There was about Desiree an aura of blatant sexuality that intimidated the older men.

"Well, not with so little clothing." He looked her up and down boldly. "I must admit you're the most seductive harem queen I've ever seen. It's a lucky thing your father is at that banquet tonight. If he saw you like this, he'd hit the ceiling."

"Oh, I can handle dear old Daddy. And incidentally, I am *not* a harem queen. I am the infamous Salome."

"Very appropriate. You have a reputation for making heads roll."

"And who are you supposed to be?"

"Blackbeard the pirate."

"Then where's your beard?"

Grinning, he reached into a back pocket and held up a bogus chin piece. "It got too itchy to bear. I think it has lice in it."

"Odd, all these coincidences about lost heads."

"How is that?"

"My mother is Marie Antoinette; she lost her head. I am Salome; I demanded John the Baptist's head. Now you, Blackbeard the pirate; if memory serves me, I believe Blackbeard was beheaded, wasn't he?"

"I thought he was hanged, but small difference; some men have lost their heads to the hangman's noose."

She grabbed his arm possessively. "As a former princess of Palestine, I claim you for my own tonight, sir. Shall we dance?"

"At your pleasure, Madam Salome." He made an exaggerated bow and swept her out onto the crowded dance floor. There was a lively gavotte in progress, and it went on endlessly. When it was over, Johnson and Desiree were winded and perspiring.

"I don't know how these old dears manage it," she

gasped. "Let's sit the next one out and get something to drink." They wended their way through the milling guests to the refreshment table, where they met Moira. Desiree pouted sullenly as Johnson bent over her mother's hand and kissed it.

"You look positively ravishing, Your Highness. I would do battle to the death to preserve that lovely head."

"And I would be flattered to have you do battle under my colors, Lieutenant." She curtsied.

"Please get me some punch, Farley," Desiree snapped.

"Your wish is my command. What about you, Madam Queen? Can I get you something to drink?"

"No, thank you, I've just finished one." Sensing the annoyance she was causing her daughter, Moira tactfully withdrew. "If you'll excuse me, I've promised this dance to Major Hawkins. I'll see you later."

Johnson ordered a rum punch for Desiree and a Scotch and soda for himself from the turbaned servant tending bar.

"Let's go out on the veranda and cool off," Desiree suggested.

"If you please."

They went onto the veranda and stood at the balustrade, looking out over the manicured lawn and gardens. Like so many palatial colonial estates, the focal point of the Government House property was its fountain. Three jets on the rim of the oval basin sent water high into the air and arching over one another. Droplets of water caught in the gentle breeze sparkled in the moonlight like jewels.

"I love to sit on the benches around the fountain and savor the cool mist wafting in the air. Come along." She took him by the hand, and they walked down the steps and across the lawn.

"Don't you find me irresistible in this costume?" she asked him.

"You and your mother are exceptionally beautiful women."

"Why must people keep categorizing me with my mother? We're not a vaudeville team: Moira and Desiree. I am my own person, just as my mother is her own person.''

"It was merely an observation. I do believe you're jealous of your mother.''

Desiree felt her face flaming; she was glad it was dark so he wouldn't notice. "That's ridiculous! I have no reason to be jealous of my mother!''

They stopped near the fountain, and Johnson faced her and placed his hands on her shoulders. Desiree thrilled at the warmth and strength of his fingers on her bare flesh; she had shrugged off the shawl, and now she dropped it on the grass.

"You're right; you don't have any cause to be jealous of your mother.''

Her eyes glistened in the moonlight. "Then how is it you pay more attention to her than you do to me?''

He threw back his head and laughed. "So that's it! You little dunce! Yes, I find her very, very desirable, but I do *not* desire her. I want to make a career out of the service. You don't think I'd be audacious or foolish enough to mess around with the wife of my general, do you?''

She tilted her head and studied him through narrowed cat's eyes. "It is the truth, I can tell. You play up to Moira to enlist favor with my father, but that's as far as you'd go.''

"I plead guilty.'' She shivered as he slid his hands off her shoulders and down her arms. "And it goes for his daughter as well. I'd never step out of line with you, Desiree . . . That name, it certainly fits you . . . Desiree . . . Desire . . . You were made for desire.''

"Do you desire me?'' she asked softly.

He shook his head vigorously. "I told you, hands off the general's ladies.''

"I don't think of myself as a lady; I'm a healthy female animal, and I do what I please. I am no longer Daddy's little girl, and I would much prefer to sit on your lap than on his.'' She slipped her hands beneath her breastplates, lifted, hunched her shoulders and let her breasts tumble free, two alabaster globes of shimmering flesh in the moonlight. Then she took his hands and guided them to her bosom. Her breasts fit perfectly in his large palms. His hands commenced shaking as her nipples grew turgid and burned into his flesh like small, hot ingots.

"I must be out of my mind!" He glanced anxiously back at the Government House. "Suppose somebody sees us?"

"Not likely, but let's be on the safe side." She led him by the hand into the shadows of a clump of mulberry trees. She put her arms around his neck and kissed him ardently, thrusting her tongue into his mouth and rotating her pelvis against him, thrilling to the surge of his manhood along her quivering belly. Johnson slipped his hands down the back of her harem pants and short skirt and kneaded her bare buttocks, teasing the cleft with his fingers. Desiree was burning with desire.

"Take off your pants, quickly." She drew away from him and flung aside the brass breastplates, then slipped down her skirt and silk pants. Johnson was naked from the waist down and was about to remove his shirt when she clutched his erect phallus with both hands.

"Don't bother with the shirt, Farley. I can't wait an instant longer!" She lay down in the grass and, still holding fast to him, drew him down on top of her. Her undulations commenced before he could penetrate her.

"God, wench, slow down!" he gasped. "I can't find you!"

She checked herself until she felt him grow inside of her. "Oh, that's good! Oh, it is marvelous! Here I go, darling! Hold on!"

It was a wild, frenzied dance of desire, the like of which the lieutenant had never experienced. She thrashed and bucked like an unbroken mare saddled for the first time; she scratched his back and bit him on the shoulder each of the four times she climaxed.

First time, indeed! he thought. He wondered whether General Flynn had any inkling of the inferno banked within the loins of his angelic daughter. Well, maybe he did suspect. After all, he was husband to the mother, and unless Johnson missed his guess, Moira Flynn was quite a fiery piece of business in the sack herself.

Jesus! How I'd like to have the chance to compare the two!

No way ever! He had already broken one commandment by bedding the daughter. If he broke the second, he'd deserve to go to hell. They lay afterward lethargically in the grass, savoring the gradual ebb of desire. The mist from the fountain dusted their hot, sweaty bodies.

Abruptly Desiree sat up.

"What is it?" He braced himself on an elbow.

She cocked an ear in the direction of the Government House. "What do you suppose all that commotion is about?"

A chorus of loud and excited voices carried across the lawn to their trysting spot. Johnson muttered, "Maybe it has something to do with us being missing."

"Don't be silly. Something's happened up there. Maybe the viceroy passed out from ogling my mother's bosom." On hands and knees she crawled to a vantage point from which she could view the house.

Her voice was concerned. "The drive is swarming with horsemen. Come on, we'd better get dressed and get up there." She put on the harem pants and skirt and breast-plates and wrapped the long silk scarf modestly around her shoulders and bosom. Johnson buttoned his pants, smoothed his pirate's shirt and searched on the ground for his eye patch, which had been knocked off in their lusty contortions.

"Never mind about it," she urged. "Let's go back."

They hurried across the broad lawn, anxiety growing as they approached the steps. Drive, veranda and steps were crowded with the viceroy's guests and helmeted horsemen.

"It's the military police," Johnson said. "Lordy, maybe there's been a rebel attack on the garrison." He ran on ahead of her and approached a uniformed captain. "What's happening, sir?"

The officer cast a jaundiced eye at Johnson's outlandish costume. "Private business."

Johnson ran his hands self-consciously down the front of

him. "Don't mind these, it's a masquerade. I'm Lieutenant Farley Johnson of the Eighteenth Lancers."

"I'm sorry, Lieutenant, but I have strict orders not to discuss it with anyone."

Desiree raced up the steps and pushed her way through the crowd into the house. The viceroy's wife came up to her; her face was deathly pale. "Oh, here you are. We've been looking all over for you. Desiree, your mother is waiting for you in Sir Sydney's study."

Desiree felt the blood rushing out of her face. "Has anything happened to my mother?"

"No, she's all right, child." She turned away quickly. "Go to her at once."

Desiree ran down the long center hall, her heart pounding wildly. The study door was open, and she burst into the room. The instant she looked at Moira, she knew something was terribly wrong; her mother had aged ten years in less than an hour. She was sitting on a lounge surrounded by the viceroy and three military officers Desiree had never seen before. Their faces were starkly grave, and a funereal miasma permeated the room, like the smell of death.

Sir Sidney had one hand resting on her mother's shoulder.

"Mother, what's happened?" Desiree went to her and knelt, grasping her hands. They were cold as a corpse's. She looked past Desiree with glassy eyes, not seeing her, not hearing her.

"Mother—" The girl looked appealingly at the viceroy. "Please, Sir Sydney, what's wrong with my mother?"

He coughed, covered his eyes with a hand as if to make his task easier in not watching her. "My dear child, Desiree, there has been a tragic accident. In Calcutta Harbor tonight, a landing craft ferrying guests back to shore from a banquet aboard the H.M.S. *Nelson*." He hesitated and shook his head in disbelief. "That landing craft . . . it exploded in the harbor. The authorities believe it was sabotage. There were no survivors."

Desiree rocked back and collapsed on her haunches. Mindless fear such as she had never before experienced welled up inside her, choking off her breath so that she could not speak but could only stare at the viceroy like a terrified animal awaiting the fatal bullet.

"Desiree, General Flynn, your father . . . he . . . he was aboard that craft. I'm sorry."

Desiree buried her face in Moira's lap, and her frame was racked by sobs of grief so heartbreaking that even the hardened military men standing by were affected.

She was in a state of shock so deep that she had no recollection of being carried upstairs by Lieutenant Johnson. Then she was lying on a bed in one of the bedrooms, dimly aware of a circle of faces peering down at her. Gradually her senses came back to life and the faces came into focus. The viceroy, his wife, Farley, and her mother were seated on the edge of the bed, stroking her hands. The tears blurred her vision again, and she shut her eyes and turned her head away on the pillow.

"Oh, Mother, how terrible for you. How terrible for both of us. But mostly for you. Two husbands dying violently in the prime of their lives."

"In the line of duty," Moira said bitterly. She sighed. "I guess the only ones who can understand why are their brothers-in-arms. Your brother, he'll understand. My father, he would have understood." She laughed hollowly. "And yes, the final irony, Brad and Sean, they understood that this could happen to them when they enlisted." She grasped her daughter firmly by the shoulders. "As for the women, they can only accept. Yes, my child, we must discipline ourselves to accept tragedy and go on living. Time heals all wounds."

Not that she believed it for a minute; they were empty words to comfort her daughter.

Chapter Twenty-one

Desiree lay in Farley Johnson's arms on a blanket spread atop a grassy knoll overlooking a small waterfall, a favorite rendezvous for the lovers since they had first made love a month earlier.

"Why must you return to the United States with your mother next week?" he asked. "Damn it, Desiree, I don't know if I can bear it without you. I love you. Stay on and marry me." He covered one of her breasts with his open mouth.

Desiree shuddered and clasped his head in her hands. "Darling, it's unfair to play on my passions as a way of persuasion. Stop it at once." She gently pushed him away and sat up. "No, Farley. I won't marry you. I never will. I'd never marry a soldier even if it means dying an old maid. I've seen what my poor mother has suffered for that indiscretion."

"I'll resign my commission."

"Don't talk nonsense. I know how much the cavalry means to you. It's in your blood, just as it is in my brother's blood. But it most definitely is not in my blood." She stood up. "I'm going to freshen up." She walked down the slope to the basin hollowed out of the earth by the erosion of the waterfall.

Johnson watched her broodingly. Her unblemished back

tapered down to a trim waist, flaring into the most perfect hips he had ever seen; the flexing of the muscles in her hard, round buttocks inflamed him even though they had just finished making love. He leaped up and trotted after her, coming up behind her in the waist-deep, churning maelstrom, and threw his arms around her, thrusting his erection between her soft cheeks and cupping her breasts in his hands.

Desiree shrieked in pretended outrage. "How dare you, sir! It's getting so a girl can't turn her back on a man. You're positively insatiable."

"I can never get enough of you."

She turned in his arms and pressed herself against him. She clasped him around the neck and threw her legs up and around him, locking her heels firmly at the small of his back. They rocked to and fro, and Desiree cried out in ecstasy as her climax began. As she peaked, Johnson lost his footing and they tumbled into the water. Desiree surfaced and blew a stream of water out of her mouth, laughing at him.

Hand in hand, they waded out of the basin and climbed the slope. While they were dressing, Desiree reiterated her reasons for accompanying her mother back to America. "Aside from my decision never to become a military wife, there is a more important consideration. My mother needs me, Farley. I need her, too. We have to turn to each other for comfort and support until the grief subsides."

"I understand, but remember, I do not intend to lose you forever. One day I will show up on your doorstep, and say, 'My darling Desiree, I've come to marry you.' "

Desiree smiled. "That's terribly sweet, Farley, but suppose my husband answers the door?"

His mouth flew open. "My God! You wouldn't? You couldn't? Marry another man behind my back? It's cruel even to suggest such an abomination!"

"All right, if it will make you feel better, I'll promise to wait for you." She laid a hand on his cheek, and her green eyes were clear as emeralds. "But there is one thing I will not promise, cannot promise. I won't vow to be true to you; celibacy is not in my nature. You must know that.''

Her candor saddened him, but he accepted what she said. ''No, I don't expect you to take a nun's vow.''

''Any more than I'd expect you to take a monk's vow. . . . Shall we be getting back? The horses are becoming restless.'' They walked down the far side of the hill to where their mounts were grazing.

The following Saturday Moira and Desiree stood at the foot of the gangplank of a slender clipper ship, the *Golden Cloud,* saying their farewells to the viceroy and his wife, Lieutenant Johnson and a few other dear friends on a quay in Calcutta Harbor.

''Will you be sailing directly to San Francisco?'' Sir Sydney inquired.

''No,'' Moira said. ''We're to put in at Osaka, Japan, as well as at Manila and Hawaii. I'm just as pleased. It will afford us an opportunity to get off the ship and stretch our legs, relieve the tedium of the long sea voyage.''

From the head of the gangplank, the second mate called down to them: ''Mrs. Flynn, we are preparing to weigh anchor. Will you please board?'' There were last-minute tearful hugs and kisses, and Johnson whispered to Desiree, ''Don't forget your promise. Wait for me.''

She kissed his cheek and turned away hurriedly, not looking backward now. Erect and with her chin set in determination, she followed her mother up the gangplank.

They shared a large, airy cabin with a porthole on either side so that they had the benefit of the sunlight both in the morning and in the afternoon. For the most part they wore informal clothing, blouses and riding breeches or the exotic, comfortable attire Moira had grown accustomed to during her years in the Far East; kimonos, mandarin jackets and trousers and the Indian kaftans. The exception was at the dinner hour, when they joined the captain and his officers at the master's table in the dining room. Then they put on more elaborate dresses and gowns.

On the third day at sea, Desiree said to her mother,

"This is terrible. I'm bored to distraction already, and we have weeks to go yet. There are just so many hours a day one can play solitaire or whist and watch the flying fishes cavort."

"I'm sure there are books aboard. Why don't you ask the first mate? It's obvious you have captivated him."

Desiree stuck out her tongue. "And you have the captain wrapped around your little finger."

"I don't know what I'm going to do with you. I think maybe we'll enroll you in a fancy finishing school for young ladies. Possibly they will be able to instill some manners and social graces into you, though I doubt it."

"That would finish me, for sure." Desiree stood up. "I shall search for Mr. Phillips and inquire about reading material."

She found Anson Phillips down in the galley, drinking coffee with the bosun. The second mate was an Englishman with pale blue eyes and a complexion so fair that he might almost have been an albino. He was most amenable to her request.

"I have some books in my cabin, and I'm sure the skipper has some as well. Come along and we'll see what we can do."

As they were leaving, the bosun said, "By the way, Miss Flynn, if you have a mind to read some old newspapers, I've got a mess of 'em in the hold."

Phillips grinned. "Sparky here is a bit of a pack rat. Hates to throw anything away."

"That's very kind of you, Mr. Bailey," Desiree said. "I'll remember it."

And she did. It took Desiree a mere week to read through every book submitted to her by the mate and captain. When that reading matter was exhausted, she sought out the bosun and asked for his old newspapers.

"I'll bring 'em to your cabin, Miss." Fifteen minutes later there was a knock on the cabin door, and Desiree opened it to a bizarre sight. Bosun Bailey was toting a stack of papers so high that they hid his face. Staggering

into the cabin, he deposited them in a corner. Mopping his
brow with a filthy bandana, he stated breathlessly:

"Plenty more where they came from, miss. You just let
me know."

"Thank you so much, Mr. Bailey. Here's a little something for your trouble." She handed him a pound note, but
he backed off indignantly.

"That's mighty thoughtful, miss, but I don't take no
gratuities for doing favors for pretty ladies such as you and
your mum." He blushed profusely and scurried out of the
cabin.

Moira confronted the pile of newspapers with amusement. "Well, I never. What is this all about?"

"I've read all the books aboard, so now I'm starting on
the bosun's old newspaper collection."

The two women inspected a dozen or so with mounting
interest. Included among the variety of journals were cop-
ies of the New York *Herald,* the San Francisco *Chronicle,*
an assortment of Hawaiian and Philippine English-language
papers, as well as some Japanese, Chinese and Indian
newspapers, also in English.

"You name it," Desiree said in wonder. "It's a clear
indication of how the White Anglo-Saxon Protestant ethic
has so long dominated the world. The British and Americans would not deign to learn the native language where
they establish colonies. They demand that the foreign na-
tionals speak and write in English."

"That's true of most colonial powers, dear," Moira
said. "Might makes right, your father always said. Power
was his obsession. Poor dear Brad."

That same afternoon Desiree stretched out in a lounge
chair to sop up the warm sunshine with a score of carefully
selected old newspapers. Somewhat later Moira joined her.
They wore loose, frothy summer frocks with short puff
sleeves, and their hair blew wildly in the strong wind that
swept over the fantail.

"These old papers make one realize just how insulated
we colonials are from the rest of the world. Things that
have taken place months before in the United States, for

example, strike me as being timely events. Except for high-level political and military business that we read about in the small provincial journals printed for the benefit of colonial settlers, such as the Calcutta *Star*, we are very much in the dark about the everyday events that are occurring around the world. I'm reading a fascinating article that says President Grover Cleveland was stricken with cancer of the mouth and had to have his upper jaw removed. It was all done in secret because the United States is in a critical economic recession, and Cleveland has been the Rock of Gibraltar that has staved off panic and total collapse. Now, after the operation, the doctors have fit him with an artificial jaw of vulcanized rubber. And he later addressed Congress and no one was the wiser.''

"How extraordinary," Moira marveled. "An artificial jaw. I wonder what medical miracles lie ahead of us. Who knows—one day they may find a way to move whole organs from one body to another.''

Desiree laughed. "Now really, Mother, there are limits to the imagination.''

Moira selected at random one of the papers from the pile with a bold headline: UNITED STATES TORN BY LABOR STRIFE. She commenced reading the related article:

ANARCHISTS PIT WORKERS AGAINST RICH INDUSTRIALISTS, SAYS LABOR SECRETARY IN FORTY-NINE STATES

Federal troops were dispatched to Indiana last night to quell rioting strikers at steel-mill plants and foundries. Cavalry units under the command of Major-General Bradford Taylor dispersed the mob, wielding rubber truncheons and sabers . . .

Moira had read on before the meaning struck her. Then she reread the sentence again with disbelief.

"Major-General Bradford Taylor!" she exclaimed. "What an amazing coincidence!"

"What's that, Mother?" Desiree looked up from her paper.

"I'm reading about the labor unrest in the United States. The government had to call in federal troops to keep order. The cavalry officer in charge of the mission is named Bradford Taylor . . . Simply amazing."

The girl sprang off the lounge and came over to read across her mother's shoulder. The article was unspectacular until the final paragraph:

. . . General Taylor was hand-picked by the War Department for this delicate assignment because of the broad spectrum of his experience. A much-decorated cavalry hero in the Civil War and the bloody Indian wars on the postwar frontier, General Taylor earned the reputation of being a skilled political analyst and diplomat on Far Eastern affairs while serving for almost ten years as military attaché to the American delegation at Peking, China. His career came near to being permanently terminated when he was charged with treason by the Chinese government, claiming that he was an American spy, and was sentenced to be executed. Under circumstances that are beclouded in mystery and which General Taylor refuses to divulge because of security reasons, he was rescued from his death cell the night before the scheduled execution by parties unknown and smuggled across the Russian border. After a lengthy journey across Russia and Europe, he arrived in London and from there proceeded to the United States. He was then reassigned by the War Department to a sensitive post in the Hawaiian Islands. Recently returned to the United States, he was awarded the rank of Major-General and appointed chief military adviser to the White House.

Moira threw down the paper. "It's incredible. It can't be. Brad alive!"

Desiree sank down on the lounge beside her mother. Her face was ashen. "I wish it weren't so, but it has to be. My father . . . to do such a treacherous thing to you,

Mother. To all of us—Pat and me. He's a monster! A heartless, inhuman beast!'' She put her hands over her face and began to cry.

Moira put an arm around her shoulders and hugged Desiree to her bosom, feeling more protective and close to her daughter than she had in years. This unbelievable circumstance was a bond that neither could ignore.

"I know, child, what you're going through. Do you know something else? Learning that Brad is alive is a greater shock than when the minister told me he was dead that awesome day in Peking. It's all so bewildering. I mean, surely Susan or Wendy must have found out he was alive. And what about Patrick? A cadet at West Point and his father a general—how could it go unnoticed?''

"Because obviously Father wanted it that way,'' Desiree said with such hate in her voice that Moira winced. The girl pounded her fists against her thighs furiously. "If I were face to face with the bastard right now, I would joyfully kill him!''

Moira stroked her hair. "Calm down, love. Anger and hate won't change a thing.''

"But why, mother? *Why?* Why didn't he let us know he was alive?''

"I don't know, Desiree. I don't know . . .'' Then with great determination she declared, "One thing I do know. Once we return to Maryland, Bradford Taylor is going to be sorry he didn't die at the hands of the Chinese!''

Chapter Twenty-two

Aunt Tillie and her sister Maud were long dead, and the old Maryland homestead had been sold by Maud's daughters, who were now living in Chicago. Upon their arrival in Washington, Moira and Desiree were invited to stay at the Collins's elegant town house at Cameron Mews in Alexandria. Wendy greeted them alone at the railroad depot. The sisters embraced with tears in their eyes while Desiree, standing awkwardly to the side, contemplated the emotional reunion.

"Susan would have been here, too, but she's not well," Wendy explained. "Nothing serious; she should be up and around within the week. And Carl is in Indiana. He's a major stockholder in some of those steel mills where all the rioting is taking place." She addressed her coachman: "Put the luggage in the carriage, Randy." For the first time Wendy became aware of Desiree. Her eyes widened. "I don't believe it! You must be Desiree!" She rushed to Desiree and embraced her. "I keep thinking of you as the little tyke in the tintypes your mother sent me from China. You're a grown woman! Mercy!"

Desiree smiled without enthusiasm. "It's wonderful to meet you, Aunt Wendy. Mother has told us so much about you and Aunt Susan. But you have seen Pat, of course. He wrote how hospitable you and Aunt Susan have been to him since he's been attending the military academy.''

''All right, Randy has taken care of your bags. Let's start back for Alexandria.''

Moira did not broach the subject most on her mind until they were on their way. She'd been both eagerly anticipating and dreading this moment of truth since the day they had learned that Brad was alive. There was only one way to approach the matter, she concluded: bluntly!

''You say Carl is in Indiana, Wendy. Is Brad still commanding the federal troops there?''

Wendy averted her face and stared out the side window of the carriage. She refrained from speaking for a long time.

''Well, Wendy,'' Moira said quietly. ''How long have you known that Brad was alive?''

''Carl has known from the day Brad arrived back in the States. But I didn't learn about it until a few years ago. In fact, it was Patrick who informed me.''

''Patrick?'' Moira and Desiree expostulated in unison.

''Yes, apparently Brad went up to visit him at West Point his first year at the academy. Pat wouldn't speak to him. In fact he tried to attack Brad and had to be restrained. He would have been expelled for attempting to assault an officer, but Brad interceded for him. He's made no further attempts to contact Pat, although he has written him letters, which Pat never answers.''

''Why didn't Carl confide in you?''

''Because Brad asked him not to. It's the one favor Pat granted to him, also: He was not to let on to you that he was alive. Last time we saw Pat he told us that as far as he is concerned, Brad is dead and that you and Desiree would be better off believing it was so. If your General Flynn had not been killed, you probably would never have found out.''

''I realize that, but there remains the central issue. Why didn't Brad want us to know he was alive?''

Wendy finally faced her. ''You may find this hard to believe, but aside from his considerable character faults, many of which Carl shares with him—avarice, ruthlessness, unconscionable ambition—there is a streak of altruism in Bradford Taylor."

"Rubbish! He's an unfeeling, unprincipled cad!"

"Mother!" Desiree clutched at Moira's arm. "Remember when Pat and I were little? At bedtime you'd read *Enoch Arden* to us? About the seaman who had been stranded on a desert island for years before he was rescued. And when he returned home, he discovered his wife had remarried and was happy and prosperous. So he left without revealing himself and died of a broken heart."

"Oh, Brad is no Enoch Arden, Moira," Wendy said. "He was not about to die of a broken heart. However, there is an element of truth in what Desiree is implying. He learned that you had married General Flynn and that you and the children were happy and prosperous, a real family."

"It doesn't make any sense! I mean, how much could he have known about my feelings, the children's feelings, half-way around the globe?"

Wendy let out her breath in a painful sigh. "He knew because General Flynn told him about your idyllic life and marriage; Flynn entreated him not to reveal that he was alive. It would have branded you as a scarlet woman living in sin. It would have destroyed Flynn's career; the British army is intolerant about scandal like that. Yes, believe it or not, Brad made the noble sacrifice—probably the only one he has ever made of such magnitude. He gave you and the children up for purely unselfish motives."

With one shock upon another, and each one more devastating than the one preceding it, Moira was aghast. "Sean knew that Brad was alive? I don't believe it!"

"Nevertheless it's true. As soon as Brad returned to America, he telegraphed you in Calcutta. Apparently General Flynn intercepted the message. There were numerous exchanges between them, and finally Brad made the momentous decision. 'It's best to let sleeping dogs lie,' was what he said."

Moira pressed her fingers against her throbbing temples. "It's too incredible! I'm sorry we came back here."

"No, Mother, no!" Desiree cried. Tears were streaming down her face. "Daddy is alive, that's all that matters. Oh, where is he, Aunt Wendy?"

"At West Point. They're holding commencement exercises three days from now. Even if Patrick won't acknowledge him, Brad wants to see him graduate."

Desiree clutched her mother's arm. "We must go there at once! I know that once Pat sees all of us together as a family once more, he'll forgive Daddy for his deception."

"I don't know. I've got to have time to think it out. Our appearance might complicate the situation between Pat and his father even more."

"No, Mother, I have never been more convinced of anything in my life. Daddy and Pat will reconcile their differences if we're all together. Another thing—Pat isn't exactly lily-white either. He knew Daddy was alive and withheld the information from us. In the matter of deception, he willingly allied himself with Daddy."

"You're right about that. The Taylor men all dance to a different piper; they make their own rules. Patrick worshipped the ground that Brad walked on, wanted to be just like his father. Well, it seems the boy got his wish," she said ironically. "As the twig is bent, so grows the tree."

"Then it's settled. We go to West Point as soon as possible," Desiree said, her eyes dancing with excitement.

Moira patted her knee. "You're right, dear. I suppose we don't have any other choice."

Moira and Desiree checked into the West Point Hotel at five o'clock the following afternoon. Moira asked the desk clerk: "Is there a General Bradford Taylor registered here?"

He put on his spectacles and consulted the registry. "Let me see . . . hmmmm . . . Yes, here it is. General Taylor arrived yesterday morning. Do you wish to have him paged, madam?"

"I think not; not just yet. My daughter and I have been traveling on trains forever, it seems. From San Francisco to Chicago to New York, then to Washington. And now from Washington to West Point. All we have on our minds now are baths and a nap. We'll inquire about the general later on.''

"As you wish.'' He tapped the bell to summon a bell-hop. "Luggage to Room 315, lad.''

After they had bathed, Moira and Desiree lay down on the suite's twin beds and fell asleep almost immediately. The girl awoke first; the room was dark. She lit the lamp on the nighttable and swung her feet to the floor. She leaned over and shook Moira.

"Mother, we've overslept. It's after eight.''

"Mercy, it seems as if I just closed my eyes. I'm too exhausted to eat supper. What about you?''

"I wasn't thinking about supper. I was thinking about Daddy. Don't you want to let him know that we're here?''

Moira pondered the question, stroking her throat to ease a rasping tightness. At last she said, "To tell the truth, dear, I don't think I'm up to the ordeal tonight. Confrontations like this are best left to a new day.''

"What a quaint way you have of expressing it—ordeal, confrontation. It has a hostile ring to it.''

"Not hostile; defensive is a more apt term. It isn't every day a woman comes face to face with a husband whom she had believed dead for more than ten years.'' She pulled the covers over her head and went back to sleep.

Moira awoke at dawn the following morning. After her bath she roused Desiree. "Rise and shine, my dear. We have a momentous day facing us. What do you plan to wear to Patrick's graduation tomorrow?''

"I haven't given it any thought. The weather is so warm for this time of year.''

"I believe I'll wear my cotton chamois popover dress. The one with the butterflies and the placet front,'' Moira said. "Why don't you wear your sundress? It's terribly flattering to your lovely shoulders.''

"Good idea, but now for my bath.'' Desiree got out of bed and padded barefoot into the bathroom. With pride Moira observed her lithe, sensual body. The fluid grace of the perfectly proportioned form incited a distant twinge of nostalgia in Moira, an element of *déjà vu*. Twenty-one— had she ever been that young? Yes, seeing Desiree, nubile, vibrant, steeped in the sensuality of youth, she was, indeed, seeing herself.

"The time has come," she said to Desiree when they were finished dressing. "Time to confront your father. Damnit! Why do I keep using that word?"

"It's all right, Mother. I'm so jittery, my hands are trembling and my heart feels as though it's about to burst."

Moira went down to the desk. "I am Mrs. Flynn," she said to the clerk. "I want to get in touch with General Taylor as soon as possible."

"Yes, Mrs. Flynn. General Taylor just went into the dining room. Would you like to leave a message for him?"

"Don't disturb him until he's had his breakfast. Then inform him that his presence is requested in Suite 315. Thank you."

Both women started out of their chairs at the rapping on the door. Moira smoothed her skirt, inhaled deeply and walked purposefully to the door and flung it open. She felt as if she were looking at Lazarus returned from the dead. Brad Taylor was even handsomer in middle age than as a sinewy, brash youth. His brown hair was graying at the temples and he was a little thinner. But he had the same impudent green eyes that were Desiree's heritage, though the glint of lechery was less pronounced now and the cleft in his chin was deeper in his fleshier face.

The two were rigid statues staring at each other, unable to speak. It was left for Desiree to end the deadlock. She rushed past Moira and embraced him, tears flowing down her cheeks and staining his handsomely tailored gray pinstripe suit.

"Daddy, Daddy, Daddy, this is a dream come true, a miracle."

"I—I—I—. . . a loss for words . . ." he faltered.

"It's a fact, I don't know what to say." And now the tears were streaming down his own face.

Moira went to him then, and the three of them were melded together in Brad's embrace, one arm around each of them, his face smothered in their perfumed hair.

When he regained his composure, he spoke, and the pain in his voice was a knife piercing Moira's heart. "A loss for words, yes, that's the rub. The thing is, there is so much to say, and I don't have an inkling where to begin." He shook his head and walked them into the room, then closed the door. He let go of Desiree and Moira and stepped back, regarding them with adoration. "A night hasn't gone by that I haven't dreamed of this moment. This impossible dream. My beloved wife and my darling daughter. I still don't believe it." He covered his eyes with his hand. "You must forgive this unmanly display of emotion. I'm a pretty poor example of a soldier."

Moira went to him and put her arms around his neck, lifting her face to him. "It's my impression that you are more of a man this moment—a finer man, a finer soldier— than you have ever been in your life. Like vintage wine, men and women, too, mellow with age."

They kissed, tenderly at first and then with a mounting ardor that caused Desiree to turn away. "I think you two should be alone to share this intimate scene. If you'll excuse me, I'll go to the dining room and have some breakfast."

Both Brad and Moira reached out to her. "It is a highly intimate moment," Brad said softly, "and you are part of it, my dear Desiree. After all, you are the creation of the most intimate experience that your mother and I have ever shared."

"And now it's time you tell us, Brad, what prompted this Enoch Arden charade." They sat down, Moira and Desiree on the settee and Brad in a leather armchair facing them across the coffee table.

He lit a cigarette and stared at the fiery coal; she saw his hands were unsteady. He began to speak, slowly and deliberately. "This is probably the most difficult task I have ever been faced with in my life. Baring my soul, exposing my shortcomings, especially to you, my daughter— that's going to be the hardest part. You and Patrick—as children you idealized me, so naturally your disillusionment is bound to be more traumatic than what your mother feels. After all, she knew me better than anyone else; she was aware of my flawed character. In those days my obsession for influence and power came before anything else in life." He reached across the table and took one of Desiree's hands. "Yes, it's true, my sweet. It even came before my family.

"I've done many things in my life that I'm not proud of. Your mother knows about them. I don't expect her to forgive me for my transgressions, but at least she will understand. As for you and Patrick, I expect neither forgiveness nor understanding. All I ask is that you try to keep an objective perspective. Loathe me if you must, as does Patrick, but at least listen to what I have to say and then judge me as you will." He looked at Moira. "How much does the child know about why I was arrested in China and sentenced to die?"

"No more than the official version: that you were involved in espionage work for the United States. Desiree and Patrick idolized you for dying a hero's death in the service of your country. This is why Pat is so adamant about not granting you forgiveness."

Brad smiled the roguish smile that had won her heart long ago on the frontier. "The idol has feet of clay; he can't accept it."

"Maybe after Desiree and I talk to him and explain . . . you know that deep inside he still loves you; the scars of his disillusionment will heal."

"No, I won't accept your intercession. This is an issue that can only be resolved by Patrick and me. But let me get on with my story. The official version of my arrest by the Peking government was true. I was engaged in espionage work for the United States and the other Western delegations there. Tz'u Hsi, the dowager empress, kept the Ch'ing dynasty in power by crushing all her political opponents. Anyone who favored land reforms, political reforms, industrialization, was branded a traitor and executed. For years secret opposition to her tyranny had been fomenting within the elite mandarin class in the Forbidden City. One of the highest ranked members of the loyal opposition was Tz'u Hsi's niece, Sun Ying. My assignment that time I went to Tientsin was to meet with some of China's most powerful warlords, along with Sun Ying and the Peking mandarins, who were sympathetic to the cause of deposing the dowager empress. Our plans were thwarted the night before the meeting, when Peking's secret military police arrested me in Sun Ying's bedchamber.''

Desiree's green eyes bored into his own. "And what were you doing in Sun Ying's bedroom, Daddy?''

"Does it really matter after all these years?''

"No more questions about that, Desiree,'' Moira said. "No, Brad, it doesn't matter after all these years. That chapter is closed. Let's be honest with ourselves, my girl, you and I are not above reproach. As Saint John said: He who is without sin, let him cast the first stone . . . As it turns out now, Sean Flynn and I were living in sin for years.''

"As you say, Moira, the chapter is closed,'' Brad said. "And now we embark on a new chapter. What about it, my dear—do you think that you and I could put our lives together again? You know, I've never stopped loving you.''

Moira touched a hand to one temple and shut her eyes. "I don't know, Brad. Right now I am incapable of making any responsible decision about anything. All I can cope with today is seeing my son graduate tomorrow.''

He got up and walked around the table, put an arm about her shoulders and kissed the top of her head. "Seeing *our* son graduate,'' he said softly. He put the free arm around Desiree's shoulders and kissed her head as well. "The two most beautiful women in the world, and they are both mine.''

Chapter Twenty-three

The older Patrick Taylor became, the more he resembled his father. "It's uncanny," Moira said. "You're the image of your father, the first time I laid eyes on him."

"I'd just as soon we leave Father out of this. I don't want to spoil my supper." They were eating in the hotel dining room the night before commencement exercises.

Moira and Desiree entreated with him, to no avail. "Don't you see, dear, that he could have disrupted our entire lives in India if he had come forward? Out of gratitude and deference to Sean Flynn, he made the supreme sacrifice."

"You buy that malarkey, Mother," Pat said icily, "but not me. Don't you understand, all these years he's deprived Desiree and me of what is every child's birthright. To have a father! To love a father. To be loved by a father. To grow up with the strong sense of belonging that only a father can provide."

"Major Flynn provided you with all those things," she reminded him.

"For God's sake, Mother, it's not the same thing at all and you know it! Uncle Sean was a prince, but he was not the father I worshipped and grieved for for more years than you ever realized." His bitterness was even more intense. "And all the while I was grieving, that selfish bastard was gallivanting around the world, living it up!"

"Hardly that."

"Mother, he was always a womanizer, even when you were together."

"How would you know a thing like that, Pat?"

His face was livid. "Because he told me. I guess he felt that confession was good for the soul. He expected me to absolve him from his past sins. I almost punched him. I wish I had."

"You would have been expelled from the academy but for his intercession."

"Too bad I wasn't. I don't need any favors from his kind."

"You don't mean that. You are about to achieve your life's ambition. Just think, tomorrow you'll be Second Lieutenant Patrick Taylor."

"We're so proud of you, Pat," Desiree said, squeezing his arm. "Imagine, class valedictorian!"

"We're all proud of you, son," Moira said, her eyes misting over. "Your father more than anyone else. Can't you find any charity in your heart toward him?"

"None."

"Then at least promise you will be civil to him at the ceremonies. Please, I beg of you, for my sake, and for your sister's."

Patrick put down his napkin and fork. "All right, for your sakes, I'll be civil. Now the two of you must excuse me. I've got to put some finishing touches on my speech." He bent and kissed his mother and sister on their cheeks. "You two really are a sight for sore eyes. Four years away from home. God, how I missed you."

"As we missed you." She stared at him, her expression firm. "As your father has missed the three of us for so many more years."

He regarded her with a mixture of tolerance and impatience. "You really never give up, do you, Mother?"

"No, I don't. And I'm not done with you yet, young man."

He laughed. "It's a lovely night. Why don't you walk me back to my barracks, and I'll give you a tour of the campus?"

"No thank you, dear. I've had a tiresome day. I think I'll hop into bed and write a letter to Bea. But you go ahead, Desiree."

"I think I will."

They parted in the lobby, and Pat and Desiree strolled through the West Point grounds, all manicured and spit and polish like the cadets themselves. "This picturesque thoroughfare is known as Flirtation Walk," Pat said. At the end of the pathway there was a stone oval dominated by an impressive statue of an Indian, green and moldy with age.

"That's old Tecumseh, patron saint of young lovers. Many a kiss has been stolen in the old lad's shadow. See that disapproving look on his face?"

"And I'll bet you have stolen your share of them, brother," she said.

"Aye." He nodded.

"Both the Callahans and the Taylors are a hot-blooded lot. I'll wager many of the maidens bussed here also lost their most precious possession."

Patrick laughed. "You might say that."

"How is your love life these days?"

"Well, I've been seeing quite a bit of my roommate's sister, Miss Candice Mannix."

She wrinkled up her nose. "Candice? She sounds like a bit of a snob."

"On the contrary, she's very much like you. I know you're going to hit it off."

"You sound exceedingly serious about Miss Candice."

"I could be; I'm not sure. Right now I've got to get my life in order. Did I tell you and Mother that my first tour of duty will be in Alaska?"

"Alaska? Heavens to be, I thought all they had in Alaska were Eskimos and polar bears."

"Word has it that large reserves of gold have been discovered up there, and that before the century ends Alaska will be the California of the north. By the way, little sister, how is *your* love life?"

"Not as active as I'd like," she told him candidly.

"Spoken like a true Callahan—" He paused. "And a Taylor. God knows our old man has been a randy sort all his life."

"Don't leave Mother out of it, lad. Did you know that she and Uncle Sean had an affair before Daddy disappeared?"

"You can't be serious. I don't believe it."

"It's the truth, nevertheless. I heard them laughing and joking about it once; I was eavesdropping, you might say."

"Well, it's water under the bridge now," he said with obvious discomfort.

"Yes, it is." And she slyly added, "That's what Mother and I have been trying to drum into your thick skull. What is past is past, and there's no point in chewing on it continuously like a dog on a dry, bare bone."

He did not respond at once. Then he took her elbow and said; "I think I'd better walk you back to the hotel."

No one could have asked for a better day to hold outdoor commencement exercises. The azure sky was cloudless, and a gentle breeze blowing in off the Hudson River moderated the midday heat of the sun. Moira, Brad and Desiree sat in the first row of spectators, due to Patrick's highest ranking in the graduating class. His valedictory address dealt with patriotism, loyalty, honor and duty, but the military theme was a showcase for his main thesis, the interrelationships among human beings in the mainstream of life. In his concluding sentence Patrick glared over the podium directly at his father:

". . . for in denigrating our fellow man and woman, we denigrate ourselves the most of all. There is more implicit in our class motto than a military code: 'We will not lie or cheat or steal nor sanction disloyalty, betrayal and deception, nor will we tolerate such infamies in any others.' For my classmates and myself, I want to thank all of you ladies and gentlemen for being here today and sharing with us this very special moment. God bless you all and God bless the United States of America.''

The applause was deafening.

Brad grimaced and muttered to Moira, ''He put that parting shot right between my eyes, eh?'' Neither Moira nor Desiree made any reply.

After the last diploma had been awarded, the cadets, now second lieutenants, let go with the traditional cheer, and their caps sailed high into the sky, darkening the air above the spectators. Then the graduates mingled with the visitors, seeking out family and friends.

The awkwardness of the Taylor family reunion was ameliorated by the fact that Patrick brought along his roommate Gerald Mannix along with Gerald's sister and parents. Anson Mannix and his wife Dorothy were a distinguished couple; he had once been the American ambassador to Spain. Moira could sense Brad's ears perk up.

The smell of power excited him as it always had; he had achieved a measure of maturity and temperance, but it was a forlorn hope to imagine that the leopard would ever change its spots. He immediately took Mannix aside and interrogated him about current foreign affairs, flattering the diplomat's ego with his old finesse.

Desiree's attention focused solely on the younger Mannixes. She approved at once of Candice Mannix, an opinion that would be reinforced as the girls came to know each other more intimately. Candice was a tall, large-boned girl, yet she was absolutely feminine and seductive; Desiree was attentive to the way she stroked her brother's palm with her index finger as they held hands. She had a broad face with high cheekbones and wide-set gray eyes, and her mouth was full and sensual. Her brown hair, streaked with blond from the sun, was tousled by the wind.

Patrick's roommate attracted a different sort of attention. Jerry was of medium height, no taller than his sister, but he radiated masculinity. Broad of shoulder and chest, slim waisted and slim hipped, he had muscular thighs that strained the fabric of his uniform. He was not handsome in the same way as her father and brother. But his rugged features—his jaw was too large and he had a knob on the end of his nose—and his infectious grin and mischievous blue eyes appealed to her immensely. And his close-cropped curly red hair was of a shade that matched her own.

His handshake was firm and genuine. "Well, when old Pat here bragged about his lovely sister, I figured he was trying to pass her off on some misguided bloke the way I passed Candice off onto him. Now that I've met you, it's clear he understated his case. I think I'm in love."

His sister chortled: "Watch out for him, Desiree. He's a shameless rake. Next thing he'll be inviting you to stroll down Flirtation Walk tonight. *After dark*, if you grasp my meaning."

Desiree laughed. "Don't worry about me, Candy. I've coped with his sort before."

Jerry linked his arm with hers. "Matter of fact, I'm not waiting until tonight. Come on, gorgeous, let's shake this mob and I'll show you the sights."

"Speaking of tonight," Patrick declared, "Jerry and I and a bunch of the fellows and their girls are going into town for a celebration. Mind if I stick you with Jerry as a date, Desiree? He can't latch onto a girl on his own."

"I'd be delighted." She looked at Jerry, her eyes dancing. "And I'll wager he doesn't ever have trouble finding a date."

He rolled his eyes skyward. "Truth is, I've been saving myself for you all these years."

As an afterthought Patrick addressed his parents and the Mannixes. "Of course, you are all welcome to join the party."

"Not on your life, Pat," Brad said jocularly. "I've been to enough soldiers' bashes in my life. They're for the young and indestructible . . . Besides, Anson and Dorothy are going to join your mother and me for dinner at the hotel."

Moira smiled cryptically, noting that Brad was resting one hand on Anson Mannix's shoulder in a spirit of comaraderie. And possessiveness!

Chapter Twenty-four

After a late supper the Mannixes retired to their room, and Brad saw Moira up to her suite. She invited him to come in for a nightcap.

"If you don't mind port," she said. "I find a glass or two before bedtime is an excellent sedative."

"When we were together, you never needed a sedative to put you to sleep," he said.

Moira ignored the remark and went to fetch the wine and two stem glasses. She tarried with her back turned until the flush had dissipated from her cheeks.

Stop behaving like a schoolgirl! she chided herself.

He sat on the settee beside her and poured the wine. "What do you think of the Mannixes?" he asked.

"Quite nice people. You certainly hit it off with Anson."

"Interesting chap, and he really knows his way around the political arena. Did you know he's up for an important post at the Court of Saint James's? Patrick could do a lot worse than have them for in-laws. Not to mention the fact that Candice seems a lovely and intelligent girl."

"I like her a good deal, and so does Desiree. Yes, from the way Pat looks at her and she at him, I believe that they are truly in love."

He put down his wineglass and put an arm casually across the back of the settee. "They remind me of you and me at that age." And his hand came down gently on her shoulder. "I've never stopped loving you, darling."

"Brad, please . . ."

"No, Moira, you're going to hear me out. What I told you yesterday—it was all true. I got what I deserved in China. Life is a high-stakes crap shoot, and I'm a high roller."

"A euphemism for 'con man.' "

"All right, so I'm a con man. However, all this is irrelevant to what I'm leading up to. Moira, darling, what do you say to you and me picking up the pieces?"

"You must be out of your mind." She tried to get up, but he restrained her.

"No, it's the only sane and logical thing to do. Look, I stayed out of your life all these years because that was the only honorable and civilized thing for me to do. You and Flynn were happy, and I had no right to act the spoiler. God knows I've spoiled enough things as it is. Another thing . . ." He took her chin in his hand and turned her face to meet his intense gaze. "That woman in Washington— I don't even remember her name, that's how much she meant to me. Yes, I was unfaithful to you, but not because I was dissatisfied with you or with our marriage. Moira, there isn't another woman in this world who excites me the way you do; there never will be. Sun Ying was just another means to an end."

"And in your lexicon the end always justifies the means. Brad, let me go, and please leave immediately."

"As soon as you hear me out. I felt like hell when I heard about Flynn's death, believe me. He was a fine husband to you and a father to Pat and Desiree. May his soul rest in peace. Nevertheless, I think it's time you give up this holier-than-thou charade. True, I'm no angel, but neither are you. Don't you know that I was quite aware that you were having an affair with Sean before I was caught with my pants down in Sun Ying's boudoir?"

Moira was disoriented and flustered. "Who told you a ridiculous thing like that?"

"Flynn; who else?" And now he turned his gaze away

from her. "You see, when he begged me not to destroy his life with you, he resorted to desperate measures to hold on to you. He told me about your affair. I can't say I blame you. I was a bloody cad, neglecting you. Flynn was always appealing to women, and he worshipped the ground you walked on. It was natural that you would turn to him for comfort, solace and passion. The past is behind us. Let's forget it. Start anew."

"A new chapter," she mused.

"Is it so unthinkable, really? I love you as deeply as I ever did, and my instincts tell me that you still care for me."

"I don't know . . ."

Unexpectedly, he embraced her and kissed her full on the mouth. She struggled, but her strength and will were no match for his. And then strength and will deserted her altogether, and she went limp in his arms. A warm sweet lassitude was pervading her flesh, along with the familiar tingling in all her nerve endings; the warmth kindling in her loins; the blazing rage of need and desire so long deprived. Moira whimpered, slipped a hand behind his head, drew him to her fiercely. His tongue invaded her mouth, titillating her tongue. And now she knew there was no hope of averting the ultimate carnal invasion. His hand slipped beneath her skirt and caressed the inside of her thighs, higher and higher, until his fingers reached inside her chemise and found their goal.

"As long as we're going to do this, let's do it right," she said. "Come into the bedroom."

As they undressed, it struck Moira with an air of wonder that what was happening felt as natural to her as if they had never been separated. They came together with the grace and symmetry of a perfect sphere. The old Grecian myth flashed through her mind—man and woman, two halves of a single entity, each seeking his and her better half.

The old magic was as powerful as it had ever been, the indescribable ecstasy, one exquisite contraction after another, his throbbing spasms threatening to tear her asunder. And then the best part of all; the heavenly bliss in the aftermath; peace, contentment, serenity.

At last Brad said to Moira, "All these lost years, all that we've been missing."

It was on the tip of her tongue to remind him that neither of them had led celibate lives during those lost years, but she held back. The moment was too beautiful to spoil.

"I think we had better get dressed and return to the sitting room," Moira observed. "Desiree should be getting back soon."

"Damn!" he cursed. "I don't want to leave you ever again."

She nuzzled his ear. "Be content with what we've enjoyed tonight. We must proceed at a slow pace, particularly for Patrick's sake."

Brad was irate. "The hell with Patrick. I've taken enough of his abuse since he's been at West Point! Another thing— under the eyes of the law, you and I are still man and wife. I have every right to sleep with my own wife."

"Hush . . ." She placed a hand over his mouth. "Please abide by my wishes, dear, and let me make haste slowly."

He sighed. "As you wish, my love."

They dressed, and not a moment too soon. They were on the settee having a second glass of wine when Desiree arrived back at the suite, accompanied by young Mannix.

"How was your party?" Moira inquired.

"Wonderful," Desiree said. "And it turned out to be a double celebration. Pat and Candice made it final tonight. They are officially engaged."

"That's wonderful," Brad enthused to Gerald. "Your sister is a lovely girl, and I'm certain she'll make our Patrick a wonderful wife."

"Thank you, sir," was the boy's reply. "And my parents and I couldn't be happier. Pat and I have been as close as brothers these past few years. It's been a long day, so I think I'll be on my way and let you people get some rest."

They said their good nights, and Desiree walked Gerald

to the door. In the hallway he turned and winked at her, framed in the doorway. "Care to make it a double ceremony?"

She arched her eyebrows. "Is this a serious proposal?"

"Quite serious. I told you I fell in love the instant I set eyes on you."

"Flattery will get you everywhere."

She was keenly aware of his hot-eyed gaze pausing at her bosom, then sliding down her body. "Everywhere," he echoed. "I have abundant aspirations in that regard. Good night, my sweet." He threw her a kiss, and she responded in kind.

Desiree shut the door and joined her mother and father. "Well, how was your party?"

"It was delightful," Moira said. "The Mannixes are very charming people. You and Gerald appear to get along quite well."

"Yes . . . As a matter of fact, he's proposed to me."

Moira and Brad exchanged startled looks. "And I thought *I* was a fast worker when I was his age," Brad said.

"You were indeed," Moira said, recalling the day he had intruded on her bath at the water hole in Texas. She yawned. "I don't want to be rude, Brad, but I really must get some sleep."

"To be sure." He rose and kissed her on the cheek and then kissed Desiree. "Good night, my darlings. I'll see you both in the morning." He stared fixedly at Moira. "And you will give serious thought to what we were discussing?"

"You can depend on it. Good night."

When he had departed, Desiree inquired: "What did Daddy mean about giving serious thought to something you were discussing?"

Moira was frank. "Your father wants us to resume our lives together."

The girl's eyes were radiant. "Mother! That's simply marvelous! Oh, I'm so happy for you. It's something out of a fairy tale." She rushed to Moira and embraced her.

"Not so fast, young lady. I haven't made up my mind."

"Don't be coy, Mother. You know you're still mad about him. I can see it in your eyes when you look at him. Of course you'll accept. After all, you still are husband and wife, legally."

"That's what Brad said, but there's more to it than legalities. I'm going to be honest with you, Desiree. Yes, I was physically attracted to your father from the start. And you're right, I still am. Our sex life was something very special, but there is more to a solid marital relationship than that."

Desiree laughed. "It doesn't hurt, Mother." Her insight was uncanny as she regarded her mother mischievously. "Matter of fact, it wouldn't surprise me if the two of you had a rather special 'party' tonight after you left the Mannixes."

The two bright spots across Moira's cheekbones betrayed her. "Don't be flip with me, young lady."

"Come on, Mother, I'm a woman, and it's clear that you and I share the same passionate nature. You've never asked me, but I don't mind telling you that I have not been a virginal maiden for some years now. In fact, that's why I may accept Gerald's proposal. It's a real encumbrance for an unmarried woman to satisfy her sexual appetite, even one as liberated as I am. I feel the urge to establish a lasting relationship with a desirable man. And if I am any judge of men, I think that Gerald should suit my requirements very well indeed."

Moira laughed and shook her head. "You are incorrigible and thoroughly wanton."

"Yes, I am, and so are you; don't deny it. Wasn't it Abraham Lincoln who said: 'A good wife should be a cook in the kitchen, a lady in the parlor and a whore in the bedroom'?"

"There is a logic to that, I must admit." A shadow passed over her face. "There is one big handicap to your father and me reuniting—the bitterness that Patrick harbors against him."

"That will pass, Mother. As a matter of fact, I thought

Patrick behaved with great civility toward Daddy at the graduation ceremony.''

''Civility, but that was all. He did it as a favor to you and me. I don't think Patrick would ever forgive me if I went back to your father.''

''That's absurd! Besides, this is your life we're talking about. Pat's going off to Alaska with Candice. God only knows how much a part of his life will ever be shared with us. You've said it yourself so many times; a soldier has no roots.''

''I suppose you have a point.''

''Then it's settled. You and Daddy are going to reconcile?''

Moira's laughter was dry as ashes. ''Nothing is ever settled, my dear. You'll learn that soon enough. Sean and I used to tell ourselves that. There are no endings, only new beginnings.''

Chapter Twenty-five

March 1, 1901

Dear Wendy,

It came as a terrible shock to learn of Carl's death. As you know, Brad was extremely fond of him, as well as being grateful for all the favors Carl bestowed on him. It has been almost two and a half years since the Spanish forces surrendered at Manila, terminating the Spanish-American War. Little did we think when we arrived here as part of the occupation army that the real war had only commenced. After Admiral Dewey's smashing victory over the Spanish fleet at Manila Bay, the American troops were hailed as conquering heroes by the Filipinos. That soon changed when Emilio Aguinaldo, the brilliant leader of the insurrectionists, discovered that the United States was not about to grant the Philippine Islands complete independence. Not only has this tragic conflict taken five thousand American lives and twenty thousand Filipino lives, in addition to thousands of wounded, not to mention the millions of dollars it is costing the American taxpayer, but it has divided our great nation such as it has not been divided since the Civil War.

On the one hand, we have the Imperialists, who espouse that by liberating the Islands, the United States has acquired the responsibility to ensure the future of this impoverished, uneducated, vulnerable population by making it a protectorate of the United States. This is a feeble excuse and cover-up for the true motivation, as expressed by Senator Albert Beveridge, who in a recent speech on the Senate floor declared: "The power that rules the Pacific in the twentieth century is the power that will rule the world. . . . Insofar as the Philippines are concerned, that power will be the American Republic now and forever more. . . ." As greatly as I abhor colonialism, I must accede that there is a measure of truth to his claim; a goodly portion of the Filipinos do favor annexation by the United States, for, as Brad points out, the traditional avaricious colonial powers—Britain, France, Germany, yes, and even Spain itself—still maintain constant vigilance with their fleets over this stricken land, waiting to pounce on the defenseless Philippines like slavering wolves if the United States withdraws its troops and navy.

On the other hand, there are the anti-Imperialists, whose principal spokesman is historian Henry Adams, and who rail that to deny freedom to any nation is contrary to the ideals and morality upon which the United States was founded. In his latest newspaper editorial Adams posed the painful query: "Must we slaughter a million or two Filipinos so that we can provide them with the comforts of flannel petticoats and electric railways?"

We have been encountering a similar dilemma in the Hawaiian Islands. "Damned if we do and damned if we don't," as Brad expresses it.

And on the subject of Hawaii, Patrick and his family are stationed on the island of Maui. Both Brad and I are very proud of him. He was with General Chaffee's army that captured Peking and crushed the Boxer Rebellion. He was twice wounded and awarded *the Silver Star for heroism as well as being promoted to major. Patrick and his wife, Candice, have a daughter, Marsha, five, and are expecting their second child just after the New Year.*

Desiree and her husband, Captain Gerald Mannix, are with the American occupation army in Cuba. Gerald served with Colonel Theodore Roosevelt there during the war and was a participant at the Battle of San Juan Hill. Their children, Daniel and Anson— named after his father—are almost identical in age to Patrick and Candice's.

Tonight General Arthur MacArthur and his sister are hosting a party for his senior officers. His wife, Mary, doting mother that she is, resides at West Point, where her son Douglas is attending the United States Military Academy. I have the distinct impression from certain veiled hints by Brad that this affair is more meaningful than an ordinary social function. Perhaps it has something to do with the elusive rebel chieftain Aguinaldo. He is the monolith around which the revolution revolves. If he were to be captured it would shatter the whole revolutionary movement . . .

General Arthur MacArthur was closeted in the study with his two chief aides, General Bradford Taylor and General Frederick (Fighting Fred) Funston.

MacArthur, as Brad liked to describe him, "was born with a bayonet up his arse and the Medal of Honor on his chest." He was indeed the consummate soldier. A handsome man, regal in his demeanor, with wavy brown hair and brown piercing eyes that could reduce a subordinate to jelly, he sported sideburns and a dashing mustache. It was rumored among his senior officers that the general harbored a secret resentment toward his son Douglas for commanding more attention from his mother than did her husband. Once, after too many brandies, he confided to Brad:

"Dougie boy is a snob and a prig and a goddamned

mama's boy. Did you know that during his plebe year, a bunch of cadets beat the shit out of him? Bully for them, the arrogant bastard deserved it!'' An expression of perplexity darkened his face. ''Thing of it is, Doug refused to rat on them, even under threat of expulsion for refusing to cooperate with President McKinley's special committee to investigate the mistreatment of cadets at the Point. He just might have the makings of a good soldier in spite of his mother.''

MacArthur, on the night of the party, was mellow and full of enthusiasm. ''Brad,'' he said to General Taylor, ''our boy genius here, Fighting Fred, has come up with a plan to take Aguinaldo that is so outrageous, so bold, so audacious, so perilous that it just might work. Before I give my blessing to it, I want your opinion. Fred, the floor is yours.''

Unlike MacArthur and Taylor, Funston did not have the classic military bearing. He looked more like a tough, grizzled top sergeant than a general. He swigged down his brandy and shoved the glass toward his commander:

''If you please, sir, a refill to wet my whistle.'' The request obliged, he stood up and began to pace. ''You'll recall, Brad, that back in February we picked up that bunch of rebels who were carrying coded dispatches?''

''Sure, the Colon Magdalo papers. We broke the code; it's Aguinaldo's code name, and the dispatches were directed to the rebel commander in central Luzon, appointing new officers and directing them to report to Aguinaldo's secret headquarters.''

''Exactly . . . Now, the message did not contain the location of those headquarters, but it said that the bearer of the message *did* know the site and would lead them there.''

''Yes, a chap by the name of Segismondo. But these people are fanatically loyal to Aguinaldo. This fellow Segismondo would cheerfully die before he'd betray his chieftain. Once we even put him up in front of a bogus firing squad, and he wouldn't open his mouth.''

Funston smiled, looking deservedly smug. ''Well, he's

changed his mind. He's finally revealed to military intelligence that Aguinaldo's headquarters are in the small village of Palanan on the northeast coast of Luzon. He's got fifty-odd security guards with him; wants to keep a low profile.''

Brad was astonished. "My God, I can't believe it. We're finally going to hook the big fish.''

"It's not all that cut and dried," MacArthur said. He refilled the three glasses and lit his pipe. "We can't just lead a cavalry charge up there like Teddy did at San Juan. Aguinaldo and his men would fight to the last man. We cannot afford to have him die as a martyr. It would set back the campaign months, years. You know how these fanatics respond to a noble cause. No, we've got to capture him alive, treat him with the same civility and respect we'd afford any other enemy commander, and persuade him to sit down and negotiate with the United States.''

"That's a mighty tall order," Brad said without enthusiasm.

"It damn well is, but now listen to Fred's extravagant plan for how we can pull it off.''

Funston outlined his plan: "You know the Maccabebee tribesmen have been feuding with Aguinaldo's faction for years. The 'Little Macs' are staunchly on our side. Now, instead of sending our own troops into that jungle—we'd be spotted by their coast watchers miles off and give Aguinaldo still another chance to escape—I intend to enlist a force of Macs and dress them up in the uniforms of the insurrectionists. Now, here's the key to the scheme. The Macs will be accompanied by a handful of American officers, unkempt, unshaven, in dirty uniforms, who will pretend to be prisoners of the masquerading rebels. The party will be led by Segismondo, the original courier who was to deliver reinforcements to Aguinaldo's jungle hideaway.''

"It's brilliant, Fred," Brad lauded the plan. "Do you mind if I offer a suggestion?''

"We welcome all the suggestions and help we can get," General MacArthur said.

"Do you remember when we overran that rebel HQ last week? They left all their gear behind them, including official stationery bearing the letterhead BRIGADA LA-CUNA, the code name of Aguinaldo's second-in-command. Suppose we sent a forged communiqué to Aguinaldo's HQ written in the same code as the letter we intercepted, advising that the men he requested are on their way, along with some American prisoners?"

Funston pounded a fist against his thigh. "Splendid, Brad! That will be the icing on the cake."

"One more thing, Fred. Assuming everything goes the way we expect and we capture Aguinaldo, how do we get him back here through enemy lines? Once word gets out that he's in American hands, the insurrectionists will put out a general alert. We'll be the object of the greatest manhunt since Booth shot Lincoln."

"It's a good point," said MacArthur, "and I think we've covered that contingency. Palanan is near the coast, so once it's a fait accompli, we'll have a gunboat standing offshore to pick up our commandoes along with Aguinaldo and any other prisoners who are captured."

"That about covers it," Brad said. "One other idea. Instead of the so-called American prisoners being dressed like officers, I say we dress 'em as privates. Somehow it seems more convincing to me."

"I agree," Funston said. "Now, as for volunteers, we'll need four men in addition to myself."

"Three," Brad said. "You don't think I'm about to miss the action, do you?"

MacArthur and Funston laughed. "Your name was on the list even before we disclosed the plan to you," Funston said. "In addition, there will be eighty Little Macs led by Lazaro Segovia and Hilario Placido posing as rebel officers."

"Excellent choice," Brad agreed. "They're one hundred percent loyal and superb guerrilla fighters."

"Any further suggestions?" MacArthur inquired.

"If I may intrude, General MacArthur?" a voice called out from the open doorway.

The startled officers swung their heads in the direction of Moira Callahan Taylor, radiant in a gown with a bell skirt, lawn ruffles and lace frills; the wasp waist was as trim as when she was sixteen.

"Moira, what are you doing here?" Brad admonished her. "We're discussing secret military operations."

"Then you should have closed the door," she replied, and smiled at General MacArthur; he was as vulnerable to her charms as any man on the post, enlisted or officer. "May I come in?"

Funston and Brad eyed the general deferentially. Mac-Arthur walked to the doorway and took her by both hands. "By all means, my dear. May I pour you a brandy?"

"I'd be most grateful, Arthur." It was a liberty that no one of his staff would have risked, calling the "old man" by his given name.

He escorted her to an easy chair and served her a snifter of brandy.

"Thank you, Arthur. And, gentlemen, I do apologize for eavesdropping, but now that the deed is done, I would like to accept your offer, General MacArthur."

"Offer?" He was puzzled.

"Yes, you asked if there were any further suggestions concerning the plan to capture Aguinaldo. And yes, I do have a suggestion that I think will enhance the credibility of the operation. In addition to the other American prisoners, I think the party should include a captured American nurse."

"Ridiculous!" said Brad.

"Far too perilous," Funston growled.

General MacArthur stroked his mustache, head cocked to one side, appraising her with undisguised admiration. At last he made an irrevocable decision.

"I think it's a marvelous idea. It adds an indefinable balance to the plan. My compliments to you, my dear. And do you have any candidates in mind for the mission?"

Her smile was flirtatious. "Now you know perfectly well whom I have in mind, Arthur. I haven't been so excited in years."

Brad was aghast. *"You?* You must be out of your mind! I won't hear of it!"

She stood up, walked over to her husband and patted his cheek. "The first time we met, I told you that nobody pulls rank on me, darling. Not even a general."

General MacArthur burst into uproarious laughter. "By heavens, Taylor, that's quite a woman you have there. Wish I were single and ten years younger."

Moira fluttered her eyelids at him. "Why, Arthur, you're not that much older than I. If I were your wife, I wouldn't leave a dashing man like you on your own."

The smile faded from his face, and abruptly he resumed his brusque official manner. "Well, I do believe it's time we put aside this business and got back to the party."

Later, after they had made love, Brad said to Moira, "You really bearded the old lion in his den with your remark about his wife leaving him alone. You know how touchy he is on the subject of her mollycoddling their son Douglas back in the States while he's all alone here in Manila. One of the reasons for his vile temper is that he's not getting any."

"Sex?" She laughed softly. "You're probably right, though why I can't understand. I was being truthful; he's an extremely attractive and virile man. There are plenty of women here who would willingly hop into bed with Arthur."

Brad regarded her with a calculating expression. "Are you one of them?"

She tweaked his flaccid organ. "Well, if you can't do any better than this, I might consider it."

He slapped her bare bottom. "I don't think he's man enough for you, darling, but there's no doubt about it, Mac does have the hots for you." He cast a sly sideways glance at her and said casually, "You know the job of chief of staff is up for grabs back in Washington. A recommendation from General MacArthur would mean a lot of points for some candidate."

She sat up in indignation. "You bastard! You haven't

changed a bit in all these years. I believe you'd actually pimp me out to Arthur to win his support for that post!''

Brad lay back on his pillow, chuckling with glee. ''I knew I'd get a rise out of you with that little joke. And speaking of getting a rise. . . .'' He reached over to pull her toward him.

Chapter Twenty-six

On March 6, 1901, Generals Funston and Taylor and three junior officers, all disguised as privates, along with Moira Taylor and eighty-one Little Macs, boarded the gunboat that would transport them north up the coast of Luzon to the landing site from which they would make the arduous trek into the jungle en route to Palanan. Moira wore the uniform of an army nurse, and she had taken great pains with her makeup; straggly hair, mud smeared over her face and arms and a pair of horn-rim glasses that magnified her eyes so that she looked, as Brad stated it, "like a boiled owl."

General MacArthur bid them farewell on the quay. It was an emotional scene as he embraced first Moira, then his officers. "You are without doubt the most gallant men I have ever commanded, and you, Moira, are without peer in courage. God willing, I will see you all again before the month is out. If you don't return safely, I shall never forgive myself."

The night was perfect for the task, the moon obscured by rain clouds and low-hanging mist over the sea. As a precaution, the gunboat steamed far out to sea so that it would be below the horizon, out of view of rebel coast watchers. For four days it steamed north and then anchored at sea until nightfall. Once again they were blessed with a moonless night, and the gunboat headed in to shore. The original plan called for the detail to board canoes a half-mile from the mainland and continue to shore, but the seas were so heavy that the canoes were swamped as soon as they were put over the side.

"Damn it, it's no go," Funston said grimly. "We're going to have to risk being spotted." To the boat's captain he said, "Take her into the beach and pray to God."

And so it seemed God answered their prayers. All eighty-seven of the party were safely landed on the wind-swept beach. Funston shook hands with the captain and instructed him:

"This is going to call for split-second precision, Hank. On March 25 you will anchor off the beach ten miles north of here and wait for our signal. If we don't contact you by dawn, you will return to Manila. All right, crew, we're on our way."

Under cover of darkness they marched up the beach toward the coastal village of Casiguran. At dawn they took to the woods. It was worse than Funston had expected. For miles they had to wade through waist-deep water and hack their way through mangrove thickets with machetes.

"You go to the rear of the column, dear," Brad gasped. "That way we'll blaze a trail for you."

Moira wiped sweat out of her eyes with a sleeve. "Nobody has to blaze a trail for this gal. Keep swinging those machetes."

Funston shook his head in admiration. "That is some kind of woman you have, Brad. She's magnificent."

It took them two days to reach Casiguran, twelve hours behind schedule.

"We're going to have to do better than this or we'll never make it back to our rendezvous with the boat on the twenty-fifth," Funston told them.

Before they were in sight of the village, their risky charade commenced. The bogus prisoners were roped together, while equally bogus insurrectionists—the Little Macs—wearing fierce scowls and carrying their rifles at the ready, herded them along the road and into the village.

The entourage received a hearty reception from the villagers, who were fanatically loyal to Aguinaldo. The elders shook hands with Segovia and Placido, posing as rebel captains, and congratulated them on their capture of the "American pigs," while the villagers spat on the Americans and hurled insults at them.

The chief declared a holiday and ordered a grand feast prepared for the "heroes." There was even a brass band. Meanwhile the prisoners were put in a hut together and guards were posted at the entryway. Some time later Placido excused himself from the celebration in order to ". . . check on my prisoners."

He conversed with Funston and the others in low whispers. "For God's sake, Placido, you've got to break this up so we can be on our way."

"I'm doing the best I can. I've sent the forged letter to Aguinaldo by a runner, informing him that his reinforcements are on the way with American prisoners. I've got to get back now before they get suspicious."

At last, four hours later, they set out again to the accompaniment of music and enthusiastic cheering. There was little daylight left, so they made camp for the night. Sentries were posted around the perimeter of the campsite, cookfires were kindled and an adequate meal was served—canned beans and meat and hardtack along with steaming coffee to cut the grease.

Huddled around the fire, the Americans discussed strategy. "The next eight miles are going to be hell," Funston told them. "The most rugged terrain in all of Luzon. Aguinaldo chose his headquarters shrewdly. It's virtually inaccessible to a large body of attacking troops. So let's turn in and get a good night's sleep, because tomorrow we're going to need every ounce of stamina and energy we can muster."

That night Brad and Moira lay side by side in their sleeping bags, with the black sky a jeweled tapestry overhead. "I wish I could sneak in with you," Moira whispered.

"Me, too, but I don't think Fred Funston would approve. I wish I hadn't permitted you to tag along. This is more dangerous than we anticipated.''

''Darling, as I've told you so many times in the past, nobody pulls rank on me, not even General MacArthur. Now, good night and sweet dreams.''

A downpour of rain woke them at dawn. There was no hope of lighting a fire, so they ate their tinned rations and biscuits cold. When she was finished eating, Moira tilted her face upward and opened her mouth wide. The rainwater was cold and sweet and more than sufficient to slake her thirst. They rolled up their gear and were on the trail by seven.

The next seven days were sheer hell as they crossed rivers booby-trapped by submerged rapids, roped together in groups of seven. The swamps and jungle, however, were the worst hazard. Some of the growth was so dense that it was impossible to hack through it with machetes. Circumventing these obstacles entailed scaling jagged cliffs, some of them sheer precipices. Fortunately one of the junior officers was a skilled mountain climber; he would claw his way up the near-vertical precipices, then anchor a thick rope to a tree on the summit so that the others could ascend.

On the fourth day they were traveling along a trail with tree limbs arching over them like a leafy cathedral when Moira glimpsed something alarming in the tree branches about twenty feet ahead of her. She screamed a warning, but it was too late. A monster snake lunged downward and locked its jaws on the shoulder of one of the Little Macs. The man screamed in terror as the rest of the reptile slithered out of the foliage and wrapped its coils around his torso. Brad, Funston and several others rushed to his aid.

''Grab the damned head!'' Funston shouted.

Brad and another officer wrapped their hands around the snake's throat, the slimmest part of its girth, and tore it off the Mac's shoulder. It was possessed of great strength, and it was all Brad and the other man could do to retain their grip as it thrashed and jerked about in rage, its jaws endeavoring to secure a hold on one of them. In the nick of time Funston swung his machete in a clean, telling blow and severed the head from the body. Headless, it still thrashed about, the unrelenting coils refusing to let go of its victim. It required ten men finally to unwrap the length of it from the Mac, now unconscious and bleeding profusely from his shoulder wound. The task accomplished, they applied cold compresses to the wound with a heavy terry cloth until the bleeding stopped. Scrutiny showed that the gash was less serious than it appeared, much to the relief of the others, for it would have been near impossible for them to transport a seriously wounded man on a litter through this primitive terrain. The trek resumed.

On the seventh day, barely able to lift one foot after the other, they encountered a band of insurrectionists, all heavily armed and wearing crossed bandoliers across their chests. Their rifles were trained on the head of the column.

Segovia held up a hand and shouted the password: "Colon Magdalo."

The rifles came down, and broad smiles crossed the insurrectionists' faces. Segovia, Placido and their leader engaged in energetic conversation in Filipino, shouting and waving their arms. Master actors that they were, the imposter officers Placido and Segovia escorted the rebels down the column and proudly displayed the seven Americans, strung together by a rope. Funston and his fellow prisoners put on a good show themselves, filthy, unshaven, their uniforms tattered, heads hanging in abject defeat. As in the village of Casiguran, they were subjected to all kinds of insults and abuse.

The newcomers were particularly interested in Moira. Despite her attempts to make herself frumpy, it was difficult to conceal the magnificent body beneath her loose clothing. She understood enough of the language to grasp the meaning of their comments.

"Not a bad piece of merchandise . . ."

"Wash her up and comb her hair and she should make a welcome addition to our whores."

The rebels led them back down the road to the Palanan

River. The Americans had to suppress their excitement. On the far bank was Aguinaldo's hideaway.

"This is an epic moment in my life," Placido said with gusto. "At last I will meet our noble and exalted leader."

"Aguinaldo has been anticipating your arrival eagerly."

The rebel lieutenant fired a shot into the air. At once people came running out of the mud huts and gathered on the bank of the river.

"There is only one boat," the lieutenant informed them. "It is safer that way; no large force can take us by surprise."

The single craft held only seven passengers, so it required more than an hour to transport all of them across to the far bank. Aguinaldo himself greeted the first boatload and shook hands with Segovia and Placido.

"Good work, my captains. This calls for a special celebration, a grand feast, but first you will come into my office and share a bottle of French brandy with me and my aides." He led the way. Aguinaldo's office was the largest building in Palanan and by far the sturdiest. The furnishings were spare but adequate—a desk, two file cabinets, a bulletin board, several chairs, and one wall dominated by a large situation map of the Philippines festooned with vari-colored pins representing the location and size of both the American and Filipino armies. Aguinaldo sat down behind his desk and gestured to Placido and Segovia and his aides to take seats. A young lieutenant served brandy in elegant crystal snifters.

The leader lifted his glass. "You are to be congratulated on your great victory over the Americans. I want to hear about it, every detail of the battle and how you came to capture the prisoners."

Speaking alternately and with vivid imagination, the two spun a breathtaking version of the fictitious battle that had Aguinaldo and the others on the edge of their chairs. In the midst of this diversion they suddenly became aware of heavy gunfire outside.

Aguinaldo rushed to the window with Placido at his side. Segovia casually withdrew to a position to the side and in back of the five aides, who were preoccupied with what was happening outside. When Placido saw Segovia standing alert with his hands on the twin pistols holstered at his sides, he made his move. In a flurry of activity he drew his pistol, swung the astonished Aguinaldo around and, clutching him around the throat with a forearm, jammed the pistol into his side.

"One false move and you're a dead man!" he snapped.

The aides leaped to their feet and went for their pistols, but Segovia's blazing pistols gunned down three of them, and the remaining two fled out the door.

Meanwhile, outside in the village square, the Little Macs, at a signal from Funston, cut down the unsuspecting rebels in a savage fire. Those who were not gunned down fled in disorder into the jungle. When the brief, one-sided battle was over, Funston, Brad and Moira went into the building where Placido and Segovia were standing on either side of Aguinaldo, who was slumped forlornly behind his desk.

"General Aguinaldo, I am General Frederick Funston of the United States Army. This is my colleague, General Taylor, and his wife, Mrs. Taylor. You are our prisoner, and you will accompany us back to Manila."

The rebel chieftain, surprisingly youthful, was a handsome man with close-cropped black hair and an expression of hauteur and dignity. He smiled wanly and replied:

"I don't have any choice, do I? I was just commending your so-called captors on their derring-do in defeating the enemy and spiriting you here as prisoners." He shook his head in wonder. "Their fiction was most eloquent. However, compared to the accomplishment of your real and considerable mission here in Palanan, the deeds they described now pale by comparison. What is it you Americans say? Truth is stranger than fiction. I can attest to it without any doubt."

The journey to the pickup spot on Palanan Bay required no more than a half-day, unlike the hazardous and circuitous route by which they had come to Palanan. A cheer went up from the Little Macs and the Americans when they emerged from the jungle onto the beach. Anchored offshore was the gunboat, its port railing jammed with relieved crewmen, shouting and waving at them. Within the hour all were safely aboard, and the gunboat weighed anchor and steamed into the open sea, on her way to Manila.

Brad and Moira stood at the rail, arms around each other's waists, watching the land recede. They were joined by Funston, who joked gruffly, "You two lovebirds at it so soon after what you've endured?"

"One of the things that makes life's hard knocks endurable. Loving and being loved." Brad kissed her unabashedly while Funston looked through his field glasses, pretending to scan the horizon.

As General MacArthur had predicted, the capture of Aguinaldo fragmented the Philippine insurrection. The end came when, on April 19, 1901, Aguinaldo took the oath of allegiance to the United States and called on his followers to lay down their arms. In return the United States declared a general amnesty for all the rebels, including Aguinaldo himself.

The following summer President McKinley was shot dead by an assassin, and the vice-president, Theodore Roosevelt, was installed in the White House.

Just before Christmas General MacArthur summoned Brad Taylor to his office. He shook hands warmly. "I have some good news for you, my boy. In the diplomatic pouch that arrived this morning, I was notified by the War Department that you are to receive a new appointment, and a prestigious one at that. Commencing June first of next year, you are to serve as chief military attaché to the American embassy in England, where you will be working hand in glove with your old friend Ambassador Anson Mannix."

Brad was overwhelmed. "I can't believe it. In his last letter Anson suggested that he might step down at the end of Roosevelt's term in office."

There was a twinkle in the general's eyes as he fondled

the bole of his pipe. "That's the icing on your cake, Brad. I have very reliable information that Anson Mannix is grooming you for the post as ambassador when he retires. With your exemplary military record and your political experience in foreign affairs at Peking, you'll be a shoo-in whether the next administration is Democrat or Republican."

"I must be dreaming." Brad clamped his head between his hands as if he feared it might float away out of sheer euphoria. "The fattest political appointment in foreign affairs: London."

"Oh, by the way, Brad, at Mannix's urging, they have also appointed an assistant attaché to serve under you in England."

"Oh? Anyone we know?"

"I should think so. Let me see." He sifted through a stack of documents on his blotter. "Yes . . . here it is. He is one Colonel Patrick Taylor."

Brad stood transfixed, gaping at General MacArthur like a figure in a tableau. "My son. . . ." His voice was barely audible.

"Your son." MacArthur rose and walked to a cabinet against one wall. "I think you require a drink, old chap. What will it be, bourbon or Scotch?"

"Anything . . . I'm too numb to taste, anyway."

Three drinks later he excused himself and rushed back to their quarters to tell Moira the remarkable news. Now it was her turn to require a finger or two or three of spirits.

"It's incredible, it really is. Imagine, you and I and Patrick and Candice, all together again in London." She lifted her glass high. "I want to propose a toast to you, Brad. Your ambition and perseverance have paid off at last."

"And to you, my darling. Whose love, understanding, patience, tolerance and forgiveness made it possible."

Moira laughed. "How is it I seem to attract men who have the gift of blarney?"

"It must be the Irish in you. How shall we celebrate?"

A familiar gleam shone in her aquamarine eyes, now darkening with passion.

Upstairs in the bedroom he watched her undress with the same rapt desire that he had experienced the first time she had exposed her nude body to him.

"Dirty old man," she teased. "Don't you ever tire of ogling me after all these years?"

"On the contrary. The quality of my passion heightens like the bouquet of vintage wine."

That night Brad and Moira explored a dozen of the sexual fantasies described in the *Kama Sutra*. They slept, and in the middle of the night, Moira was awakened by the light flicking of his tongue in her navel. She moaned and grasped his head in her hand.

"Darling, enough is enough. I am thoroughly exhausted, and I'm sure you must be, too."

He raised his lips and spoke to her softly, almost with reverence. "That's not what I had in mind, my sweet. My desire has been totally spent. I merely want to demonstrate my consummate adoration of you. Not as a sex object but as the equal partner we spoke of in the ancient Greek myth. My other half, my better half." He bent to her face and kissed her chastely.

For a long while they lay side by side, holding hands, each consumed in his and her own reveries.

"Why are you so tense?" she asked him.

There was a prolonged silence before he answered her. "All this unexpected good fortune—London, Patrick and his wife with us . . . in a way it's frightening. Do you realize how many years it's been since I've had a real relationship with my son?" He sat up, swung his legs to the floor, and reached for his cigarettes. "Damn it, he hates my guts!"

She rolled over and placed a hand on his shoulder. "That is not true. Patrick doesn't hate you. What he feels is the same sort of frustration and resentment that you do, that you never shared a conventional father-son relationship. All those years lost between you." Her voice cracked. "I feel it, too. Not that I didn't care deeply for Sean. But he was my second choice. I too regret the years that you and I lost. Brad, be patient with our son. I know you love him, and I know just as well that he loves you, too."

He covered his face with his hands and began to sob; she had never seen him cry before. "I love Patrick more than life itself. I don't demand that he love me that way in return. Just that he abandon this fruitless and senseless vendetta he's been waging against me all these years."

She stroked his back and assured him. "Brad, I am certain that this new association you and Patrick will be sharing when we go to London will help you find a common ground to renew the bonds that existed when he was a child and worshipped the ground you walked on. I am not a proponent of the old myth of feminine intuition, but I am a wife and a mother. In the same manner that you and I are a unit, a family entity, so Patrick and Desiree are also parts of the whole. We are a loving family, no matter what superficial intermissions imply. We love each other and we always will."

They fell into a deep, peaceful sleep, wrapped in each other's arms.

Chapter Twenty-seven

The Twentieth Century

Dear Wendy,

   You no doubt are wondering why I date this missive "The Twentieth Century." It is symbolic of a galvanic change that has been transfiguring England—yes, the whole world, I think—since the death of Queen Victoria and the ascension to the throne of her son Edward. An astrologer acquaintance claims that the year 1900 marked a mystical numerology for the entire solar system. There is indeed—here, at least—an aura of rejuvenation, excited anticipation, a sense that we are moving into new and revolutionary times that hold the gift of awesome promise along with an undercurrent of apprehension and danger.

   As his mother, the Queen of England, was a woman of her times for forty-four years, so Edward is a man for the new times that are upon us. "Victorian" connoted pomp and circumstance, ultraconservatism, a society in which women and children were meant to be seen but not heard. "Edwardian," like the new king himself, suggests liberalism such as has never been known in England. Frivolity and fast and irresponsible living are common, in this wanton, libertine age.

When he was the prince of Wales, King Edward accrued an international reputation that was the bain of Victoria's existence. His sexual exploits were legion around the world. God only knows how many bastards he sired; there is a reliable rumor that he is the father of Lilly Langtry's illegitimate child. It is a well-known fact that he suffers from venereal disease. No matter; his presence on the throne opens the new century with a refreshing breath of cool, crisp, stimulating air.

I believe I told you in my last letter that after Brad resigned as ambassador, he and his predecessor, Anson Mannix, became associated with Cecil Rhodes and now own considerable shares in the fabulously rich Kimberly diamond fields. In addition, Brad owns a seat on the London Stock Exchange as well as a seat on the Amsterdam Diamond Exchange. He has realized his youthful ambitions beyond his wildest dreams. Ironically, in this life we lead there is a price on everything, and with burgeoning success he becomes more and more remote from me and his family. I don't believe he spends more than two or three weeks in England a year. To be sure, he wanted me to join him in his incessant peregrinations around the world in search of further material acquisitions and the power they bestow on him. But I have done sufficient globe trotting in my lifetime and prefer to remain in London with my son and daughter-in-law and my beloved grandchildren. All of us have become quite Anglicized, and I consider our country estate in Kent a permanent residence. I want to die and be buried here in England, my adopted land. Patrick, a full colonel, is chief of US Military Intelligence in the British Isles and also serves as military charge d'affaires to the American consulate.

I received a letter from Desiree last week. Gerald, now a brigadier general, is assistant commandant at the military academy at West Point.

To return to what I said about the Victorian era

*with regard to women and children—meant to be
"seen but not heard": With the advent of the Edwardian
Era, women are coming out of their cocoons in droves,
social butterflies as it were, very much to be heard as
well as seen. The newly proclaimed freedom is reflected in the new feminine wardrobe. In the old days
even the well-kept courtesans wore plain flannel drawers. Edwardian underclothing, known as lingerie from
the French, features a wide variety of shocking lace
and satin and silk fripperies, teddies, chemises, frou-
frou slips, transparent blouses with picot-trimmed neck-
lines, diaphanous nightgowns and bed jackets and a
marvelous new invention called the brassiere, a flimsy
garment to replace the rigid corselet, designed to
support the bosom with a minimum of material and
maximum of body freedom. All of it is brazenly calculated to inflame male passion. And with great success, I may add.*

*English women are a common sight on the tennis
courts, on golf courses, on ski slopes in Switzerland.
Last year a woman athlete won the all-comers ski
competition against an otherwise exclusively male field.
I ride to the hounds every Sunday morning. And,
what's more, I drive my own motor car, as do several other ladies of my acquaintance. Prime Minister
Asquith complains that when motoring it is impossible
to differentiate between the sexes, as we drivers are
all swathed in sealskin coats, goggles, and hats tied
on the head with scarves.*

*I have become deeply involved in the Women's
Social and Political Union, an organization dedicated
to the enfranchisement of women and their equality
with men in every other endeavor. The organization
was founded by a Mrs. Emmeline Pankhurst and her
two daughters, Sylvia and Christabel. There is bitter
opposition—some violent and physical—against the
WSPU movement at every level of society, from the
lowly laborer to the most distinguished members of
Parliament. However, we are making haste slowly,*

*and more and more of our liberal legislators are
espousing the cause of female liberation; not to mention the members of the prestigious Fabian Society, a
literary clique whose members include the illustrious
George Bernard Shaw, H. G. Wells and Sidney Webb.*

*There is a young member of Parliament who is
zealously opposed to the WSPU. I had the dubious
pleasure of meeting him at a recent rally at the Free
Trade Hall for passage of a Women's Enfranchisement Bill. . . .*

A majority of the members of the WSPU wore drab
brown dresses with hobble skirts, high-button shoes, and
round pillbox hats perched primly on their heads. When
reproached by some of the more militant members for her
frivolous attire, Moira informed them politely but firmly:

"I refuse to adopt a uniform of conformity; that is one
of our foremost causes—breaking out of the mold of conformity that has been conferred on women by men. It is
detrimental for women to try to appear to be what we are
not—men. I take pride in my femininity, and it enhances,
rather than detracts from, sexual equality." She nudged
Sylvia Pankhurst slyly. "You know what the French say
about men and women: *Viva la difference!*"

For the meeting at the Free Trade Hall, Moira wore a
brightly banded broomstick skirt in long tiers of crisp
seersucker; her hair was tied back with a green ribbon.

When the women got out of their carriages at the hall,
they were hissed and jeered by an unruly mob of men who
were restrained behind police barricades. A good many of
the members were shaken by this savage display of hostility. But Moira held her head high and stared with unblink-
ing disdain and repugnance at her detractors as she ran the
gauntlet to the main entrance. The abuse hurled at them
was vile and obscene:

"Anarchists!"

"Whores!"

"Lesbians!"

Once inside the hall, Emmeline consoled her disconcerted cohorts: "Don't let their kind ruffle your feathers, ladies. Actually, they are more to be pitied than reviled. Don't you see what it is? The emergence of women as equals and partners threatens their masculinity. That crowd out there, they're all weaklings and cowards. And they are in a distinct minority. The majority of men, despite the fact that they are vaguely uncomfortable with the idea of female equality, are fair-minded and reasonable. They will learn to live with our equality, and, yes, they may even come to like the concept. Think of the responsibility it will lift from the struggling male wage earner's shoulders when his wife can contribute to the family income. Never fear, we shall achieve our goal."

The members of the Central Committee of the WSPU sat in chairs arranged in a semicircle on the stage at the front of the main hall. In addition to Sir Edward Gray and two other members of the House of Lords, there was a member of the House of Commons, a good-looking, stocky chap of about thirty-five with a dour, brooding expression as he contemplated the "upstart females," as he had described the militants. His name was Winston Churchill.

When Mrs. Pankhurst, the first speaker, addressed the assembly, she was loudly booed from the gallery.

"Damned Bolsheviks, that's what you are!"

"Rioting, picketing, throwing bricks at the PM's house!"

"We learned our lessons from your own union organizers," she shouted at the hecklers. "Do you recall when Parliament and the press were accusing the unions of blatant Marxism?"

A burly, unkempt man in the front row stood up and shook his fist at the women on the stage. "You call yourselves suffragettes! What you really are is untouchables! Stealing the bread and milk out of the mouths of the babes of honest working men!"

Moira Taylor rose and strode to the front of the stage. She glared at him stonily until he dropped his eyes, then inquired: "And what is your occupation, my good man?"

He swung from one foot to the other and scratched his

whiskers before replying in a small, sullen voice, "I'm a manure collector."

"A street sweep, is that what you are." She let her gaze roam around the room and smiled at the hostile audience. "Let me assure you—whatever your name is—and the rest of you distinguished gentlemen—that you have absolutely nothing to fear from us, my friend. There isn't a woman on this dais who would think of stealing *your* job away from you."

The quip touched a chord, and there was intermittent laughter from the crowd. And as the forum progressed, Moira could sense the mood of the gallery subtly moderating. Mrs. Pankhurst had warned her speakers before the session:

"The important thing to remember is not to lose our tempers and resort to what our foes smugly refer to as female hysteria. You all are familiar with the crude misconceptions they foster about our sex—such as that once we obtain the vote we will stop menstruating."

The women of the WSPU were models of restraint and reason that day, fending off the charges and accusations and insults they were subjected to with good humor, intelligent wit.

When it was Moira's turn to speak, she promptly became engaged in a spirited debate with the MP from Manchester. As the exchange grew more heated, it degenerated into a duel of strong personalities in which both contestants lost their objectivity.

Red-faced, he shook his cigar at her. "You are a witch, madam! You would turn England back centuries and have her ruled by a race of fanatic Amazons!"

"No, it's you who would turn back time," she retorted. "You would have women restored to being chattel, such as they were in the Middle Ages, no better than livestock or other material possessions!"

"You fly in the face of God, madam!"

She mocked him. "Mr. Churchill, do you believe God is a man or a woman?"

An audible gasp of shock filled the hall. Churchill's face

flamed even brighter. "You blasphemous woman. It's gospel that our Creator is of the male gender, not that he is a man in the literal sense. But the Good Book states very emphatically that God created man in his own image."

Moira shrugged. "Well, there you have it." She looked around the semicircle of WSPU women. "No wonder the lot of women has been so miserable beginning with Day One!"

Pandemonium was rampant in the packed auditorium. The veins in Churchill's temples were swollen; his eyes bulged with outrage and disbelief. At last he found his voice; it trembled with emotion.

"Are you married, madam?"

"Yes, I am, if it's any of your business."

"Then your husband should give you a proper thrashing, a vigorous caning."

"You pompous ass!" Eyes as dark as a stormy sea, Moira glared around the dais and spied an umbrella at the side of one woman's seat. Leaping up, she snatched the umbrella and, brandishing it like a sword, advanced on the flabbergasted Churchill. He got up and put his chair between him and this madwoman.

"What the devil do you think you're doing?" he asked in dismay, and kept backing away as she stalked him around the stage. Her show of spirit and determination and her refusal to be bullied either by the spectators or the distinguished members of Parliament earned the respect of a goodly number in the crowd; they began to clap, stomp their feet, whistle and egg her on.

"Go on, girlie, let the cheeky bastard have it good!"

"Don't let fatso push you about!"

Among the women of the WSPU there was consternation. Even Emmeline Pankhurst and her daughters were flustered. Mrs. Pankhurst got up hurriedly and tried to intercede between Moira and the cowed MP. Moira shoved her aside gently and continued the pursuit.

"Madam, I beg of you, get hold of yourself!" he pleaded. Relentless as a stalking tigress, she backed him to the very edge of the stage. Then, eyes gleaming with triumph, she lifted the umbrella with both hands and brought it down like an ax on the top of his head.

"Agggghhhhh!" Crying out like a felled ox, he toppled backward off the platform into the first row of spectators. At that moment three English bobbies came rushing from the rear of the hall and leaped onto the stage. A wild melee ensued as they endeavored to subdue her. It was no easy task. She was a large, strong woman, with her strength fired by adrenaline.

Galvanized by the sight of their sister suffragette being manhandled by the policemen, the ladies cast off their inhibitions and joined the fray.

"Bravo!" shouted Emmeline Pankhurst. "Let's teach them a lesson or two!" She leaped up, and to the amazement of the audience, she produced a small bullwhip from her handbag and commenced lashing the bobbies.

Within minutes the Free Trade Hall was the arena for a donnybrook that involved almost every body in the place, as the union members chose sides and did battle. Pugnacious chaps, they required small excuse to join in a "bloody good fight," as one combatant exulted while the police led him away.

A troop of bobbies had to be summoned before the "fighting hellcats" of the WSPU were finally subdued and carted out to the paddy wagon to be taken to jail.

Emmeline and Moira stood at the back of the wagon, waving to the cheering crowd of unionists.

"Spunky bunch, you got to give 'em that," one man said to another.

"Sure are, mate. And you know something—there is something to what that Pankhurst woman says about the rough treatment the union got when we first stood up for our human rights."

"Blimey, you said it, Jack. Got to admire anyone, male or female, what stand's up for his or her rights!"

Chapter Twenty-eight

The suffragettes were herded into a common bullpen along with at least a score of other female prisoners, most of them prostitutes. Many of them had been confined for more than a week with no opportunity to wash, change their clothing or comb their hair. The place was infested with lice, roaches and other vermin, and the stench of mass body odor and a line of slop buckets against one wall was overpowering.

"This is abominable, inhuman!" Moira gasped. "I wonder whether Mr. Churchill or his fellow MP's have ever seen the inside of a hellhole such as this."

"I doubt it," Emmeline said. "And I for one am glad that we have had the opportunity to see it."

"Are you mad, Mrs. Pankhurst?" a woman with less intestinal fortitude railed. "I shall never forget this nightmarish indignity as long as I live." She began to weep. "James warned me what would happen to me if I got involved in your movement. Ohhhhh . . . why didn't I listen to him?"

Pankhurst regarded her contemptuously. "Stop your whining, Ella. That's just what the men expect us to do under duress—weep and faint. The reason I am glad we have the opportunity to witness this sewer is that it makes me aware that there are injustices aside from our own cause that society must be compelled to rectify: poverty, prejudice, tyranny, the plight of the dispossessed such as these poor creatures. There must be equal rights and justice for all, not just for a privileged few. And that is truly what the WSPU stands for—justice for all!''

One of the inmates came up to them. She was a pretty child of no more than fifteen, rouged and powdered, and the lines of experience etched into her face were as descriptive as the lines on a contour map: drunken father, slut of a mother, starved and beaten as a child, forced out into the mean streets to survive, and surviving the only way she could, by selling her sole possession—her body.

''Blimey, you gals must be high-priced hookers,'' she said with respect. ''Pound at least.''

Moira and Mrs. Pankhurst smiled, and Emmeline said to her, ''No, young woman, we are incarcerated here for alleged sins of the intellect rather than for sins of the flesh.''

The girl gaped at her in open-mouthed bewilderment. ''Cor, whatever does that mean?''

''I'll try to explain it to you. When you get out of here, you may care to join our movement. It would be of enormous benefit to you. . . .''

Moira smiled and whispered to one of the other women, ''Good old Emmeline, she can't resist proselytizing even in the pokey.''

She turned at the rasping sound of a key in the lock of the cell's door. A fat warder swung the barred gate open. ''Come on, you tarts from the WSPU. Someone's posted your bail.''

''It must be my husband,'' said Mrs. Pankhurst. She put a hand on the shoulder of the young prostitute she had been counseling. ''Now don't forget, my dear. As soon as you are set free, come and see me at our headquarters. And if you like, persuade some of your friends to come along, too.''

''Thank you, ma'am. I'll see what I can do.''

The members of the WSPU filed out of the cell and followed the warder down the dim, dingy corridor to the booking room. A uniformed sergeant sat behind a high desk conversing with, of all people, Winston Churchill.

"I don't believe my eyes," Moira exclaimed.

The desk sergeant fixed them with a jaundiced eye. "Mr. Churchill here says he doesn't want to press charges again' you, *ladies!*" He uttered it with obvious distaste. "God only knows why he's being so lenient. You're still facing civil disobedience charges, but he's posting your bail on that as well."

Churchill cleared his throat and rubbed the bulbous tip of his beet-red nose. "The fact is, ladies, I feel in some respect that I share the burden for the eruption at the Trade Hall. In retrospect, some of my remarks were intemperate and rude."

"They certainly were," Moira said coldly.

Churchill paid the bail, and the group left the prison. "I have hired two carriages to transport you ladies to whatever destination you choose. The fare is already paid."

"That's very generous of you, Mr. Churchill," said Mrs. Pankhurst. "We accept your apology, and I think we owe you our apologies in return. Don't you agree, Moira?"

"I suppose so," she said reluctantly. "My behavior was not exemplary either, Mr. Churchill." She smiled and extended her hand.

He grasped it in both of his and beamed at her. "I am very grateful to you, Mrs.—" He hesitated. "I regret I forget your name."

"Mrs. Moira Taylor."

"Taylor?" His brow furrowed in thought. "By any chance are you the wife of Bradford Taylor, the former American ambassador?"

"One and the same."

The other women had already boarded the carriages, and Mrs. Pankhurst called to Moira, "We're eager to get home, my dear."

"Yes, I'll be right there." She said to Churchill, "Thank you again, Mr. Churchill. I must be going."

He placed a hand on her arm. "No, wait, Mrs. Taylor. Would you do me the honor of allowing me to drive you home? My car is around the block. I would really like to talk to you in more depth. I realize you have an image of me as a bigoted ass, but it's not true. In spite of our differences, I have great admiration for Mrs. Pankhurst and you and the general principles of the WSPU. It's your methods I disapprove of. The doctrine of the end justifies the means. Militancy is so unfeminine, and femininity is a trait I revere highly."

"Is it femininity or submissiveness you revere? They are not the same thing."

Churchill burst out laughing. "Here we go again. All right, I won't object if you lecture me, but will you accept my offer of a lift?"

She hesitated and glanced up at Mrs. Pankhurst. "You go along without me, Emmeline. I think I will accept Mr. Churchill's offer."

"I'm grateful, Mrs. Taylor." He tipped his bowler to Mrs. Pankhurst and the other women and told the cabbies to be on their way. Then he offered his crooked elbow to Moira, and she slipped her hand inside. He escorted her to the corner and turned right. "There she is—isn't she a beauty?"

"Positively handsome." It was a sporting car with a tonneau large enough to accommodate four passengers in the rear and two in front, covered by a patent leather roof. The chassis was black and polished to a mirror luster and trimmed with chrome and brass. He opened the side boot and handed Moira a linen duster and a pair of goggles. She donned them, and he helped her up the step, then went around to the driver's seat and climbed aboard. As they drove away from the curb, she studied his profile. He was a very attractive man, she decided, stocky, but unlike some heavyset men, he wore his clothes well. He looked quite dashing in his gray striped suit, checked vest and slim trousers; his boots matched the sheen of the car.

"I know your husband, General Taylor. We belong to the same club. Haven't seen him of late. Is he well?"

"Brad is as healthy as a horse. As for seeing him, we

rarely see him, either. He spends a good deal of time abroad.''

''Yes, he's a very energetic man. Ambitious.''

''Ambitious; quite.''

He glanced sideways at her, contemplating the note of dissatisfaction he detected in her voice. Impulsively he asked her, ''Mrs. Taylor, will you have dinner with me tonight? I'm genuinely interested in the suffragette movement, and I do advocate that women should ultimately achieve the franchise.''

''Do you now? I do not like the inference of the word 'ultimately.' Ultimate in akin to infinity.''

''No, I didn't mean that. What I do mean is that Rome wasn't built in a day. Social revolution is not accomplished overnight. It must progress step by step. The point is, by your brash, militant acts you terrify the diehard reactionaries, who, like it or not, still wield the power in government. And you provide them with propaganda that enables them to suppress your progress—like those union members who were so hostile toward you at the Trade Hall. What do they know about the feminist movement? And at heart they couldn't care less. They are brainwashed by the editorials they read in the newspapers and the speeches the politicians make in the union halls. The crux of it is, the only way you can fulfill your goals is by working for them in a subtle, quiet way. To use a military metaphor, outflank the opposition. If you agree to be more temperate in your endeavors, I give you my vow that I will support enfranchisement for women at a time when it becomes attainable. The time is not ripe yet.''

''I'll think about it.''

''We'll talk more about it at supper this evening.''

''I haven't made up my mind to accept your invitation, Mr. Churchill,'' she replied haughtily.

''I entreat you . . . and please call me Winston.''

She baited him. ''Well, I suppose it's harmless enough. You do not appear to be a rake.''

His smile was enigmatic. ''No comment. I'll pick you up at eight.''

* * *

Lolling in her bath, Moira tried to define her sentiments about Winston Churchill. He was a martinet. He was a snob. He was irritating. Yet there was something indefinable about him that she liked.

He's got to be twenty years younger than you; is that the answer? You're flattered that a virile young man is attracted to you?

Yes, and why shouldn't I be?

It's been a long time since you've made love. You're a bit randy. You're entertaining the possibility that you and young Churchill may end up in bed together.

Years ago Brad and Moira had come to a tacit understanding with regard to their sexual lives. Neither expected the other to remain celibate during their prolonged separations. It had been two months since Moira had terminated her affair with the duke of Kent, at the request of his brother King Edward, who threatened to vacate the duke's title unless she promised never to see him again. For years the king had been endeavoring to seduce Moira. Admittedly she had been tempted; after all, how many women had the opportunity to sleep with a king? The deterrent had been her certain knowledge that Edward had syphilis.

She shuffled through every gown in her wardrobe twice before she selected a country print pinafore of jade green and white with a ruffled underdress. It was a youthful dress that made Moira look five years younger.

To make herself look younger still, she let her long, raven hair, remarkably unstreaked by any gray, flow down her back, clasped at the nape of her neck by a simple black velvet ribbon.

When she was finished dressing, she appraised herself in her vanity mirror. The aquamarine eyes were as bright and clear as they had been when she was sixteen. The aristocratic aquiline nose was just as proud and slender. The olive skin was still unblemished. She patted the underside of her chin with the back of a hand. So many women developed sagging jowls. Highly satisfied with herself, she took her wrap and went downstairs to wait for her suitor.

What an odd way to describe him, she mused. *Suitor? Why, I hardly know the man.*

At one minute before the hour of eight, the front door chimes sounded. The maid admitted Churchill and led him into the parlor, where Moira was sipping a sherry and reading a copy of the London *Times*. She put down the paper and rose to greet him.

"Mr. Churchill, and in evening clothes, no less. You should have warned me that this was a formal affair. My outfit is patently unsuitable."

He grasped her hand, bowed and kissed her fingers. "Unsuitable? My dear Moira, you could triumph in high society wearing sackcloth and ashes. You look positively ravishing." There was a twinkle in his rakish blue eyes. "And I wish I could."

"*Mr.* Churchill!" Moira feigned indignation. "You are a naughty young man. I knew it was a mistake to accept your invitation."

"Winston, please, my dear. And stop referring to me as a young man."

"But it's true. I'm almost old enough to be your mother."

"Nonsense, and stop fishing for compliments. You know perfectly well that you don't look a day over thirty-five. Besides, chronological age is irrelevant. The true measure of one's age is here." He touched a finger to his temple. "We're as old as we feel. And tonight I feel twenty and you are eighteen."

"Flattery will get you nowhere, sir."

"Would you care to wager with me?"

"Do you know, I do feel rather girlishly giddy tonight. Power of suggestion. Where are we dining?"

"An old inn, far out in the countryside. The John Peel Tavern." He frowned as an odd expression spread over her countenance. "Is anything wrong?"

"No, no, it's just a curious coincidence. A long time ago, when we resided in Maryland, there was an inn with

the same name. My husband used to frequent it with
. . .'' She let it trail off.

*Charlotte Collins . . . One of Brad's first stepping
stones on the route to success.*

"Shall we be off then?"

She picked up her wrap.

"Allow me." He draped it around her shoulders.

The trip in his motor car lasted well over an hour. The
John Peel Tavern nestled in a bower of maple and pine
trees, a typical old English inn constructed of massive
timbers, unpainted, and bleached white by the sun and
handsomely mottled by the elements. A wooden sign swung
in the breeze above the front door, bearing the emblem of a
curved bugle and the inscription: Do you ken John Peel . . .

The eerie coincidence was perpetuated when they walked
into the foyer; the atmosphere matched the inn's namesake
in Maryland. Dark stained wood paneling and heavy draperies across the windows created a dim, intimate atmosphere, which was enhanced by high-backed secluded
booths. The whitewashed ceilings were spanned by massive oaken beams. A majestic bar was stained to match the
walls and decorated with ornate carving.

They were greeted by a slender young woman, primly
garbed in a black hobbleskirt and a white starched linen
blouse fastened demurely at the throat with a black velvet
string tie. She addressed Churchill in a flavorful Irish
brogue.

"Mr. Churchill, it's a pleasure to see you again. It's
been so long. We feared you were bored with us."

"Never, Marion. The fact is, I've been swamped with
parliamentary business. I would like you to meet Mrs.
Moira Taylor, wife of the former American ambassador,
General Bradford Taylor."

Marion clapped her hands to her cheeks. "Mercy me!
Are you the woman who is affiliated with Mrs. Pankhurst's
WSPU?"

"Proudly, one and the same." Moira extended her hand.
"It's a pleasure to make your acquaintance."

The two women shook hands, not a common practice in

the era. "Well, I am proud and honored to make your acquaintance, Mrs. Taylor. I am absolutely awed by the WSPU and its extravagant goals. Imagine, women having the right to vote and achieving equality with men."

"It's our birthright, Marion, don't you agree?"

"Agree? I agree one hundred percent. It's just the boldness of your cause that I wonder at. Do you know that the Irish—both men and women—endure the same kind of subjugation from the English as do the female sex?"

"I was saying that very thing this afternoon in the jailhouse. The cause of the WSPU is not restricted to female suffrage. It is the cause of all of the world's oppressed peoples. Marion, why don't you attend one of our meetings next week? I can vouch that the experience will give you inspiration and courage."

"I just may do that."

Churchill threw up his hands. "That will be enough of that! Mrs. Taylor, I did not bring you to supper to encourage you to launch a conversion campaign at one of my favorite London haunts. Especially when your first subject is the most attractive, most able hostess in all of England. As well as being the *compleat feminine woman*." He treated Moira to a lifted, superciliously raised eyebrow. "May we have a corner table, dear Marion?"

"To be sure, your regular booth, sir." She led them through the dining room, where parties of two or more were dining in supreme luxury. Men and women were garbed in evening wear. Silver champagne buckets graced almost every table. Marion seated them at a booth far removed from the general company. "I'll send over my assistant, Carol, to take your order, Mr. Churchill."

As she turned to leave, Churchill patted her comely rump with the back of his hand.

"I'll forget that happened, sir," she said impishly.

"I believe I misjudged you, Winston, when I surmised that you were not a rake. You do behave with untoward familiarity to the opposite sex. How would you feel if a lady came up and pinched your bottom?"

He chuckled. "Dear lady, I would consider it one of the

high points of my life. Please feel free to help yourself.''
He winked at her across the table and took a cigar from his
inside coat pocket. ''Do you object?''

''Not in the least.'' Moira removed a handsome gold
cigarette case from her purse. ''Just as long as you don't
object if *I* smoke.''

He gazed at her with open admiration. ''Gadzooks!
What a marvelous, headstrong, courageous woman you
are. They say that beauty is only skin deep. Yours, dear
Moira, goes right down to the bone.''

''I thank you, sir.''

They looked up as another young woman approached
their table. ''Good evening, Mr. Churchill,'' she said with
a radiant, dimpled smile; she was attired similarly to Marion.

Churchill let his gaze run up and down her svelte form.
''Well, my top priority would be highly improper, so let
us settle for a bottle of champagne—Moët is a fine choice.''

She blushed prettily and curtsied before departing. ''Winston, you really affect a cavalier attitude toward the ladies.
I'm shocked.''

''No you're not, Moira,'' he said casually, eyeing the
girl's undulating backside as she retreated from the table.
''I must say, Carol is a well-developed Calapygian cutey.''

''Whatever on earth might that be?''

He smiled and lit his cigar. ''Well endowed in the area
of the derrière.''

''You are positively outrageous, sir, and I do believe I
will take a carriage home.''

''Nonsense. Tonight you and I—as my American mother
says—are going to paint the town red.''

''I think we had better settle for pastel pink. By the
way, who is the proprietor of this establishment?''

''Why, Marion and Carol.''

''What enterprising young business women they must
be, to own a regal place like this.''

Churchill laughed and tapped his ash into a crystal tray.
''Oh, they are enterprising and ambitious, that's for sure,
but not primarily in the world of commerce.'' His face lit
up in lusty good humor. ''The fact is that Marion and

Carol were kept women before they acquired the John Peel Tavern.''

"And very well kept, I must say," said the astonished Moira.

"You might say that, my dear. They both were courtesans to the prince of Wales before he became King Edward."

"That is shocking."

"You see, after Edward ascended to the throne, he was compelled to curtail his romantic activities, but, being the thoughtful, grateful, generous fellow that he is, he did not forget his mistresses. He made Marion and Carol a gift of the John Peel Tavern."

"And cheap at that," Moira said, "considering that those poor ladies must spend the rest of their days in the dark shadow of his social diseases."

The dinner was superb: consommé a la princesse served with sherry wine; red snapper a la dauphine; pommes duchesse; salad de concombres; fromage de Roquefort; and fruits assortis, all served with Moët champagne.

"Would you care for a brandy with your coffee?" Churchill inquired.

"No thank you, Winston. If I eat or drink another drop, I shall split my gusset."

"I should like to see that . . . I'll wager you wear French underclothing; right now I'd say you have on black lace."

"You are a wicked man. My undergarments are of no concern to you."

"A situation I intend to rectify as soon as possible."

Moira laughed and patted his hand, which lay extended on the table. "Winston, you are like a naughty little boy out to shock his mother. Well, you are not succeeding. I am virtually unshockable. In fact, I could relate a few anecdotes that might well shock you."

His eyes glowed. "Try me."

As the meal progressed, Moira and Churchill had drifted into a mood of comfortable, casual camaraderie, the sort that exists ordinarily between longstanding friends.

"I wish to hell you'd stop thinking of me as a son.

Naughty little boy indeed! I assure you, my dear, if you permit me the opportunity, I will arouse feelings within you that are anything but maternal. Your marriage has to be unsatisfying.''

"You presume too much, sir.''

"Come off of it, Moira. You said yourself that you see Bradford only infrequently. A vibrant woman like you— certainly those brief excursions cannot slake your obvious lusty appetites?''

Moira covered her eyes with her hands, laughing to the point of tears. "I don't believe you, Winston. What do you know about my so-called lusty appetites?''

"I intend to find out. Do you know, I have never been attracted to any other woman so urgently as I am attracted to you? Here, let me have your hand underneath the table and I shall prove it to you.''

"Now you've gone too far. I am not the type of woman who fondles men underneath the tablecloth.''

"How many lovers have you had during the past year?''

"That is none of your concern. I am seriously thinking of joining a religious order and embracing a vow of celibacy.''

"God forbid!''

Marion approached the table. "Did you enjoy your supper?''

"Delectable,'' Moira said. "Down to the last morsel and drop of coffee.''

"Will there be anything else, Mr. Churchill?''

"I think not, Marion.'' He stared at Moira across the table, his eyes smoldering with passion. "At least, nothing more that is on your menu.''

Chapter Twenty-nine

Outside the inn he assisted her into the car. The step was a high one, and Moira hiked her skirt above her knees. Churchill brazenly ogled her shapely limbs.

"Lovely, absolutely lovely," he said.

"Lecher."

"I admit it. Never can resist a pair of artistic legs."

"I thought you were a derrière man?"

"That as well. After all, they all join together so esthetically." He started the car and drove around the graveled driveway to the main road. "Are you in a hurry to get home?"

She thought about his question. The night was balmy; there was a full moon; and the wine had made her lightheaded. Then there was the restlessness that always afflicted her with the coming of spring as the vibrant body juices pulsated in her veins like sap rising in the maples that were budding on either side of the road.

"What do you have in mind?" she asked him.

"There's a little lake not far from here—Silver Lake."

"Yes, I've heard of it. It's a popular gathering place for young people, isn't it?"

"I feel very youthful tonight. How about you? Care to kick up your heels? There's a pavilion out over the lake where some of the more notable dance bands play on Fridays and Saturdays.''

"I'd love it, Winston. I feel like dancing tonight."

"Did you know," he said, "that since the coming of age of the motor car, adultery has increased tenfold in the United Kingdom?"

"Mercy, now why should that be?"

"Simple. In the horse-and-buggy days, men and women were restricted to their own towns and villages. Rarely did one ever venture further than a ten-mile radius from his or her own locale. The motor car has extended that range immeasurably. For example, tonight you and I have traveled some thirty miles from home. It is highly unlikely that your London friends would have chanced upon our surreptitious rendezvous at the John Peel.''

"Surreptitious rendezvous?" Moira was amused. "There is nothing surreptitious about it. My entire household staff is aware that you and I are dining out. Really, Winston, you have the imagination of a romantic novelist."

"I've been advised that I should put my flair with words to practical use."

Their dialogue took a more serious direction. "Since the death of Queen Victoria, have you sensed a distinct alteration in the lives and attitudes of the British populace—the fiber of the nation itself?" she asked him.

He turned to look at her, the cigar jutting at a rakish angle from a corner of his mouth.

"You're extremely perceptive, my dear. Well, your Mrs. Pankhurst and the WSPU are typical of the radical transformation that has been taking place in Britain in a few short years. The dramatic expansion of unionism . . . women's liberation . . . the uprisings in Ireland and India . . . the accelerating tension in Europe, Russia, the Middle East. My own feeling is that we—the entire world, not merely England—are sitting on a gigantic powder keg. The fuse is lit and burning. Our dilemma is that we don't know just how long or short that fuse is. But time is running down, and the explosion is inevitable. The only thing that remains to be determined is how, when and where the impact will first be felt. To quote my American mother once more, we are all waiting with bated breath for an accident that is preordained to happen.''

Moira shivered and hugged her arms across her bosom. ''That is a chilling hypothesis, Winston.''

''It is, because I am totally convinced that Armageddon is almost upon us.''

The pavilion at Silver Lake was entertaining a large clientele that evening. The dance floor was built on a large pier stretching out into the lake. There was a circular stage in the center of the floor. Gracing it were four musicians playing piano, bass, drums and saxophone. They were black men.

''My word!'' Moira exclaimed. ''I've never heard music like that before.'' She commenced clapping her hands and shaking her hips. ''It's positively infectious. I can't stand still.''

''They call it New Orleans jazz,'' Churchill informed her. ''Buddy Bolden and his band. They just came over from the Continent. Unfortunately the dance floor is so packed, you could toss a handful of shillings into that mob and not a one would strike the floor. There's an old joke that one night in the wild melee a girl became pregnant and didn't even know she had been jazzed.''

''Jazzed?''

''Pregnant she was. 'Jazz' is a colloquialism for sexual intercourse.''

''How quaint. I rather like it.''

''Sex?''

''None of your affair.''

''I hope to make it my affair. Since we can't dance, would you care to take a stroll around the lake? It boasts some lovely scenery.''

''I'd like that.''

They walked down the beach, away from the pavilion.''

''It's plain why they call it Silver Lake,'' Moira observed. ''The sand gleams like silver in the moonlight.''

Churchill pointed across the lake. ''The water, too. It's the effect of the moonlight filtering through the branches of the weeping willows and white birch trees overhanging the bank.''

Churchill lit a cigar and inhaled. The tip glowed cherry red. Moira said, ''You truly fancy those, don't you?''

''My second favorite addiction,'' he said with clear innuendo.

They engaged in idle chatter concerning mutual friends and families. ''I'm grateful that you attacked me with that umbrella today,'' he said. ''I've been hearing about you for years, and somehow our paths never crossed.''

''I've *never* heard about you,'' she said impudently.

He regarded her with an owlish stare. ''Oh, but you will, my dear. You most certainly will hear about Winston Churchill. My name will become a household word in time to come, and not just in England.''

She sighed. ''You sound very much like my husband, Winston—consumed with ambition.''

''There are two classes of people in world society; those who are born to lead and those who are born to follow. I happen to be a natural leader.'' Suddenly he pinched the ash off his half-smoked cigar. ''Now from here on, we must be very quiet. Pretend you're walking on eggshells.''

''Whatever for?''

''I am about to introduce you to a live demonstration of the phenomenon I was describing to you earlier. The link between motor cars and adultery.'' He took her by the hand and led her up the slope of a grassy knoll, touching a finger to his lips. ''Speak only in a whisper and stay low when we get to the top.''

''What on earth are you up to? I believe you must have had too much of the grape.''

''Never mind, you'll see for yourself.''

At the hilltop there was a thick growth of scrub pine trees. They wended their way through the grove and stopped short of the grass that grew down the far side of the hillside. Moira was puzzled at the sight of at least ten motorcars parked at intervals and at various angles in the clearing at the foot of the rise.

''I don't understand,'' she whispered.

Churchill chuckled softly. "There's the proof I spoke of."

She could make out dark silhouettes of men and women sitting in the autos, some in the front seat, some in the back. "What on earth are they doing out here in the wilderness?"

"For a reputed woman of the world, you are painfully naive. Look there, directly below us."

She fixed her gaze on the car that was nearest to their vantage point, bathed in luminous moonlight. The top was down, and reclining on the rear seat were a man and a woman with their clothing in disarray.

Moira's cheeks were hot with embarrassment. "This is outrageous, Winston. We're no better than Peeping Toms. I don't know when I've felt so humiliated."

"Quite." His hand stroked the curve of her back and settled on her buttocks. "But exceedingly titillating, don't you agree?"

"You're disgusting!"

"Don't deny it, Moira. Haven't you ever been curious about the sexual habits of our fellow bipeds? I mean, when we are having sex, it is a purely private and subjective experience. We don't see ourselves performing. We are deprived of the long, objective view. Now, from our present viewpoint, we can gain total enlightenment. See there, he's about to effect the *coup de grace*."

The woman let out a long, tremulous sigh as he entered her, and then they began the rising, rhythmic tempo of lust.

Moira was in a state of mind that bordered on somnambulism. She was vaguely aware of his hand hiking up her gown in back and slipping between her bare thighs. "Stop it at once," she gasped. "You have no right!"

"Don't play games, my dear. Watching that couple has excited you as much as it has me. Aha! And here is the incontestable proof." His fingers slipped beneath the legband of her chemise.

"You sneaky bastard!" she said. But she offered no

resistance when he pressed her down in the thick, sweet-smelling grass and kissed her throat and her temples.

"This is sheer madness," she protested, though not too convincingly.

"Do you wish to remove your gown to avoid incriminating wrinkling or grass stains?"

"Perhaps that would be wise."

In no time the two of them had divested themselves of their clothing. Moira lay back in the soft summer grass and spread her thighs. She was fully aroused even as he entered her, and somewhat shocked by the lust that had captivated her at the sight of the strange man and woman fornicating. She savored his penetration, inch by inch, and reached her first climax even before he had achieved total entry. She maintained a plateau of desire that enabled her to attain four orgasms in quick succession.

"You are the most magnificent woman I have ever bedded," he whispered at the height of his second climax.

"And you are *one* of the best studs I have ever bedded," she replied testily. "Another error, Winston. Men perpetuate the notion that *they* are laying women; the dominant role in the sexual act is their prerogative. It's not accurate . . . As a matter of fact, I just laid *you*!"

He rolled on his back in the grass and began to laugh.

"You'd better restrain yourself," she warned him. "They'll hear us below."

"Let them come up and watch, for all I care. After all, we were the first ones to peep, as you so delicately phrased it. Care to have another go at it before we leave?"

"I think not, Winston. It's a long drive back to London, and quite frankly, I am thoroughly exhausted." She laughed and tweaked his diminished member. "I feel like a cat ready to curl up after devouring a warm saucer of cream."

"When can I see you again?"

"Let's not make long-range plans. I do expect Bradford to return next month."

He bent over and kissed her on the cheek. His voice was intensely sincere. "I want you to know that this is not a one-night stand, to quote the old lady again. Too bad about our spouses. We could have made it permanent and ideal.''

"Winston . . .'' She patted his cheek. "What about all your burning ambitions? If your political enemies found out about us, they'd break you, just as they broke Charles Parnell over his affair.''

"Damn!'' He sat up and pounded a fist on the ground. "It's the old axiom that the worst tyranny in the world is the tyranny of the weak over the strong. The public mind is so inflexible, puny and self-righteous. We in politics who serve the public are greater slaves to their power than they are to our mandates.''

"It's always been like that, Winston. Take Brad, for example. The personal sacrifices he has made to attain power and wealth have been enormous. He's quite literally lost a family to his ambition.''

"A pity, but every man has a price, and the tragedy is that that price is so small. I wish you and I could go on like this forever.''

"There is no such thing as forever. Everything has a beginning and an end.''

The idyll of Winston Churchill and Moira Taylor continued to the very eve of World War One.

Chapter Thirty

June 28, 1914—THE ARCHDUKE FRANCIS FERDINAND, HEIR PRESUMPTIVE TO THE THRONE OF AUSTRIA, AND HIS WIFE, THE DUCHESS OF HOHENBERG, WERE ASSASSINATED IN SARAJEVO, BOSNIA, TODAY. . . .

Winston Churchill hurled the London *Times* against the wall. "The arrogant fool! Bearding the lion in his den is tame sport compared to a Hun archduke preening himself in public in the geographically damned Balkan Peninsula! For centuries it's been bridge and battleground for all the great European wars of history, a jigsaw of small countries, all fiercely nationalistic, whose boundaries shift from one war to another. Small wonder that the poor devils are possessed by ethnic paranoia."

He stood at the window, chomping on his cigar, glaring out across the spacious gardens of Manorhaven, the Taylor estate in Kent. Moira rose from the settee and came up behind him, placing her hands on his broad shoulders.

"Winston, I know very little about politics and international intrigue, but I fail to comprehend why one more political murder in an area where they train assassins as casually as the civilized world trains doctors, lawyers and teachers should evoke such an apoplectic rage in the first lord of the British Admirality."

He turned and embraced her. "My dear Moira, ever since Austria-Hungary annexed Bosnia six years ago, I have been predicting that the Balkans are a time bomb destined to blow up all Europe. There hasn't been a month in all that time without at least one serious border incident between Austria-Hungary on one side and Serbia and Bosnia on the other."

"But how does that involve Great Britain?"

He hurled his dead cigar into the fireplace. "It's. a Chinese conundrum, my love. Multilateral treaties, mutual assistance pacts, so much hodgepodge it overwhelms the mind. If the German ambassador pisses on the Italian minister in the men's room, before the week is out England could be at war with Germany."

"That is really a hyperbolic metaphor, dear." Moira laughed and hugged him.

"It is a grim fact of life. Let me project a hypothesis of the events that will transpire within the next month or two. First of all, Austria-Hungary will submit an interminable list of demands to Serbia, including the impossible condition that Serbia and Bosnia suppress by military force all anti-Austrian radical demonstrations.

"Now at this point Russia gets into the act; it has a mutual assistance pact with Serbia. Isn't that asinine? A pact of mutual assistance between a bear and a mouse!

"Now France also has a mutual assistance pact with Russia; that is somewhat more practical.

"Italy has a secret pact with France, avowing that neither will enter into any conflict in which the other is a participant.

"And Germany is totally committed to backing Austria-Hungary in the event of war.

"When we first met, I spoke of the imminence of Armageddon. I am dreadfully afraid that the moment is upon us, my darling."

She came into his arms and they embraced quietly and contemplatively.

*　　*　　*

Winston Churchill's prophecy was accurate. On July 28, after Serbia and Bosnia rejected the impossible demands of Austria-Hungary, the latter declared war on Serbia. The whole precarious balance of power on the Continent collapsed like a house of cards.

Russia declared war against Austria-Hungary. Germany declared war against Russia. On August 3 France and Germany were at war. When Germany violated Belgium's neutrality on August 4, Great Britain declared war against Germany. Within the year Italy would side with the Allies, while Turkey would support the Central Powers.

On September 1, 1914, Patrick Taylor resigned his commission with the United States army and enlisted in the British armed forces. When he broke the news to his mother at dinner that evening, Moira looked at his wife, Candice.

"What do you think of his decision?" she asked.

"I'm terrified for him, but I support Pat in his very difficult moral decision."

"I applaud your understanding and tolerance, Candice, my dear. I've been an army brat or an army wife from the day I was born. My father was killed at the Little Bighorn. I thought for years that Pat's father had died in China. Sean Flynn was killed in India. And now my son is going to do battle in Europe. I've got a thick skin; it must be more painful for you, dear."

Pat, seated at the head of the table, with Moira and Candice sitting across from each other, reached out both hands and clasped theirs.

"The two women whom I love and cherish and admire more than any other women in the world. I'm grateful for your support in what is, quite frankly, a very momentous decision. Edmund Burke said it most eloquently: 'All that is required for the triumph of evil is that good men remain silent and do nothing.'

"His credo inspired the revolution that won us our freedom and gave birth to democracy. In this perilous moment in history, the threat of tyranny and subjugation hangs over our heads like a sword of Damocles. Not just over England but over the whole world. Kaiser Wilhelm makes no bones about it; he seeks world domination.

"It will only be a matter of time before the United States will join in the fray on the Allied side. There is no room in the American mentality or morality for tolerating the iron-fisted demagoguery of the Central Powers any more than there was for tolerating George the Third. The way I see it, the sooner the better, and I intend to be in the front ranks of the defenders of world freedom."

"Well said, my beloved son." Moira's eyes were dewy. "And my beloved husband. I have never been more proud of you than I am right now."

They were having coffee and brandy in the study when the maid came in. "Mrs. Taylor, Mr. Winston Churchill would like to know if you can see him?"

"By all means, Sara. You should have shown him in directly."

She and Patrick rose as Churchill entered the room. He shook hands with Patrick, bent to kiss Candice's hand and kissed Moira on the cheek.

"Sorry to barge in on you like this," he apologized. "I realize this must be a very eventful night for all of you. And an emotional time." He nodded at Patrick. "You are not without celebrity, Pat. The word is out that you have enlisted in His Majesty's Royal Dragoons."

"I have, sir, and proud to be a member of the team that is going to kick the Kaiser's butt to hell."

Churchill laughed, his voice deep, resonant and rasping: "Bully for you, lad!" He clapped Patrick on the shoulder. "In any case, congratulations, Colonel Taylor. I am certain your illustrious father will be as proud of you as these ladies are when he learns of your decision."

Patrick avoided Churchill's gaze and maintained an icy silence.

Sensing the tension, the first lord of the British Admirality cleared his throat and lit a cigar. "As a matter of fact, my dear Moira, my presence here is motivated by a matter relating to Bradford."

Patrick consulted his pocket watch and said, "I really

think we must be off, Candice. I have a morning ahead of me that would equal the labors of Hercules."

"I'll see you to the door," Moira said. "Excuse me for a moment, Winston."

"To be sure." He shook hands with Patrick and said solemnly, "I hope to see you again before you're off to France. If I don't, the best of luck and God bless you. My intuition tells me it's going to be a long, hard war."

Patrick smiled. "We'll do our best on the land. Just see you hold up your end in the British navy."

Churchill chuckled. "You have my word for it. Good night, my dear Candice. And please give my love to your delightful children."

"Thank you, I will, Uncle Winston."

Moira walked with Patrick and Candice into the foyer. "Good night, my darlings. I realize how busy you will be in the next few weeks, Pat, tying up loose ends before you enter the service, but if you get a breather now and then, don't forget to come and visit with your old mother."

Both Patrick and Candice laughed. "Old, Mother?" Pat scoffed. "You are still the belle as well as the bellwether of London society." He kissed her cheek and said in a low, sly whisper, "And just so the two of you don't think you're pulling the wool over anyone's eyes, it's apparent *he* is still an ardent admirer of yours."

Moira slapped him playfully on the cheek. "Don't get impudent with me, young man. You should be ashamed of yourself."

"Well, I'm not. After all, I am a product of the Callahans and the Taylors. Now you'd better get back to Winston."

She closed the door behind them and went back into the study, where Churchill was pacing back and forth, rolling his cigar around in his sensuous lips. His high brow was rippled in thought.

"Oh, there you are. Fine son you have, Moira. Candice, too."

"They make a perfect pair," she agreed. "Now what is this matter you want to speak with me about relating to Brad?"

"General Taylor is on his way back to England."

She was astounded. "How do you know?"

"Diplomatic pouch arrived today at the Home Office from South Africa. The cliché is that the son follows in his father's footsteps. Brad's turned it around. He's about to follow in Patrick's footsteps. He's going to fight for England and the Allies as well. Surprised?"

"Just for an instant, but not really. Brad has always enjoyed a good, honest fight for a worthy cause. I wonder . . ."

"You wonder what?"

"I wonder if the worthy common cause will bring them any closer together?"

Churchill hunched his shoulders. "It's a possibility. I don't know. I followed my father into politics, but I still think he was a son of a bitch!"

There was a long, uncomfortable pause before Moira broached the subject that was haunting the two of them: "Now that Brad is coming home—the war and all, your herculean responsibilities as lord of the admirality, as well as my own responsibilities and duties to my husband and my son—I imagine it would be prudent for us to stop seeing each other; for the time being, at least."

"At least. . . ." His expression was tormented. "For the time being. Moira, my darling, you are and will always remain the most memorable and cherished woman I have ever met. But the two of us are far too intelligent and realistic to nourish the fable that when this war is over, you and I can pick up where we left off and resume our perfect relationship as if nothing had ever intervened. 'For every thing there is a season . . . a time to live and a time to die.' You and I, we've had our full share of living, but now the dream is finished—dead." He poured himself a full tumbler of brandy and downed it in a single quaff. He sat down and leaned forward, rubbing his eyes with the fingers of one hand. "And then there is my wife—Clementine is pregnant again. And Randolph; he's three. Damn it, Moira! You above all appreciate the intimacy and cohesion of family. Do you understand what I feel for you?"

She placed a hand across his lips. "No, Winston, you don't have to say it. I do know. I feel the same way about you. And I also appreciate and revere the inseparable oneness of flesh and blood . . . Brad . . . Your Clementine . . . I believe we could deal with that dilemma. But the children—Patrick . . . Desiree . . . and my grandchildren. No, we are bonded together for all eternity, just as you and Clementine and Randolph and whatever children you produce from this moment forward are bonded."

He looked up and reached for her hands. "Moira . . . there is one final obligation we owe each other."

"What might that be?"

"What else? A final tryst."

"Winston, it's out of the question. The servants . . ."

"No, no, I don't mean here in your home. Tomorrow night I would like to have supper with you at the John Peel Tavern, where we first met, and then—"

She completed the thought for him. "And then we'll retire to that grassy knoll where we made love for the first time."

"Exactly. Are you game?"

"I wouldn't miss it for the world. What time will you pick me up?"

"Why, eight o'clock, of course, the same time I came here that day we first met. And if it is still a fixture of your wardrobe, I would like you to wear the same gown you wore that wonderful night—a green pinafore, if memory serves me correctly?"

She regarded him with astonishment. "Indeed it does. Winston, you are a remarkable man. With all the pressing affairs of state weighing down upon you, you still remember what I wore that night so many years ago. I'm profoundly touched."

"I will never forget a detail of that night as long as I live. Not even the dogs of war can obscure that cherished memory."

They walked over to the broad window overlooking the gardens, arms linked around each other's waists. The lawns and silver maples flanking the drive were iridescent in the moonlight.

"You see," he said quietly. "Even the moon remembers our night. It's obliging us by shining full."

Briefly tears blinded Moira's eyes. "I think you'd better go now, or I'll relent and risk letting you spend the night here."

"I understand." He embraced her tenderly. She walked with him to the door and stood in the open doorway, watching him descend the steps to his waiting hansom. As the cab receded down the drive, Moira walked to the porch railing and looked up at the stars. Softly she began to recite:

"Star light, star bright, the first star I see tonight.
I wish I may, I wish I might get the wish I wish
tonight."

And what wish would that be, she asked herself?

To be transported back in time, lying in the sweet summer corn with Bob Thomas? Or with Brad the first time they made love in the tepid water of the Texas lagoon? Or together with Sean in the tent on the Chinese hillside above the Boxer pagoda?

And dear, sensitive Winston?

They, these four, were the only men in her life whom she truly cared for.

All the wishing in the world could not recapture the immediacy of life's past joys.

Nor end the tragic, damnable war!

Chapter Thirty-one

Newly commissioned Brigadier General Bradford Taylor arrived back in England in early December. His hair was silver gray, and he was thinner than when she had last seen him. The lines of age had added character to his handsome face. He embraced Moira with an ardor that had been absent in their relations for a long time.

"God, luv, you're a sight for sore eyes," he told her. "And as gorgeous as always. You're like a sorceress who cannot be touched by age or death."

Moira laughed. "Would that that were so, but I am only too aware of the inroads of age. You're looking well yourself, Brad. How was your voyage?"

"Interminable. I thought I'd go mad with ennui. I spent most of the trip in the ship's wireless room, listening to the war bulletins. Gad! It looked very ominous for a time there. The kaiser is a brilliant tactician, we've got to give him credit. When the Germans cut off Metz and swept through Belgium and Luxembourg, it seemed inevitable that they were going to isolate the channel ports from the Allies. Why they withdrew after decimating the French on the Marne is an absolute mystery to me. Maybe an act of a beneficent God. In any case, it afforded the British and French the reprieve they needed to pull it all together again.

"We nicked Jerry at Liege and then at Mons, and he was finally stalled at Verdun, Rheims, Soissons and Ypres." His expression became grave. "Any word from Patrick?"

"He was wounded and decorated at Ypres. You wouldn't know that, of course."

His color was ashen, and she noticed his hand shook when he lit a cigarette.

"Christ! Badly wounded?"

"Never fear. In his last letter from the hospital, he was quite chipper and expressed the hope he'd be returned to his outfit within two weeks. Would you like a drink, Brad?"

"A very strong drink."

"Come into the study." She told the butler to carry his bags upstairs, and they went into the study. Brad went to the server and poured himself three fingers of Scotch, then splashed soda into the tumbler. "What are you having, my dear?"

"A little sherry will be fine." She seated herself on the sofa and smoothed her skirt.

He brought over the drinks and sat beside her. "We've got a lot of catching up to do and not much time to accomplish it."

"Do you have your orders yet?"

"Yes, I've been to the War Office in London before motoring out to Manorhaven. I'll be leaving for France on New Year's Eve."

"That's not much time, but at least you'll be here for Christmas. Naturally we'll be spending it with Candice and the children."

"I've been looking forward to that. Too bad Desiree and her family can't be here. It may well be the last holiday we'll be together."

There was an unaccustomed wistfulness in his voice that touched her. She laid a hand on his sleeve. "That's not like you, Brad. You used to be the eternal optimist."

He smiled a bit sadly. "The passing years beat it out of you, Moira. When we're young, the horizon is infinite, but with the advancing years we become all too aware that the end of the road is in sight. . . . But the hell with the end of the road. This is today, and there's still plenty of life to be lived." He put an arm about her shoulders and drew her against him. His voice dropped an octave. "By the way, where did the butler take my bags? That is to say, are you and I sharing common quarters tonight?"

Moira looked up into his green eyes and was thrilled to note they had not lost their glint of lechery. She smiled and lifted a hand to stroke his cheek. "If you'd like."

His smile now was like the rising sun. "I was afraid you might have grown tired of waiting for me."

She laughed, a deep, throaty laugh. "What leads you to believe I was sitting here waiting? I've found ample diversion to occupy me during your long absences."

"I imagine you have." He kissed the top of her head. "I saw Winston briefly today. We had a drink at the club. He told me about the bizarre circumstances of your first meeting."

"Dear Winnie." The memory of that day elicited an affectionate chuckle. "Did he tell you how I batted him over the head with an umbrella at the WSPU meeting, and that the Pankhurst committee and I ended up in the pokey?"

Brad laughed. "It must have been hilarious. Then after all that he bailed the lot of you out."

"Yes, and we've been dear friends ever since. Would you like to have a bath now? I'll speak to the cook about dinner. Anything special you'd fancy? The larder is still amply stocked; the German blockade has not exacted any drastic effect on the economy as yet."

"Well, it's tightening like a noose around Britain's neck. Churchill told me today that within another year all of our tight little island will be on spartan rations. As for tonight, you surprise me." He stood up and walked to the server. "I think I'll take another drink upstairs with me."

They retired early. Moira bathed and anointed herself with perfume and powder and unguents; the only obvious signs of the aging process on her flawless skin were rough, dry patches on her elbows and knees and shoulders. Before she slipped into her nightgown she inspected herself in the mirror on the back of the bathroom door; pinched her thighs and buttocks; lifted her breasts with the backs of her hands.

"Still some tone remaining in the old girl," she observed wryly.

Her nightdress was a cool confection of voluminous, soft white lawn with a daring, wide neckline piped and bowed in pale pink above a deep flounced collar touched with a frosty eyelet. Feeling as giddy and nervous as a new bride, she went to Brad, lying in the big canopied bed, naked but for a sheet draped modestly over his loins.

"God, it's miraculous! I always see you the way I did the day I intruded on you while you were bathing at that water hole in Texas."

She laughed but was flattered just the same. "Then age has badly affected your eyes." She kneeled on the bed and flipped the sheet back. Her eyes widened. "However, more to the point, it certainly hasn't affected the reflexes that really are meaningful." Without further ado she bent over him, clasped his upright phallus tenderly in her hands and enveloped it with her lips.

He climaxed and then accommodated her in kind.

They made love three more times that night.

And their passions never ebbed during the entire three weeks before Brad was to be shipped out to France.

"I feel as though we've gone back in time and recaptured that first month of our honeymoon," he said.

"Yes, I feel that way too." But she was lying and he was lying and they both knew it.

What they were experiencing now was desire born of fear and desperation, the frenzy of the dying, feeling that if they tried hard enough they could cling to immortality.

The truth was that Brad and Moira were both convinced that once he left England and went to war, they would never see each other again.

Christmas was happy but subdued; Patrick was somewhere in the trenches in France, and Brad was due to join him in another week.

"Do you think you'll be seeing Pat?" Candice asked him as she bid them good night on the doorstep.

"I expect so," Brad said. "I'm assigned to the inspector general's office for the time being, and my first site of inspection will undoubtedly be in the Ypres sector."

On New Year's Eve, Moira and Candice and her family were on the docks at Plymouth to say farewell to Brad. It was not a melodramatic occasion; everyone smiled and laughed and pretended that he was off on a gay lark. When he kissed Moira for the last time before heading up the gangplank, the others averted their eyes.

He kissed her and whispered in her ear, "When I come home, things will be different. I'm tired of scurrying around the world. I'm going to settle down at Manorhaven and become a gentleman farmer."

"I can't wait."

He strode briskly up the ramp, and Moira did an about-face and walked back along the quay, her head held high and her back straight.

It was the last day in May of 1915 when the maid came into the sitting room where Moira was entertaining Candice at tea time.

"Madam, Mr. Winston Churchill is calling."

"Bring him in and set another place."

The instant she saw Churchill's grim, gray expression and the manner in which he held onto the doorway, Moira knew his reason for coming to Manorhaven.

Her voice was brittle. "Do come in, Winston, and sit down. Tea?"

"Whisky neat, if you please." He reached inside the pocket of his suit coat and removed a letter. He held it up. "Patrick requested that I deliver this to you personally. It came this morning with the special dispatches from Paris. It's from the front at Ypres."

"Is Pat all right, Uncle Winston?" Candice asked tersely.

"Pat is going to be fine, my dear. He's been wounded, but not seriously."

"But Brad is dead," Moira said tonelessly.

Churchill's jaw sagged forward on his chest, and silently he placed the letter in front of Moira. She opened it with her knife and unfolded the sheets of cheap, lined notebook paper. She read the contents aloud without emotion:

Dear Mother,

I will not prolong, with evasions and euphemisms, the agony and suspense you must be feeling as you read this. Father is dead. He died in a display of heroism the like of which will never be surpassed in this war or any other war, past or future. He was here to review our division on the eve of the second battle of Ypres. The Huns have been on the defensive in this sector ever since we whipped their butts last November. Desperate because of their inability to sustain a new offensive against our now-seasoned troops, they resorted to new depths in barbaric warfare: the introduction of lethal mustard gas into battle. Those British soldiers who were without benefit of gas masks died in droves in a most hideous fashion. I have seen men with their limbs blown off and decapitated by shell fire, but the long, agonizing, suffocating death that gas inflicts on its victims makes the former forms of dying seem merciful by comparison.

At midnight the division's big guns let go with a synchronized salvo that made the earth tremble as if in the throes of a giant earthquake. Moments later the German trenches and fortifications were transformed into a wall of fire that stretched in either direction for as far as the eye could see. The terrifying barrage went on all night.

Our boys went over the top just before dawn, wending our way through enormous shell holes, scorched underbrush and blackened tree stumps and torn barbed wire, infiltrating the German defenses. By the time the sun lifted above the horizon, our brigade was overrunning the whole plateau, mobbing the enemy's command posts, bayoneting machine-

gunners from the rear and dropping grenades into pillboxes. To the right and to the left our Tommies poured through the gap, driving a wedge through the heart of the Kaiser's "impregnable" defenses and into the center of town.

Father and his aide, Major Somers, and I were at the point of the spearhead with Company A. When we reached the village square, all hell broke loose; we had blundered into an ambush. On four sides of the square there were German machine-gunners lying in wait for us behind the parapets of the buildings flanking the square.

On all sides of us British soldiers were dropping like flies. I bawled an order to take cover, and Father and I and the major dove into the closest shell hole. Fortunately for our brigade, the terrain was pockmarked with deep holes that provided excellent cover from the fire of the German machine guns. The hazard was that unless we could extricate ourselves within a reasonable period of time, the enemy gunners would juggle their positions on the rooftops until ultimately they were set up in the right locations to exploit our vulnerability.

"There's our biggest problem," Father told us, pointing to a building with a heavy concentration of Germans on the top floor. His eyes picked out a low stone wall that ran along the top of a high rise behind the occupied building. "You two start firing and distract them while I'll see if I can make it up behind that wall."

He crawled out of our hole, squirming like a snake on his belly across the open ground, with machine-gun bullets kicking dust out of his field pack, ducking into one hole after another along the way while we kept up unceasing fire aimed at the Germans. Miraculously he reached his objective, and while the major and I looked on in awe, he picked off one German after another in the most amazing display of sharpshooting I have ever witnessed.

Then, ducking into the building's rear door, he climbed the stairs to the top floor and burst into the room where the surviving Germans were holed up, two in all out of the original seven. As Father confronted them, they tried frantically to swing the muzzles of the guns in his direction. Firing from the hip, he shot one between the eyes, and then his rifle jammed. Leaping across the room, he swung the rifle like a club and brained the remaining German.

Now, manning the German machine guns, he trained one and then the other on the Germans in the other buildings who were on lower levels than he was. In no time at all the Germans held up the white flag, and the day was won, thanks to Father's incredible heroism. Or so we thought.

While we were assembling our prisoners in the square, there was one Hun we had overlooked, crouched at a cellar window in one of the racked buildings. In one last defiant gesture this sniper took careful aim and fired a last single shot. It had Father's name on it.

As he lay dying in my arms, I begged his forgiveness for the shabby treatment I had meted out to him for so many years. I told him in essence:

"Father, you must believe that I never stopped loving you. I was bitter and heartbroken because I thought you had abandoned mother and Desiree and me and did not love or want us anymore. It was a natural response from a grieving child but unforgivable in a mature man. I must live with that guilt until the end of my days. If ever I can become half the man that you are, Father, I pray that my own son will harbor toward me a small measure of the great love and respect I feel toward you at this moment."

He smiled up at me as the light faded from his eyes and spoke in a barely audible voice. "I love you dearly, son, I always have; you and your sister and

the very special love I feel for your mother . . . Tell
her we will meet again; she'll know what I mean."
Then he took my hand and kissed it at the moment he
passed into eternity.

She paused and looked first at Candice and then at
Churchill. "What we've said so often—an archaic age has
passed on along with an archaic queen. I shall always
nourish nostalgia for that sweet century that brought me so
much happiness; and yes, sadness, too. The world will
never be the same again. Life will never be the same as it
was. And maybe in a sense that is a good thing. One can't
stop the world from turning any more than King Canute
could stem the advancing tides of the sea. The universe is
eternal, but mortal man and his ideas and his mores and
the society he inhabits at any given moment in time—all of
it is impermanent. Our lives are no more than an impersonal blink of God's eyelids. Now if you will excuse me, I
must go to my room and draft a cable to notify Desiree
that her beloved father has departed from this world."

Churchill came to her and put an arm around her waist.
"My dear Moira, the tears will dry, and once more there
will be laughter and happiness within these walls. More
than that, within the whole world."